THE MOSAIC SWALLOW

THE MOSAIC SWALLOW

Hendrik Hoitinga

Printed in the United States of America
ISBN 978-1-967279-02-9 (hc)
ISBN 978-1-967279-00-5 (sc)
ISBN 978-1-967279-01-2 (e)

2025.02.10

This book is printed on acid-free paper.

Blue Ink Media Solutions
1111B S Governors Ave
STE 7582 Dover,
DE 19904

www.blueinkmediasolutions.com

TABLE OF CONTENTS

DEDICATION
&
ACKNOWLEDGMENTS

For Peter;
That road trip back in '73, Though 50 years
ago it be, Still stirs the memory

Thanks to;
Gilly, my wife, for her love, patience and understanding. Margaret
Alison, for her friendship, inspiration and encouragement.
Author's favourite passage of Scripture;

'Trust in the Lord with all your heart, And lean not on
your own understanding. In all your ways acknowledge
Him, And He shall direct your paths'.

Proverbs 3; 5-6

BOOK 1

The Searcher

PROLOGUE;

Toronto Airport, Canada

Sunday 19th May 2019

Alison Hudson apologised as she bumped into the man.

He smiled, was about to make some sort of witty remark, but she had turned and was gone. He watched as she reached a nearby departure gate and noted that she was heading for Halifax. He himself turned and walked along to his gate, unlike the lady who was in a rush and who's face, he now recalled, registered stress, he was in no rush. Plenty of time to get to his next flight, Seattle. He had ordered a car and would drive to his destination in Oregon from there, staying overnight in Portland.

Myrtle Creek, Oregon, USA, Monday 20th May;

"Who are you?" The tone of her voice was challenging. As he was walking up the pathway, the door had opened and she had come out. She now stood on the porch. Her stance defiant. Even though he was still at some distance, he could see her eyes were focused and glaring. There was a determination that clearly flowed from her. A determination that suggested strongly that she was not to be crossed. He frowned slightly, but kept walking towards her, wondering who she was. Smiling as he drew closer he then stopped, three feet away from the bottom of three steps that led onto the porch.

"Hi, I am Thomas Klaassen, and who might you be?"

"Saw your car stop outside," she answered, indicating the vehicle he had arrived in moments ago. "If your selling, I ain't buying. Better you leave," she finished, her eyes never once wavering. He looked into those eyes, a very deep blue, kept the smile on his face and reached into his jacket pocket. She was wary of his movement, but stood still and firm.

He took out a bunch of keys. "Here, catch these keys" then threw the bunch at her. Her reflexes were quick, she caught them deftly with her right hand, her eyes only very briefly leaving the man that had come up the path.

"One of those, fits the front door," he said "I'll step back a bit, let you try," and keeping eye contact with her, took two steps back, all the while still smiling at her. She held his gaze for a bit longer, then looked at the keys in her hand. She selected one, then, throwing him another glance, turned and inserted the key in the lock. The key slid in smoothly and as she turned it, the tumblers worked. She took the key out again and turned to face him.

He stayed where he was; studied her. This was an unexpected turn of events.

Who was she? He guessed she would be in her mid-twenties, around five foot four, though scruffily dressed in jeans and a t-shirt that bore the name of a football team, revealing a rather scrawny figure, he was in no doubt that it wouldn't be wise to mess with her.

"Robert was a good friend of mine," he said, deciding to stay where he was, hopefully putting her at ease.

"How come you've these keys?" she asked, glancing down at the bunch in her hand.

"I had a letter from Robert, shortly before he died," he answered, then moved towards her again. "I have the keys; picked them up this morning because he has given me this house." Reaching the bottom step, he looked up at her, "So, the question is now, who are you, and what are you doing, in my house?" Thomas held out his hand as he mounted the first step. She threw the bunch back. He caught it.

"Claire," she said, her faced slightly flushed now, her stance more relaxed and he noted her eyes had softened. "I...I live here."

"How about we go inside. I really would like a coffee, and you can tell me your connection to Robert." She led the way inside, through the hallway, then turned to the right into the front room, which, through an archway, led to the dining room at the back and then, turning left, through to what was a modest, kitchen. He had closed the front door behind him and followed her, relieved that he had gained her trust, at least a little.

She turned, having grabbed the ready brewed coffee and retrieved a mug from a nearby tray, pouring the liquid, she asked, "How do you have it?"

"As it comes, no sugar, thanks."

"Are you…are you going to sell the house?" she asked, her voice no longer defensive but quiet, pushing the mug towards him, then pouring one for herself.

"I don't really know, to be honest. I received the letter from Robert, via his solicitor. It was a shock to find out he had written it only a few days before he passed. The letter, giving the name and address of the solicitor where to collect the keys, is somewhat cryptic, but that wasn't a surprise, knowing his condition. How long have you lived here then?"

Thomas took hold of his mug and took a careful sip.

"Three years. He saved my life you know. Said I could live here. I do the housecleaning and the cooking. Did have a job for a while across the road at the gas station, but it closed, about six months ago." She paused, then went on, "I could do the same, you know…"

He noticed her look of concern, then decided he would like to have a look around the house.

"Show me the house, please," he asked her.

Placing her mug on the kitchen counter, she said, "Okay." Thomas could see that the house was indeed very tidy, and clean. It had a second lounge on the ground floor, as well as a toilet off the entrance hall. Upstairs were four rooms. She first showed him the master, explaining she had fully cleaned the bedding and had taken all Robert's clothes, as per instructions, to a local church. She then showed the room in which she slept. Again it was tidy and clean and had a cheerful look about it. The third room was a guest room with two single beds and the fourth was locked with a numbered keypad.

Thomas looked at Claire, questioning with his eyes.

"I don't touch this room," she said, pressing the combination on the pad. "It's where Robert worked. He gave me the code for the door only a few days before he died."

She opened the door and stood aside.

Thomas took it all in. It was a big room. It had two large desks, one by the window and the second at a ninety degree angle to it. There was a leather high-backed chair and Thomas could see by the marks on the carpet that Robert would obviously wheel from one desk to the other. Two walls were lined with six bookcases, then there was a couch with room for two, and a low coffee table separating the couch from a large and comfortable looking leather chair. Furthermore, as well as a desk lamp on each solid wooden desk, there was a standard lamp next to the coffee table and the last item Thomas noticed as he scanned the room, was a small refrigerator. Then, taking in more details he saw that on one of the desks stood a large monitor in front of which was a keyboard and on the other desk numerous trays and folders, a printer and a laptop.

"Wow" he said softly. Then, still taking it all in, he said, "I recall a sentence in the letter he wrote to me," turning to look at the young blonde woman next to him, "it said, 'Find case 1988, and look'."

"This is what he does," Claire said. "This is how he saved me. He found me, it's what he does, he finds people." Then, as an afterthought, she said, "he never mentioned you."

Thomas said nothing, taking it all in as he stepped further into the room. He knew how his friend was, knew that this was precisely how his mind worked.

"I was his best friend, at school," he answered, still looking around the room and at the many books on the shelves, "many years ago. We kept in touch, but not so much over the past few years. I moved to Sweden."

"I guess that's why you weren't at the funeral?" Claire asked. Thomas looked at her; answered "I was away. Long haul flights, Shanghai, Tokyo, Hong Kong, Melbourne, Sydney. By the time I got home, there was a letter from the solicitor, which contained the letter from Robert. I left home immediately, flew across yesterday, drove down from Seattle and I went to the graveyard last evening … sorry I missed the funeral."

Claire nodded an understanding, "They called him 'The Searcher'," she said.

T H E   P R E S E N T ;

Myrtle Creek, Oregon, USA

Sunday 26th May 2019

Thomas stood on the front porch. A quiet morning in a quiet town. Sipping his first coffee of the day he reflected on these past days. The letter from Robert had been quite a shock. Over the years he had kept in touch, usually once a month, just a quick call, a quick chat. Robert wasn't much for chatting, this he knew.

But in those brief conversations, he had never mentioned what he was really up to.

Thomas had assumed, as Robert had on occasions said he was really into history that it was general history that he had been referring to.

What he had really been doing for the past two decades, since early 2000, according to Claire, had been delving into the history of missing people cases.

Six days ago, when he had first arrived, had met Claire, and been shown around the house he had inherited, he had been blown away by Robert's room with all the shelves and shelves of folders and books. Later that day, upon another look at, and investigation of, this room where, according to Claire, Robert spent practically all day every day, he noticed the sign that was placed on one of the two large desks. 'Search Engine' it simply stated. In the evening, having spent time in talking with Claire, she told him that over the years Robert had successfully tracked, traced and found more than thirty-five missing people. She also explained that Robert would not take on any cases where the person had been missing for less than a year. She, however, didn't elaborate on her own story of how she had been found.

That evening Thomas made up his mind. Robert had asked him, in that letter, to look at a case. It was time for a change. This was the opportunity. Staying the night, he had left the following day to head back to Stockholm in Sweden, to his apartment there. He was a pilot for the Swedish Airline SAS. He informed his boss of important family business he had to attend to and so resigned.

Thomas then organised a firm to pack his belongings and an agency to place his apartment up for sale arriving back at the house in the town of Myrtle Creek, just under two hundred miles away from Portland, his home town, where he had met Robert at high school, on the Saturday. On his return he had again contacted Robert's solicitor in nearby Roseburg and had been able to finalise the paperwork, despite it being late afternoon on a Saturday. He also then discovered that, not only had Robert given him the house, but there was a substantial amount of funds coming his way. Claire was very happy to be staying and keeping house for him. She was a nice young lady and he looked forwards to the day when she felt that she could tell him her story.

Thomas, now forty-four, was single. Piloting jets all around Europe, he had spent his younger years with an attitude of work hard and play hard, conquests on his mind with a string of fair maidens scattered throughout western Europe. This was while working for a Spanish Airline. There had been a time though that he thought he had found the one. Someone to create a stable life with. But, as he had played with the heart strings of many women, she played with his. One day she was gone.

Taking stock of himself that day, he resigned, left Madrid and looked for a new job, a new home, a new him. Landed up in Stockholm. The birthplace of his great-grandfather and mother.

He heard the door behind him open and turned to see Claire coming out.

"You okay?" she asked.

"Yes," he answered, finishing his drink. Then looking at her, said, "I was once again looking for a new direction–a new start. Robert has given me one, I'm going to look at case 1988 as he asked me to. First though, breakfast."

"You must have been a very good friend," Claire said, expertly preparing an omelette for Thomas, "I mean, to give you a house and all."

"Do you have any idea about his sister?" Thomas asked, "I believe she went to San Francisco many years ago, but, then disappeared? Is that why he started this search activity?"

Claire placed the omelette in front of Thomas, "No, I think his sister moved away to San Francisco in 2009. I also know that he wasn't close to her. He started looking for missing people, around the turn of the century, maybe it was a New Year's resolution. I don't know. He was, well you know I guess, he was not very good at talking, he was caring, but, well, you know, lived in his own little world really, what is it that he had?"

"A type of Asperger's Syndrome," Thomas answered, tucking in to his breakfast. "He wasn't diagnosed until he went to high school. He was always very good at focusing on certain things, good at maths, a logical mind, but lacking in social skills. It meant he was an easy target for bullying. I liked him, thought he was a great character. We got on well."

He was about to reflect on the day they met, when Claire broke into his thoughts, "I'll need to get some groceries and other stuff. Also, perhaps you can tell me what you would like to eat, so that…"

"Claire," Thomas interrupted, "I appreciate your willingness, doing the housework, the cleaning that's plenty, getting groceries and stuff, all good, but you don't have to cook. Well, apart from these omelettes, which taste great, but, you know, I can look after myself. Want to look after myself. Cook for you sometimes. Anyway, what I'm trying to say is that, well as far as I'm concerned, this is your house as much as is it mine, okay?"

Claire, nodded. Not knowing what to say, she smiled and nodded, fearing that if she were to try and talk that she would burst into tears. Armed with his second coffee of the day, Thomas went upstairs and into the room he now referred to as, 'The search engine', and sat at the desk by the window.

The case that Robert had mentioned in his letter was in a folder on the desk clearly labelled at the top right-hand corner with the title; Case 1988.

It was there, ready for him. It had been there when he had first entered this room and had been overwhelmed by the bookcases full of folders and books and had not even taken in the very file that lay in plain sight.

Robert had obviously been aware of an illness that would bring an end to his life. The way he had written the letter, confirmed that.

Giving the combination of this room to Claire a few days earlier, also confirmed that. It was also obvious, for whatever reason that this case was particularly important. Sitting down in the comfy leather desk chair, Thomas placed the mug on a coaster, then reached over and took hold of the file, opening it.

He began to read.

Outside someone was watching, observed the young woman leaving the house and getting into her battered VW Passant station car and set off in the direction of town. The figure then exited the car, strolled over to where the car belonging to Thomas Klaassen was parked, quickly ducked down and placed a gadget of sorts next to the exhaust pipe, stood upright and walked on, almost in a fluid motion, then turned, crossed the street, double backed to where their car was and got back in. The ignition turned the engine on and the car moved away.

THE PAST;

Period 1–Part 1

The year 1814–Colombia

With snorts and heavy breathing, the four horses stopped almost simultaneously.

The four men, perspiring as much as their horses, looked down from the hill upon which they had arrived with sighs of relief. Below lay the river. The Sumapaz river.

Water for the horses, a little bit a shade from some low shrubs and rocky outcrops. The leader, a man named Philippe Castagnet, looked across to his companions and smiled broadly, then set his horse in motion, slowly stepping down the hill towards the river, whose sounds reached their ears. The horses too, smelled and heard it, their ears turning towards the sound. With an occasional snort the four dark brown coloured horses stepped almost in single file, and upon reaching the river's edge, the riders dismounted, with an effort took the saddles and saddlebags off and led the animals to the edge, choosing a spot where they would be able to safely drink.

Philippe and the others then set about filling their water flasks with fresh and cool water, also splashing themselves. The evening was coming. The light was fading.

The horses, having had their fill of the water, wandered around and began to graze on the light covering of some type of pampas grass.

They had been riding all day. Sometimes just at a walk, but often a light trot. Resting briefly only three times prior to their arrival at the river's edge.

They would set up camp here. Philippe stood and looked at the flowing water and looked at a map in his hand.

They were doing well and he was pleased. They would cross the river in the morning and tackle the next stage of their journey.

All carefully planned. All worked out in the finest detail…

It had been a couple of hours before dawn when they had quietly slipped out of the city of Bogota. The streets were quiet. Though there had been tension in the region, and there had been some unrest and even skirmishes, the last couple of days had been relatively calm. The four riders, going just by the light of the half moon and stars, left the city behind. It was cold in the night air and the horses, perhaps sensing the need for quietness, seemed to be tiptoeing along the dirt road out of town. Each man had a roll, containing a blanket, clothes and provisions, tied just behind the saddle, and each man had a set of saddlebags. So began their journey that brought them to this point…

The saddles had been placed on the ground and the saddlebags were draped over several rocks. Two of the men had fetched dry wood, a third was preparing a pot of strong coffee that soon would be heated by the fire. Philippe turned, tucked the map away and looked at the four saddles and the sets of saddlebags.

They had done it. Al they needed to do now, was to travel a further distance of close to three hundred miles, hopefully, over the next six days.

A fire was soon lit and the night fell quickly. Their faces shone dimly by the light of the flames. The sound of the river flowing and the occasional snort of a horse could be heard along with the gentle crackling of the fire.

Earlier that day

Jose de Garagoa stood on the balcony of his hacienda. Hands in pockets, he stared out over his land. Three miles away was Bogota city. His wife of 12 years wisely kept silent as she knew her husband was not in a good mood. In fact, he was angry. First he had learned that four of his horses had been stolen. Fine horses, cavalry horses that he and his team of rebels had liberated from the Spanish some months ago. Stolen from under his nose.

That wasn't the worst of it. A rider had arrived from the city earlier in the morning, had come galloping up the long road leading to the house, only moments after Jose had learned of the stolen horses. The Patron, as he was locally known, had a house in the city, set right amongst other larger buildings in the main street. Here he kept acquired treasure, paintings, artefacts, jewellery.

He also kept a mistress there.

The rider, sweating from the ride and flushed with worry as to what his master would say, haltingly stuttered out the news. The house had been broken into and the Patron's study had been burgled. The chest, containing gold coins, had been forced open, the contents gone.

After a verbal explosion, Jose had gathered some of the men and barked out his commands, to find out what exactly had happened, how it had happened, who had been so brazen in doing so and most importantly, where had they gone? He had not once considered the welfare of his mistress.

That had been nearly two hours ago. It was now a little after midday. His wife, Dacha, sat quietly in the cane chair. Inwardly she was amused at his distress.

He had spent more time in his house in the city these past months. She knew he had a mistress there. Wondered if she might be involved in whatever had happened, wouldn't that be amusing, she thought to herself, and had to concentrate hard not to smile.

It was more than an hour later that two of his men rode up to the house and reported. Not much information. There had been four men, most likely Spanish, who had left the city in the early hours of the morning, heading north.

It appeared they had only broken into the house to gain entry to his study and had taken the coins, obviously knowing that they were there. Nothing else was touched or taken. Apparently his mistress hadn't even been woken, had slept through the whole thing. By nightfall there had been no further reports as to the whereabouts of these four men.

The following day Philippe and his men had once again set off before the sun had fully risen, had carefully crossed the river and were on their way to a town some forty miles away, Girardot. Though traversing through a terrain that was known to receive much rain throughout the year, it remained dry.

The going was good and stopping briefly only once, they came to a farm just north of the town just after midday and made straight for the large barn.

The doors opened and a man came out.

Pleased to see him, the riders dismounted and there were handshakes and hugs all around. Inside the barn were six horses.

Meanwhile, to the south of the city of Bogota, Caprice dismounted and studied the ground.

She cursed under her breath and showed her fury to the ranch hand who was sat on his horse, looking down at her, waiting instructions from the fiery tempered daughter of the Patron. She stood up and looked at the sky.

Rain was coming.

Taking another look at the tracks she'd found, she drew a conclusion, standing up, she voiced her findings to the young ranch hand, "They doubled back, left the city heading north, but, as these tracks tell us," she said, looking down, "they are in fact heading south."

Caprice swore again, and scowled up at the young man she had ordered to accompany her as she mounted the horse. She had already told the young lad that one of the four horses that had been stolen had been hers. A fine animal.

Moreover, she knew that as her horse had been separate from the other three, it had been carefully chosen. She knew who had taken it.

When she heard the commotion yesterday morning, she confessed to her father that she'd been having a dalliance with a Spanish guy, Philippe. Told him she had been leading him on, teasing him and flirting with him. She knew that it must have been him. Later in the day, she told her father she would take a ranch hand with her the next morning. She would track them down, she was very fond of her horse.

He had understood.

She turned her horse around, and headed back to the hacienda. She would need provisions and a spare horse, as well as a weapon. She would take her father's long barrelled shotgun and extra ammunition. She knew how to use it.

"I will hunt you down Philippe," she said, spurring the horse underneath her into a trot. The ranch hand struggling to keep up with the pace.

T H E   P R E S E N T ;

Myrtle Creek

Still Sunday 26th May

Case file 1988 contained several documents. There was a newspaper article, a police report, a weather report, then several sheets type written by Robert. There were a dozen or so photographs and two computer discs.

Settling himself on the couch, mug of coffee on the small table beside him, Thomas, having flicked through the contents of the folder, then commenced reading in the sequence Robert had placed the information. The newspaper article first.

'Tornado sweeps through archaeological dig. Four dead, 17 injured' was the headline.

Thomas checked the date: 1988, hence the name of the case file he surmised, and read the article. He was only just starting to read the police report, when there was a 'ding'.

Curious, he got up and went over to the desk and noticed that there was a cell phone-like piece of equipment attached to the main computer.

This was lit and the screen had just one word on it. 'Message'.

Figuring that as it was connected to the main, what Robert called his 'search engine' Thomas fired up the computer, knowing, by instructions left, the password. Entering this he saw the big screen lit up, showing a background picture of an idyllic beach scene with palm trees. The picture disappeared as another screen came to view.

'Message Board' showed in big letters as the heading. Below it an icon was flashing beside the symbol of a bell. Thomas moved the mouse and clicked.

Immediately a message came on the screen.

Thomas read it, read it again, sat back, then read it again, before getting up, leaving the room and calling out for Claire.

Moments later he returned, Claire in tow, and gestured to the screen.

Claire glanced at Thomas, then sat herself in the chair and read the message.

> *'Robert, urgent, probable abduction, female, depart Plymouth Mon noon, arrival Bilbao Tue 1.30. Company J. Inverno. Send help'. DP.*

Claire looked up at Thomas.

"Do you know what this is about?" he asked her, but before she could formulate an answer, he went on to say, "I thought Robert only looked into cases that were over a year old, so what is this? Who is DP, and what does it mean, 'send help?'"

Thomas, perhaps not really expecting an answer, began to pace the room.

Claire stood up from the desk chair, waited until he stopped pacing, and caught her eye, gave her his attention. She then spoke.

"Robert does … did, the searching, he would be in here every day, usually all of the day. It was his life. When, … when I was rescued, it was the police who freed me, but there was someone else, a woman. She did not say who she was, but told me about Robert and how his investigation led to my rescue.

"Determined to find out who this Robert was, I searched, asked around and found him, knocked on his door, and, well, stayed. Anyway, Robert must have connections all over, helpers I suppose.

"This DP must be one of them. As for sending help, I have no idea who you might call. Looking at the time mentioned," Claire said, again looking at the screen, "it seems there is little. Plymouth, I think, must be in the UK and I know that Bilbao is in Spain …"

"Yes," Thomas agreed, "and looking at the schedule, it has to be a boat, a ferry perhaps. Claire, could you possibly search for the quickest way I can get to Bilbao, preferably before Tuesday?"

"I will investigate and check out the Plymouth – Bilbao connection and this company, J. Inverno."

"Of course," Claire answered, saying as she exited through the door, "A woman is in danger. We must do something."

"We must do something", Thomas whispered as he tried to get his head around all that was happening. Obviously, whoever this DP is doesn't know about Robert's death. A reply to his urgent e-mail was also needed.

'*DP, Robert passed. Will follow up on request. Stand by. TK*', he typed on the screen below the message and pressed reply.

As the incoming message had been brief and somewhat cryptic, Thomas felt it best to do likewise. Not much later he found out that there was a ferry service between Plymouth and Bilbao, and had just found details of a trucking company, based in Santander, called J. Inverno., when Claire called from downstairs.

Thomas went down. She had placed her laptop, actually a spare one Robert had given her, on the dining room table, notepad and pen by her side and looked slightly flushed and pleased with herself as she began to tell him what she had found.

He looked at his watch when she had finished speaking, "That leaves me little time. I'll get my credit card. We'll book this. Well done!"

Forty minutes later Thomas got into his car, waved to Claire on the porch and set off, destination, Portland airport. From there he was booked on an evening flight to Atlanta. He would overnight in a hotel near the airport and was scheduled to fly out just after 4 pm the following day. The flight would arrive in Bilbao a little after 8 am, Tuesday morning.

The ferry was due to arrive at 1.30 pm, giving him probably around three hours to disembark, go through customs and hire a car. As long as the flight was on time that should be time enough.

The instruction he had received from Robert, with regards to logging into his computer system, he left with Claire. There had been no reply from DP.

Thomas asked Claire to update him should another message from DP come in, then he'd packed a suitcase, wondering what it is he hoped to do once in Bilbao.

Forty minutes into his journey, the car that had been parked in his street, was five cars behind and now maintaining that distance between them.

T H E   P A S T ;

Period 1–Part 2

The year 1814–Colombia

There was rain in the air. But that was fine, knowing the severity of a downpour in these regions, it would wash out their tracks. Philippe was again pleased with the progress they were making now that there were five of them on fresh horses, and with a spare horse as well. It had taken them a little longer than anticipated, to find a good place to cross the Magdalena River. Had it rained earlier, it would have been even more difficult, but once on the other side the pace was good and they were eating up the miles.

The destination on this third day was Cajamarca, some sixty miles to the south west.

Philippe led the team, set the pace, sometimes a short jog, a short run, then back to a walking pace before once again going to a trot. The horses were fit; the ground was easy. He spoke little. Sometimes he would hear his men chatting, laughing at times, then there were miles and miles of just silence. Horse and man, each with their own thoughts. The fit horses easily carrying the rider and the weight of the gold in the saddlebags. It began to rain, very lightly.

Philippe knew that by now the pursuit, for he was sure that the Patron, Jose, would not let this go without some sort of effort to capture them, would likely have picked up their trail. How far would they go, he wondered, as he once more broke into a trot, his men following suit.

At a little over six foot, he was of sturdy build, with dark hair, bronzed skin, brown eyes and a smile that made many a fair maiden blush. He thought of the lovely Caprice.

Caprice: she would make sure that she would be among a team that Jose would send, He was sure of that. She would find the barn, would find her horse, would find the note he left her. They had some good times together, riding, dining and dancing. Making love.

Yes, he was sure that a team would be chasing them. He was also sure that once they tracked them for a distance, they would likely figure out where they were headed.

But they had a big head start, and with fresh horses, this next stage would no doubt see them even further ahead. Still, as the rain began to fall more heavily, he acknowledged that they still had many miles to cover and it wouldn't be entirely impossible for the Patron to send a solo rider to head for their final destination and gather some men to form a team to apprehend them.

He shoved the negative thoughts from his mind. For now they were well on their way and what's more, at the pace they were going, it would be highly unlikely anyone could overtake them. Furthermore there was a team of six men preparing things ahead of their arrival, which would hopefully be in three days' time.

Philippe once more slowed to a walk and thought about the need to stop for a meal, a drink and a rest, particularly for the horses.

It was also raining as the team of five men and one woman, reached the outskirts of the town of Girardot.

Caprice, a good tracker, seeing the spoor leading to the north of the town instructed the young ranch hand who had been with her the day before, to stay with her and for the rest of the men to go into the town and ask around. She would follow the track to the north.

The men, an assortment of labourers in the employ of the Patron, followed her orders and rode away, hoping at least for some shelter and some food as they had been riding now for a day and a half, much of it through the night.

Caprice followed the tracks and fifteen minutes later saw the large barn.

Setting her horse into a gallop, she reached it in no time, dismounted and taking the rifle from its sheath, approached the barn doors.

She could hear the noise of horses inside and opened one of the large doors.

Four horses. Among them, her own. There was no one around.

Putting the rifle down, she approached her own horse, speaking to him, rubbing his face, patting his neck as she cast an eye over the animal.

He was calm, as were the other horses, They had feed and drink available.

Walking around her horse, checking him all over, she then noticed a piece of paper, folded and stuck into a slit in the wooden box that made up the stall.

The young ranch hand had also entered the barn by now and saw the Patron's daughter as she retrieved a piece of paper.

Taking it, unfolding it, and reading it, Caprice cursed.

Then, she led her horse outside and began to unsaddle the horse that she'd been riding, she spoke aloud. "I will hunt you down Philippe!"

This to the amusement of the young man who carefully hid his smile.

T H E   P R E S E N T;

Somewhere over the Atlantic

Monday 27th May

Booking first class not only allowed Thomas the security of a seat on this flight to Bilbao, but also afford him the luxury of space as he opened his laptop to commence his search. Though having purchased these flights on his own credit card, he thought about the funds that Robert had left him. Not one to spend much on himself as his life was all in that room, the funds, mainly given by grateful families, grew into a substantial amount.

Thomas had slept surprisingly well, had arranged a late check out and left for the airport at 2 pm. He was used to flying, had flown many hours with a Spanish airline before working for the Swedish airline. He knew Bilbao a little, but had never stayed overnight there.

The first thing he began to arrange, after take-off and a nice dinner, was to book himself a car for when he arrived. Next was to do some further research on the freight company based in Santander, J. Inverno, and during the flight he discovered that it now belonged to a woman, a Miss Juliette Inverno, who had inherited it from her father.

They had a fleet of ten trucks and regularly transported goods to and from the United Kingdom, Germany and Denmark.

He sent an e-mail to Claire, asking if she had any more communications from this mysterious DP. Then, already over half way on the journey, he sat back as the jet crossed the skies over the Atlantic Ocean, and thought about his friend, Robert.

You're quite the man Robert, finding all those missing people. How did this come about, Thomas wondered, and thought back to when he first met him.

Lincoln High School, in the North-West district of Portland. The year 1990. Thomas had arrived as a new pupil as his folks had moved from a different part of the city. It was his first day, first lunch in the school's canteen. Sitting at a table he noticed a couple of lads prompting another boy to "Do it–go on."

The boy, gangly, not very tall, with quite ruffled brown hair and brown eyes, after some more goading, got up and headed for a group of three girls who occupied a table.

They were the only ones at that table, despite there being room for five more. Thomas watched, and, through conversations he'd already had during his first morning, knew that these were the ABC girls, their speciality, bullying.

He noted the two lads who had prompted this guy, whose name he would soon discover, was Robert, were watching in amusement.

Robert approached the three girls, and addressed the one in the middle, this being Barbara, as they always sat or walked in the same formation, Alison, Barbara and Cynthia, hence their reputation as the ABC girls.

Thomas took a bite of his sandwich and watched, as it seemed, did many others for there was a hushed silence. What followed had not been very nice. After Robert had asked the girl in the middle, Barbara, if she would like to go to the school dance with him, which was in two weeks' time, the three of them began to berate and belittle him with a flow of unkind words audible to everyone.

It was Thomas who moved first and walked over to where Robert, now quite flushed with embarrassment, stood frozen to the spot.

"Come on, leave them to it. They get their kicks from belittling others, but they are nothing more than cowards." Thomas looked each of them in the eye, then steering Robert away, turned to look at the trio once more and said, "Your amusement today, will one day turn to sorrow…"

A stewardess broke into his reminiscing asking if he would like another coffee.

Two rows behind Thomas, the person that had placed a gadget under his car, sat quietly, enjoying a glass of wine. The powerful jet engines droned on, pushing the craft towards the European continent as daylight began to fade.

THE PAST;

Period 1–Part 3

The year 1814–Buenaventura

In a tavern near the waterfront, Henry Hopkins slowly sipped the lukewarm beer as daylight began to fade. It had been another hot day. The tavern was only half full. The situation in Colombia had been tense for some time, with Creole fighting Creole. The Spanish were on the back foot and there was talk about Simon Bolivar and his army gaining much ground in the region.

Henry, who had been unable to speak a word of Spanish upon his arrival in South America, landing in Caracas in 1803 and travelled on to Colombia. Now, nearly eleven years later,–spoke it fluently.

He had been working in a silver mine that lay between Bogota and Cartagena and during that time had rarely set foot in either the current capital or the large seaport.

Recently he had picked up on the various battles that were raging in the region, and figured that the time was right to move on, head further south, maybe even into Peru. He sipped some more of the local brew.

Standing only around five foot six, he was sturdily built and those who knew him, would not cross him. Though a very like-able man, he certainly wasn't one to be hassled.

Buenaventura.

He and his team of four men had located stables on the edge of town and had stalled their horses and three wagons there. It had been early afternoon when Henry headed into the city leaving the men

29

to rest up and guard their horses and equipment. They had already travelled many miles through some rugged terrain and were grateful for a rest and a bed to sleep in, which had been sourced shortly after their arrival.

Henry sipped some more beer and thought back bringing to mind that sea journey that brought him to the South American continent; remembering how he had been so sunburned and had purchased several large brimmed hats at the ports trading post. This had been in Caracas, Venezuela. From there another journey by ship to Cartagena and then onwards to the mines which he had heard about. Upon his arrival at the mine, all those years ago, it had quickly become obvious that Henry had a vast amount of knowledge, which he had gained working in the tin mines of Cornwall. He was soon made into a team leader with a group of nearly two dozen under his control.

It was also during this time that he met fellow Cornishman, Richard Trevithick, a pioneer in the area of steam. Henry spent some time with him. They were an interesting looking pair with Henry a sturdy five foot six and Richard standing six foot two. They bonded well and quickly, and Henry purchased two steam pumps from this brilliant inventor, with the intention of using them in the future, already thinking about setting up his own business.

Then recently, feeling more and more that it was time to move on, he had the idea to head for Ecuador, having sourced some knowledge on mines near the city of Quito…

Looking out over the harbour, the oncoming dusk creating a soft glimmer on the water, he was pleased that he had decided to move on.

Ecuador was not that far away now. He was pleased with the team of men he had picked. These four had been part of his team for the past three years.

They were hard working, reliable and trustworthy. When Henry had spoken about his plan, they had unanimously agreed and were enthusiastic about this adventure.

Henry finished his beer, got up and left the tavern, looked out over the ocean and wondered about the events of a little earlier.

There had a been a commotion in the city, at the harbour front. In fact, there had been a gun shot and much shouting.

Then, as he had been walking along the waterfront, in search of a tavern to quench his thirst he saw the ship. It had left its moorings and was sailing out of the port. A small two-master, the sails already set and catching the wind. She was fast, Henry observed. He watched for a moment or two, then resumed his walk to later hear about what had happened when a group of men entered the tavern, excitedly chatting away.

The Spanish had for a time kept a stronghold in Bogota, not only housing a garrison there but it was also where they minted the silver and gold coins to pay the soldiers and purchase goods. A local uprising and a strong force of Creole had sent the Spanish retreating to the north. From the conversation, Henry learned that apparently this stronghold was ransacked and destroyed and a local and powerful landlord, the 'Patron', a certain Jose de Garagoa had found a chest of gold coins, which he promptly confiscated.

Now it appeared that it was this chest of gold that had now been stolen back by a group of Spanish soldiers. This according to a lone rider, who had traversed the country to warn the port authorities of this theft. However, the warning had been in vain. The robbers had easily overpowered the two men who had tried, somewhat reluctantly, to stop them. One them firing a shot that had been well wide of the mark.

As he walked back towards the stables, Henry thought about this occurrence and figured it must have taken quite some planning for it to be stolen from Bogota, at least three hundred miles away, transported to this port, a ship waiting and heading to who knew where. Henry smiled as he reflected on the account the men in the tavern had given of this commotion, and of the fact that the port authorities had quickly launched a small vessel in pursuit. Though what they thought they might accomplish against a ship armed with four cannons, was beyond him.

They would have no chance however, to even catch up. The much faster schooner was well away. Henry couldn't wait to tell his men of this event.

They would spend the night here, pick up fresh supplies then head towards Quito in Ecuador, over five hundred miles away.

The schooner, aptly named 'Flecha' meaning arrow, was indeed, well away.

Philippe was pleased and standing on the deck near the stern watched the land disappearing in the distance.

He had expected that there might be some resistance; figured that somehow word might have reached the city of the Spanish horsemen heading their way with stolen treasure. The single rider, on a horse that was lathered in sweat, had arrived only moments before they were all set to board the schooner. Though the young man had begun to shout some sort of warning, as he dismounted, he practically collapsed to ground with extreme fatigue.

The resistance was weak and futile. An elderly man with a rifle, picking up on what the young rider had shouted, had tried to persuade them to stop, aided by a port authority man, but these two were quickly overpowered once the man had fired his rifle.

Both men were then–pushed off the dock into a small fishing vessel.

By the time they had extricated themselves, the schooner was away.

They scrambled to get a vessel into a pursuit, but were quickly resigned to the fact it would never catch the fleeing schooner.

Philippe smiled, thinking how well they had done.

They had safely reached Cajamarca on the third day, and had then ridden just over sixty-five miles on the fourth day to reach the town of Zarzal. Day five saw the team ride, carefree, through the countryside on a hot and sunny day to arrive in Buga in the late afternoon. On the sixth day they crossed another big river, this one the Cauca River.

It had taken them a while to find a suitable place to cross as it had rained the previous evening, but once on the other side they made up some ground and reached the outskirts of Buenaventura in the early evening, another day's journey of around sixty-five miles. On the seventh day, after waiting until mid-afternoon and a suitable tide, they rode into town, arrived at the dock, unpacked, dealt with the port authorities and set sail, leaving the city of Buenaventura, its name meaning 'good fortune', behind in their wake.

Well, certainly good fortune for them. After a very brief hiccup in the proceedings, mission accomplished…

Philippe briefly thought about Caprice, then turned and headed for his cabin, where, the gold coins were now safely put into a strongbox.

Eight hundred of them.

In order to distribute the weight evenly, they had carefully counted a hundred coins into each side of the saddlebags, thus each man carried two hundred, a weight of around 100 pounds. Four of them, a total of eight hundred coins, minted in Bogota around 1770. These were Charles III coins, with the inscription *IN-UTROQ- FELIX – AUSPICE – DEO* around the edge. Philippe was in no doubt that these would hold and likely increase in value.

They were heading north for Mexico. And as the sun set the seas were calm and a soft breeze was assisting the schooner to slide smoothly through the water of the Pacific Ocean.

THE PRESENT;

Myrtle Creek

Monday 27th May

Armed with a fresh bottle of still water, Claire went upstairs, punched in the code and entered the room. She switched on the lights, placed her bottle on the desk and fired up the computer. It was a little after 8 am.

She had woken at 7.30, decided to get up straight away, showered and dressed, and then went downstairs to fix herself some breakfast. Typing in the security code Claire sat back for a moment and thought of her changed circumstances.

When she finally tracked down the man responsible for her rescue and knocked on his door, he had been welcoming and friendly. Her decision to stay and be the housekeeper had been accepted and she felt safe, secure and happy for the first time in a long time. But although Robert was a nice man, he was very much living in his own world, practically living in the room she was now in. When Thomas had asked how it came about that Robert came to do this, came to search for missing people and successfully so, she didn't know.

It was different now. Thomas was so different.

She had been a little in awe when he had said he would go and answer the call of 'Send help'.

Claire was determined to be more than she was before, more than Robert had allowed her to be, always adamantly saying this was his role in life and that he would do so, alone. His attitude in that didn't take away the fact that she thought the world of him. After all, if it hadn't been for him…

The screen came to life, the scene of the beach and palm trees and a very blue sea.

It was different now, Thomas asked for her help, and she would certainly help. Moreover, she was also determined to find out more about Robert, even hopefully find her own case amongst his files. There was no new message, nothing from the mysterious DP. Thomas was flying into a situation. She needed to help, in some way, in this, probable abduction?

Claire set about to do research to, in some way, assist Thomas.

She began by searching what Robert had on his 'Search Engine' computer.

In particular she was aiming to find out who this DP might be. The message had been so cryptic, so short, probable abduction? Wasn't he sure? A female? Who was she? She would check the newspapers from England for any possible news on that.

Meanwhile some 440 miles to the south, in San Francisco

It was Memorial Day.

Millie Parker stood with her arms folded and looked out over the vast Pacific Ocean. A soft breeze was gently tugging at her hair. Her eyes were moist and there was a frown on her forehead as she thought of the many events that ran, randomly, through her mind. Not too far behind her was a wooden bench, one she had sat on, over thirty years ago, as a twenty-one-year old, sitting between her grandparents, her mother's parents, well, step-parents, as they had adopted her from her mother's sister. She had been crying then, for her mother had been killed in a tornado in New Mexico.

Millie stood quite still, trying hard to reassemble all her thoughts into some form of logical pattern. Being Memorial Day, a nation remembering the fallen throughout the wars, she felt it appropriate to come here. Her grandparents were long gone now, buried here also, in this cemetery on a hillside to the north of the city.

In fact, her father had arranged it so that they lay either side of her mother. Her father was now in his mid-eighties; had never been the same man since his wife, her mother, Emily, had died.

He sold the mining company in Harris back in 2009 and had moved here to be close to her, his only daughter.

Millie took in a deep breath, flicked some of her brunette hair away from her face and reflected on her own life.

She had gone off to Milan, as planned, at her father's insistence as he moved to Canada, to the town of Harris where he took over the company mining business. She spent two years studying fashion and tailoring. Had then fallen in love with a likeable rogue as she travelled back to America. Lived together with him in Miami, where he was from, but three years later had left him behind and moved back to San Francisco. Having also studied art and literature and finding no success in establishing a career in fashion, she applied for, and was accepted, as a teacher in a fashionable and elite girls school.

Hearing some people behind her, she turned and smiled at them as they walked by, then turned once more to face the sea, remembering when her father had stood on this very spot that day. Where had the years gone.

The breeze coming in from the ocean was pleasant on her face and she again pulled some hair away from her eyes and tucked it behind her ear.

Taking another deep breath, she reached inside the handbag that was slung across her shoulder and retrieved a letter.

She had received it ten days ago, but had only found and opened it yesterday, after coming back from a short holiday. She drew the note from the envelope and read it again. It was very short, somewhat cryptic, it read; *About your mother's death in 1988, can you help with some information I am looking for? Regards, Robert Pentegrass.*

Then there was a contact e-mail address.

Millie put the letter back.

Robert Pentegrass, Pentegrass, she knew that name, but couldn't think from where.

Making a decision, she retrieved her phone, rechecked the contact e-mail address on the letter and sent a message.

In Myrtle Creek a 'ding' alerted Claire of an incoming message.

Millie put her phone back into her handbag.

She again began to wonder what this might be about and again, as she looked out over the ocean, many other thoughts began to mingle in her mind.

Once more reassembling those thoughts into some form of pattern she fixed her thoughts on her great-grandfather. Thinking of the history about him that she knew, his name was Carlos and he had arrived by ship from Acapulco and settled here back in 1924.

〜✦〜

THE PAST;

Period 2

The year 1823–Acapulco, Mexico

Philippe Castagnet walked into the store on the waterfront, nodded a friendly hello to the young man who was behind a counter arranging a number of fish hooks into a wooden display box, and had a look around.

Zoltina Huanca asked if could be of any help and came around the counter to greet his customer.

"I am in need of some fishing equipment, and, I believe you hire out your vessel?"

Nine years. It had been nine years ago when Philippe had traversed practically the breadth of Colombia with the gold. Nine years since he and his men had successfully reached Buenaventura and had set sail for Acapulco. All had gone well, smooth sailing, a buoyant crew in a joyous mood, until a day out of their destination. In the evening before their arrival the weather turned, the sun had set and the wind increased. The sun and its light, had given way, to darkness. The seas changed, and within minutes the wind rushed at them. They had not even time to lower the sails.

The waves dramatically increasing in height and power, the sails ripped to shreds, the schooner floundered and was pushed by the wind and waves onto the shoreline. There was nothing anyone could do. At the mercy of nature the ship was swept closer and closer to the shore. A rocky shore.

The men held on to what they could, soon seeing the white of the froth on the wave tops as they rolled against the rocks. There was nothing to do, but get ready to abandon ship when the moment presented itself.

Nine years ago.

"Yes, it is the one directly opposite,' Zoltina said, pointing.

Philippe looked through the window of the store, he had spotted the vessel before entering, wondering if that was indeed the boat he could hire.

It would do very well.

"Yes that will do fine," he said, turning his attention to the fishing equipment that lined the walls. Twenty five minutes later he had agreed a price for the hire of the boat and had purchased what he needed.

Nine years!

As he left the store, thanking the young man who, after some friendly chatter and bartering, he had discovered was originally from Peru, and indeed a very knowledgeable and likeable young man, Philippe headed for the tavern not far from the dockside where they were waiting. All this time had passed.

Taking another quick look at the vessel he had just hired from the young man who's grandson would, nearly a hundred years later, travel to San Francisco, Philippe walked back into the town centre, thinking back to that fateful day…

So destructive had that quick storm been. He recalls jumping ship, when he gave the word to do so,shouting the command and watching his men, through the rain make the jump before he did so himself, he remembers shivering as the water had not only been seething, but cold. It was like a cauldron. He was sure at the time that he was going to die.

After what seemed like forever, but was likely no more than minutes, he was first struck against some rocks, then swept onto the beach itself. When he opened his eyes, he realised that he was breathing, he realised that he was alive. He was in pain, a lot of pain. All down one side. He was bleeding.

Making an effort to sit up, he managed, but it was very dark all around.

The wind had subsided and the sea was calm, he could hear the waves gently lapping onto the shore. His eyes slowly adjusted and the clouds broke to reveal a few stars. He carefully felt along his body, where the pain was, the left side of his chest was partly laid bare, his clothes having been shredded and he recalled his crash against the rocks.

Part of his trouser leg was also torn, he felt blood, both on his chest and his left leg, but grimacing as he tried to get up, he knew that nothing was broken.

To his relief, the leather skin water bottle, the same one that had served him well on his horseback journey from Bogota, was intact.

He opened it and drank, but then immediately felt dizzy. He managed to screw the lid back on the water bottle as he sat on the sand and then his eyes rolled upwards as he passed out.

Some time later, he opened his eyes, blinking several times, and noticed dawn was breaking, he sat up and saw that the sea was calm and the sky was clear. He made an effort and stood up, waited until he felt steady on his feet, then straightened up, relieved that he felt stronger.

Philippe gingerly walked along the beach, searching the shore, searching the sea. Nothing. He was alone.

No sign of his four horsemen; no sign of his six crew men. Not even a sign of any debris. Stopping, he looked for some time, scanning the shore, scanning the sea. Then he turned, and just as gingerly, walked the other way for a while. But nothing. Not a thing. He was alone. It was as if the ship never existed. It was as if he had just been deposited there, on a small stretch of sandy beach …

… Pushing those memories aside he entered the tavern, spotted where they sat and headed over.

"Well?" Caprice asked.

THE PRESENT;

Bilbao–Spain

Tuesday morning 28th May

During his flight he had pulled up a map on his laptop to get his bearings as to the whereabouts of the docks. He found out which dock the ferry would berth in, and studying the road maps, knew where he had to go in order to await the truck.

The N-644 led to the port, it was the only road in or out, so he was sure he would find a spot from where he could spot the J. Inverno vehicle.

Driving away from the airport in the rental vehicle, Thomas followed the instructions he had put into the satellite navigational system and reached the spot he was aiming for. A quick look around and he found the ideal spot and parked and waited. What exactly he was going to do, he had no idea. He would follow the truck, then see what developed. It was exactly 2.15 pm when he spotted it.

Forty minutes later, it all went wrong.

He was glancing at the navigation screen, and noticed that they were about to enter the town of Ampuero. It was a lovely forested area. Although he was pleased with his progress, he still was unsure as to what exactly he should do when the truck, now less than three hundred yards ahead, stopped. Where would it stop? Would he be able to get near? Would he be able to see what might happen?

Glancing at the screen, he was thinking about these things, when he sensed and heard a car engine. The vehicle, a pickup truck, with what sounded like a very powerful engine, was suddenly beside him, despite approaching a bend on the windy road. Then it swerved into him. The heavier vehicle shunted him aside and Thomas was suddenly off the road, slipping down a low bank. The brakes seemed to have no effect at all, nor did the steering, though a desperate pull on the wheel did manage to make a slight difference, and he narrowly scraped by a large tree. But then another slope took the car, still travelling at some speed, down and along.

The rear end lost control and swerved, but the undergrowth slowed the vehicle quite rapidly now. The crash was almost like a soft crunch, but Thomas felt the impact as the passenger side of the car scraped a large tree then they slithered to a stop. The engine cut out, and beside the ringing in his ears, all was suddenly quiet. Such had been the low impact against the tree, the air bags had not been deployed.

Thomas was angry with himself. He had been too assured, too confident. He had been spotted. Moreover, his ordeal was not yet over, for he noticed two men scrambling down from the roadside, heading for him.

Thomas released the seatbelt, opened the door, then stumbled out. His foot slipped and his head hit the top of the door. What to do now, where to go he thought, feeling somewhat dizzy.

The men, struggling slightly, working their way through the undergrowth, seemed to be unarmed and now only about fifty metres away. Stay and fight? He was pretty fit, albeit a little shaky right now, but there were two of them, and from this distance, he could see their determination. Run? But where to? Forty metres and the lead guy suddenly had a knife in his hand.

Thomas felt he had no option. He had been careless, had been spotted, but now he had to somehow turn the tables.

The second guy had stumbled on some tree roots, and was ten metres further behind. Thomas had to act, and act now. Pushing himself away from the car, he lunged forwards, towards the lead guy. This action surprised the man, who, Thomas saw as he drew closer, was, though stockier in build, about six inches shorter than him.

He slowed his advance, unaware that his friend behind him had once more been tripped by roots and had fallen to the ground.

Thomas however, had noticed. This gave him extra confidence and an incentive to charge. Picking up a short sturdy looking branch he lunged forwards.

Holding the branch and beginning to swing it, hopefully to aim for the man's knife hand, it was Thomas who stumbled and tripped.

He rolled but the branch he had picked up crumpled on impact.

The man with the knife advanced, but was then suddenly struck.

Thomas rolled over again. He'd seen something flying through the air, and tried to scramble to his feet.

A figure had suddenly appeared.

A second large pine cone flew through the air and connected.

The knife man was down, having stumbled backwards and tripped and was stunned, bleeding from a wound on the side of his head.

The second man, had himself regained his feet and seen what was happening. He turned around and scrambled back towards the road.

Thomas, though back on his feet, felt even more dizzy and his legs were trembling.

Managing, just, to stay upright he saw a figure approach him.

It was a woman.

Meanwhile in Myrtle Creek

Six-thirty in the morning, Claire stirred, then flung back the duvet cover and got up. She showered and thought about the e-mail she had received from Millie Parker the day before, a connection to the 1988 case file Robert had been working on, and the one he had asked Thomas to follow up on.

Claire dried herself, dressed and wondered how Thomas was getting on.

She had breakfast, then took a mug of tea up to the work room and fired up Robert's search engine.

Robert obviously felt that this Millie Parker might have some answers with regard to the events surrounding her mother's death, but answers to what.

After reading the e-mail the previous day, she had written back, explained that Robert had since passed, but that her mother's case was being looked into. She also wrote that she would check the file and get back to her as soon as possible as to what it might be that had made Robert curious.

It had been late into the evening when she finished reading the files that Thomas had started to read before the urgent interruption. Discovering some typed up notes amongst the papers, she found why Robert had been curious.

This morning she would contact Millie, and ask for her number to speak to her in person. Robert's findings and suppositions may not be totally founded on facts, but Claire knew Robert well enough to understand his workings out, and felt that there was certainly reason for further investigation, hence the importance he placed on this case file for Thomas to continue with.

Taking a sip of her tea, Claire then sent another e-mail asking Millie if she could speak with her. She would then be able to say that it may not have been the tornado that had killed her mother.

Back in Spain, near Ampuero

"Go and get you stuff from the car. We need to get away from here," she said, the words breaking through his confused mind. "Come on, quickly," she prompted, taking him by the elbow and steering him towards the rental car which stood forlorn in the thicket. She continued to speak to him, "I have already contacted the police, and given the number of the car that drove you off the road. Get your luggage and stuff, back to my car."

Thomas complied, her voice was strong, resolute. The grip on his arm firm. Who was she? Where had she suddenly come from?

He was shaken, more than he first realised. The shock of being forced off the road, ploughing down an embankment, scraping shrubs and trees, and coming to a standstill. Then getting out, hitting his head on the door frame, seeing two men heading towards him. He recalled seeing the second man tumble, seeing the first man, knife in hand coming at him fast.

He opened the rear door, grabbed his briefcase from the back seat.

Despite the trip down the embankment, and subsequent scrape against the tree, the briefcase was still where he had placed it.

She had let go of his arm, opened the driver's door, and found and pulled the lever to open the boot.

He remembered he had picked up a branch, but then had himself stumbled.

"Come on, I've got your case," she said, then moved back towards the road.

He followed.

"So, who exactly are you?" he managed to ask, also realising that he seemed somewhat out of breath and still rather dizzy.

"Time for explanations later. Got to get you back to my car," she said, turning to see him struggling behind her. He was pale, and she noticed he was bleeding a little from a cut just above his left eyeline.

She also noted that the two men were scrambling back up the embankment, but heading in the other direction, back to their vehicle. She was glad of that.

She reached the road; there was no traffic. She heard sirens in the distance.

"Here, give me your briefcase. Get in the car." she said. He handed it over and did as she asked.

She opened the boot, placed the suitcase and briefcase inside, slammed it shut and stood by her driver side door.

A police car came into view, from the town of Ampuero only a mile up the road.

She waved them down.

THE PAST;

Period 3

The year 1828–Hermosillo, Mexico

It was the evening after the celebrations. It was warm and a little humid. Philippe sat in a cane chair in the garden at the back of the stone house. The celebrations had been organised as the town, which had been their home now for the past five years, had its name changed, from Pitic to Hermosillo.

Philippe had been drawn to this region as the people here were very supportive of the Spanish. It was still warm and he was about to take another sip of cold beer, when his son appeared from the house, followed by his older sister and bringing up the rear, Caprice, his lovely wife.

Three-year-old Juan came to say goodnight. It was well past his bedtime. He leapt into his father's arms and kissed him on his forehead. Philippe held him tight, briefly, kissed him on his cheek and released him.

Their daughter, whom they had named Louisa, came next, far more grown-up, far more sophisticated, and with an air of confidence, she smiled at her father, then leaned over and kissed him on his cheek. Though now nearly eight years old, she was tired too, and it had been a long day. She headed after her brother, back into the house.

Caprice sat herself onto his lap, He encircled her with his arms.

They looked at each other. Philippe had fallen in love with her the first time he saw her, now more than fourteen years ago. She had been resistant at first, but had then seen something in his eyes, something in the way he spoke and something in his nature. She too, fell in love. She leaned forwards, they kissed, both of them lost for moments as time stood still, as the world around them seemingly dissolved.

They had each other, they had their children, they had all they needed … Caprice drew back, smiled at him, kissed him briefly on his lips and thought back, to that day in the barn, all those years ago …

Having cursed a lot, when unsaddling the horse that had brought her there, she told the young ranch hand to go into town to fetch the others, to overnight in the barn, and set off back home in the morning, taking three horses back with them.

She herself would follow the trail on her own horse with a spare. She would hunt him down, to the ends of the earth.

The young lad, seeing the fury in her eyes, left quickly. When he had disappeared from view, she set about to ready herself for the next phase of the plan.

A plan she and Philippe had made less than three weeks ago.

She was alive with excitement as she saddled her own horse. Caprice then made a quick search in the barn, found another saddle and other equipment, a blanket roll and a pair of saddlebags; provisions, prepared in readiness for her coming and for her onward journey.

Though perhaps it was fraught with danger for a woman travelling alone, she relished the adventure. She was self-assured and capable, she was armed, she was determined.

She felt happy, and for the first time in a long time, felt free. As she rode away from the barn that afternoon, knowing her destination, she recalled the wind in her face, recalled how she played the part of an angry young woman, played the part of a woman with an urge for revenge. She felt she had played it well as she rode away, circumnavigating the town of Girardot and heading south west.

Away from her home, away from a step-mother who showed little love, away from a father who was very controlling and cruel. She was free!

She followed the route that Philippe had planned and was alert and cautious, sleeping well away from any town, and only once venturing into one, early one morning, to replenish her provisions.

She made extremely good time, alternating the horses, and reached the stables on the north edge of Buenaventura only a day after Philippe and his men.

She had been a little wary when she saw some men there attending to three wagons and a number of horses. They gave her plenty of attention, but then this one man stepped from the group, sensing her discomfort, perhaps, and spoke to her.

"Looks like you have had long journey," he said, smiling and walking up to her horses. He spoke in Spanish, but this wasn't his native tongue, though he spoke it very well. Not only that, as he caressed her lead horse she sensed his goodness.

"A fine animal, this one," he said. Then after taking a cursory look at the second horse, looked at the woman, then said, "The stable patron is not here at present, but I can assist if you wish."

She nodded at the man, feeling instantly relaxed, then wondered and asked, "I have indeed travelled far. This is the end of the journey for me, at least on land. You like this horse. Obviously you appreciate a good horse, would you be interested in purchasing it?"

Henry walked around the animal, noticed the long barrelled shotgun tucked into a special sheath attached to the saddle and asked, "and the shotgun?" noticing it was very similar to the one he already had and might come in handy.

"That too I will no longer need," she replied.

Henry and the young woman bartered to an agreed price, for the horse, the saddle and the shotgun. The second horse she would leave as payment for the stable owner.

The weapon would indeed prove useful and help save Henry's life and the lives of his men a little over five years from that time in a confrontation with marauding bandits.

"Henry, his name was Henry," Caprice whispered, as she got up from his lap. "Come on, let go inside. It's getting colder."

"I'll be in shortly," he answered, watching her go inside the house.

He too, began to bring to mind the events of the past.

The coming back to consciousness when on the beach was the first thing he began to recall, and not for the first time. Over the years he had often thought of that moment. The pain he felt; the realisation that he was alive, the realisation, after walking painfully up and down the beach that he was alone.

He could not understand it; could not perceive that there was no wreckage. There were no bodies, nothing but an empty ocean on a clear and beautiful morning.

He felt emotional. He felt drained. He had pain in his chest and his leg was throbbing continuously, but after some time he also realised that he was hungry. Philippe dragged himself to his feet once more, and headed inland, to find a farm, a village, a town, anything.

It wasn't until he had walked up the gradually sloping bank to the ridge when he noticed two things. First, as he reached the brow and could see what lay ahead, he was pleased to see what looked to be a village in the distance. Then, as he turned to look once more at the sea behind him, he spotted the rocky outcrops. Initially, in the dark of the evening, they had thought that the rocks were the actual shoreline. He could now see there were a series of rocks some distance away that protruded above the sea level and stretched more than fifty metres. Somehow, he must have been pushed through a gap by the severity of the wind and waves and washed onto the beach.

It appeared the others had not been as fortunate. He seemed to be the only survivor, His ten men were gone. The ship was gone. The gold was gone.

Philippe turned and headed for the village which he estimated was a couple of kilometres away. But he had gone no more than a hundred metres or so when he blacked out again and dropped to the ground.

He shivered, suddenly felt a little cold, and got up from the cane chair to head inside the house.

Later she lay in his arms, listening to his breathing. She thought how he had been quite nostalgic earlier, as had she, thinking of their lives together, the past, and how they got here, to this point, with two lovely children.

She loved him so much, and knew that she meant the world to him.

Caprice sighed and smiled as she once again took herself back in time.

She was about to leave Henry and his men, wishing them a safe and prosperous journey, but Henry insisted that he go with her to make sure she was safe and help her secure passage to Acapulco where she was aiming to go.

She smiled her thanks.

Not much later, with the extra funds she now had thanks to the sale of her horse the saddle and her father's shotgun, and with the help of Henry, she secured passage on a Spanish Galleon that was due in a few days' time and a safe inn until then. She thanked Henry, and as she settled into her room looking through a small window overlooking the harbour, thought of Philippe.

Four days later she boarded the Spanish Galleon and five days after that, the ship sailed into the harbour of Acapulco.

Caprice stood on the foredeck, scanning the dock area ahead. Her heart skipped several beats when she saw him.

Saw the tall dark haired man she was so much in love with, saw his broad smile. He was waving

She lifted her head from his chest, briefly watched as he slept, so peacefully now, but there had been times when his mind had been troubled.

She kissed him lightly on the forehead, then turned and settled in to sleep.

THE PRESENT;

Near Ampuero, Northern Spain

Tuesday evening 28th May

They had left the hotel and she had driven out of town, heading south, then after less than three miles, she looked for, found and turned into a parking area in this forested region. There were no other vehicles.

She had been quiet, had not spoken other than to say to him, "Okay, let's go."

Getting out of the rental car, she spoke, "This way, follow me."

Thomas, feeling refreshed, followed her. It was early evening and the light was fading. He thought back, to around four hours earlier, when she had told him to stay in the car whilst she dealt with the police.

Her Spanish was quite good Thomas observed, glad he was sitting down. He still felt a little shaken, a little dizzy, and incredibly curious as to who this woman was who had so deftly plucked him from danger and was now confidently speaking with the local police. He noted that she made no mention of the two men, and that she wanted to get this man to a local doctor. She also informed them that she had spoken to the rental company and could they pass on their report to them. She gave them her contact number and got in behind the wheel. The policemen, both slightly shorter than her, nodded and smiled and took it all in, agreeing to all she asked. Whoever she was, she sure had a very commanding way about her, as well as being rather attractive.

Once in town, she stopped the car in a roomy plaza, then turned, took hold of his chin, turned his face towards her, looked briefly into his eyes, studied the cut on the side of his head and said, "Stay here. You'll be fine. I'll get something to dress that cut, then we'll plan our next move."

With that she was gone and he watched as she crossed over to a shop with a green medical cross hanging above it.

"Our next move?" he said softly to himself. "Who are you lady?"

She was back within minutes, smiled at him and turned on the engine. "There's a small hotel just around the corner. We'll go there," and pulled away.

The hotel was indeed just around the corner and she parked the car.

Turning again to look at him, she took a linen handkerchief from her handbag, pressed it gently where the cut was and said, "Just press it lightly until we get inside the lobby, then I'll see to it when we get to our rooms. Can you manage your own luggage?"

"Ahh, yes, of course," Thomas answered and got out of the car.

Each with their own baggage they entered the hotel lobby, Thomas struggling a little carrying his case and his briefcase with one hand, whilst keeping the handkerchief pressed to his forehead, until they were inside the lobby where she did all the talking, renting two rooms for two nights.

Cash in hand she paid for them, signed a ledger, then turned and smiled.

The rooms were adjacent and though basic, were clean and tidy and each had an en suite as well. She unlocked the door, and gave him the key. "I'll be there in a few minutes. Don't lock the door," she said and moved to enter the other room.

Thomas placed his case on the floor, put his briefcase and the room key on a small table and had just sat on the bed, again pressing the now bloodied handkerchief to just above his eye.

She entered the room, closing the door behind her, and with some medical equipment in hand sat beside him.

Once again taking hold of his chin, she took the handkerchief away, then looked into his eyes and studied the wound.

"You have a slight concussion," she said, then proceeded to dress the wound with some antiseptic, which stung, and placed a plaster over it. Finally she wiped away the streaks of blood and some additional ointment gently with her own handkerchief.

"Get some rest," she said, looking at her watch. "I'll come and see you in an hour." With that she left the room.

Whether it had been an hour or not, he didn't know, but when he stirred to wakefulness she was sitting at the end of the bed.

"Hi," she said, "I'm Cynthia Barnes, but please call me Tia."

Thomas frowned, the name rang a distant bell.

"Here," she said, fishing a chocolate bar from her handbag, "eat this. Sugar, energy. It will be good for you, until dinner time. First, we must talk. Well, I will talk, you listen, okay?"

Thomas unwrapped the bar and began to eat it.

He was feeling quite well really, the short nap had done him good. He ate and looked into her eyes and still had a feeling her knew her from somewhere.

It was all very well to say to just listen, but he had questions, "Are you one of Roberts helpers?" he asked, between mouthfuls before she could begin to speak. Her look told him everything. He was to shut up and listen.

"Okay, okay, listen. Right, off you go."

"I think that you recognised my name, though perhaps not from where. Well, you knew me, I knew you, way back in high school ..." she could see that Thomas had connected the name and was about to say something, "Don't speak, not yet. Wait until I have finished, okay?"

He nodded and continued eating the chocolate bar. "I was one of the three ABC girls. Oh what fun we had, but oh how I regret that time, regret who I was, what I, what we did.

"I remember you sticking up for Robert on several occasions, not just because of us, but with other bullies as well. It seemed the school was rife with them at that time."

She paused very briefly, again looking at him, "Anyway, you have to know, maybe you remember that I, well, didn't ask, but suggested that you take me to the dance. More of an order really. How I remember it, as if you could have no option than to comply."

After a slight pause, then, "If you recall, there were three boys, who came at you, attacked and beat you, one day? Well, I watched; I smiled; I was satisfied. I had arranged it."

Again Tia paused for a moment, Thomas noticed that her eyes, a light green in colour, were slightly moist. She held his gaze for a moment, then looked down.

He finished his chocolate bar and kept silent, there was more to come.

"Whilst it felt good at the time," she said, still looking down, "that evening I cried. Felt ashamed of what I had done." After another short pause, Tia looked up, into his eyes again, then, sighing a little, she continued, "Time passed. I had a younger brother, and when he went to the high school, for his first year, he was bullied, possibly because I was his sister … probably, because I was his sister … It was about, two months into the school year …" He noticed she was now close to tears.

"He began to shut himself away in his room, after school. He, he looked at me differently. Then one day, he left home, in the evening. Mum found a note.

He had gone to the river, threw himself of the bridge into the Willamette river."

Tears rolled down her cheeks now.

Thomas remained silent.

"Suicide by drowning," was the verdict. The note, and mum allowed it to be read in school a few days later, read "To all you bullies, I am going to kill myself, hope this satisfies you."

The school, the students, everyone; there was silence; there were tears.

I cried every night for at least a week. I had a part in his death, me, my attitude, my bullying of others," through the tears she looked at Thomas. "I am so sorry," her voice barely a whisper.

Thomas remained silent, he felt there was still more to come, more for her to explain. Best not to speak just now.

Cynthia took out a small handkerchief, wiped the tears away, blew her nose. Appreciating his silence and composing herself, she continued, "I left school. I wanted to put it all behind me. I got a job, then, later continued to study from home." She sighed, took a deep breath, and composed herself a little more. "So, years passed then one day, about ten years ago now, I ran into Robert.

I recognised him, but he didn't remember me. I found out later that he had some form of Asperger's Syndrome, I also remember how we belittled him that day, and how you came to the rescue.

Also, I will always remember what you said to us, when you took Robert away. You said, and I still remember it, word for word, 'Your amusement today, will one day turn to sorrow.'

She looked at Thomas, he looked back, but stayed silent.

"It sure did turn to sorrow, didn't it. It also turned to sorrow for Alison, Ally, one of the three. She got into a relationship, had a daughter and one day her daughter was taken from her, abducted, by the girl's father and new girlfriend, and you know what that girlfriend, or wife actually, turned out to be Robert's sister, Sandra.

"What a small world we live in sometimes," she said, her voice a little stronger again, and went on, "Anyway, I met Robert. We got talking and I found out what he did. He searched for missing people, boys and girls, men and women, who had either been taken, or had run away. It was a sign for me. I had to help. I was financially very secure, but that's another story, so, I became Robert's helper, his eyes and ears on the outside, for he rarely went out anywhere.

"So, for almost a decade now, I got to know a little about how he works. He trusted me, gave me directions, clues as to where to look, where to go. He was good at his research. Over the years, we assisted in the rescue of many missing persons. Also found a few that, well, where it didn't end that well.

"Claire was one of the successful ones. On her own bat she found Robert, went to work for him that was a good thing."

Tia paused for a moment, sighed, took another breath, then continued, as she could see that Thomas was still listening intently.

"His illness came suddenly. His death even more so. I was devastated, lost, but he wrote me a letter. In it he asked me to do something. He obviously knew that he was dying, close to the end. He asked me, to watch over you."

Tia gave another deep sigh, wiped away a few more tears, reached over and took hold of Thomas's hand, then said, "So, I am your guardian angel."

Another brief pause, then Cynthia continued, smiling and her tone once again upbeat, "You were so fast, I had no idea where you were heading when you left. Had to think on my feet. Managed to get on the same flight to Atlanta. Robert had given me a code to access his e-mails, so I was able to open an e-mail, figuring it may contain some info as to what was happening, the one from the UK. I discovered what you were up to, then. When in Atlanta, I too booked a flight to Bilbao, also took out a rental car and kept an eye on you, wondering what you were going to do … What were you going to do? Did you have a plan?"

Thomas kept hold of her hand, gripped it tightly for a moment, feeling tears building up behind his eyes and wondering if he even had a voice to speak. Then, clearing his throat, said, "Well, no actually. When we first read the e-mail, it sounded like something needed to be done. I felt I had to try at least to see where it might lead."

Then, after a pause as he looked into her tearful eyes, said, "Thank you, for sharing. That was a tough time for you back then, but you know, we all do things in life that we come to regret. I'm sorry about your brother."

With his right-hand thumb wiping another tear from her cheek, he said, "Thank you for coming to my rescue."

"But," again clearing his throat, "what do we do now? There is a woman is danger, what can we do?"

"We'll think about that. Tell me, I think Claire must be helping? I did see her at the funeral, but I kept my distance. How is she?"

"Yes, she's a good young lady. Robert very much liked to work alone, given his condition that was understandable, but she wants to help, so, she's helping. Who, by the way, is DP?"

"I don't know. As you said, Robert kept a lot of things to himself. When I saw that e-mail that's the first I ever heard of a DP. Also, whoever it is, had no idea that Robert had passed, so, not a very close contact."

She got up from the bed having let go of his hand, said "I'm just going to freshen up. I'll knock on your door in half an hour, then we'll go and grab some dinner somewhere," and with that she left the room…

Thomas closed the passenger side door and followed Tia as she crossed over the road and walked into the woods on the opposite side.

He soon caught up and was at her shoulder.

After a few minutes, walking along a narrow dirt path, she said, "I do know where I'm going. I checked out some maps. Not far from here, you'll soon see," glancing at him and giving him a brief smile.

Thomas smiled back, then, with the trees making the fading light even darker, took in the woman beside him. She was tall, probably around five eight or nine. Her hair was dark brown, cut quite short. Dressed in denim jeans, a light rain jacket, feet in ankle boots and a checked cotton shirt beneath the jacket, she was rather attractive, he observed for the second time.

"Nearly there," she said, then they stepped out of the woods and below them, was the valley.

The light was stronger now that they had left the forested area.

Thomas took in what he saw before him.

Nearest to them, no more than about six hundred metres away, stood a large building. He could see the road leading up to a big courtyard in front of it.

And there, reversed into the loading bay, was the J. Inverno truck. There were two smaller buildings beyond the large warehouse.

Beyond those was a wooden fence. It stretched all the way from the second of the small buildings, up to another road that wound itself further along the valley to reach the hacienda-type ranch that lay some hundred metres or so from the nearer buildings. Then, to the far right of the valley, stood another, what looked to be a large hanger of sorts. Outside it, stood a plane.

"He has his own plane," Thomas observed.

"Of course, you're a pilot," she said, her voice just above a whisper, though they were well away from where anyone might hear them.

Thomas took in more of what he saw. A large orchard stretched along the rear, behind the nearer building, all the way to the rear of the hacienda itself. Though at a distance, and with the light now fading quickly, he could see the hacienda was large with many porticos, courtyards and a balcony that ran along the front of the first floor.

"Wow, quite the estate," he said, looking at Tia.

Meanwhile, over five thousand miles away in Myrtle Creek

Claire blew out her cheeks and sat back in the leather desk chair. Her eyes were moist. She had been on the verge of crying, when she heard Robert's voice.

The two discs that had been in the case file, were recordings of telephone conversations. After receiving the e-mail from Millie Parker, she had delved into the case that Thomas had begun to look into before the urgent communication from the mysterious DP had sent him flying off to Spain.

Case 1988.

She had read through the newspaper report, through the police findings, and through the notes Robert had written. Then she had inserted the first of the two discs to suddenly hear Roberts voice. The first call, first recorded conversation, was to a woman whose name was Nueva Santos.

"Ah, Mrs Santos? Mrs Nueva Santos?"

"Yes?"

"Ah, my name is Robert Pentegrass. I assist the Portland and Oregon police in investigating cold cases of missing persons. In doing so, I came across a report about a Mr Eddie Philpot, and I believe, you worked with him, in your student days, both working with a Mrs, or I should say Professor, Emily Parker. This was in 1988?"

"Yes sir, I was there. You are of course referring to the tornado tragedy, I will never forget?"

"Yes, of course. Sorry to, well relive that time, but, as I have been looking into this, the subsequent disappearance of this Eddie, may I ask you a few questions?"

"Yes, of course. But what do you mean his disappearance? He survived, went back to, well I don't know where to. Are you saying he disappeared?"

"Yes Ma'am. Sorry to ask, but can you talk me through what you remember of that day when the tornado came?"

In her home in Albuquerque, the now forty-nine-year-old Nueva, married with three children, sat herself down on the stool by the breakfast bar. Something was suddenly nagging at her, causing her to frown, and she began to think back, then began to tell what she remembered, of that day a little over three miles from Silver City, New Mexico.

Nueva had momentarily stepped from the main tent. It was the middle of the day.

It was hot. Inside the tent they had been carefully sifting through, and recording, the findings of the dig. She was very pleased to be there; chosen to assist Professor Parker on recently discovered, believed to be Mayan, ruins of a lost village.

Earlier, they had been told of a tornado in the region, but it was still several miles away and heading north, and there was no reason for concern.

However, there was suddenly a change.

The stillness from only moments earlier was no longer. The almost oppressive heat seemed to suddenly cool down, and the wind began to toy with Nueva's long hair. Looking at the sky, then looking into the distance, she first froze to the spot. A tornado, in the distance, but seemingly drawing closer. It was huge, towering high into the sky.

Her first instinct was to head for the professor's trailer. She got her feet to move, ran across the dirt, and reaching the trailer practically flew up the two steps and banged hard on the door.

"Professor Emily!" she shouted.

The door opened and as Nueva was about to explain, she could see that it was not necessary, for the professor looked beyond the student, her eyes widening, her mouth open.

Nueva turned. The tornado was huge, it was coming in very fast and already the wind was beginning to disturb the dirt on the ground around them.

"Quick, come inside," Emily Parker, said, grabbing the student and literally pulling her inside the trailer and shutting the door. Such was the speed of the tornado, there wasn't time to do anything else. No time to warn anyone else.

The sudden roar like that of a dozen approaching diesel trains boomed all around.

In her home in the kitchen, Nueva stopped, paused, as she recollected what happened next.

"Thank you for talking to me," Robert said, "I know that this must be rather difficult for you."

"Yes, no. Well, it's okay, or, maybe," Nueva managed to say, then closed her eyes and began to tell what happened next.

"After she dragged me inside and shut the door, she told me to get under the table, which was her makeshift desk. She then got under it with me, but then but then she got out, reached over and grabbed a folder from the table top, then got back under and"

After a long pause, Robert prompted her. "Ma'am?"

"Sorry, yes. Well, I've just remembered something, something I had never considered, never thought about. Well, it was such a chaotic event you see, afterwards, later, when I saw Professor Emily's body, well, it wasn't there."

"What wasn't there Mrs Santos?" Robert said, prompting her once more.

"The sound was horrific," Nueva said, she had paled a little, telling and remembering. "Then the whole trailer was shaking, then it moved, then something else was flung against it, the noise, it seemed to never end when it finally stopped I was by the door of the trailer. Professor Emily lay at the other end of the trailer. The table had moved, but was still upright.

"There were many boxes and other stuff all strewn about the place, but, she spoke to me, the professor,"

"Check on the others" she said. She was bleeding from a wound on her head, but she spoke to me. Also, the folder, the one that she had grabbed just before, she had it clasped to her chest.

"Well, I went outside. The trailer had been damaged by another trailer that had been blown against it. I saw that the main tent was completely gone. I heard cries and crying. But people were alive, well, most of them.

"I walked around and helped, and spoke to my fellow students. I remember crying. Well, it was, about well I don't know, fifteen minutes or so, later, I went back to report to the professor. Her assistant, Mr Alfredo, who had been in the other trailer, he had died. Then two of my fellow students, had also passed.

I was shaken and crying and hurt. Went back to see the Professor but she had also died I couldn't believe it. I could see that she was dead. I didn't go near her body, I just knew but here's the thing. Now, thinking back on it all, the strangest thing, the folder, the one she had been clutching, was not there.

"How did I not remember that until just now?" she said, after another pause.

"You were in shock, Mrs Santos. Friends had died. People you knew had died. You were in shock. Don't blame yourself for not remembering, but thank you so very much. That detail could well help me in solving this case."

After more pleasantries and surprisingly comforting words from Robert, for whom this was not like his usual self, Claire thought, given his condition he normally showed little compassion, the call ended.

The second disc was a short telephone conversation with the administrator of the University in Albuquerque which had been the sponsor of the dig in Silver City.

In it Robert asked if there were any findings on the dig, or if indeed work had continued on it after the devastating tornado had hit the site.

The administrator said he would look into the matter and would be pleased to forward anything he might find.

Claire wondered if anything had been found, if anything had been forwarded, and if so, where might that be. One thing was for sure, the notes Robert had written, about his suspicion on the death of the professor, were indeed warranted. The conversation she had just heard between Robert and this woman, Nueva, certainly confirmed it. When the young student, obviously in shock, had left the trailer to check on the situation, Emily Parker had been alive, and moreover had a folder clasped to her bosom.

Claire was sure now that foul play had indeed occurred.

The folder very likely containing important findings that were worth killing for. Her assistant in the other trailer, was also dead. Was his death due to the tornado, or was he too killed?

Claire looked at the clock on the wall and realised it was getting close to lunchtime. She had promised to ring Millie Parker late morning. Reaching for her phone, she looked at a sheet of paper and dialled the number.

When Millie's phone rang in San Francisco, in the darkness somewhere in the countryside near to the town of Ampuero, Thomas and Tia slowly made their way towards the hacienda.

They had made their way down the hillside and reached the orchard to the right of the large warehouse. It was fenced, but the fence was a low three plank wooden structure and there seemed to be no security cameras within their sight as they moved carefully among the citrus trees towards the west of the valley and the hacienda.

Since observing the valley from their hillside vantage point, neither had spoken.

Tia was leading. Having googled the area, she knew the rough layout of the main house. They reached the end of the orchard run. A stone wall was before them. Slightly to the right a wooden door would lead into the courtyard beyond.

"I want a peak over the wall," she said, her voice low, looking at Thomas.

He understood, placed himself with his back against the wall, which was over seven feet in height, cupped his hands together in front of him and felt her hands on his shoulders as she stepped into the clasped hands and heaved herself up.

"This courtyard is clear," she said, stepping down again, her face inches away from his, "There is another archway, leading to the next courtyard. Let's go."

Tia made her way to the wooden door, tried the iron door handle and pushed.

It opened, made no sound and she went through. Thomas followed.

Tia moved quickly towards the next archway, her soft-soled boots making no sound at all on the tiled floor. Thomas was right behind her, then moved to a position on the opposite side of the archway. Both peered through.

They were at the back of the large house. Whereas there was a balcony that ran the length of the house at the front, Thomas had observed, from quite a distance away, at the back there was only a small balcony.

He briefly thought it strange as the view from this side over the valley was surely a better one. There was a sound of music softly permeating through the air. But there were no lights showing on this side of the house, with the exception of one lamp, from inside an extension to the house on the right-hand side. No sign of any cameras, no sensor detectors.

Tia looked across at Thomas in the dimness, then gestured with her head and moved swiftly to the rear of the house, almost pressing herself to the stucco wall. Thomas followed. She then moved around past Thomas and headed for the extension where the light shone through the vertical blinds.

The addition to the original house proved to be a gym.

Peering through a gap in the blinds she saw the spacious floor, and noticed two walking machines as well as two exercycles. There was an array of other equipment dotted around the edges, but then she saw the woman. Thomas saw her too.

Her wrists were tied together and the rope ran upwards where it was attached to the end rafter. The light, from a single lamp on a wall at the other end showed she was dressed in crumpled and dirty clothing.

Her shoes had been kicked off and she hung there, slouched, her stockinged feet just touching the wooden floor. Her head was slumped, her hair, bedraggled, hanging limply like a curtain.

Thomas noticed that there was a door leading to the outside, "Psst," he said, and walked around the corner of the building to where the door, a single door, led inside. Here there were no blinds and he could see the whole room, right to the far end double doors. No one was about, only the woman, who hung there, not six feet from where he stood.

Tia saw it all too, then whispered, "What are the chances of this door being unlocked?"

Thomas tried the handle. Pulled towards him and the door was indeed unlocked.

It opened. They looked at each other briefly, then leaving it open, they both entered. There was no sound of any alarm, no sound of anything. They couldn't even hear the soft music any more. Tia walked around to the front of the woman, brushed her hair aside and lifted her head to see the woman's face.

"She's unconscious," Tia whispered. "Hold her up as much as you can. I'll untie her hands. Thomas nodded, walked around to the front of the woman, then encircling her with his arms, lifted, making sure he was close enough to her face to stop her crying out should she awaken.

Tia stretched and worked on the knotted rope. It took a little effort, but with Thomas taking the strain on the rope, she managed to undo it.

Thomas then shifted his position slightly and with a heave lifted the woman over his right shoulder. The fireman's lift.

It reminded him of his pilots' training, many years ago. He learned this in case of emergency evacuations. He moved towards the door through which they had entered and Tia, having picked up the woman's shoes, followed, though just as she was about to exit, she noticed the handbag.

It had to belong to the woman otherwise it wouldn't be here. She quickly snatched it from the floor, then left the building, softly closing the door. She said to Thomas, "Back the same way."

He set off. The woman was a lightweight. He figured her to be no more than about five foot four, and, judging by her face, which he had kept an eye on whilst Tia was untying the rope, she was in her early or mid-sixties.

He also noticed that one side of her face was reddened, most likely caused by several hard slaps. "Who was this woman?" he thought as he moved through the first archway. Tia was right behind, then passed him quickly in order to open the wooden door leading to the orchard. Letting him through she closed the door and was right behind him as they made their way back to the car.

She too was wondering who this woman might be and why they had gone to quite some trouble to abduct her, even to the point of running Thomas off the road and coming at him with a knife. She was glad when they reached the end of the orchard and was amazed how easily Thomas climbed over the wooden fence, still carrying the woman over his shoulder.

Going up the hill was a bit harder, and by the time they reached the edge of the forest, Thomas stopped for a moment, transferring the woman onto his other shoulder, then said to Tia, "Lead the way. That way I can trace your footsteps."

Tia, having been the leader all this time, acknowledged his request and led the way into the wooded area. The car was not far away now, and despite the difficulty in moving through the now dark forest, they reached the road, crossed it and got to the car.

THE PAST;

Period 4

The year 1858–On the Colorado River near Yuma

Juan Castagnet kept his horses calm, talking to them, stroking them, constantly going from one to the other, his voice soft and calm, influencing the horses to be the same.

There were eight of them, fine animals, good stock, healthy, robust and well trained. As well as the horses there were two wagons sat upon the barge, ever so slightly rocking as it was being towed through the shallow waters of the Colorado river.

The magnificent paddle-steamer towing them was about a hundred and twenty feet in the length, with two decks, the chimney belching out smoke. It easily chugged along, towing the large barge as well as with much cargo on board. The rear paddle wheel churned up the waters.

At first it had been the noise of the steam engine that Juan felt might be of concern to the horses, but he led them onto the barge easily, and as he kept giving them attention, and an occasional treat, they were fine. Even the large paddle wheel thumping into the water didn't seem to faze them. They weren't far away from Fort Yuma now.

Juan felt the slight breeze on his face as they went around another bend in the mighty river. He reflected on the Fort's history, and the fact that it had been founded nine years ago, information he had picked up prior to boarding the barge, for it had been nine years ago that he left the family home when he was twenty-four.

Juan glanced over to the covered wagon, not only full of equipment for his trade, for he was a blacksmith, but also his personal belongings as it was his home. Six of the eight horses, were for the Fort. He had also sold horses to them previously, a total of fourteen in fact. But this time, as the fort had no blacksmith at present, they were employing him for three months.

Later that day, after leading the horses off, and harnessing his own two horses to the wagon, he rolled it off the barge. He was given a spot by the river near the Fort where he could set up his camp and there were two buildings he could use for his blacksmith services. Juan was well pleased. He received his payment for the horses he delivered, and once his own horses were settled and fed, sat on the back of his wagon. The light was fading, so he sat close to the lantern he had lit and again opened his father's journal. Though he had already perused the thick book that had been given him several times, there were still areas which he either had not read properly or missed altogether.

His father had begun to write this journal around six months after he had been shipwrecked, but began by telling the story of when he had first laid eyes on Caprice. He wrote about falling in love, about the plan he and Caprice made, the detailed planning of the theft of the gold, the journey to the coast, and the sea journey to what he had hoped would be Acapulco, and how he would wait at the dock every day until the day she arrived. But then there had been that sudden and violent storm.

Juan fixed himself something to eat and drink, checked on his horses, then settled down to read some more, commencing where his father wrote about the evening before that fatal storm.

*I am very pleased. The sea journey is going
well, Acapulco about a day away*

Even though it was over six months ago, Philippe remembered it as if it happened only days ago.

Whilst it was relatively quiet, he brought four of the seamen into his cabin, leaving two to keep an eye on things. His four horsemen were in the galley, preparing dinner as they were on kitchen duty during the voyage.

Philippe had opened the gold chest earlier and had drawn out what he needed.

He paid each of the six seamen six gold coins each, a substantial amount which they could get by on until such time as they found their next passage.

His four horsemen, he paid eight coins each and for himself he put twelve aside, which he secured in a pouch tucked beneath his clothing around his waist. The remaining seven hundred and twenty gold coins remained in the secure locked chest. Then came the storm, late in the evening.

Juan skipped a few pages and continued reading from the time his father had found himself alone on the shore, no sign of the wrecked ship, no sign of his men, nothing. Then seeing what looked to be a village ahead, turning to see that the rocks they had crashed into, were quite some distance from the shore and then stumbling and blacking out again as he made his way down a small hill.

The sound stirred him. The sound and the smell. Then he felt a breeze. It was a horse. He opened his eyes, and saw the animals head, right by his face, the nostrils blowing in his face. The horse snorted a little, then lifted its head and stood, as if waiting. Philippe, painfully, brought himself to a sitting position, realised he was talking to the horse, "Alright boy, I'm up, I'm up," then as he took in this horse, noticed it was saddled. But, where was the rider?

He forced himself to stand, then went over to the horse and took the reins, all the while talking, "So, my friend, where is your master, or your mistress? Come on boy, take me there."

And as if the horse sensed what was required, it started to move, pulling him in the direction of the village ahead. He hadn't gone too far, his movements slowly feeling steadier. His legs, though a little wobbly, carried him onwards. His head was throbbing. His chest was hurting.

But it was only moments later when Philippe noticed a body, on the ground; the body of a young girl. She had obviously fallen, had a cut on her head and was unconscious. With all his effort, he lifted her.

She was surprisingly light but there was no way he had the strength to mount the horse or even place the girl upon it.

He had let go of the reins and the horse walked on.

Philippe, making sure he held the girl securely, slowly followed.

What he had first thought a village, was a small settlement. Several old buildings, a larger farmhouse, two small cottages and a barn that held two wagons and a variety of equipment. He heard a voice, a woman's voice, and saw her. She was running towards him, but whatever language she was speaking, he could not understand. A man was now also hurrying towards him.

The horse had stopped. Philippe stopped. The woman came up and held out her arms, he placed the girl into them and then, suddenly feeling quite dizzy again, stumbled and collapsed a third time …

… Juan turned a few more pages, the next part of his father story was, he felt, pretty mundane stuff. He had been sixteen years old when he had asked his father what he was writing almost every day, and had been shown the journal. There were definitely many boring bits, and what he called soppy stuff.

Sitting on the back of his covered wagon, reading by the lantern that shone brightly upon the pages, Juan smiled and he turned to the more interesting parts of his father and mother's journey …

… The next day, a recovered Philippe told them how he needed to get to Acapulco as his soon-to-be wife, was due to arrive at some point in the next week he hoped.

The man of the household, now a farmer, used to be, in charge of the horses, all the tack and saddles in the Spanish army, and most importantly, he was a blacksmith, a trade and expertise that came in very useful.

He had settled in the region when his regiment disbanded, and were scattered by the Creole uprising. He stopped when he saw a young woman knocked aside in a skirmish, helped her and subsequently stayed.

She took him in, kept him hidden for a while in her rough dwelling, and they later moved closer to the coast and set about building a new home for themselves. With help from the woman's brother and father, they set up a small farm with some cattle and a few goats, then planted alfalfa, ideal for the conditions in which they lived, and which had many uses, as well as being a great source of manure.

They built a cottage, then two barns, and another couple of buildings that could house the animals when the conditions were too harsh for them to be outside.

They had been living there now for nearly fifteen years.

The woman's father had since passed, but the brother had taken a wife and they, along with their first child, made up part of the homestead. The Spaniard, whose name was Carlos, and his Creole wife had two children, a girl of three and their eldest, a girl of eleven, who had been the one Philippe had carried home.

They told him to take one of the horses, travel to Acapulco, a mere six miles away, to await his woman.

Philippe said he would return with her

Juan arched his back, then settled to read the part of his father's story about the gold. As a boy, this was a great adventure story. He found the right page and continued reading the writings of his father, taking him to that time and place.

Armed with a letter written by Carlos, Philippe found the stables that were owned and run by a former compatriot who had served with Carlos. Here he not only stabled the horse, but was also given a room. Every day Philippe would go to the harbour and check on expected vessels. Three days after his arrival, he was more than excited as he watched the Spanish galleon come into view.

The very same day, hitching the horse to a buggy, courtesy of Carlos' friend, he brought Caprice back to the homestead. Although it was only Carlos who spoke their language, Philippe and Caprice were soon part of the homestead family, helping and working around the farm. Carlos had already been told of the shipwreck that had brought Philippe here. He was also told of the cargo, specifically the gold coins that were meant to set up their new life in Mexico, and between them they set about to figure out how to retrieve them from the sunken schooner.

Carlos was a very handy and knowledgeable man. The cattle and goats were left in control of his wife and her sister-inlaw, while he and her brother worked the land Carlos also used his blacksmith skills, built a forge, built a plough and secured an anvil and other equipment from Acapulco. The brother was handy with woodwork.

Early one morning, Philippe took Carlos to the shore and as they came over the hill, the one he remembered crossing over on that day, they saw the rows of rocks some hundred metres from the shoreline. He pointed them out to Carlos. They spent some time in discussing, first of all, how to get to the rocks, then how to proceed and search under the water for any wreckage.

Later that evening, Carlos, his wife Rosena, her brother Marcos and his wife, Chantale, and Philippe and Caprice, talked through how they might achieve this salvage. It turned out that both Caprice and Chantale were good swimmers.

Four days later, the weather was suitable, and with Rosena staying behind to watch over the children, Carlos, Philippe, Marcos and the two women, Caprice and Chantale, headed for the shore.

The three men were carrying a small boat between them. These little boats, made of straw, referred to as Cabalitto de totora, literally meaning boats of straw had been in use for centuries in this region and throughout South America, particularly in Peru. Marcos had procured one from Acapulco two days ago. They also took some chain and a grappling hook as well as some netting. First they set off from the shore with the equipment. Marcos and Philippe headed for the line of rocks and hoped to find some sort of perch on the other side of them where they could set up.

Philippe came back to take the two women across and Marcos, then sailed back to fetch Carlos.

The sea was calm, they found a wide strip of level stone, ideal for their purpose and Caprice and Chantale stripped to their underclothes and went into the water, which, according to both ladies, was quite warm. They were successful on their very first dive, the wreck was right there, broken in two. With the aid of the grappling hook, and the chain, forged and made by Carlos, the two women worked together with just one aim, to find the chest. They located it after their fourth dive and then managed to attach the hook to it. It took the three men nearly forty minutes to haul it to the surface.

Juan smiled, closed the journal and looked over his shoulder to where a large trunk stood, next to his own anvil.

The trunk, should anyone be curious enough to open it and look inside, contained hammers, nails, tongs, some other tools and many, many horseshoes.

However, beneath all that equipment, was the very chest hauled from the sea that day. Juan closed the flaps to the wagon, blew out the lantern and prepared for sleep.

THE PRESENT;

San Francisco

Tuesday afternoon 28th May

Millie sat on one of the benches scattered around the grounds of the boarding school for girls, situated on the northern outskirts of the city. The elite school, founded way back in the early 1900s, schooled girls from as young as eight years old up to eighteen, and had a capacity of two hundred and fifty, though it had originally only been built to accommodate a hundred.

The school proved popular and grew very quickly, both in size and reputation, in the 1930s. Prior to the Second World War, it was extended to house 160, and a new wing of classrooms was also built at that time. Further extensions in the 1980s added some further buildings, including a laboratory and new library, and meant they were able to house 250 pupils.

It was a cloudless day. The sun was warm and bright as it made its way towards the horizon. It was a little after 2pm.

"Hi Miss Parker," a voice said and Millie turned to see the approaching girl. Millie smiled and stood up, "Thank you for seeing me Theresa," then, gestured, "please. take a seat."

"You're coming up to your final year here. How are you feeling about that?" she asked the dark haired girl.

"Good," Theresa, known to her friends as Terri, answered, frowned slightly, wondering what this might be all about.

"I think that the recent events, the revelation with regards to your mother and what happened to her, well, they must still be quite fresh in your mind. Quite an adjustment for you. It seems you have dealt well with the change of circumstances, however, that's not why I asked to see you. I am in need of your mother's assistance. I thought it best for you to be here as well. I have spoken to her on the phone and she will be here any moment."

Before Terri could even begin to formulate a question, her mother came into view.

Both Millie and the girl stood up, the latter walking up to her mother, giving her a hug, then walking back towards where her teacher, Miss Parker, was waiting.

After they all sat down on the bench, Millie sat herself a little sideways and looked at them both, "Thank you for coming Miss Hudson. I have just discovered something rather upsetting that happened to my mother, and, well, you may have information that might help me. I can see that you are wondering what this is about, but please, bear with me. I will explain," the teacher said.

After a brief pause and seeing that she had their attention, she went on, "So, back in 1988, my mother, she was a professor in archaeology and geology, well, she was on a dig in New Mexico and a tornado struck.

"Along with three others, she was killed that day."

Millie paused briefly, looking at the mother and daughter. "Now, earlier today, I found out that it may well have been that she was murdered ..." Millie again paused, seeing the reaction on their faces and hearing an intake of breath. "I know, you're thinking what might this have to do with you. Well, I am hoping you can help me. Now, I know, obviously, from the police reports and from the headmistress, all about how Theresa was taken from you, back I believe, in 2009, and," looking at the young girl, "that you were told that your mother was dead."

"I also know that the persons responsible were your biological father and his wife Sandra Pentegrass. Now, this is where, hopefully, Miss Hudson, you might help. You see, I had a letter, a few weeks ago, however, I didn't open it until a few days ago when I came back from a short vacation, the letter was from a Robert Pentegrass."

Alison Hudson, though she preferred being called Ally, coloured slightly, then said, "I, yes, I knew Robert, a long time ago, at high school."

"Did you also know a Barbara Philpot?" Millie asked.

Colouring a little more, Ally answered, "Yes, yes I did. Not a great time. Not great memories," she added.

"Well, Mrs Philpot, Barbara's mother, contacted Robert. You see Robert was helping the police, chiefly in Portland, with the search for missing persons; cold cases. Mrs Philpot heard about this and got in touch."

"Did Barbara go missing?" Ally asked.

"No, not Barbara, but her older brother, Edward, or Eddie. You see, he was at the very scene, the archaeological dig in New Mexico, and he went missing from there that very day, and according to research that Robert was doing, he might well have been involved in the death of my mother," Millie paused.

After a moment or two, Alison took hold of her daughter's hand, and began to speak, "I ran with a bad circle in those days," she said, still with a deep colour in her cheeks. She looked at her daughter, then at the teacher, "There were three of us. We called ourselves the ABC girls, A was me, Alison, the C was for Cynthia, the B was for Barbara. She was the main influence. She was bad. I am ashamed of how I behaved back then. We were young. I was stupid. Anyway, Robert, bless him, was one of our victims, if you like. Not nice, Terri, I'm sorry. Barbara was not a very nice girl, the B was also for Boss, and she bossed us around.

"I didn't know she had an older brother, but, if he was anything like her, then he too was probably a bad lot, but," focusing on Millie, "how can we help?"

"Sadly Robert passed away recently," Millie said.

She let that sink in for a moment. "Another person you might remember, is a guy called Thomas Klaassen?" Millie asked, having had a long conversation with Claire.

Alison frowned, then recalled, "Yes. Yes I do. He was Robert's friend I recall." She had no idea whatsoever that it had been this very man she had bumped into at the airport in Toronto eight days ago.

"Indeed, he was. Well, apparently he has taken over doing what Robert had been doing for nearly twenty years. The police referred to Robert as 'The Searcher'. "Currently Thomas is away on the continent, but there is also someone else involved, who, for the past ten years has been helping Robert. She too is in Europe somewhere, her name you will also know, as you have mentioned her already, Cynthia, Cynthia Barnes."

"Really?"

There was silence on the bench for some moments. Birds were chirping away, the afternoon sun was shining down on them and a breeze coming in from the nearby ocean kept the temperature down a little.

"I will help," Ally said, still holding her daughter's hand, "but, I still don't know how I can help?"

"This morning" Millie replied, "I had a long conversation with a young lady. Actually, I don't really know how old she is, but she sounded young. Anyway, her name is Claire, she informed me of all the background and of all the people involved. She also told me that she herself was one of the many people who Robert found over the years, then proceeded to tell me how she had sought him, Robert, and that she had found him and decided to stay with him. She became his housekeeper and cook. You know I guess that Robert had a form of Asperger's Syndrome?"

"I discovered later, yes," Ally replied.

"Well, anyway, Claire is now more deeply involved, assisting the woman called Cynthia and this man called Thomas. They, as I said, are currently in Europe, Spain to be exact." Millie continued to explain, then focusing her attention on Alison, "So that aside, Claire told me all about the report Robert had started to make, at the behest of Mrs Philpot, and of course he found out all about my mother and the dig in New Mexico. She related all that Robert had found out to me this morning.

Well then, there are two things that need to be followed up on. One is what documents we can find about the dig from the university at Albuquerque. Who were the sponsors? Secondly, we need to track down Mrs Philpot, and/or Barbara. This in the hope of finding more leads to the whereabouts of Eddie, and, possibly more important, the whereabouts of a folder, last seen clutched in my mother's hands as the tornado struck," Millie finished. Then taking a deep breath she stood up and gazed into the distance for a moment, reliving all that Claire had told her, and picturing in her mind, how it must have been for her mother.

There was silence for some time.

Then Ally released her daughter's hand and also stood up. For a while she, like Millie, seemed to stare into nothingness, then turned, and looking at them both in turn spoke, "You know, I remember Thomas. He was a nice lad. I also recall what he said to us one day. He said, and I remember his words now, quite clearly, all these years later, 'Your amusement today, will one day turn to sorrow.'"

Ally took a deep breath, then said, "I will track Barbara down. If anyone might know something, it will be her."

Millie held out her hand, which Ally took, and said, "Thank you. Thank you so much. I will go to Albuquerque. We'll stay in touch."

"Yes, we will," Ally answered, then putting her arm around her daughter who had also got up from the bench, said, "Yes, I will be careful," seeing the concern in Terri's eyes, "but, just as someone helped us, bringing us back together, so I must help Miss Parker," And, with a nod to Millie, they turned and walked away, back into the school building.

Millie watched them go, thankful she had the help of Alison, then turned and looked at the sea in the distance. She would take some compassionate leave and organise her travels.

Millie took out her phone to ring Claire to update her on the results of the meeting and how things were going to progress from here. It was at that same moment, back across the Atlantic and in the town of Ampuero that between them, Cynthia and Thomas carried the woman into the hotel and laid her down in Cynthia's room. It was nearly midnight.

T H E   P A S T ;

Period 5

The year 1859–Tucson, Arizona

Juan had, for some years now, yearned to go to Tucson. He'd heard of the wild lifestyle, the fabulously beautiful women, of fortunes to be made.

But, during his time working for the Fort at Yuma, where his initial contract turned from three months to six and then nine months, he was told of other stories, stories of lawlessness, of heartache, of men becoming destitute through gambling and becoming addicted to alcohol. Keeping these stories in mind, Juan arrived late afternoon at the stables run by a Jeremiah Prudence, Juan had been given this place and this man as a contact who would see him right and be able to put work his way.

Jeremiah was well into his fifties, Juan guessed, a stout man with a barrel chest and arms the size of small tree trunks. His face was weather-beaten, his eyes a piercing blue, his whiskers grey, matching what hair he had left on his scalp. His face was round, and Juan had an instant liking to this man. After reading the introductory letter, by apparently a distant cousin, Jeremiah pumped Juan's hand and clapped him on the back, welcoming him, assuring him he could stay as long as he liked and that there was plenty of work available.

Juan stowed his covered wagon safely behind the stables to the side of the attached house where Jeremiah lived with his wife, and felt at ease and at home almost instantly. He was looking forward to his first visit into the town.

Jeremiah gave him a horse to go into town with. His own horses were grazing out back. They deserved a rest after pulling the wagon from Yuma, a distance of over two hundred miles, during which time, fortunately, Juan had encountered no problems.

Riding away from the stables, Juan thought about and was thankful for his father, who survived the shipwreck, collected Caprice from Acapulco and reclaimed the chest of gold from the sea. His father and mother had stayed with Carlos and the family for nearly nine years. They worked on the small settlement and learned new skills. It was Carlos who had taught his father all about becoming an all-round blacksmith, and so in turn, it was his father who had taught him, when they were living in Hermosillo.

Juan reached the edge of town, already the sound of piano music reached his ears. He stabled his horse at a place recommended by Jeremiah, as it would pay to have a bit of security for the horse and equipment, there being 'rough elements' about, warned his new boss.

At six foot three Juan was taller than the average man. Also as he was solidly built, not many would care to even think of crossing him. His tanned, clean-shaven face was handsome, his brown eyes deep and warm, his hair combed back and almost black. As he grew older he became more and more like his father in appearance.

He knew that he attracted women to him, but still had to meet one that touched his heart. Hopefully, whilst in Tucson, this might happen, as he was beginning to think about settling down and raising a family.

The 'Golden Nugget' was the most popular tavern in the town, according to Jeremiah, but not the friendliest. He suggested a better one to check out would be the 'White Parrot' on account of the white parrot owned by 'Tucson Joe' who acquired it from a passing traveller. Though Joe had acquired it, it hadn't been long before the parrot flew out one day and never returned. The name however, stuck.

Juan strode through the street, on the left the piano music and laughter came from the Golden Nugget.

He passed the new stagecoach building, then saw the sign for the White Parrot.

Before he got there, three ladies were approaching him, dressed in colourful outfits, they made a beeline for him, surrounding him, and trying to coach him to come along and they would show him a good time, two of them hooking their arms around his.

"Sorry ladies," he said, smiling at them, his voice deep and firm, "not this time, meeting a friend," and with that he nodded to each of them and released himself from their hold to continue on his way.

Puffing his cheeks with a sigh of relief he approached the tavern and the ladies continued on their way, crossing over, he had noticed, to the other side of the street towards the Golden Nugget.

He entered through the double swing doors and took in the surroundings.

To his right was the bar. The counter ran about seven feet right up to the outer wall, at a right angle the bar than ran about double that, to the far end. There was a steel rail running along the bottom, about three inches from the floor where one could rest one's feet. There were several spittoons placed at intervals.

Beyond the wide counter, there were rows of bottles and a large mirror. On the left side of this mirror, which had scalloped edges, a white parrot had been painted.

There were four men at the bar and one barman behind the counter. He had fair hair, a round and jolly face and blue eyes that sparkled. His smile, when he did, showed uneven teeth and a couple of gaps.

To his left as Juan walked up to the bar, were several small round tables, each surrounded by four chairs, and a piano stood at the far end against a staircase leading up to the next floor. Two men and a woman sat at one of the tables, all of them turning to face the stranger that had entered.

It was quiet in the place, most punters no doubt favouring the more popular tavern across the road.

The quiet atmosphere suited Juan and he greeted the barman, nodded to the men at the bar and ordered a whisky.

"New in town stranger?" the barman said, filling a glass and moving it across the counter.

"Juan," he answered, "working with Jeremiah for a spell."

"Call me Joe" the jovial barman said, "first one is on the house."

Three quarters of an hour later the atmosphere changed a little in the White Parrot.

Having ordered a second drink and passing the time with an occasional chat with the barman, Joe, and with two of the men who stood at the bar nearest him, both older than him and both local farmers, the swing doors opened.

Four women entered, two Juan had met earlier when they were hanging on to an arm each in an attempt to steer him to the tavern across the road.

The other two, in similar dress, one who's hair colour was red and the other dark brown followed the direction of the finger of the blonde-haired woman leading the way, pointing at him. They all entered and sat around the first table, giggling a little, whispering a little and stealing looks at him every few moments.

Juan, having observed them for a few moments, turned and finished his drink. He was starting to feel a little uncomfortable. The two farmers nearby were seemingly somewhat amused. Joe was about to address Juan, when a woman descended the staircase. Her hair was blonde and long, with curls. Her dress was of a fine material in a pale yellow colour and the blouse underneath was white with a frilled collar.

Juan watched as she came down the stairs, noticed her walk, noticed her clothes and noticed her confidence and her slight smile, as she took in the scene.

Here was a woman of class, he thought to himself, and kept his eyes on her as she headed for the bar.

"This is Magdalena" Joe said to Juan, "my daughter."

"Lena," the woman said, stopping right in front of Juan and giving a nod.

"Pleased to meet you ma'am," Juan managed to say, feeling a dryness in his throat.

The woman smiled in return, then turned and headed for the table where the four women sat, "Well ladies, can I get you any drinks?" looking at each in turn, her blue eyes catching each of them as they looked up at her.

THE PRESENT;

Ampuero

Very early morning–Wednesday 29th May

Thomas knocked softly on the door to Tia's room.
It opened.
"I've been thinking," he said, entering as she opened the door wider for him to come in. He noticed the woman was still, seemingly unconscious, lying on the bed.
"Dangerous," Tia said. Then as he turned to look at her, she smiled at him. She noticed he looked tired and a little pale. Not surprisingly, seeing as he carried the woman from the hacienda through the orchard and woods, back to her car, probably a little over a mile.
"They will soon notice, if they've not already, that she's gone, and will, I have no doubt, follow up. I also believe that this family, what did you say their name was? Thermos?"
Tia softly closed the door. "Teremos", she said, smiling at him. She noticed that he must have taken the plaster off, revealing a reddened mark above his right eye, "Gregor Teremos, and his family"
"Yes well, him, them. They'll will have influence. I mean, look at the place. It's massive, no doubt producing a large income for this area. They will be influential. This means that they will have found out about the rental car. They'll have my name, and," Thomas said, bending down to take a closer look at the woman on the bed, "they'll have yours too."

"Agreed. We are not safe here, but with her still comatose, what can we do?"

"I wonder who she is? Why did they go to a lot of trouble to bring her here, and string her up like that. It's obvious they needed something from her," Thomas said, his voice barely above a whisper.

"Yes, indeed, though what that could be, well, until we speak to her, we won't know," Cynthia answered.

"She may of course have told them, whatever it was they wanted to know. She looked pretty drained. She must have said something."

A soft voice from the bed spoke, "I told them but, not the truth" the woman on the bed sat up.

Her face was very pale, her eyes were wide open and she took in her surroundings. "Who are you guys?" her English had a bit of an accent. Thomas thought it had an Australian sound to it and wondered, although she had been taken from London, if she was a tourist.

"I'm Tia, he's Thomas," Cynthia said and sat on the bed by the woman, "Who are you, and what's this all about?"

The woman swung her legs across and onto the floor, then stood up, though almost immediately sat back down on the bed again.

"Phew, quite dizzy doing that." Then, looking at Tia and Thomas in turn, she said, "I heard most of what you have just said. I heard a knock on the door. It woke me, but not knowing where exactly I was, I pretended to still be out of it they know who you are?"

"I knew of your abduction," Thomas said studying the woman's face and inwardly agreeing with his first observation that she would be in her mid-sixties. "I tracked you, tracked the truck, but there were others. I was obviously spotted and subsequently run off the road. Thankfully, Tia, here, who was also aware of the situation, came to my rescue–a damsel in shining armour." He smiled across at Tia who smiled back.

It was then she who again turned to the woman and continued "I dealt with the police, regarding this incident, so, the police have my name, and of course his too, though they are not aware of what we are doing here."

"But," Thomas again took up the conversation, "Cynthia here also gave them the licence plate of the vehicle that ran me of the road, belonging, no doubt to your kidnappers, so, they will know that something is up, and, with the influence they have, we can't rely on the police to be on our side."

"Well, you are right. They have. They are a powerful family in this region. They made a point of telling me that. You are right also that we therefore shouldn't rely on the police. We are not safe here," the woman replied.

She stood up again, this time managing to stay on her feet, then, after a moment, she again looked at them each in turn, "Thank you, but somehow, we need to leave here, leave this region, and that, is not going to be easy." She held out her hand, "Victoria Lange"

Thomas shook it, then in turn Tia shook her hand also.

"So, I've been thinking," Thomas said, giving Tia a look, "I think I know the best way for us to get out of here."

"You do?" Tia asked.

"Short C-23 Sherpa."

"I beg your pardon?" Tia asked.

"It's the plane we saw. It's a Short C-23 Sherpa, it's a 'STOL'. That means short take-off and landing capability. You saw, the runway was not very long. I bet it's fuelled up. I can fly it, we just need to get there"

Both Tia and Victoria looked at him.

"Go back there?" Tia asked,

"We can leave here using your rental, sure, but how far are we going to get? The local police no doubt will be on the lookout soon, if they're not already."

"So? It's still the middle of the night. We can get to the plane. Once on board, we're away," Thomas said, smiling at each woman in turn.

"You make it sound so easy," Victoria said, "but you two did get me out, so,"

Looking at Tia, Thomas said, "you had a map. You know how the hangar and the plane were on the far side of the valley when we were on that hill. Is there a road that might get us closer?"

Cynthia thought for a moment, picturing the map in her mind, then said, "Go and pack your stuff. We'd better move right away. Its already coming up to 1.30 am." Turning towards Victoria she added, "Once we're on the way, you better tells us all you know, as to why you were abducted."

"Of course," was the reply.

Twelve minutes later they had left the hotel through a side door through the kitchen, without anyone seeing them.

Tia opened the boot. Thomas, who had carried all the luggage, leaving Tia to guide and hold a still weak Victoria, now placed the luggage inside and closed the boot as softly as he could.

Once in the vehicle, Tia started the engine and Thomas turned around to give Victoria a bottle of water and a couple of biscuits which he had retrieved from his own luggage a little earlier, figuring she wouldn't have eaten or drunk anything for some time.

"Thank you." After a gulp and several bites as Tia drove out of the small town, she asked "So, how did you know, I mean, about my abduction?"

"All in good time," Thomas said, holding on as Tia turned the car on to the main road and sped towards the forest area. There was no traffic, and no one spoke as the car drove smoothly on the tarmac surface.

Then Thomas held on again as Tia suddenly turned the vehicle off the main road and onto a narrow dirt road that entered the forested area.

The clock on the dashboard read 1.55am. Tia switched off the headlights, slowing right down, and navigated by the car's smaller sidelights.

Meanwhile

At the departure gate in the San Francisco airport, Alison Hudson was deep in thought. It was time to put some wrongs right. It was time for a confrontation; time to step up to the plate and time to show who she really was, the real Ally.

A little over three hours earlier she had said goodbye to her daughter and had shaken the hand of the teacher, Millie Parker.

That Miss Parker's mother most likely had been murdered was an interesting development, for, it hadn't been that long ago Ally herself had almost been killed.

With fondness she thought of her rescuer, the tall handsome Dutchman. Her recollection was cut short as the announcement to board the plane came over the airport announcement system.

Earlier, once back in her apartment, it had taken her less than twenty minutes to find the whereabouts of Barbara Philpot.

Still in Portland, she now ran a flower shop in the north-west suburb of the city. As she still had her maiden name, Ally assumed that she had never married, though of course she could well have a partner. She found no evidence of any children.

Having confirmed this fact, she booked her flight and started packing. Looking at her watch, and knowing her arrival time in Portland, Ally realised she would not be in time to visit Barbara today.

Ally packed her laptop and decided she would do some more research whilst in flight, mainly to see if she could find any more information on the Philpot family.

As she settled down in her first class seat, Alison was grateful that she was financially very secure, she had her daughter back after more than ten years, and was thinking about the conversation with Terri's teacher Millie.

What a small world. Barbara's brother Eddie, somehow involved.

And Robert. Poor Robert, on the receiving end of her taunts all those years ago. Again she thought what a small world it can be, as it was Robert's sister, Sandra, still believed to be in Hawaii somewhere, who had been part of the plot that had taken Ally's daughter.

Alison took in a deep breath, sighed, then strapped herself in ready for take-off. The plane taxied, stopped for barely a few seconds, then the engines roared and the jet thundered down the runway, the wheels left the tarmac and Alison was pushed into her seat as the plane soared into the sky, leaving the city below and behind.

Back in the city below and behind

Millie had arrived home from school and set about preparing some dinner first of all. Second she booked a flight, or as it turned out, two flights, the first to Phoenix, then onto Albuquerque. Having done that relatively quickly, she then booked a hotel, ate her dinner, and after clearing up in the kitchen, packed a case.

She had settled down to watch a movie in the hope of stopping the thoughts milling around in her mind, when, about halfway through, she suddenly realised that she needed to bring Claire up to speed and wrote an e-mail to her, updating her on the proceedings so far.

Earlier in Myrtle Creek

Claire received a message from Thomas, 'We have her, need to move on, be in touch'

"We?" she thought, reading the message again. "Who's we? And why the need to move on?" Seeing the time on the message she realised it must be after midnight for them. Where did they need to move to, and why?

"Thomas, Thomas, couldn't you just give me a little more information!" she said aloud.

2:05 am–Three miles from Ampuero

"Stop" Thomas said.

Tia had been concentrating on driving on this narrow dirt road that seemed to be getting narrower. Thomas had been looking past her to the left, trying hard to see anything through the dense trees, but had spotted a clearing.

The car stopped and Tia looked at Thomas by the light of the dashboard.

"Back up a little," he asked.

Slowly the car reversed, Tia focusing on the road via her side door mirror until she heard him say, "Stop," once more.

"Okay, let me just check," Thomas said, getting out of the car.

He walked around the front of the car, headed into a clearing and came back almost immediately.

"This is the place," he said to Cynthia who had lowered the window. "The ground is firm, the clearing is wide enough and more importantly, it runs straight into the valley. I'll guide you"

Thomas walked backwards and beckoned Tia onwards.

By the dim parking lights she could see him and trusted him to keep the car from plunging downwards or into a rut, but, after less than forty seconds, when he beckoned her to stop, she could see where they were.

The valley lay before them, a slight slope and they would be on even ground. Ahead was the big hangar, which had a single lamp giving light around the aircraft.

"Okay, no time to lose. We have to take advantage of this opportunity. Well done for finding this road," Thomas said, getting back in the car.

Then, glancing at Victoria in the back, he again focused on Tia, "I'll go down there, and get into the plane. Now, see there is a cargo door at the rear of the plane?"

Tia looked, and in the light from the lamp on the building, she could see what Thomas meant, "Yes" she answered, then looking back at him.

"When you see the ramp coming down, drive and take the car straight inside. Don't worry about anything else. Just get this car up and into that plane, okay?"

"Understood," she said.

Thomas leant forwards, towards her, quickly kissed her on the lips, then exited the car.

"I don't recall ever having that effect on men," Victoria said, leaning forwards and looking out between the front seats. She watched as Thomas quickly moved down the slope, then made his way towards the hangar.

Tia smiled and watched him too.

She kept the engine idling. The last thing she needed now was for it to conk out.

Thomas walked quietly up to the side of the hangar. He had already checked that there didn't seem to be any security cameras about, just the single lamp on the front of the hangar that shone onto the plane. All was quiet.

He stood on the corner of the building for a moment, double checking everything that he could see, then, having formulated a plan, he set to work.

First he walked over to the wheels and pulled the chocks away, making sure they were well out of the way. He then pulled out a flap below the cockpit, stepped onto it and opened the cockpit door. Moments later he was inside, closed the door, and quickly looked out of the windows towards the hacienda, No sign of any life.

So far so good.

He slipped between the seats and into the cargo hold behind the cockpit, briefly feeling in the semi darkness for a light switch. Two wall mounted lights instantly came on. The hold was empty. Excellent! He then took a look at the rear cargo ramp mechanics, saw how to lower and raise the ramp. Obviously it could only be done from this point, which he thought might be the case.

"Right," he said aloud to himself, "engines."

Back in the cockpit he studied the control layout, saw what he needed to do, and, closing his eyes, set to the starting sequence. First, ignition to the control panel. A flick of a switch.

A lovely sound reached his ears and he opened his eyes to see the panel lit up. In the darkness all around it was like a Christmas tree. Time to move quickly now.

Port engine, start.

From the clearing, Tia noticed the lights when they came on in the cockpit. Both women were silent. Both were tense.

They heard the sound of an engine, and saw the propeller beginning to spin.

Surely they would hear this in the house, Tia thought, her eyes now solely focused on the cargo door.

The port engine was warming up nicely, and quickly too, Thomas saw on the instrument panel. Excellent, time to open the cargo door. He slipped from the pilot seat through to the rear and pressed the control button. At first he thought nothing was happening, but then the motor kicked in and the door began to open. Thomas moved quickly back into the cockpit and switched on the starboard engine.

He took another look out of the window, and was relieved that there was still no sign of anything or anybody coming from the house.

The port engine was up to speed, the starboard engine was warming up. Thomas quickly checked over the rest of the instruments. All seemed to be fine and plenty of fuel.

He then slipped into the cargo hold again, in time to see Tia drive the car towards the plane. Stepping to the side and heading for the ramp controls he waited.

The car hit the ramp, shot up it and once inside Tia slammed on the brakes to halt the vehicle only inches away from the bulkhead. Thomas pressed the close button.

Tia realised she had enough room and reversed a little to give Thomas room to re-enter the cockpit, then killed the engine.

Thomas gave her a thumbs up as he slipped back into the cockpit. As he sat down, his eye caught movement. Two men were coming from the warehouse building at the far end of the valley.

No sign of life as yet from the house. "Time to move," he said to himself, then revved the engines, checked the dials and moved the plane.

Tia slipped into the cockpit, sat herself down on the co-pilots seat, saying "I've told Victoria to stay put."

"Well done you. Strap yourself in, there are men coming," Thomas said, also putting on his seatbelt and turning the plane slightly, facing it straight on to the runway.

The men were still some way off, and neither seemed to be armed.

"Here we go," Thomas said, thrusting the engines to full power, then gripping the controls and pushing them forwards.

The plane's engines roared, almost immediately. The plane surged forwards and shot across the runway picking up speed very quickly, and as the plane thundered down the short runway, Thomas saw through the side window that the two men had stopped and someone was coming from the house. But they were too late.

Focusing on the runway, just a dim strip of hard packed dirt under the night sky as he hadn't dared switch on any landing lights, Thomas kept the plane on the ground as long as he dared. The forest loomed ahead of them.

Then, pulling on the levers, Thomas pulled the plane up. The trees now seemed to come at them rapidly, but the craft lifted skywards, cleared them, and Thomas had already pressed the levers to bring the landing gear up.

He banked the plane to the west, then looked at Tia and grinned.

Moments later he banked the manoeuvrable plane to the north and headed for the sea directly in front of them, keeping the aircraft low.

In Portland

Alison's plane had landed and she had picked up her luggage and headed for the taxi rank.

THE PAST;

Period 6

The year 1861–Tucson, Arizona

From the moment he had first seen her, striding so confidently and beautifully down the stairs, he somehow knew, this was the one. But then, as she was introduced and he briefly looked directly into her eyes, he wondered if she could possibly develop any feelings for him. Now, nearly a year later, he knew for sure.

Juan was loading equipment into his covered wagon, his home. It had been his home ever since leaving his folks in Hermosillo when he was twenty-four, he was now almost thirty-six. But this would be a final journey in the old wagon.

After checking over the wagon, checking the harnesses and the horses, making sure he had all his belongings, he sat on the back of the wagon, where, on many an evening he had sat reading, thinking by the light of the lantern.

He looked out across the field and thought back to that day that evening, his first time entering into Tucson, entering the White Parrot.

"Lena" she had said, her voice soft, yet strong. She had looked into his eyes, she had nodded and then had gone over to the table where the four ladies had taken a seat. After taking their drinks order, she walked back towards him. Passing him by, she again looked into his eyes, then, again her voice so soft, she said, "If you have any intention of capturing my heart, you'd better be good." She smiled again and then sorted out the drinks for the four ladies, who were all looking at him. Juan finished his drink and watched her for a bit as she gathered the drinks onto a silver tray.

Then, as she was returning to the bar, he stood up.

"My father knew, with certainty, when he met my mother, and so it was. I know, you are for me, and so it will be," then smiled and nodded to her as he left the tavern.

His heart was racing. He wanted to stay. He wanted to turn around. Had he been too assured, too arrogant? But, he had meant every word. Juan went through the swing doors and headed home. Yes, he had met the woman he felt was the right one for him, but, he also knew that it wasn't going to be easy.

"You'd better be good", she had said. Was it a challenge? He thought so.

He had better be good, very good indeed. Taking in a deep breath he passed by the saloon across the road where the piano was still honky-tonking away and the sound of laughter reached his ears.

The following day, while Juan was working on reshoeing a horse at the stables, a man rode up. He stayed on his horse, a black mare, and spoke, "Hey, you!"

Juan looked up at the man, he was smartly dressed in a suit, wore a white Stetson and had a revolver hanging by his side. His face was pale, his eyes a grey colour and he had a black moustache above his thin lips. Juan took an instant dislike of this man, but politely asked, "Yes sir. Can I help you?"

"You stay away from my woman," he said, his voice trying to sound menacing, but failing. He followed on with, "Won't warn you again."

Then he kicked his spur into the horse and turned around.

Jeremiah had come out to see what was happening, and watching the man disappear from view, he turned to Juan, "One day here, and already making enemies?" he asked, smiling.

"Who is he?" Juan asked, and continued shoeing the horse.

"Rancher, wealthy, nasty. Name's Calhoen, Joseph Calhoen"

"And who does he think his woman is?" Juan asked, finishing one hoof and starting on the second hind leg.

"Guess you must have met Joe's daughter, Magdalena. He has designs on her."

When Juan didn't respond, Jeremiah added, "Be careful."

Later that day, when he was sure that his work was up to date and after checking with Jeremiah he asked if he could leave for a bit as there was something he wanted to check out. This was fine with the old man and he wondered where the young man was off to in the middle of the afternoon.

When evening came, Juan once more rode into town, once more stabled his horse and once more strode through the town to the White Parrot.

Greeting Joe he ordered a drink and Joe obliged, and when placing the drink before him, whispered, "watch your back" then nodded and went back to where he had been conversing with a group of three men.

Juan watched the mirror behind the bar. In it he could see a mirror that was above the piano by the staircase, and in that he could see the swing doors.

Less than ten minutes later he saw the doors open and saw the man enter. He wasn't very tall. The two men who followed him in were almost a foot taller.

The talking stopped as the tension built. Trouble was looming.

The man, Juan now knew to be Joseph Calhoen, walked up to the bar, "How about that deal Joe," he said, "wouldn't want you to lose any more customers now, would we."

Then looked at Juan, smiling.

"There will be no deal," the voice soft, and yet strong.

She had appeared from somewhere and had answered before her father could, standing beside him behind the bar and looking at the man directly.

"Now honey, you know how I feel about you. Wouldn't want your pappy to get hurt now, would you?"

"Sounds like a threat there mister," Juan said, finding his voice was calm and he felt confident of what he could achieve.

"Ain't none of your business son," came the reply.

The two men who had followed Calhoen into the tavern now placed themselves either side of Juan. Joe said nothing.

Juan was wary and again looking into the mirror, he could see that there was a shotgun of sorts tucked underneath the counter. Joe was getting ready for trouble.

"That black mare you were riding this morning, Mr. Calhoen," Juan said.

Joseph Calhoen turned, frowning. "What of it?" he barked, his voice once again sounding raspy and without depth.

"I know horses, Mr Calhoen, and that mare–I know it's markings. I know who it belonged to. I wonder, there is a garrison close by. I worked at Fort Yuma. I have contacts, do you really want me to get in touch with them? They don't take kindly to horse thieves you know."

Joseph Calhoen coloured bright red. He tried to stare at Juan, but found he couldn't. He turned and stormed out, not saying another word. His two henchmen following quickly.

For several moments there was a stillness. No one spoke.

"I'll have another Joe, please," Juan said, breaking the silence and smiling at Lena to whom he then said, his voice low, barely above a whisper, "Might not be good enough yet, but, it's a start, right?"

She looked at him, her cheeks ever so slightly coloured, then found her composure and answered, "It's a start,"

Then nodding her head at him, she turned to disappear from where she had moments earlier appeared.

Joe brought the drink, then reached out his hand to pump Juan's hand vigorously. He had no words to speak.

Not much later Lena showed herself again, caught Juan's eye and gestured for him to follow her.

Up the stairs she went, up the stairs he followed. Standing by a door she then opened it and entered. He followed, she shut the door, then walked over to one of the two windows in the room which was a lounge. There were three old leather armchairs, a small table, some old cupboards, a couple of oil lamps. She spoke, "He'll not stop for anything now. He's riled, and he'll want revenge. Who are you?"

The colour had crept back to her cheeks, he could see she was concerned.

Moreover, he could sense that she was angry.

"I can handle Joseph Calhoen," she went on to say, her voice strong and with a hint of fearless determination. "the situation, though not ideal, was balanced. You've rocked the boat mister, all in order to win me over?"

Staying standing by the door, he looked directly into her eyes as she glared in anger at him, then, trying to keep his voice calm, he spoke.

"He came to see me this morning. Warned me. I didn't like him, and found out who he was, but I have a few contacts in the area, so learned more about him. Know your enemy. He threatened your father. He was menacing, but no more than a bully. You might accept a situation that's balanced, but I do not. You let folk like that take an inch, they'll take a mile. I take it he frequents the Golden Nugget?"

"He owns it," she said, quite stunned at his response.

"Right then, I'll go and find him, and make a deal to leave your father and you, alone."

Juan turned, and was about to leave, but she said, "Wait, please." She waited until he had turned around to face her, and found her heart was suddenly racing. She felt her anger subsiding quickly and realised that no man had ever spoke so strongly to her.

"Are you sure?" she asked, her voice no longer with an edge, but once again soft.

He again looked into her eyes, no longer glaring, but he was sure he detected a sparkle and he could feel his heart beating in his chest.

"I'm sure. After all, as you requested, in order to capture your heart I better be good," he said, smiling at her.

It was then, as he was about to turn and leave the room a second time that he noticed the painting, on the wall, above a small fireplace.

It was around eighteen inches wide and probably three foot in height.

The frame was gilded and ornate wood, surrounding an oil painting showing a man standing next to a black horse. Juan strode over to it, and took in the quality of the painting.

"Pa won it–poker game," she said. "A traveller, Spanish guy, former soldier I think, more than ten years ago now."

"It's a very good painting," Juan said, admiring the horse, then looking at the man in the painting. His coat was a magnificent red in colour, but it was not the uniform of a soldier, or a conquistador, but, seemed regal, perhaps a dignitary, a king even, Juan glanced over his shoulder into the interior of the wagon. It was there, the painting all wrapped and secured by a woollen blanket. Again he briefly wondered about its history: who had painted it, most likely a Spaniard, he thought, perhaps an Italian.

But how had it got here, and who had been the guy who lost it in a card game.

Juan jumped from the back of the wagon onto the ground.

The lovely Lena came to greet him. "Ready?" she asked. Putting an arm around his neck then drawing close to kiss him briefly on the lips.

Her eyes sparkled and she was flushed with excitement.

"Ready. Silver City here we come," he answered once she had released her lips from his. He held her tightly, then helped her get up onto the wagon.

It was still early in the morning, but two hundred miles lay between them and their destination. She too glanced into the covered wagon from her seat, saw all his equipment, her own treasures, and of course, though securely wrapped up, the painting, a gift from her father.

❧❧❧

T H E   P R E S E N T ;

Over the Bay of Biscay

Wednesday 29th May

"I stole a painting," Victoria said. She was standing in the doorway to the cockpit. The lights from the instrument panel showed her face to be still rather pale.

"Thirty years ago," she added.

They were flying low over the water. The Bay of Biscay. Amongst the many instrument on the panel, she noticed a clock that read 3:16 am.

For a moment anything else drifted away, just the illuminated dials, the lit up number 3:16.

She knew it well, the verse from scripture, a well-known verse, John chapter 3 and verse 16. "For God so loved the world" she thought, the beginning of the verse resounding in her mind.

The engines droned on, the propellers thrusting the plane onward, and the stars giving a little light in the darkness.

Everything happened so quickly. When she stirred, in the hotel room, trying to grasp how it was she got there, then the realisation and the urgency to get away. The trip in the car down the narrow dirt track. Watching in silence as the man left to try and board the plane, the plan, the ramp, the manner in which they spoke about it. They were positive, self-assured, yet, realistic. Their voices were soft and the tone was that of determination. They knew the danger. They had known about her abduction. They had rescued her. But such had been the urgency in planning and executing a getaway, there had been no

98

time to talk, no time to explain: for them to tell her how come they were there; for her to tell them why it was she had been taken.

John 3:16, "For God so loved the world" the clock on the instrument panel ticked over.

Victoria saw that the woman, Tia, was looking at her. He, the tall blond man, Thomas, was concentrating on flying the craft, peering at the various instruments, and peering out of the cockpit windows.

"It was a commission" Victoria said, looking directly at Tia. "Chap by the name of Johannes Acker. He was a dealer, an art dealer, he approached me. Heard about me; somehow found me, which, of course as a burglar, was pretty worrying, especially as I was wanted in several countries. Anyway, he spoke to me, in a tone that suggested I take up his offer, he then explained how he was involved in returning art to their rightful owners. Art the Nazis in the war had looted. Some, he told me, were able to be resolved through the courts if there was enough proof or provenance. For this particular painting, he said there wasn't, and I was to get it for him and all would be well. On top of which a fee of five thousand euros.

"So, feeling I had no option really, I took it on. This was back in the summer of '89, as I said, thirty years ago. The painting was on loan. It hung in the museum in Bilbao, a painting by Titian, of a man standing by a black horse.

The man was Charles V, and the painting was on loan to the museum from, guess who, yes, the Teremos family."

Before Tia could make any response, Victoria went on, "By the way, you mentioned earlier, about Gregor Teremos. Well, actually, he was the one who started the orchard, but it was his son, Alberto, who had acquired the painting and it was he who loaned it to the museum."

"I see," Tia said. "Still, you say it was acquired, does that mean they stole it?"

"This is it," Victoria answered. "I was told it was part of Nazi loot, but as I prepared for this theft, I did want to find out a thing or two. Thus, I knew it had been Alberto who loaned the painting. I don't know where he got it from, but I don't think it was stolen loot at all.

"I began to have my doubts. Anyway, I felt I had no choice, did the theft, then put it behind me.

"I had a thousand euros up front, for expenses and so on, and never saw the rest. Never heard from this Johannes Acker ever again. My instruction were to drop the painting off into a locker at the Gare Du Nord railway station in Paris.

"I was given the key for it. There was an envelope there, I placed the painting inside, then took the envelope and left.

"Not wanting to hang around, I quickly boarded the train for the airport. I had already stashed my luggage there and had purchased a flight to London. Didn't want to take any chances of being double-crossed. Discovered on the train that the envelope contained just one proper banknote; the rest were paper cuttings."

The plane flew on in the darkness, the propellers droning evenly in the night sky.

"Though he told me the name of the Jewish family to whom it had originally belonged was Milgram, I could find nothing on them either.

"I moved to Australia and lived there for the next twenty five years, returning to London five years ago."

"And then the Teremos family found you," Tia surmised, "but what, after all this time, could they hope to find?"

"Well, when I realised where I was, and was strung up and slapped about by a woman telling me she was Letitia Teremos and that no one crossed her family, I figured out what it was about. However, though I thought about telling her about Johannes Acker, for some reason, I don't know why, I didn't. Besides that was thirty years ago. He was already in his sixties then; is probably dead by now, so, I told them another story altogether." At this she smiled at Tia, then explained, "Told her about a very nasty character, from Lille, horrible little man. He crossed me. He came to mind, so told her all about him as being the man behind the theft, and that I only just stole the thing."

"Then what happened?" Thomas, who had been listening whilst still watching all the instruments, asked. He had made sure that the radio was switched off. He wanted no communications from any airfield tower as he flew across the water. He wanted to land this thing before daylight. Then get the vehicle out and be on their way. Based on his knowledge of the air routes in this area, he felt that Brittany was close enough.

"She slapped me some more, then left me hanging there."

"So" Tia was beginning to ask, but Thomas interrupted her.

"Land ahead. Victoria, please get back into the car. Tia, help me look for a level field, near to a road."

Realising that this would not be an easy feat, Victoria said, "Good luck guys, and thank you," then stepped from the cockpit, closed the door and got back into the car.

Tia saw the land.

It was low lying land, with no obvious big hills or mountains, lots of trees though, she saw as they were nearly upon the coast.

Thomas flew even lower, then to slow the craft down further and in preparation for a quick landing, put the landing gear down.

The drag immediately had an effect as they flew over land.

"There!" Tia suddenly called out, "to the left, a meadow, next to that field of, corn or something, see it?"

"I see it," Thomas said, banked the plane, and came in lower. He flew only just above the tops of the trees, then saw the meadow closer, it ran slightly uphill, but that was okay, the ground seemed firm and suitable.

"Can you see any roads?" he asked.

Thomas reduced the power, manoeuvred the flaps, watched the instrument panel and kept his eyes on the ground ahead through the cockpit window. It was still too dark to see if there were in ruts in the terrain, then, at the last minute, he switched on the landing lights. The whole meadow lit up and Thomas landed.

Tia held on tight, and held her breath.

Wheels touched the ground, a bump, then they were down. In the bright light Thomas had already seen that the meadow was glistening.

The ground would be wet and slippery.

The front wheel touched the ground. He applied the brakes.

"Wheels slipping a little," Thomas said, "wet grass"

But he controlled the plane and it slowed down. He heaved a sigh of relief.

"Remind me to kiss you," Tia said, also breathing again. "I did see a road, track really, just ahead beyond that hedge that's coming up."

The aircraft stopped well before the hedge. Thomas cut the engines and the light, then went out of the cockpit into the cargo hold, "Get ready to drive out," he said to Tia, moving quickly towards the rear and operating the ramp control.

The ramp lowered, Tia started the engine and twisting around, backed the car down the ramp.

Thomas closed the ramp, moved back into the cockpit and climbed from the craft the same way he had entered, making sure all the controls were switched off. Taking a look around, he saw a gap in the hedge and an iron gate which was closed. He ran towards it. Tia, having seen it too, switched on her headlights and headed in the same direction.

A chain was looped around a post, but it was not locked and he unhooked it and opened the gate. She drove through and he closed the gate before getting into the passenger seat.

"Look," Tia said, smiling at him as he got in and fastened his seatbelt, "there's a town, nearby," pointing to the navigation screen in the car.

"Well, off we go then m'lady," he answered. "Find somewhere to have breakfast, I'm hungry!"

Tuesday evening

In her hotel room in Portland, Alison was hungry. She had ordered room service, as she did not fancy going to the restaurant, and it should be arriving any minute.

Portland. City of roses. Her home town.

It felt strange to be here. From the moment she landed, her mind was flooded with memories. Memories of her schooldays, ones she had pushed to the back of her mind for years. Memories of her brief relationship with Julian, still painful; of the time when her daughter was taken, so cruelly, so quickly.

Taken by Julian and his wife Sandra.

Sandra, the sister of Robert who she, along with her bully friends Barbara and Cynthia, had treated badly. Was that the reason she had teamed up with Julian?

Strange how she had never thought about the connection before. Had that really been the reason to take her daughter? Revenge?

She shook that line of thought from her mind, then visualised again the time she, when on the trail to find her daughter, had been abducted, and left for dead on the edge of ledge, in a narrow canyon.

A knock on the door shook her out of her thoughts. Food!

Whilst eating her dinner she returned to her previous thoughts about the man who had come to her rescue. Although it already seemed to have occurred a lifetime ago, it had only been less than four weeks ago!

Her thoughts then turned to her daughter's teacher, Millie. Poor woman, having all these years believed her mother to have been killed by a tornado, only to find out she had in fact been murdered. She was looking forward to confronting Barbara in the morning. What might she know about her brother, about his disappearance, about the missing folder. Finishing her meal, she decided she needed a chat with a good friend. Searching on her phone, she found the number and pressed to connect. "Hi Chrissie, it's Ally"

In Albuquerque

Millie was of the same mind, having reached her hotel and not feeling up to going out again, she too ordered room service.

In the morning she had an appointment with the dean of the university. She had spoken to him earlier prior to leaving home. She had been informed that the administrator had retired recently, and that a new one had not as yet been appointed.

He also informed her that the communication from Robert Pentegrass, the phone call that had been made, had indeed been noted, but somehow, nothing further was done about it. He apologised and looked forward to meeting her in the morning. He would see what he could find out.

She had thanked him and had then set out to fly across from San Francisco.

En route she thought about her father. After speaking to Alison and Theresa, and then having secured her compassionate leave, Millie had quickly called into the residential home where her father lived. His mind was going, but he did recognise her. Smiled. She made some small talk, but did not mention anything about what she had learned. He wouldn't comprehend and any mention of her mother, she knew, would often upset him.

She sighed, as the plane descended; she missed the father he had been.

THE PAST;

Period 7

The year 1862–Silver City

Lena was happy. Though she did miss her father, he had insisted that she go. Thanks to Juan and his army connections, all was settled and peaceful in Tucson. The White Parrot saloon was thriving, as was the Golden Nugget. They were no longer enemies, but friendly rivals, each with their own clientele.

Landowner Joseph Calhoen was dead and buried.

It had been quite an intense time. That first evening when the wealthy rancher had the encounter with Juan, he'd quickly withdrawn, but the following day he made a decision to call Juan's bluff. At least, he thought it was a bluff.

Juan who had a feeling that it hadn't been the last time he would need to confront Calhoen, set out early that afternoon.

After the treaty, the old fort had been taken by the Americans only a couple of years earlier. Juan rode up to the Fort, Presidio San Augustin, which was slowly being dismantled. The outer walls of the fort had already been taken down.

He knew a small garrison was now stationed there, and he rode into the camp to speak to the commander.

Introducing himself, and passing on a greeting from the Fort Yuma commander, to prove he had been working there for the past nine months, he explained the situation in the town. Juan told of the landowner Calhoen and the black mare he had been riding, which

Juan had recognised by the markings, and knew that this horse had belonged to a captain in Fort Yuma. Juan knew horses.

The commander took in what he was told and said he would take action should any trouble arise. He told Juan that there had been quite a bit of cattle rustling in the Yuma area some seven months ago, and horses too had been stolen. He thanked Juan for the information. Satisfied, Juan returned to his work.

Later in that same day, trouble did indeed arise.

Lena sat on the cane chair on the front porch, lovingly rubbing her tummy. She was expecting their first child.

Having only moments earlier kissed and waved goodbye to Juan, she'd sat herself down in the chair. Taking in the early morning sun, she reflected how it all came about that they were now here. In the smaller, but lovely town, Silver City.

The mine attracted many from far and wide, and though a good sized camp was set up, many of the men would regularly come in to visit any of the four saloons.

Juan, had sourced and purchased a set of stables on the west side of town, in the direction of the mine, and had already established good business.

The house had belonged to her mother, who had long parted from her father but had not forgotten her only daughter. She passed, strangely, on the day of the big fight, and a messenger had arrived a few days later to bring Lena the news, as well as documents to state she now owned a house.

It added to their wish to move. Especially after the big fight.

Closing her eyes, she thought back, to that evening, and rubbing her knee she could feel the scar beneath her cotton dress.

His third evening heading into town. It felt like so much had already happened. He was not happy with the noticeable tension, feeling that his very presence had been the cause. The previous evening, having calmed an angry Lena down, he had been distracted by the lovely painting, and they had just sat and talked, though often each disappeared into their own thoughts for some time.

In the end, they both agreed to wait and see what happened next.

Stepping towards the White Parrot on this third evening Juan was upbeat and eager. The only reason for that, he knew, was Lena.

He thought about her almost constantly, smiling as he remembered when he had first seen her descending the stairs.

He hadn't been long in the saloon, having greeted Joe and also noting that there was no one else in the place, when Lena had come up to him, had kissed him on the lips, a quick kiss, then looked up at him.

He could see the concern in her eyes.

"Trouble brewing?' he asked, looking from her to Joe.

He nodded, a look of concern on his face too.

"They are going to come and destroy this place," she whispered.

"Joe," Juan said, "go up to the garrison camp, Tell them I sent you and that trouble is about to happen."

Joe nodded and left, not uttering a word.

Juan then looked at Lena, taking her face between his hands, he kissed her on the forehead, then said, "Find somewhere safe, and stay put."

"This is my fight as much, if not more, than yours," she replied. "I'm not running"

Juan could see the fierce determination in her eyes.

"Well then, let's take to fight to them. Let's go to the Nugget."

Lena was about to reach over for the shotgun under the bar, but he stopped her, "No, leave it. We go unarmed. It will surprise them; see what develops."

"Let's go then," she said and linked her arm with his and they left the saloon to head up the street and then across to the Golden Nugget.

In the morning sunlight, Lena smiled as she again began remembering that evening, picturing the scene, recalling the turmoil and chaos, the sudden hush as she and Juan pushed through the swing doors

They all stared. Lena was surprised that there were so few. She had expected a large crowd, but there were only some. Most folk, she guessed, hearing what trouble may be brewing, had wisely stayed at home.

To her left, occupying several of the tables on that side of the saloon, were the four women who the day before had come into the White Parrot. There was also a woman sat on the piano stool and she counted two more ladies in the group, seven altogether.

Juan sized up the situation. Joseph Calhoen was sat on a tall bar stool, probably designed for him to make him seem taller. He would prove no trouble. The two men who had followed him into the White Parrot the previous evening were standing either side of him. There were two barmen behind the counter and a further three men milling around. All of them were totally focused on Juan.

"I'll take the women," Lena said. "You take the men." her voice no longer soft, but loud enough to be heard by all, furthermore delivered with such confidence, it made Juan believe that this would be a piece of cake.

"Deal," he said.

She then ran and launched herself, diving headlong onto the first table.

The move surprised everyone, including Juan, but it had the desired effect.

Create chaos, was on Lena's mind.

No time to turn and walk out, though that would not have been on his mind.

As Lena landed on the table, grabbing two of the women as she did so, the table collapsed and they all crashed to the wooden floor.

Juan decided the best ones to take out first, would be the two men either side of Calhoen.

He was upon them before they had time to register his approach as they had been totally absorbed by Lena flying through the air.

Best form of defence, Juan was thinking, is to attack. A fast blow connected to the first man's jaw, and as he crumpled to the floor, Juan was upon the second man.

Juan was a blacksmith, using his arms and hands, hammering and bashing metal upon an anvil.

He was strong and his momentum took the second man down.

Getting up very quickly, he looked at Joseph sitting on the bar stool, and noticed his face had paled and his eyes were wide open.

Juan headed for the group of three men.

Only one of them noticed him coming, the other two were mesmerised by the scene on the other part of the saloon where Lena, having taken two women down, had risen up to attack the next two.

The woman on the piano, sat frozen, her hands clasped to her mouth.

Juan moved, and again using his momentum, drove himself into the three men.

One them banged his head on the stair post and was out cold, the other two fell to the floor but one of them, the one who had seen Juan approaching, managed a fist to the side of Juan's head. A glancing blow, but still one that threw him off balance.

There were two women near these three men, and though they'd also been totally focused on Lena, now grappling with two women, they suddenly moved into action. One of them, seeing Juan stumble off balance, jumped on his back. The other decided to flee the scene altogether and ran up the stairs.

The weight of the woman suddenly upon him, brought Juan tumbling to the floor, where he rolled right over the woman who had been on his back, then rolled again as the man, having taken hold of a chair, was aiming to smash it down on him. The chair smashed into bits and a glancing blow struck his upper arm, but Juan was agile and found his feet again before the man came back at him. Juan's left arm was throbbing, but his good arm was fine, a well-connected blow pummelled straight into his assailants face, breaking his nose and spurting blood in all directions.

Lena in the meantime had easily dealt with three of the women. The fourth was now upon her, but with a deft move, Lena threw her off, pushing her against the second table, which fell over leaving her tangled up for the moment.

Lena stood up, took a quick look at the lady at the piano, who sat, still with hands clasped to her mouth. No threat there. She had also seen one lady run up the stairs. That left just one. Lena saw that she was about to get up again and attack Juan from behind with a chair leg.

The man with the broken nose had managed to grab hold of Juan and together they crashed to the floor, destroying another round table in the process.

This left the space clear and Lena moved fast, placing herself between Juan and the last woman. This one was sturdier, looked to be more dangerous and Lena knew overcoming her would not be easy, but she strode forwards nonetheless, thinking that no one was going to mess with her man.

Joseph Calhoen, had regained some sense of control over his body, having been frozen, was sat on the stool, totally surprised at this sudden attack.

He had not expected this, and had hoped to walk down the street and demolish the White Parrot with the aid of his men. Looking around, he saw that this was now highly unlikely. Three men were already down and out, the two barmen had totally disappeared, and there seemed to be just two fights still raging.

Two men, one he noted with blood all over his face, were rolling around at the bottom of the staircase, and not too far away from them two women were locked together.

This was Joe's daughter, he noted, the one who had flung herself across the room like a diver would into a river. The other, was his own daughter.

He tried to find a voice to encourage her, but found he couldn't speak.

Then remembered his pistol. At least he would have the pleasure of killing the Mexican. Sweat on his forehead, he struggled to control his shaking hand, but got hold of the pistol to draw it out of its holster.

Juan was hurt, his arm throbbed, and he had crashed into the stair post, dazing him The man beside him was groaning softly, blood everywhere. Juan sat up and saw one fight was still in progress. His Lena was rolling and entangled with another woman.

Then he noticed Calhoen, the gun coming out of the holster, saw his face, saw the intensity, and saw his eyes wide open and full of hatred.

The gun was lifting; was pointing at him.

Juan sat and looked; there was nothing he could do. He couldn't move, wouldn't be able to avoid the shot. He watched the man's eyes, then, just as there appeared to be a smile forming on the rancher's, now red face, a shot rang out.

The four women had struggled back to their feet, their clothes dirty and ripped and two of the four had smudges of blood on their faces.

Some of the men were coming around to a sitting position and Lena and the other woman stopped fighting, still clinging on to each other's hair.

Then Juan saw Joseph Calhoen topple forwards to the floor. Confused he turned around to see where the shot might have come from.

The woman on the piano stool had a gun in her hand. Half a smile on her face, which was almost deathly pale, and eyes wide open in shock.

With some effort Juan got up and stumbled over to the fallen man. Turning him over on to his back he could see the shot, fired by a small calibre weapon, had struck the man right in the heart.

There was no mistake. He was dead, probably already so by the time he toppled off the stool. There had been a silence in the room ever since the shot had rung out. The man with his broken nose stopped groaning, holding on to his bleeding nose and sitting upright.

Lena and the other woman untangled themselves from each other, then both stood and came towards where Juan was kneeling on the floor.

"Is he?" Lena managed to ask, her breathing still laboured from all her exertion.

Juan looked up at her, "Yes," he simply said, then looked at the woman still sat on the stool by the piano, gun still in her hand.

"He was just going to shoot you, just like that, I, well, I didn't mean to kill him, just.

Juan nodded at her, then the swing doors opened and the sheriff entered, along with two men.

Lena faced her adversary, "I'm sorry Kitty," she said, then the two women, whom only moments against had been wildly clawing, scratching and fighting each other, now embraced. Lena knew this woman was Joseph's daughter.

The sheriff quickly sized up the situation, saw the gun and walked over to the woman. His two men helped to get some of the others to their feet, and as if right on cue, the town doctor entered the saloon.

On the cane chair, the sun getting warmer by the minute, Lena smiled at the memory.

Sad that Joseph Calhoen had to die, despite him being a nasty man. But what a night; what a brawl; what a fight. The bruises and cuts she carefully tended to later were all worth it, for the whole situation in town changed.

Juan had been the catalyst, the proverbial straw that broke the camel's back. He had been the tinderbox that ignited.

The town settled down. The woman who had shot Joseph was cleared of any wrong doing as she had, according to the sheriff, acted justly in preventing an unarmed man being shot. She was also Joseph's sister, and had been under his thumb for many years. For her it opened up a whole new life.

A week later, Lena's father, Joe, proudly walked his daughter down the aisle of the small church. A beaming Juan was awaiting his bride.

And Kitty, Joseph's daughter, was amazed, surprised and overjoyed, when Lena came to the ranch one morning, both women still sporting a few bruises, and asked her to be the bridesmaid.

Lena sighed, then got up. There was work to be done in the house.

Later that first week after their arrival in Silver City, Juan and the expectant Lena set off on a flat wagon, pulled by two horses and headed about three miles from the town centre. On the back sat a chest. It was covered with a blanket, and beside the chest was a box full of square marble stones.

These were mosaic tiles in a range of colours that Lena had found in a small outhouse of her new property. This gave her an idea, to work in together with the idea her husband Juan had.

He had found the right place. It was a barren piece of land, it wasn't on any route, and although he had noticed some remnants of what might have been a settlement at one point, there was nothing there now.

With the mid-afternoon sun making regular appearance through the cloud cover he stopped the horses and let the reins hang loose. His horses were well trained and stayed put. He helped his wife from the seat and then proceeded to shift the box. It was heavy. Lena walked around the ground, then found the best spot.

"Here," she said, then getting on her knees she used her hands to create an even space in the sandy soil.

Juan shifted the box to the edge of the wagon. Then he grabbed the box of tiles and also placed that on the edge. He called Lena over and together they lifted both the chest and the box to the floor. From there Juan dragged it to where they wanted it.

He was sweating when it was all in place. He opened the chest.

Taking the cloth cover away, he revealed the gold coins.

He took a few out, let them run through his fingers, then put them back.

As he'd learned from his father's writing, there had been eight hundred coins, which first belonged to the Spanish. They had been liberated from them by the 'Patron', Caprice's father, then after planning it together Philippe and Caprice had plotted and planned the robbery. After taking the coins out of Bogota, across the country to Buenaventura, they had loaded it aboard a ship in a newly sourced chest and headed for Acapulco.

He, his father Philippe, had paid his men, and also put some aside for himself in a leather pouch which survived the shipwreck and was still tied to his waist when he came around on the beach that morning. Seven hundred and twenty coins were still in the chest when they hauled it from the sea.

None of it had been needed by the time they left Carlos and his household nearly nine years later. Although he and Caprice offered a hundred coins to Carlos, they refused to accept, stating they had all they needed. Using some of the coins from the pouch, Philippe hired the vessel to sail them up the coast to land eventually up in Hermosillo as he'd needed the boat to carry the weight of the gold safely.

Philippe, himself, sailed the vessel back to the Peruvian from whom he had rented it, and then returned to their new home by horse.

They had enough to live on, and the chest remained sealed, the coins untouched.

Juan's sister was offered some for a dowry when she was getting married, but she refused, saying it would not enhance her life as she wanted to achieve a happy future working together as a couple. Though she loved her parents very much, and knew of the history of the gold coins, she didn't want a reminder of that side of her history.

This left the chest for Juan. His father gave him the remaining two coins from his pouch and this was all he needed. During his travels across Mexico and into America, during his time in Yuma and then in Tucson, Juan had used these last two coins to purchase his first horses. The chest remained closed.

Juan offered a hundred coins to Joe, Lena's father, but he too refused to take any, saying he had all he had, and had even begun to take an interest in Joseph's sister, who had taken up playing the piano at the White Parrot.

So the chest and its contents stayed intact.

Jeremiah, who was also offered some of the contents, said no, happy with his lot, and having those would not improve his life, he said.

And so the chest, still containing seven hundred and twenty coins, came along to Silver City. Juan and Lena had no interest in it either, as they too had all they needed, each other and a child on the way.

Having the coins was a weight he no longer wanted to carry.

It had to be buried, to be found perhaps, by someone in the future.

Juan had found the spot and Lena had come up with the idea to lay the mosaic tiles over the top once the coins were buried.

They both set to work, working for the next hour to dig a square hole in the loose and sandy soil.

Then they laid the coins down, and after a light coating of soil, Lena began to lay the tiles, using her creativeness to form a pattern with the dark and light shades of the marble tiles, often wondering, as she played with a pattern, as to where these tiles had come from.

It was getting dark when they finished. Lena stood up and looked at her work, Juan came to stand beside her. Whilst she had been creating the pattern, he had gathered the soil to cover it all. They both looked down. Lena had done a beautiful job and the pattern she had made from the mosaic tiles was obvious.

It was a bird, a swallow with its forked tail.

They held each other and stood for a few moments, then Juan set about covering it all with the soil he had gathered.

It would be a 126 years later when Professor Emily Parker would uncover the hidden treasure.

❦

THE PRESENT;

Albuquerque University

Wednesday morning 29th May

The dean had welcomed Millie warmly, and passed her on to a woman who was the temporary administrator. She was then handed two box folders, given a place where she could sit to read and, if required, she could make copies of whatever it was she needed. Furthermore, after only a few minutes, someone came in with some refreshments.

The folders contained many legal documents, insurance schedules, and the list of students who would be assisting Professor Parker. Then there were maps and timing schedules, lists of all the equipment that was to be used, the insurance schedule and details of the two trailers and several tents, including a large canopy tent which was to house the finds.

Furthermore there were details about the vehicles, about the transport company, and documents about the various landowners' permission and grants.

Millie found a folder amongst the many papers which held the notes by the various students and then, finally, another separate folder. In here she found notes from the Professor herself. Her name was stencilled on the front.

For a moment Millie held her breath. Seeing her mother's name so boldly written on the front caused her eyes to well up.

Letting out a sigh, she composed herself, then opened the folder.

The first thing that struck her, was a sketch, in fact several sketches and again her eyes welled up. She had often watched her mother sketch, fascinated by her artistry. This was indeed her mother's work. She knew that for sure and struggled to hold back the tears. Millie sniffed, then worked her way through the drawings. They were all detailed plans of the dig, the areas in which items had been found, a compass in the top right-hand corner depicting the direction of the land.

Then, along a strip at the bottom of each sheet, a quick sketch of each item discovered.

Millie came across a sheet that was stuck to the others. She peeled it loose, figuring it had been accidentally attached through the heat and perhaps a drop of spilled jam or honey. She remembered how her mother enjoyed blueberry jam.

This sketch was different. It wasn't a plan of the ground, but a picture of a swallow and beneath it she read the details that it was made up of mosaic tiles, each tile measuring 2.5 centimetres and covering an area of one square metre exactly.

The swallow was very descriptive, showing the distinctive forked tail in dark shades.

The sketch seemed out of place as it didn't relate to the other drawing in any way, and after having gone through the rest of the notes in the folder and finding nothing else relating to it, Millie began to wonder.

Could it be, she was thinking, handling the single sheet once more that it had mistakenly found its way into the wrong folder that this perhaps, was supposed to be in the folder that had been taken?

After searching through all the paperwork, including weather reports and police reports regarding the tornado, and medical report about the wounded and those who had died, she could find no other reference to the sketch of the swallow.

After she'd made copies of what she hoped might be relevant, documents, Millie then handed the two box folders back, with thanks, and quickly saying goodbye to the dean, she left the campus. She had been there just over three hours.

Feeling very strongly about the sketch of the swallow that had been created from the mosaic tiles, she'd made a copy of it, but had also taken the original.

Walking back to her hotel she pondered about her finds. Would anything be of help? Nothing she had found directly pointed to any foul play.

Yet, what was the folder about that had gone missing according to the woman Robert had spoken to? Was it to do with the mysterious mosaic swallow?

Also, though no expert, she had taken copies of the medical reports on all four victims. There might be a clue in those, especially with regard to the deaths of her mother and her mother's main assistant, Mr Alfredo. She would need to get a medical expert to check these. Feeling hungry and in need of lunch, she wondered how Alison Hudson was getting on. Would she be more successful in finding out what happened to both the missing lad, and the folder?

In Portland

Alison had parked the rental car directly across the street from the flower shop. She had arrived early, and spotted Barbara coming up the road and unlocking the shop. It was a little before 8.30 am and, according to the sign in the window, the store was to open at 9.00 am. Did Barbara have any assistants, Ally wondered, noticing she had unlocked the door, but had gone into the small shop without locking the front door.

Ideal.

Ally got out of the car, ran across the road, opened the door and entered. She then turned and twisted the door lock and locked it. The electric sign that would notify anyone coming or going, was not yet turned on.

Ally walked briskly towards the back, then through a door into the large storeroom. Barbara was at the far end, entering an office, but turned and shook as Ally called out "Barbara Philpot!"

The woman visible paled, fumbled with her office door keys, fumbled with her handbag, but lost her grip on both and they fell to the floor.

Ally walked right up to Barbara, wondering how it ever was that she'd been so afraid of her. She was much shorter, still quite thick set. Her hair was dyed red and she wore false eyelashes that seemed to Alison, to look rather ridiculous.

"We did bad things," Ally said, stopping only inches away from her. "I was a scrawny fourteen-year-old, and you were the boss, but, I am no longer a scrawny fourteen, and you and me, we are going to have a little talk."

"And you'd better answer my questions, understood?" Ally added.

Barbara, a little colour coming back into her face, nodded, unable to say a word. She was about to attempt to pick up her bag, but Ally stopped her.

"Leave it" she threatened, "your brother, Eddie, tell me where he is."

Barbara frowned, "Eddie?" she asked.

To the left of where they stood, there was a large long trough against the wall, obviously for watering, preparing and washing plants and flowers. It was made of concrete and ran about five feet in length and was almost a foot wide.

Ally grabbed Barbara by her upper arm forcibly and easily steered her towards it. "I'll have no hesitation in dumping you in there, and giving you a dousing. I should have had the courage to do that when I was younger." She stopped by the trough, but maintained her grip, and went on to say, "Your mother contacted Robert. Do you remember Robert, Robert Pentegrass?"

"We gave him some stick, didn't we? Well, she went to him, to ask for help in finding your missing brother, not knowing of course, how we treated the lad at school. Still, he very likely would not have connected that fact, nor have connected the name. Anyway," Ally continued, still holding tightly to Barbara's upper arm, "I know that your brother went missing from an archaeological dig in New Mexico, but I also know that he was up to no good. He stole something, then went missing, so, if you don't want me to ram you into this trough and soak you, you better spill, tell me all you know. The front door is locked, so, talk!"

Ally was surprised at how bold she was, but also a little concerned at how angry she was at this woman who now stood quivering before her.

Not everything was Barbara's fault. She had to acknowledge her own part. Still, if this was how to get some answers, all well and good. She kept her grip on her arm. Barbara was clearly in some pain and her face registered concern and fear, but, she found her voice, and said, "Mom went to see Robert?"

"Yes, you see" Ally explained, "Robert assisted the police to locate missing persons; had been doing so for nearly two decades; was known for it. Your mom no doubt heard about it. Used to by the way, Robert died a few weeks ago"

Barbara dropped her head, looked at the floor and was possibly hoping it might swallow her up.

"Eddie was scared," she finally said, looking up again and directly at Ally. There was moisture in her eyes now, she was on the verge of tears.

"He called me," she said, closing her eyes now as a single tear escaped and rolled down her cheek. "It was the day after the tornado had struck, which I remember hearing about. He was scared, said he owed money to someone and had been instructed to steal something."

"A folder?" Ally interrupted.

Barbara opened her eyes, her tearful eyes, and looked at Alison, "Yes. He said he was supposed to take it the day before, but hadn't found the right opportunity, then, when the tornado struck, he saw his chance. There was chaos, so, he said he took the file." Barbara paused here for a moment.

Another tear rolled down her face and Ally decided to release her grip.

Rubbing her arm, Barbara looked up again at Alison, then said, "He then broke down. Cried over the phone. He had done some bad things, but, he said the file he needed, this folder, the person was holding it tight. Wouldn't let go, so, he said he grabbed something and hit her, he rang me the following day because he didn't know until then that he had killed her"

Both women were silent for a while, it was Ally who spoke first, "Do you know what happened to the folder, or perhaps what was in it?"

Barbara wiped some tears away, sniffed a couple of times, then again rubbing her arm which was obviously painful, she looked at Ally and said, "I have it"

Ally looked surprised, and said, "You have it?"

"Eddie was scared, but he wasn't going down for murder, so, he posted a parcel to me. The folder is inside it. Then he went on the run. He said he needed to get as far away as possible." After a brief pause, a few sniffs and still rubbing her upper arm, Barbara said, "I received it a couple of days later. I hid it away; wanted nothing to do with it. Didn't open it, didn't want to be connected in anyway."

"Wait a minute," Alison interjected, "but you were what, about twelve? Didn't your mother know?"

"Mom was hardly ever home. She worked nights, slept in the mornings, or slept somewhere else. I was usually just by myself, it's probably why I became."

Ally saw the pain now in Barbara's face, not from being hurt just now, but the pain of the memories, of being unloved at home, and having to fend for herself.

She could now understand better why she had become that bully, had lashed out at those who had all that she didn't have, inflicting punishment, making others miserable to counter her own sadness.

"So, you hid it. Where is it now, and where is your brother?" Ally asked, more sympathetic now, realising why she had been as she was, back at high school.

Ally looked around, the tidy storeroom. There were many flowers and bouquets and shrubbery and pots. It was very cheerful.

The shop itself also was neat and tidy and the smell was very pleasing. She looked at her watch, it was 8.45 am.

"Sort yourself out, get ready to open the shop, but then tell me what else you know." Holding Barbara by both shoulders she looked her in the eye, "Okay?"

Barbara nodded, and when Ally let her go, she sniffed some more, gathered her bag and keys and unlocked the office.

"Anyone working for you?" Ally asked.

"No, I run it by myself."

"It's a lovely store."

"Thank you."

Ally headed back through to the shop and looked at the various flowers and plants.

Barbara came through with bit more colour in her face and though her eyes were still a little red. She managed a smile and unlocked the shop, turned the sign around then went behind the counter and switched on the electronic beam sign and the register.

"I never heard from Eddie again," she said, opening the till drawer and putting the float in. I'm sure he is no longer alive. As for the folder, the parcel, it's still in the house, my house now."

"Mom is shacked up with someone. We're not in touch. Haven't spoken to her in years. Surprised she went to ask about Eddie? When did she do that?"

"Not sure exactly. I can find out, but likely a month or so ago," Ally replied.

"What's in the folder?" Barbara asked.

"Don't know. A friend is looking into that. I hope it will help solve a mystery, though we now know that it was your brother who killed Professor Parker, not intentionally though," Ally added.

"Thank you," Barbara answered, then smiled as a customer entered the shop.

Ally wandered around, then, as Barbara said to her to make a coffee for herself, she took did that, and made one for Barbara also. Though she still felt some animosity, she was beginning to appreciate the circumstances which surrounded her at the time.

"Thanks," Barbara said, taking hold of the mug of coffee as the customer left the shop. "I sometimes close at 1.00 pm for an hour, to get some lunch. Also, if I have any deliveries, then that is when I do them. I have none today, so far anyway." She took a careful sip from the mug.

"My house is not far from here. We'll go and get that parcel then, if that is okay?" After a pause and another sip, she continued, "And, I am soo sorry for who I was. I can't turn to clock back, but, if I can help you, well."

Ally nodded and sipped her coffee. Looking out the shop window onto the street, she pondered. It was surely Eddie who had killed Millie's mother, but what was so damn important in those files that the professor had grabbed and clutched so tightly.

In Albuquerque

In her hotel room, getting ready to check out and fly home, Millie was wondering the same thing.

What had been in that folder that was so important, and, did it have anything to do with the sketch of the swallow?

Whilst across the Atlantic

Both Thomas and Cynthia were on their laptops, scrolling and searching. Victoria was in the kitchen, cleaning up after dinner. It was nine in the evening, though still quite light outside.

After landing the plane in the very early hours of the morning, they drove through the meadow onto a dirt track, reached a main road, the D69, and found that they were close to a place called Soullans. Looking at the satnav in the car, Thomas felt they should travel to a slightly bigger town and so they headed for Challans.

It was Tia who came up with the idea of renting a cottage, a holiday let. Though many might be occupied, it wasn't the height of summer yet so the possibility of obtaining one would be feasible. This would mean they wouldn't all have to register as they would have needed to going to a hotel.

In the town of Challans, which lay about 270 miles south west of Paris, Tia successfully secured a cottage, explaining to the estate agent that they were on an impromptu search for any chateaux that might be for sale and needed a base.

Not an unreasonable story as Tia knew that foreigners from the United Kingdom and also northern Europe were frequently searching for a reasonably priced French estate. Ideal. They purchased groceries, also some fresh clothes for Victoria and after settling in, both Thomas and Tia promptly fell asleep in their bedrooms.

Victoria set about doing some housework. She asked them both for any laundry which she washed along with her own rumpled and dirty clothes.

Just before going to sleep, though by now extremely tired Thomas sent an e-mail to Claire. Then, he asked Victoria if there was anyone she needed to contact who might be worried or concerned. She said no, so they went to bed.

That was eleven hours ago.

In Myrtle Creek

The 'ding' on her phone had woken Claire. She looked at the digital clock on the bedside table. One am.

The message was from Thomas. She punched the app and a message appeared.

Again it was brief,

'All safe, escaped bad guys, not out of the woods, sleepy, talk later, love Thomas'

Claire read it though twice, then put it down and lay back on the bed. She growled and whispered aloud, "Why not tell me a little more?

"All safe, who's all? Escaped bad guys. That sounds interesting. How many bad guys? Not out of the woods, what did that mean?"

Pleased to have heard from him, as it was of course a big relief, she shook her head, then smiled, turned and had no trouble now in falling asleep.

Present time in France

"Anything?" Victoria asked, bringing through a tray with coffee and desserts.

"Wow that's looks yummy," Thomas said, looking up from his laptop, then referring to some notes he had written, said, "Found the painting, well, at least confirmed its existence. Found the article where it records that it was stolen from the Bilbao museum of art, back in 1989. It also says that, to date, the thief has not been captured, nor has the painting ever surfaced."

"And I have been trying to trace this Mr Johannes Acker," Tia said, eyeing up the lovely dessert that had been placed on the table. "He was indeed an art dealer and did work with the French police to get stolen Nazi art back to their proper owners, but, according to a report here, he died in 1990, in Lucerne, in a boating accident."

"Really?" Victoria said, pouring out the coffees for them.

Thomas sat back, reached for his dessert and sighed. "It seems we're stuck for the moment. For one, we can't find any trace of the painting. It's perhaps why the Teremos family searched for and captured you, in the hope for any information. Then, we have the dilemma of probably being sought by the Spanish police, so what can we do next? At least you are safe." he added.

"We are no longer in Spain, so that's good," Cynthia said, "we could go to the police here in France, but this, of course, would bring trouble for you Victoria, being an art thief and all."

"I believe that finding the painting, finding out more, if we can, about Johannes Acker, and more about how the Teremos family acquired the painting in the first place might help." Victoria said, her voice soft and with concern on her face. "But, it seems we have come to a dead end. Above all, I don't want you two to get in any trouble, so, this needs some thinking through."

"Agreed," Thomas said, tucking into his raspberry and cream dessert. "Also, there is a DP in the UK somewhere, who knew of your abduction, who alerted us, well, alerted Robert, but obviously didn't know about his death, so, who is DP?"

Victoria sat down and sipped some of her coffee and all three fell silent for a bit.

"Right," Thomas said, "Time to ring Claire, and speak to her. We haven't been the best at keeping her informed. She might have an idea as to how best to proceed. Robert may have some contacts in his files that she might be able to uncover."

"Don't forget to tell her about me, and give her my love," Cynthia said.

"Will do," Thomas replied and pressed some numbers on his phone. "I'll put it on speaker." He stood up and walked over to the window.

Darkness was falling and he figured it to be around lunchtime back in Myrtle Creek.

"Thomas! Thank goodness! I have a thousand questions, who's 'we' and who is the abducted woman? Why, was she abducted? Escaped from the bad guys? Who? Who are these bad guys? And not out of the woods? What does that mean?

Claire ran out of breath after delivering that barrage of questions which made Thomas smile, as it did both Tia and Victoria who heard it clearly.

"Breathe Claire," Thomas said," I know. I'm sorry, I should have told you more earlier, but everything happened so fast, so listen up and I'll run through the scenario." He smiled at Tia and Victoria, then continued, "To answer your first question, the 'we' is a woman called Cynthia, she was the one who was at your rescue and spoke to you. One of Roberts helpers. She sends her love. Now, she was also sent a letter by Robert telling her to look after me, which, I'm glad to say, she did."

Thomas finished the update by asking Claire to send the following message to DP, *'Abductee rescued, need transport back to UK, help'*

Then in closing asked Claire if she could find out if Robert had any knowledge or contacts with the art world as they wanted information on a painting by Titian, a portrait of King Charles V standing by a black horse, then he ended the call.

THE PAST;

Period 8

The year 1895–Boston, Massachusetts

Franck Huysen, his wife Anje and their twelve-year-old son Joachim had arrived in New York just under a fortnight ago, had then travelled by horse and wagon on to Boston.

They had fled Europe. Fled their home town of Ghent and had sailed from Antwerp. Anje was Jewish, and all over Western Europe, tension was mounting.

Although he'd initially thought to start life anew in New York, on the voyage over Franck had met a fellow refugee, a Dutchman.

They had bonded, and after only a few conversations, had decided to work together. The Dutchman, his name Moshe, had worked for some years at the Weeskamer, an auction house in Amsterdam. Franck was a dealer in art. It seemed provident. They shook hands and agreed to start a business in Boston because Moshe had connections there, mainly in the shipping industry.

And so it was, just four months after their arrival that the business was set up. Though Joachim was only twelve, his father was determined for the boy would take over one day and so the company he started, he named Franck Huysen and Son.

Franck had brought quite a selection of paintings and a few sculptures with him and with Moshe running the auction side of the business, Franck scoured the city and surrounding area, hoping to persuade people to sell through his auction house.

It was in the beginning of November when a woman entered the building. Under her arm, wrapped up in a colourful woollen blanket, she carried a painting. Moshe, first took in the appearance of the woman, who was well dressed and, he estimated, in her early thirties. He watched as she unfolded the blanket to reveal the work of art.

Moshe knew art, knew artists, had studied books. Not letting anything show, he examined the piece.

It was around eighteen inches in width and thirty six inches in height. It was on a canvas stretched over a light piece of wood. It had no frame.

Moshe carefully looked at it, studied the back, then, looked at it some more.

There was a little damage around the edges. He surmised that there was once a frame which had been carelessly taken off.

But the painting in general was good. He knew the artist. He was sure this was a work by Tiziano Vecelli, better known as Titian.

The vibrancy of the red coat, the use of the almost purple blues. The face of the man, whom Moshe felt was Charles V, was full of expression. The horse was beautifully painted, though Moshe had not known of Titian painting animals before. Figuring this work was painted in the early 1500s, he was sure of the artist. This was indeed a work by Titian.

Finally standing up, he looked at the woman.

"Where you get this piece," he asked, his English, though much improved since coming to Boston, was still broken and sharply accented.

"It originally belonged to my grandfather, Joe Wheeler. He won it in a card game about thirty-five years ago from a Spanish guy travelling in the area. This was in Tucson," she answered. "It was then given to my mother as a wedding gift. Now it belongs to me."

"Interesting," Moshe said, after a moment or two, taking yet another look. He took it from the table and propped it up against the wall, stepped back and took it all in.

The horse was indeed painted beautifully, the figure standing by the horse, he knew almost certainly was King Charles V.

"The Spanish connection is good," Moshe said. "Is very nice piece, very good artist, will sell very good price."

"You know this artist?" the woman asked.

"Yes ma'am, this is by Titian, famous Italian painter. We will sell at good price, yes?"

The woman nodded.

Moshe took the lady into the office where he wrote down some details and explained to her that the auction would be held in nine days and was this all right with her.

She nodded again, and explained that she had recently arrived in the city and was looking forward to the day of the auction.

Moshe led the woman out and then turned to once more view the painting she had brought in. He wondered who the man had been that had lost this lovely piece of art in a card game, and how had he acquired the painting, this man from Spain.

THE PRESENT;

Teremos Hacienda–Spain

Wednesday afternoon 29th May

Letitia Teremos. Forty one years of age. She stood five foot four inches, was slim built, but kept herself very fit, cycling and walking every day on her machines. Her hair was almost black, and she had it in a ponytail as she stood in the gym.

She looked at the rope that lay on the floor and brought her mind back to Monday when she had brought the woman here, and had her strung up on the overhead beam that formed part of the roof structure.

Once the two lads had done so, she had ordered them to leave.

She was annoyed. She had been told of a man following the truck. The lads had spotted him soon enough as they were driving well back as a backup precaution. She had been pleased that she had ordered this. She had planned the whole operation, a plan she had been working on for almost a year.

That had been a good precaution, however, to have got out of their vehicle with the intention of seriously harming this man was not in the plan. Running him off the road, all well and good, but they should have left it like that.

She had told them so in no uncertain terms.

Who was this man that was following them, and, who was the woman that had come to his rescue. Those had been the questions in her mind, on Monday afternoon.

After having strung the woman up, Letitia took hold of her face, and noted she was still quite drugged. She would return.

In the meantime she would find out, about this man, and this woman. The police chief in Ampuero was summoned. He had learned about the car run off the road, and recognised the license plate given of the pickup truck involved, which he knew to be owned by the Teremos family, so he knew why he had been summoned …

… Now she stood where the ropes still lay … Letitia walked over to a heavy leather punchbag suspended from the ceiling and proceeded to pummel and kick it for several minutes. Grabbing a towel from a shelf, she wiped her face and arms, then draped the towel around her neck and went over to pick up the rope … she was angry.

First of all, at the woman; the woman she had sought and found. The woman who had been the one who had stolen their painting.

She had planned her revenge well. The abduction had been perfect. The travel well organised and executed. It was just that last bit when it was discovered they had been followed.

But she was more angry with the fact that, although she had slapped the woman several times, had grabbed the woman's face hard and could see the pain in her face, yet she had not told her the truth, though indeed at first when she had told the story, it had not sounded like a lie.

Leaving her hanging there, Letitia had gone to the main house, where she ordered her cook to make her dinner and had sat down, put some music on, and opened her laptop to begin searching.

First, to check on the story that the woman, the thief, had told her.

This soon led to a dead end, for the man she had accused of being the planner of the theft had died quite some time ago, and she had been unable to find any associates or the possible whereabouts of her painting.

She did find that the man had a police record for dealing in stolen pieces of art, which had given her some hope that the story told was the truth. However, in searching further, she discovered that the man had been in prison in Belgium at the time the painting was stolen from the museum.

It couldn't have been him; the woman had lied.

Frustrated, she turned her attention to the names she had written down, the names the police chief had given her. The man, whose car had been driven off the road, was a Thomas Klaassen, from Stockholm, Sweden, and the woman, who had reported the accident, was a Cynthia Barnes from Portland, Oregon, US.

So, who were these two, why were they there, and how were they involved?

She had wondered about going back to the gym to slap the woman around a bit more, but she was tired, and went to bed. That would keep until morning.

A little over three hours later.

"Senorita, senorita!" the housemaid called out, banging on the door.

Letitia stirred, then woke fully, looked at the clock which showed it to be almost 2.30 am.

She got up and went to the door, saying, "What is it Maria?"

She opened the door and her maid, Maria, was there in her dressing gown, with her face red from excitement, "Oh Senorita, the plane, someone is starting the motor."

Letitia, rushed to her wardrobe, opened it to grab a dressing gown and ran across the hall to the side of the house where the balcony ran along its length. She entered the dark lounge and ran over to the window. She could see by the light shining from the hangar that both propellers were turning, then the plane moved and turned into the runway.

From the corner of her eye she saw two of her hands coming from the direction of the warehouse where their living quarters were also situated.

But the plane's engines were now on full blast and it shot forwards and began to barrel down the runway.

Letitia open the door to the balcony, saw that her manservant had come out of the house, armed with a shotgun. But it was too the late. The plane lifted off, the wheels tucked in, then it banked away to the left.

Cursing all the way, Letitia ran down the stairs and headed for the gym. Cursing some more as she saw the woman was gone.

Holding the rope in her hands, she looped one end around one hand, then grabbed another part of the rope which she looped around the other hand.

"You will pay," she said, in a loud whisper, tightening the rope between her hands. "Whoever you are, you will pay." Throwing the rope into a corner, she left the gym and headed for the front door. Having calmed down a little, she spoke to her manservant.

"Tell them," she said, nodding to the two men who were standing outside and looking perplexed, "to get back to their quarters. There is work to be done in the morning. You too, get back to sleep. Leave everything to me."

Letitia then bounded up the stairs back into the lounge, and picked up her phone.

Waking up the police chief, she told him of the theft of her aircraft, likely by the two foreigners, and to get onto air traffic control and find it.

Fixing a coffee for herself, she paced the floor for some time, watched the sun come up, then dressed and walked over to the hangar.

She kicked the chocks that lay there. Who were these people?

Finally, late morning, she decided to have a lie down, stripped down, got into bed and promptly fell asleep.

She woke nearly three hours later.

Surprised that she had slept so long, she showered, dressed and once more opened up her laptop. As the screen came to life, the clock on it showed it to be nearly two in the afternoon, nearly ten hours since informing the chief, but, strangely, no word, and no sign of the plane, her plane, anywhere.

Her plane, she mused, thinking back as to how she got to this point in her life.

Letitia's father, Alberto, and her older brother Ramon, had both been tragically killed in a boating accident, nearly three years ago.

The Teremos Orchards were well known in the country and abroad and sales were steady, but Letitia wanted the high life, travelling to Paris, to Rome, to New York, staying in the best places, living the high life, parties and gambling. Las Vegas and Monte Carlo were favourite haunts. Meanwhile the farm manager, Ronaldo, ran the business.

But the money ran out, and Letitia came home one day to discover that her manager was going to leave. He had warned her of her spending and she'd told him just to worry about the business, and that her own affairs were her own affairs.

This had been a wake-up call. This had called for drastic measures.

She knuckled down, focused on the business, persuaded Ronaldo to stay and spent some time in actually learning the business.

With her spending now curbed, and with the sales steadily increasing as she secured extra customers, she discovered she rather enjoyed her role in the business. The company grew again. She bought the plane after taking flying lessons, and having set the family business back on an even keel, she began to look for better profits.

And better profits lay in drugs. She still frequently rued the days when she had so carelessly spent so much money, particularly gambling in Monte Carlo.

THE PAST;

Period 9

The year 1947–Monte Carlo

Roberto Solari stood back, put his brushes down and stretched. He looked out of the window of his attic studio. The sea was blue and calm, and the sun was heading for the horizon. He noticed several small boats and saw a couple of fishing boats heading back to shore.

Life was still pretty hard, though the war had been over for nearly two years. There wasn't the abundance that there once was, but it would return, he thought, lighting a cigarette. A steam whistle blew, and moments later he saw the train pulling away from the station that he could just see through the window on the left.

His apartment ran the full length of the house and was divided into three sections. Where he stood now, by one of three window, was the largest area, his studio, where he worked. Through a small door he could enter the middle section, a small kitchen, a table and a small sitting area. There was also a door to enter the narrow corridor and stairs leading to the floor below.

The third section was also quite small, and housed a double bed and a wardrobe.

He would wash in the sink in the kitchen and had to go down to the next landing to go to a toilet. There was a shower also on this landing that he could use if he so wished. It was home and it suited him fine. It certainly was a better place than the rooms he had previously, this, courtesy of a sizeable commission he received in copying a painting.

He was a street artist, able to do quick portraits of tourists, and the tourists, mainly wealthy ones, were coming back.

Roberto turned from the window and looked at his current work. Another commission, another copy. He had two easels side by the side, the original on the right, his work on the left. It was starting to come together.

He had been approached when he was visiting his local cafe, where, most mornings, he had a light breakfast and a coffee.

The man, a young man, in his mid-twenties, joined him at the table. "Heard about you. A friend of a friend, Jan Smettens, said you are a decent artist. I need a painting copied, yes or no? I have no time to lose."

"Yes."

Fifteen minutes later Roberto let the young man in and took him upstairs to his fourth floor studio. The man had a parcel under his arm.

Once upstairs, Roberto took the parcel, unwrapped it and put it on the easel.

He studied it for a while.

"Can you do it?" the man who had not introduced himself at all, asked.

"Yes, three weeks," Roberto answered, still observing the painting.

"Two weeks," was the answer and he placed an envelope of a small table.

Roberto looked at the young man, looked at the envelope, picked it up and peered inside. "Two weeks and I make it good. Seventeen days and I make it very good," he said.

Eighteen-year-old Roberto held the man's gaze, who turned and replied, "Very well, seventeen days." Then he left the apartment.

Roberto didn't even look at the man again, just heard the door shut and again took in the painting. It was very well painted, the horse was beautiful, and standing beside it, the man was splendidly dressed, in crimson and purple, Roberto knew this figure. He had come across other portraits of this man, Charles V who was either a king or an emperor.

He studied the work for a while and became also sure that it was a work by Italian artist, Titian. The face of the man, Charles V, was painted with such care and showed great expression. It would be the hardest part of the painting to get right, Roberto thought, studying the work closely for quite some time before gathering the various colours that he would need and selecting a suitable canvas to use from his available range. He was happy to find one that matched in size.

Once outside, the man who had visited Roberto, walked across the road, entered a phone box, inserted some coins, and pressed a button to dial a number.

"Johannes here" he said, "seventeen days. Get the paperwork ready." Then he hung up.

Leaving the phone box, the young man looked up at the apartment building.

In seventeen days he would be back.

THE PRESENT;

Challans–France

Wednesday–nearly midnight

"We should go back," Thomas said, having entered Cynthia's bedroom and was standing at the end of the bed.

Cynthia sat up in bed. She hadn't been asleep. She was just lying there, thinking, about Thomas mainly.

"Go back? Go back where?"

"Take the plane and return it," he said.

"Take…Are you crazy?"

"No, at least, well, no, not crazy. Hear me out. We got Victoria out. She's safe, but, you and I are now wanted by the Spanish police. Sure, we can tell the story, our story, but, how influential is this Letitia woman. I feel we need to go back and set things right. We do have leverage."

Tia sat and looked at him. He had come into her room. She had hoped he would come, and he had, but not for the reason she hoped for. Go back? Surely a death trap.

"What leverage?" she asked.

Thomas walked around and sat on her bed, looking into her eyes, and said, "We'll send Victoria to Paris. She can go to the British Embassy or Consulate there, and tell her story. Interpol will be involved. In the meantime, we fly the plane back. They'll not expect that, and they won't touch us, with the information that we tell them, they won't dare."

"You're crazy," she said. "Better let Victoria know." Then she smiled, leaned forwards and kissed him briefly, saying "that's the kiss I still owe you, now, shoot, get ready."

After dressing quickly, Cynthia opened up her laptop, and bought tickets on line for Victoria to get to Paris. Also, from an inner compartment in her handbag she retrieved some American dollars she could exchange for any expenses.

The train would depart for Paris late morning. It was at that moment, as she handed Victoria the cash that she realised something she had totally forgotten. Victoria hadn't asked about it. She probably assumed that the Spanish woman had it at the hacienda, but it wasn't there. Cynthia had taken it, grabbed it from the floor of the gym as they left, with Thomas carrying Victoria over his shoulder.

The long walk, through the orchard, then across some fields and into the woods. It was dark, but she had led Thomas back to the car. She'd seen how Thomas was now struggling to carry Victoria much further, had put the handbag down to open the rear door of her car and had helped Thomas place Victoria on the back seat.

They had left.

"The handbag," she suddenly exclaimed.

They both looked at her. Cynthia explained, "Oh Victoria, I'm sorry. I did have your handbag. It was on the floor in the gym, but, I put it down on the ground when we reached the car to get you inside. Totally forgot about it until just now, so sorry."

"Hey, don't worry, didn't have much in it, … thought the Spanish woman must have it, …"

"Credit cards? Keys?" Thomas asked.

"Yes, but look, you guys were rather busy at the time, rescuing me! Don't worry about it."

Cynthia gave Victoria a code that she needed to punch into a machine at the station in order to retrieve the tickets, then gave her a hug. Thomas was busy getting their luggage in the car, shivering in the night air, then he also gave Victoria a hug.

Five minutes later Cynthia drove the rental car back to where they had landed the plane. It was now a little after midnight.

They reached it, having only once taken a wrong turn; a great feat on a dark night.

Cynthia pulled up to the gate and Thomas got out to open it.

He could see that the plane was there, untouched, and looking forlorn in the darkness. She drove through and Thomas closed the gate. Next he jogged towards the plane.

Once again he entered via the cockpit and set about lowering the ramp, switching the cockpit lights on and briefly checking that nothing had been tampered with.

Tia gunned the engine, drove the car up the ramp despite a little slip in the grass. Thomas closed the ramp and re-entered the cockpit.

He checked the fuel gauge, which he had remembered showed almost a full tank and sighed with relief to see there was still ample fuel left. Then he started the engines. Port side first. This time there was not such urgency. Starboard side, all running. No problems on the instrument panel, all was as it should be.

Next he swung the plane hard port, hoping he had enough clearance to turn around before the hedge ahead.

Cynthia had strapped herself into the co-pilots seat and said nothing. She could see he was concentrating fully. The look on his face suggested it might be a tight run thing to get the plane up to speed on this wet meadow.

Thomas, feeling that all was now ready, looked at her, smiled, then blew out his cheeks again, "Okay, here we go. It's all or nothing."

All or nothing, Cynthia thought to herself, looking through the cockpit window into the dark night. Her stomach muscles were tight, but was this because of the situation they were in, or because of the man sitting next to her? As she had looked at him earlier, while he was checking all the dials on the instrument panel, totally absorbed in the preparation, she had realised she had such strong feelings for him.

A man, who when he was a young lad, she had treated so badly.

He revved the engines as high as he dared before releasing the brakes and pushing the stick forwards.

The plane picked up speed rapidly, despite the wet grass, but the end of the meadow loomed closer and closer in the light of the front landing gear.

Several bumps, then the wheels were off the ground, Thomas switched the light off immediately. He wanted to return as stealthily as they had come.

He once again sighed with relief when they had gained the height he wanted.

Tia realised she had been holding her breath. She too exhaled and took in fresh air, then glanced at the man next to her. The man had, without hesitation, flown across to help a woman in trouble, any way he could.

Yes, she thought, sighing, she was falling in love.

It wasn't long before the plane flew low over the Bay of Biscay.

Meanwhile

At the same time, though with a nine hour time difference, Alison Hudson, on board the plane from Portland, and on the descent to San Francisco, also puffed out her cheeks, having just read through the findings in the folder, the one that Professor Emily Parker had so tightly held to her chest that fateful day.

She had received the folder, which was still inside the parcel bag that Eddie had sent from Albuquerque, which Barbara had never opened, from Barbara at her house only blocks away from the shop. She had then booked her return flight and had thanked Barbara. Neither spoke as they walked back to the shop.

But Ally then initiated the move and they hugged, briefly, before she crossed the road back to her rental. She promised she would keep Barbara informed, especially if she found out more about her brother Eddie.

She also gave Barbara her number, if she ever wanted to just chat.

It wasn't until she reached the airport that Ally opened the parcel and took out the folder. Once her flight had reached altitude and she could use her phone, she rang Millie, told her of the findings in the folder and asked her to come to her apartment, and gave her an approximate time and then texting her the address.

Millie said she had also uncovered some information, so they could compare notes.

After landing and getting a taxi, Alison once more called Millie, saying she would home in twenty minutes.

Back over the Bay of Biscay

In the darkness of the night, Thomas flew low and keeping the city of Bilbao well to his left. They headed overland, then banked to port, almost skimming the treetops, before banking to starboard again. The town of Ampuero lay ahead, and after banking a final time, Thomas switched on the landing lights.

Ahead was the hacienda, the warehouse, the orchard, the main house and the runway. Wheels down.

"Senorita, senorita!" the housemaid almost screamed, once again banging on her mistress door.

"What?" Letitia asked, having opened her door. She was wearing fine cream coloured silk pyjamas.

"The plane, Miss, it come back!"

"What?"

Thomas landed successfully, then rolled the plane further towards the hanger, and set about turning it around, almost placing it exactly as he found it.

"Does the phrase, 'lion's den' come to mind?" Cynthia asked, unbuckling her seatbelt.

Thomas smiled, unbuckling his own, then said, "Get in the car, I'll lower the ramp." He moved past the car to the rear and controlled the mechanism.

The ramp descended. Tia was in the car, started it and reversed down the ramp. Thomas flicked the lever, and was back in the cockpit when he saw a woman leaving the house, by herself, rifle in hand.

The propellers slowed to a stop.

Thomas switched of the cockpit lights and then moved back into the cargo hold.

Here he opened the side hatch, unfolded and lowered the steps and switched off the lights in the hold.

Meanwhile Tia drove around to the side of the plane, careful to avoid the plane's wing and propeller. She too noticed the woman heading their way, rifle in hand.

Thomas walked down the steps and beckoned for Tia to come and join him.

She cut the engine, got out of the car into the cool of the night, which made her shiver, walked over to stand next to Thomas at the bottom of the steps and waited.

Letitia had dressed quickly, twisted her long dark hair into a ponytail, put on a pair of boots, grabbed her father's rifle and headed downstairs.

Her driver and manservant was by the front door, awaiting her instruction.

"Stay here, and tell them," she had opened the door and seen two men coming from the warehouse direction, "to go back to sleep. Work to be done tomorrow. I've got this."

"Very good, Miss."

Wearing tight jeans, a checked shirt that wasn't tucked in and a determined look on her face that registered both surprise and anger, she prepared the rifle and strode towards the plane.

She saw the twin propellers slow, noticed and heard the car come down the ramp, then walked briskly. She saw the car come around from the back of the plane. Then a man walked down the steps from the plane. She was thinking about getting the rifle ready to shoot, but changed her mind when she saw that he was waiting.

Letitia, quite confused as to what was happening, strode on, and noticed the woman get out of the car and join the man at the bottom of the steps.

She kept walking, angrily, and decided to raise the rifle in readiness when she was about twenty feet away.

It was then that man spoke.

"We've returned your plane Miss Teremos," the man said. He was confident, his voice was strong and assured and he was smiling.

"We had a parcel to deliver to the British Embassy," the woman said, also full of confidence and smiling, "perhaps we can talk about it?" she then suggested.

Letitia, usually used to being in total control, was both wary and unsure.

"Or we could just get in our, our car and go home," the man said.

"Come inside" Letitia said, lowering the rifle. "Leave the car there." She kept her eyes on them as they moved away from the plane.

"Don't suppose you could rustle up some coffee could you?" Thomas said, reaching the woman who stood still and observed them both, "No trolley service on this flight," he said, taking Tia's hand, still full of confidence and smiling.

"And I would really like to powder my nose," Tia said, also smiling.

Briefly looking from one to the other, the Spanish woman turned on her heels and said, "Follow me."

Hopefully her voice sounded assured, she thought, as she felt totally at a loss at present. Who were these two? Yes, she knew their names, a Thomas Klaassen and a Cynthia Barnes, but, to come back here, to be so brazen, so confident, they obviously had a good reason to behave in this way. But, as they made their way to the house where her driver stood by the open door, she heard no police sirens, so, best to stay calm and hear what they might have to say.

"Prepare coffee and take it into the lounge," she said to the man by the door, handing him the rifle. Then turning to the maid who stood, looking a little pale, in the hallway, by the stairs, "Maria, show this lady where the bathroom is please." Then, noticing Maria's worried look, added, "It's all right Maria and then make sure the guest room is ready."

Briefly focusing on the man as the maid led the woman away, Letitia said, "Follow me please," and headed up the stairs.

He followed her up the wide staircase, amused at the fact that she had said please.

Turning left they entered a large lounge. Letitia switched on the lights in the large room and gestured for him to sit down.

Back in San Francisco

Darkness was beginning to fall as Ally unlocked the front door and nodded to the waiting Millie, who saw her taxi arrive and had got out of her car. Ally entered, turned on the hallway light, invited Millie in, and closed the front door.

Then proceeding through to the living room, and turning the lights on she said "Please, make yourself at home. Can I get you anything?"

"Later," Millie said, holding a folder in her hand, "curiosity has to be fed first."

"Absolutely," Ally said, dropping her overnight bag and taking her coat off which she flung on a chair. Then, retrieving a folder, she sat down on the two-seater couch and Millie settled in the single armchair.

"Okay, how about you go first Millie," Ally said, placing the folder beside her and looking across at the other woman.

Millie stared at the folder that Ally had placed on the couch and after a moment or two, she whispered, "Is … is that blood on the cover?"

Ally frowned, then also looked and realised, "Oh Millie, I am so sorry, yes. Of course I noticed the smudges, never thought it well, I suppose."

"It's okay Ally," Millie responded, her voice back to normal, "I saw it and just froze for a moment. Sorry for being so melodramatic."

"No, not at all. I should have anyway do you want me to go first?"

"No, I'm good," Millie said, then taking her eyes away from the folder, she looked directly at Alison and began. "Right then. Well, I found out a lot about the dig that my mother was running in New Mexico."

Millie shifted slightly in her seat, took hold of her folder and spoke, "Found all the details of the university's involvement and financial support, the students who were assigned to the dig, all the insurance details, and that it was run by my mother assisted by a Mr Alfredo. He also died that day."

Pausing briefly, Millie's eyes were drawn again to the folder that lay on the couch, but she refocused on Alison and continued. "Then I discovered some papers from my mother, and some drawings. Many of them were creased, smudged and ripped, presumable damaged by the tornado, but, other than some details of the size of the dig, the placement where several Mayan artefacts had been founds, some topical drawing of the various excavations that were being carried out, I found absolutely nothing, though. Well maybe, but I can't figure it out. A separate sketch that seemed out of place," Millie said.

After another brief pause she continued,

"It was stuck to another sheet. I thought it might have belonged in another folder, perhaps the one that had been so important for my mother," she glanced briefly at the folder that lay next to Ally, "I took it away with me, and though I also made copies of all the other relevant documents, I could still find nothing that suggested why there had been foul play. I'm still not even sure if foul play ever happened."

"Oh, it happened all right," Ally said, reaching for the folder and opening it.

Then looking directly at the woman opposite her, who, she noted had lost a little colour since her arrival, said, her voice softer, "I'm sorry to say, but, your mother was indeed murdered, although, it wasn't intentional. A young man, Eddie, desperately wanted a folder your mother was clinging to. He hit her to take it from her, but the blow was too much. He discovered only the following day that your mother had died."

Ally let that sink in for a moment, cross with herself for not even realising that the marks on the folder were surely blood stains.

Then she spoke again, making eye contact with Millie, who's eyes were moist, and said, "This guy, a young lad really, was Eddie Philpot, the older brother of the woman I went to see. She told me that, when she was twelve, he called her, very scared and crying, as he hadn't realised he had killed your mother."

"He then said that he was posting something to her, and would she hide it. He was going on the run, as some bad people were after him."

"Wow," was all Millie could manage to say, appreciating the newly found friendship she had in the woman across from her, who had herself faced a traumatic event when her daughter had been taken.

"She never heard from him ever again. She hid the folder, or rather, she hid the parcel that her brother had sent. Inside it was this folder."

"Really?"

"Yes, it was still inside the parcel bag that her brother sent from Albuquerque. Now, you should have it, though, now that I think about it, it may be worthwhile giving the cover of this folder to the police, they may discover"

"Yes that's a good idea, we should," Millie agreed, then, "Sorry, please, go on"

"Before I hand it to you I would like to read something I found, and the reason this information was so important. May I?"

"Yes, of course. Absolutely. I'm all ears."

"It is about a note your mother found, on the dig," Ally said, then taking hold of a sheet of paper, she said, "It's written in Spanish, but on the plane, I translated it, and this is what it says,

> *No amount of gold will equal the satisfaction of challenges overcome.*
>
> *No amount of gold will bring the growth in our nature and character when difficulties are faced and conquered. No amount of gold can measure the value of true love. We leave it here, as we have all that we need and what we want is still an aim and a purpose that we may strive for to obtain a true sense of worth.*
> *Juan and Lena Castagnet.'"*

"Wow," Millie said, "so, does that mean then, where it said, we leave it here, they are referring to gold?

"Also, who are, or rather, who were these people?"

"Yes, to the first part of your question, in your mother's folder she describes it in detail. She found a small area beautifully covered in mosaic tiles, these had been carefully placed, goodness knows how long ago and there was a scene created by these tiles that of a"

"Swallow?" Millie interrupted.

"Yes, how?"

"That's it that's the connection! The sheet of paper I found, the one stuck to another sheet, it depicted a drawing my mother made of a swallow, and, at the bottom, it had the dimensions. Let me find it. It's the one original that I took,"

After a quick rifle through all the papers, Millie found it. "Here it is!"

"There, look, she wrote 'mosaic tiles, 2.5 centimetres in size and depicting a swallow', then drew it.'"

Ally leaned forwards, took the sheet and looked at it.

"This connects it alright," Ally said, then continued with her findings. "Well, underneath these tiles, as your mother carefully looked beneath several that had been disturbed, was a layer of gold, in the form of golden coins, Spanish ones, dating back to the early 1800s."

"A layer of gold coins? Surely worth killing for," Millie said, her voice a whisper.

"It is also where your mother found a thin leather purse, inside which, was this letter, this message, written by hand in Spanish. As to the second part, I have no idea as to who these folks were, this Juan and Lena Castagnet, and your mother, obviously, because of the tornado, had not yet commenced researching that," Ally finished, putting the papers back inside the folder. Then handing it over said, "You keep it all together with the information you have found, and take it to the police." Then, remembering the parcel bag which she had discarded at the airport in Portland she wondered now if she should have kept that.

Millie took the folder, opened it and flicked through the many sheets, the writing, the drawings, all by her mother.

Ally noticed Millie was beginning to cry, ever so softly.

Getting up and placing a hand on her shoulder, she bent down, whispered, "I'll get us a drink" then, squeezing her shoulder gently, headed for the kitchen.

Back at the hacienda

The manservant brought in a large silver tray upon which was a cafetière of coffee, three cups with saucers, a jug of milk and a bowl of sugar, along with several tea spoons. Cynthia had in the meantime returned and sat herself next to Thomas.

Not much had been said after Letitia had gestured for him to be seated.

Thomas made straight for a large leather three-seater and looked around the room.

It was lavishly furnished. There was another leather couch, a two-seater, and also two single armchairs, all of the same set.

There were several bookcases, some glass display cabinets which held what looked to be porcelain figures, a few paintings and a tapestry on the wall, two beautifully carved oak standard lamps, a Tiffany lamp on one of the four small tables and a drinks cabinet against the far wall.

Three large windows looked out over the patio and orchard to the rear, and two windows flanked a set of doors on the opposite side leading to the balcony.

Thomas, just before sitting down, could faintly see the light of the hangar shining onto the plane and Cynthia's rental car.

He also figured that this is where the music must have been coming from when he and Cynthia had crept along the wall towards the gym.

Letitia sat herself in one of the single chairs opposite him, and decided not to say anything until the woman returned.

When she did and sat next to him, she eyed them both, looking from one to the other.

Then taking a deep breath, she spoke, "So, why have you come back? Are the police about to come and take me away?"

"Contact your police chief. We know you must have a lot of influence in these parts. Tell them the plane has been returned, and that there was a misunderstanding," Thomas said.

"And make sure you also tell them to clear our names from any enquiry. I'm sure you know who we are. This is Thomas, by the way, I am Cynthia and you are Letitia, and Victoria is safe and well."

"So…" Thomas spoke again, "until you have done that, we will enjoy the coffee that is about to be brought in…" as the manservant entered.

Letitia again looked from one to the other, then glanced up at her man, after he had put the tray down, she said to him, "Will you get their car and bring it around to the front," then looked at Cynthia.

Tia nodded and took the keys from her handbag and threw them at the man who deftly caught them.

"Then bring their luggage to their room."

"Si Senorita" he replied and off he went.

Letitia looked at the clock on the mantelpiece. "We can't do much more until the morning. I'll get Maria to take you to your room. Finish your coffee first," then she got up and left the room.

Thomas and Tia looked at each other and both raised their eyebrows, "Still in the lion's den I reckon," she said.

"But we have the whips, surely? She was definitely pale and uncertain, on guard and wary, but troubled."

"Agreed," Tia answered, "but my question is this, who is going to have the bed?"

Back in San Francisco

Millie sipped her glass of white wine. She had calmed down. To first notice the stains on the folder and guess this was possibly her mother's blood, then to have it confirmed that her mother had indeed been murdered, was quite a shock, even though, according to Claire, Robert had suspected this to be the case.

"Do you think this Eddie is still alive?" she asked Ally, who was also sipping a glass of wine.

Contemplating what to make for dinner, as she was suddenly rather hungry, Ally replied, "I don't believe he is. We're talking 1988, over thirty years ago. He told his sister he was on the run. I'm sure they, whoever they are, must have caught up with him, or else, surely, he would have contacted his sister by now. What I would like to know is who it was that knew about the discovery of gold."

Then continuing to speak whilst getting up from the couch, "Who was it that organised Eddie to get the information in the first place, and, where is he or she or they now."

"I was thinking that," Millie answered. "My mum made the discovery. She detailed the area, she drew the picture of the mosaic swallow and she wrote about the gold coins. So, to take that time, and looking on the map as to where the other excavations took place, there had to be someone close by who knew of this, who watched this. My suspicion is it has to be one of the other students who were on site."

They both fell silent for a while, Alison having entered the kitchen, was rummaging in a cupboard broke the silence. "Let me rustle up some food, I'm hungry."

"I'll help," Millie answered, getting up. "Listen, how about we split up the tasks again. For me, it's important to find out everything about the death of my mother. We know why. We also now know who, but not who was behind it all, so, I will investigate everyone who was on that dig further, from the students to the truck drivers who shifted the equipment and set up the camp, also, any university teacher who might have an involvement."

Entering the kitchen, Millie continued, "If you could perhaps follow up on the gold itself, and the tiles, as to how they got there, and, most of all, who were Juan and Lena Castagnet. Sounds like a French or Spanish name. Could you do that?"

"Absolutely. My thoughts exactly, and I know a guy who's very good at research. I'll get him to help."

"Okay, but, with this gold involved, I sense it could be a dangerous road we are stepping onto. Is your guy going to be okay with that?"

"Oh, yes, most assuredly. Furthermore, totally to be trusted. He rescued me from death and was the man who helped me find Theresa," Alison replied.

"Oh wow, I was put into the picture, with regards to what happened with Theresa," Millie said, "I remember the police detective who came around to the school, but I wasn't given any details, other than that it had been Theresa's father and his wife who had taken her all those years ago. The wife confessed all then fled to Hawaii?"

Millie, seeing the look on Ally's face, then went on, hoping to lighten the mood a bit, "But this mystery man, who rescued you, I sure would like to meet him one day."

Alison smiled at Millie, but could find no words to say.

"First I will call Claire," Millie said, picking up her phone, and in an upbeat manner said, "I'll let her know what we have uncovered so far and what our plans are. If it wasn't for Roberts initial findings, we would be none the wiser. Keeping her in the loop is important."

"Tell her about me, and could you ask her to pass on a greeting to Thomas?" Ally said, "and Cynthia too. I haven't seen her since her brother died."

Millie nodded, noticed in the reflection of the mirror on the kitchen wall that Alison's thoughts were far away, and punched in the numbers.

THE PAST;

Period 10

The year 1989–Bilbao, Spain

Thirty-five-year-old Victoria Lange checked herself in the full length mirror.

She was dressed from head to toe in black: soft black ankle boots with a deep thread rubber sole, tight leggings, a zip-up black training jacket, underneath which she wore a black turtle-neck jumper, and to finish the outfit, a black vinyl hood, fitting tightly around her head down to her neck. Her auburn hair securely tucked away and there were only three openings, two for her eyes and one for her mouth.

She checked that her breathing was good when breathing in through her nose, the hood was porous enough to let the air through. She then donned a pair of black gloves.

At five foot five, she was slim in build and very fit.

This was the part she enjoyed, the part that gave her a thrill. It was exhilarating, dangerous. The adrenaline kicking in. All the ground work was done, the preparations were done, the casing of the museum completed.

Time for action.

It was a little before 3.00 am. It was raining lightly and as she left her apartment, via the balcony at the rear. She sensed the atmosphere of a city that was asleep.

The night was dark, the rain obscuring any stars. Perfect.

With the agility of a cat, she stepped onto the railing of the small balcony, then reached up, grabbed the edge of the roof and swung herself up and onto it.

The apartment had been chosen with care, after many days of searching and preparation. Victoria silently moved across the flat roof, then leaped onto the roof of an adjacent block of flats with the ease and grace of a panther, again moving silently along it to the far end.

A lone taxi travelled along the road below. A few lights were on here and there.

The rain fell softly.

Checking the road below once more, she stepped over to her right, and grabbed hold of the handle attached to the zip line that she had installed three days ago, also during a dark and wet night.

Sliding across the road she reached the old building. The museum.

Untying this end of the zip line now, she climbed seven feet higher, then re-attached the line, to create a downward angle for a smooth return journey later. Checking it was all secure, she moved around the roof structure and reached a wooden platform outside a wooden door.

When she'd checked the full details of the old building, she had discovered this area and found it ideal as it gave entrance to an old loft area that was no longer in use.

She opened the door, and after closing it behind her, felt for and found the switch that she knew was there. Victoria flicked on the lights.

Two fluorescent tubes attached to a beam lit up the loft space which was less than three metres wide and two metres high, but ran for over eleven metres and contained various odds and ends.

There were some broken chairs, a couple of stepladders and, what gave Victoria an idea when she had first visited, three copper coloured posts and a length of red rope, often used in museums to cordon off an area.

Victoria started setting up the next phase of her plan.

Fortunately the object she was after was on the top floor of the museum, one floor below. She walked down the wooden steps from the loft and cracked open the door at the bottom which she knew was not alarmed.

The floor was not in total darkness. Several small lights gave the area a dim appearance. Two cameras to disable next.

She walked back up the wooden stairs to where she had stored the equipment she would need, took out a torch and a spray can.

She went down the stairs, through the door, then moving quickly, hugging the wall, she reached camera one, sprayed the lens, and moved to camera two, again spraying the lens. In the adjacent room, there were again two cameras and she took care of them both.

She then headed back to the loft. She had time to work now. There were no sensors on this floor, however each painting that hung on the wall was alarmed.

Victoria next brought down the three copper coloured posts. Though a little awkward to carry, they were not heavy. These she placed around the area where the object of her quest hung.

Next she went back, brought the thick red rope and a stepladder.

She positioned the stands, threaded the rope around them, and was pleased with her work.

The stepladder she placed by the painting.

Next she went back to the loft and fetched the frame she had made. It was an identical frame to the one surrounding her picture, at least, identical at a quick glance, and it was much lighter weight.

She leant it against one of the copper posts and, taking her torch from a pocket in her jacket, she climbed the steps.

From her other pocket she drew out some wire. Using a tool which she extracted from the back of her torch, she spliced two wires onto the ones that were there, then spliced the other end of the wires she had brought further down and proceeded to cut the wires in between.

It remained silent. No sirens or alarm bells going off, no noise.

Victoria lifted the frame from the hook that secured it, carefully lifted it down the steps and placed it on the floor.

She drew out another set of wires which she spliced onto the live wires, and connected the other ends onto the wires she had placed on her new frame, Connection made, she cut the painting free.

Again it remained silent. No alarms ringing, no noise. Taking her new frame up the steps, she hung it upon the hook, then tucked the extra wires away so as not to be easily noticed, being careful not to break the connection.

Stepping down, she took the painting she had come for back into the loft.

Then she went back to retrieve the stepladder.

She left the rope cordon in place.

Back in the loft, she checked the time on her watch.

Excellent.

She went downstairs again, closed the door to the loft, went back up and proceeded to wrap the painting securely. The spray she had used on the cameras, was a dissolving liquid, it would initially set, forming a foamy substance, but in time, and through warmth, it would just dissolve.

Once the painting was wrapped, Victoria tucked all the tools of her trade into a soft black leather satchel. This she slung over her shoulder.

Tucking the painting firmly under her arm, went out the door onto the wooden platform, closed the door and made her way to where the zip line was secured. It had stopped raining, but the cloud cover was still such as to create a dark night.

Checking for traffic below, she took hold of the handle with her right hand, made sure the painting was securely tucked under her left arm, thinking to herself that it weighed a little more than she had anticipated. She swung back across the road. The muscles on her right arm straining to hold her, the painting and the satchel and Victoria sighed with relief when she had reached the other side.

Later, after the museum had opened, they would find the cordoned off area surrounding a picture, at least, surrounding a frame.

For some time this caused no concern, assuming it was something the museum was working on. Some visitors took a look at the inscription on the wall that mentioned the painting and that it was on loan.

It wasn't until early afternoon, when an assistant noted the scene, became curious and asked the curator about it that the discovery was made.

Baffled by this cordoned off area, they investigated and it was soon discovered that the frame was a copy, the painting itself had not been cut out but stolen in its entirety and despite screening footage of security cameras, no one was any wiser as to how the theft had occurred.

By the time the museum had, with much embarrassment and a string of apologies, notified the owner who had loaned the painting, Victoria was already in Paris.

THE PRESENT;

Paris

Thursday–30th May

Sophie Louise Pontiac sat back in her office chair and smiled.

She twisted her chair around so she could face the window. It was sunny and clear. She thought about the man who had just called her. Sam.

Perhaps a romance that could have been? Through him though, she did meet Martijn, the Dutch policeman, and a brief romance blossomed.

Very brief. She was very happy in her work and living in Paris. He was very happy in his work and living in Amersfoort.

They had some lovely moments, had some lovely days and nights, but had parted, friendly and without regrets. He was a lovely man.

She twisted her chair back around to face the desk.

Sam had called, had a favour to ask, she would get on it straight away. Whilst a romance with him had never blossomed, she would be forever grateful as he had come to her rescue when stuck in a tricky situation.

To work then. She glanced up at the clock on the wall and noticed it was just before noon.

He had asked her to see if she could find out anything about a painting by Titian, a portrait, 18 inches wide by 36 inches in height, originally with an ornate gilded frame, it featured Charles V wearing a long red coat or garment, and some kind of head covering in purple. He was standing by a horse. It was dated fifteen hundred and something, and had been sold in 1947 through the Franck Huysen auction house in Boston.

After chit chat, and asking to be remembered to Chrissie, she said au revoir and hung up.

Boston

"Well? And how is the delectable Sophie?" she asked teasingly.

Sam gave her a scowl, then said, "She says hi. Come on, let's have breakfast, then we, or rather I, can get on with what my other girlfriend has asked me," smiling teasingly he headed into the kitchen before she could throw something.

The previous evening Alison had called him. She had briefly outlined the situation that she found herself in, with regard to her daughter's teacher and the killing of Professor Parker, the teacher's mother. And all of it to do with the finding of gold coins underneath a layer of mosaic tiles.

Ally had asked Sam to try and find out who Juan and Lena Castagnet were, and had explained about the note left.

Sam was intrigued. First of all the name of Parker was familiar to him and he wondered if there was any connection there with his research on an earlier case. Second, he asked where this archaeological dig was.

He made some notes and handed the phone over to Chrissie, who chatted with Ally for some time.

It hadn't taken Sam long at all to find the name.

A woman by the name of Caprice Jeanne Castagnet sold a painting at the Franck Huysen auction house, and Sam thought about that coincidence, noting that the woman sold a painting by Titian, and this is why he had decided to contact Sophie the following morning as she was the manager of the Fine Arts Auction House in Paris and could possibly helpful in trying to track this painting down.

Although Sam had discovered the name of the person who sold the Titian portrait, the buyer was listed as anonymous, however an added notation mentioned the person, a man, was from Paris.

Looking at the dates, Sam then set about tracing back in time, judging this Caprice Jeanne Castagnet would most likely be a granddaughter of Lena and Juan.

Figuring that the Titian had likely crossed the ocean as the new owner was from Paris, he left that research to Sophie and began a search into who the Castagnets who, according to Ally, had buried a lot of gold coins, way back in 1862, might be.

Somewhere near a place called Silver City.

T H E   P A S T ;

Period 11

The year 1989–Near Silver City, New Mexico

Simon Lightfoot looked over the white painted fence. A fence that enclosed just over an acre of land. A three plank fence with posts every six feet, there was only one gate, or rather a set of two gates. Simon walked around to where these were and looked at the noticeboard that was erected just inside the fence to the left of the gates.

A monument really, an oversized spade lay beneath the board on the ground, and there were four names engraved in the handle. Fresh flowers had been placed there earlier. He had laid a bunch himself.

A year had passed. A year since the tornado ripped through here and a year since four people lost their lives.

Simon was the last one remaining, his old BSA motorbike was parked close by. 'Professor Emily Parker, Donald Alfredo, Kathryn Smith & Josie Morton' was carved into the stone handle of the sculpture, then on the blade of the spade it had the details of the excavation dig and the date of the tornado strike.

The noticeboard above it told of the ground being a sanctified area and to be kept without disturbance in memory of those whose lives were lost.

Simon looked around and remembered the television footage.

Josie Morton, aged seventeen, had been his girlfriend.

Nineteen-year-old Simon walked on, past the gates which were padlocked. He had wondered why there were gates in the first place if this area of ground was to be left undisturbed, and was told that it was in order, from time to time, to ensure there was no unwanted rubbish or weeds, access was needed.

Simon turned to look around him. All the others, and there had only been about a dozen or so, had left.

A member of the Albuquerque University staff had made the journey to say a few words and a prayer, leading to a short time of silence.

Simon had spoken to a few of them, but mainly kept to himself and made a point of studying those who had come.

He walked around the perimeter, studying the ground both inside and outside of the wooden fence, it's white paint shining brightly in the early afternoon sunlight.

He could see nothing that made him suspicious, yet, something was not right. The reason he was closely observing those who had come today was because of a letter he had only recently been given.

It had been unopened, it had been addressed to him. It had been amongst the Josie's personal belongings which had been returned to her family.

He had not been liked. At a tad over six foot, he was gangly, had long wavy brown hair, the beginnings of a beard and whiskers, a golden earring and a tattoo on his upper arm. On top of this, he was a high school dropout, rode an old motorcycle and worked in a garage, and he was white.

Not the kind at all for the daughter of a well-to-do family. A black family.

At the funeral he had been virtually ignored, though definitely noticed, as he was only one of two white men, the other being Josie's faculty teacher from the university.

On that day Simon had recalled a song by the band Hot Chocolate, titled Brother Louie, from 1974 and how things hadn't really changed a lot.

Then, just about a fortnight ago, while working in the garage and taking a break, smoking a cigarette on the courtyard, he noticed young Raphael, Josie's little brother.

He was being picked on, harassed. Three youths, two of them male, were in the young boys face, also giving him an occasional push.

Never one to shy away from a fight, one of the reasons he was often in trouble at school, Simon flicked the cigarette away and walked towards the group.

At first the three turned and focused on him, calling him a selection of names and tried to be as threatening as they could. However, getting no response and beginning to realise that they might have bitten off more than they could chew, they backed down, then turned and walked away.

Simon looked at Raphael, who looked back up at him. Then Simon turned and headed back to the garage, not having said a single word.

Later that same day, Josie's mother came into the garage and sought him out. Handed him a letter, said sorry, and quickly left again.

None of Josie's family had come to the memorial service.

Simon made his way back to his motorcycle, leaned himself against it and once again pulled the letter from the pocket of his leather jacket.

When he had first read it, he had been touched and concerned.

Touched because her words were poignant and romantic. He had a special place in his heart for her, and she made ever so clear by the words she had written, had a special place in her heart for him.

She wrote about her anger at her mother and father, how she had been forbidden to see him, how they had in no uncertain terms referred to him as a no good loser.

After she'd written all of that, no doubt wanting to express her feelings and releasing that through her words, Josie then wrote about the dig she was on with the very nice Professor Emily. She wrote that she had been chosen to work in the professor's team and then told of an incredible find, one that she had to keep secret for now.

But, she explained, as this letter was not going to be posted for some time yet, she wanted to write about it, and so in her letter she told of the day when there were just three of them, the professor, herself and a student named Conrad.

Leaning on his bike, reading, Simon paused, fished out a packet of cigarettes, lit one, then pulled another piece of paper from one of the pockets in his jacket.

Unfolding it, he looked at the list of names.

Research he had done as to who exactly, had been involved in this dig.

Among the names, Conrad Shelton. Seventeen.

Folding this paper up and putting it back in his pocket, Simon continued to read.

Josie described the event: the moment, when they, the three of them, uncovered a mosaic that they believed to be a floor. But as they carefully brushed the soil and sand away, it was revealed to be a square no more than a metre. In fact, she wrote, they measured it, and it proved to be exactly a metre square, and it was made of beautiful tiles that revealed a picture of a swallow.

This was not Mayan. This was Roman the professor said, but, here is the exciting bit that has to be kept secret. In one corner there had been a disturbance, likely caused by an animal, and this revealed underneath several loose tiles. A layer of gold!

All placed so neatly; golden Spanish coins.

Also, carefully uncovering a little more, they found a thin leather bag. Inside was a letter, written in Spanish.

The professor at this time, as it was beginning to get dark, asked her and Conrad to help replace the tiles, keeping the thin leather bag out, then to cover the whole area over again with the soil.

She explained this was an important find, but one that needed to be very carefully investigated and so it was not to be spoken about until she said so.

Josie then wrote some more about how she missed him and dreamed about riding on the back of his motorcycle with him.

Simon put the letter back in the envelope, put it back in his pocket, took a few more puffs on his cigarette then flicked it away, and got onto his bike, kicking it to life.

As he rode away he wondered if that mosaic square was still there, somewhere, or if someone had discovered it, and taken it away?

With the wind in his face as he headed back home, Simon recalled the news on the television that day.

The day the tornado hit.

The professor had died. So had Josie. That left only one person, who definitely knew about the gold.

Conrad Shelton.

THE PRESENT;

The Hacienda, near Ampuero, Spain

Thursday 30th May

A small television was on in the spacious kitchen. Thomas was listening to the news as he was fixing himself and Tia some breakfast, though it was already nearly lunchtime.

Maria was assisting and preparing some croissants and jam. She explained in Spanish that the jam was from their own orchard.

Placing the drinks and the food on a tray, Maria handed it all to Thomas who took it upstairs to the lounge.

Letitia stood there, wearing the same jeans and shirt she wore earlier, when she had been holding the rifle and pointing it at them as they stood on the steps of the plane. There was a difference in her now as she stood looking out the window.

She turned as she heard him enter.

Tia was seated on the same three-seater as before and Thomas placed the tray on the low table in front of the leather couch.

She looked up at him and smiled. Grabbing a plate and placing a croissant upon it, she bit into it. She was hungry. Despite not having had a very long sleep, she felt fresh and full of energy.

"Mmm, this jam is delicious" she said, looking at Letitia who had come away from the window and had placed herself in a single chair opposite them.

"Thank you" she said, her voice soft. Going by her appearance, she had not slept much either, and she showed signs of stress and anxiety.

Thomas sat down.

"So, what happens now?" she asked, looking from one to the other.

It was Thomas who answered, "You went to a lot of trouble. No doubt a lot of planning and research too, to find out about this painting, why?"

"My men …" she began, her cheek bones colouring a little, "should not have come after you. They, they thought they did the right thing. I'm sorry."

Thomas and Tia ate their food and sipped their drinks, neither responding.

"I will tell you," Letitia said, standing up and walking back to the window where she had stood before, looking towards where the plane stood outside the hangar.

"You are a good pilot," she said, turning to look at Thomas, then, closing her eyes briefly, she began to speak. "Three years ago, my father and my brother died. An accident, on a boat, off the coast of Biarritz. I was, well, not very good. How do you say it, spoiled rich kid? I drank, I gamble, I go everywhere…But, all change. The business fell apart. I was spending too much." She stopped briefly, reflecting, having turned to once again to look out the window.

"One day I wake up," she said, turning to face them again, "I wake up in hotel room in Cannes. No memory, I…well, came home. Was now determined to make it all right. Worked hard, studied, got my aviation licence. That's my plane out there." Pausing briefly, she then continued, "I did think about increasing our income by dealing in drugs, much money, but then my, well my father's manservant, took me to my father's room. I had not been in there, also not in his nor my brother's room, since…" another brief pause.

"Well," she continued, having taken a deep breath, "he showed me my father's desk, and said for me to read through all the papers. I would understand, he said…That's when I found out about the land deeds."

Letitia walked back to the chair, sat down and leaning forwards, she continued, "A long time ago, there was a dispute over land that we, our family, owned. A parcel of land that lay adjacent the river, nearby. We use that river. It supplies water for our orchard, an important piece of land, but the title deeds of this document also prevent anyone from placing any dam on the river that would decrease the flow of the river alongside our land.

"A new landowner had come, had purchased land on the other side of the river and had built a dam to obtain water for his farm. Also, this farm, was growing poppy, for use in drugs. A new family was trying to control the region, but my father and my grandfather were well known and well liked, had much influence. They produced the deeds and the new landowner was forced to take the dam down.

This was not well received and threats were made to my family.

All this I found out through all the paperwork that Augustus, my manservant, made me read."

Letitia again stood up and walked over to the window. Then she turned, looked at them and went on, "We have, I have, a close relationship with the local police and council. I hear from them about the new owners of the land next to the river. Apparently a granddaughter, who, having studied law, was going to challenge the wording of our deeds. This was almost a year ago. They have been stopped so far, but pressure is on and there will come a time when I will need to fight this in court, and this is where the trouble begins…"

Letitia once more sat herself down, pleased that both the man and woman were listening to her so attentively. "At the time of the original trouble, and facing threats of this hacienda being burned to the ground, my father had an idea, and I only found this out just over a year ago. He placed all the original documents on the back of a painting, the one by Titian, then he offered this to be on display for the public, to the museum…"

"The painting that was stolen by Victoria," Tia said, intrigued by the story, "but that was a long time ago. Why did your father not mention it?"

"I don't know. Perhaps, as the threat at the time, went away, and really has only reappeared since his death, I guess he wasn't concerned."

"And so you researched and tracked down the woman who stole it, in order to trace its whereabouts. That took some doing, I'm sure," Thomas said, also intrigued by the turn of events.

"Nearly seven months. It was actually a friend of mine, Juliette, she owns the transport company now. Inherited from her father. She had remembered an incident when she was in Australia. Anyway, it helped to locate this, Victoria, then months of planning, but, all to no avail. She did not tell me the truth, did she?"

"No," Tia answered.

"But," Thomas added, "she did tell us about it and we have done a little research, also curious as to where this painting might now be. The man who hired Victoria, a man named Johannes Acker, died some years ago. We do have some friends who are also looking."

"I spoke to the police chief this morning," Letitia said. "Your names have been cleared, though he did say something about flying without authorisation. I will fix that."

"We will need to contact Victoria," Thomas said, looking at Cynthia, "ask her to drop charges under the circumstances."

"Agreed," Tia answered, then looking at Letitia.

She looked rather relieved, "And, she could be a useful friend in finding your painting."

"You think she will agree to this?" Letitia answered, quite surprised as to how friendly these two strangers were.

"She is on board a train bound for Paris soon," looking at her watch. "Actually, she is on her way now. We will need to intercept her before she goes to the embassy," Tia said.

"I'll call Claire," Thomas said, even though it would be the very early hours of the morning in Myrtle Creek.

Thomas stood up, pulled the phone from his pocket and pressed some numbers.

It seemed like she had only just fallen asleep when the phone rang. "Yes?" she sleepily answered.

"Sorry to wake you Claire" Thomas said, "We need to reach someone in Paris. Do we know anyone. Did Robert have anyone there, do you know?"

Claire shook the sleepiness from her head, thought for a moment, then answered "As a matter of fact, Cynthia's school friend, Alison, has a contact in Boston, who has a contact in Paris. What needs to be done?"

Thomas was momentarily dumbfounded, "Cynthia's school friend? Alison?" he asked.

Claire, fully awake now, and rather pleased with herself, smiled and answered.

"Why yes Mr Thomas. Whilst you and Cynthia have been hijacking planes and rescuing damsels, I have been following up on the case file that you started, if you recall? Well, very intriguing I tell you. The upshot is that…no, never mind right now. Obviously your request is urgent. What needs to happen?"

Thomas looked at Tia who was frowning. She had been listening in on the conversation as Thomas had his phone on speaker. "The woman, the damsel we rescued, is on board a train for Paris. She is heading for the British Embassy there. She needs to be stopped from doing so. Circumstances have changed. I need to speak with her, can you arrange this?"

Claire, full of confidence and enjoying her new found role, said, "How do you mean? Last I heard she was with you two. Where are you then?"

"We are back in Spain, we returned the plane…"

"Of course you did…" Claire interrupted, raising her eyes to the ceiling.

"Long story," Thomas said. "Will fill you in later, but we need to speak to Victoria, Her full name is Victoria Lange. Think you can help?"

"Absolutely! Leave it with me, I'll get on it straight away. Can I ring you back later?"

"Please. Yes, thank you, and well done you," Thomas said and ended the call.

"She did say Alison?" Tia asked.

Thomas smiled. "Apparently Claire has been as busy, if not more so, than we have. Yes, school friend?"

"Yes, one of the gang. One of the ABC girls, Alison Hudson, how is she involved?"

"I don't know. This has to do with the case that Robert expressly wanted me to investigate, which I did start, until, well, this. Seems she is well into it."

"Well, well," Tia whispered to herself, "Alison Hudson."

Thomas finished his croissant, stood up and said to Letitia, "There's not much we can do now until we hear from Victoria. Hopefully someone can get to her in time. How about a tour of your business? And where did you buy that plane?"

"Good idea," Tia answered, making sure she stood next to Thomas and feeling a tinge of jealousy as she noticed the Spanish woman, more relaxed now, smile at Thomas. "Keep ourselves occupied while we're here. When in Rome and all that."

THE PAST;

Period 12

The year 1997–Rome, Italy

Christina Small sat on a cushioned metal chair at a wrought iron table and looked across at the majestic Trevi Fountain.

She sipped her latte and tried to get over her disappointment and concern.

Her green eyes took in the scene before her, the busyness, the tourists, the cars, the buses, the many scooters.

She wondered if she ought to throw a coin into the fountain: apparently something one did in the hope of a wish coming true.

Twenty-five-year-old Christina, who preferred to be called Chrissie, finished her drink, checked her watch and sighed. Time to check out of the hotel and head back to the airport.

She walked the busy streets, her mind in somewhat of a daze, not even noticing the many admiring glances she received.

Recently her father had passed away. Recently she had discovered, hidden in a box underneath the stairs of the family home she had now inherited, a letter from an art gallery in Rome, stating they were looking forward to meeting him.

Him being her grandfather who had disappeared without a trace in 1946.

She had contacted them and visited the gallery earlier. They had found the correspondence, but, also stated that although they had been expecting him, he never showed up.

The five foot six blonde, dressed smartly, was deep in thought, wondering what had happened to her grandfather all those years ago. She took little notice of the man, who suddenly appeared around the corner, coming down the steps that lead to her hotel, and only narrowly avoided colliding with her.

He was in a hurry.

As Chrissie mounted the steps leading to the lobby, behind her a car screeched to a stop and two men got out, quickly pursuing the man who had almost bumped into her. But with her mind elsewhere trying to shake her disappointment, so she didn't notice. She went to her room, checked she had everything, then checked out.

Even two hours later, when she was at the airport awaiting her flight back to Boston, she didn't pick up on the news on the television, showing a picture of a man, brutally shot and killed only a short while ago and asking if anyone might know this man.

Conrad Shelton was dead.

THE PRESENT;

Boston

Thursday 30th

Sam was doing his best to make an omelette, but was somewhat hampered by Chrissie who had snuggled up behind him, placed her arms around him and was nuzzling into his neck.

He was about to turn the gas off and forget about the omelette, when a phone on the kitchen table buzzed.

Reluctantly Chrissie untangled herself from Sam and answered, seeing by the number that it was Alison.

"Ally?"

"Hi, listen. Millie just called me, she had a call from Claire, in Myrtle Creek, who had a call from Spain. It's urgent that we talk with Sophie in Paris…" Ally began.

"Hang on Ally," Chrissie said, put her phone on speaker and called Sam. "Okay, talk."

"Can you reach Sophie? She needs to get to the railway station and intervene. She needs to stop a woman from going to the British Embassy…"

Sam, hearing the urgency in Ally's voice, switched the gas off and whilst still listening to the conversation, grabbed his own phone and started dialling, having spoken with Sophie only a little earlier.

Twelve minutes later both Chrissie and Sam ended their calls.

Thomas, in Northern Spain, had woken Claire in Myrtle Creek, who in turn had woken Millie in San Francisco.

She, having grasped the situation, woke Alison who then in turn rang Chrissie and Sam in Boston.

Sam then got hold of Sophie in Paris for the second time that morning.

In Paris Sophie googled the train times, and looked at the clock on her wall. Seeing the timetable and again looking at the clock, she realised that although she could get to the station on time, it would be tight, and then to try and locate a woman amongst a throng of people would be very difficult indeed.

She had a name, but has no idea what she looked like.

Sophie picked up her phone and rang for a taxi, then grabbed her coat and bag and left her office. Thinking on her feet, she made up her mind and exiting the auction house as the taxi pulled up, she got in and gave instructions.

She would head for the British Embassy instead. She quickly checked on her phone for the address as the driver only knew roughly where it was.

She arrived at her destination and, checking her watch, noted that the train would have just arrived at the station.

Sophie paid the taxi, got out and waited close to the gates that led to the Embassy.

Fifteen minutes later a taxi pulled up and a woman got out.

Sophie approached.

"Victoria? Thomas and Cynthia need to speak to you urgently"

Unsure for a moment, Victoria sized up the woman as the taxi driver retrieved her small suitcase.

"I will call them now, so you can speak to them?" Sophie said.

"Yes, of course"

Sophie dialled a number she had been given by Sam, then as it was ringing, handed the phone over to the woman. Victoria nodded her thanks to the driver, then said, "Thomas?"

"Victoria," Thomas said, then putting the phone on speaker, "you haven't gone to the embassy yet have you?"

"No, I'm just outside it. This French woman stopped me and rang you, what's going on?"

"The woman is Sophie, you can totally trust her. Go with her. I'll tell you why…"

Thomas then related the story, with Tia occasionally chipping in with some added details. Victoria listened, trying hard to push away the noise of the traffic and ignoring the pedestrians walking by. She glanced occasionally at the French woman she now knew to be Sophie.

Then, frowning, she said, "No, it's not right. When I took the painting that night, I took it back to where I was staying. I knew that the ornate gilded frame was not the original and that it would be cumbersome to travel with, so I took the painting out. Believe me, it was only the painting. There were no deeds, no other papers tucked in anywhere, it was just the painting…"

After a pause, Thomas said, "Okay, well, could you work with Sophie? Still need to hopefully find the painting. It does belong to the Teremos family."

After ending the call both he and Tia looked over to where Letitia sat. She too had heard the conversation and sat looking quite perplexed.

"So, where are the deeds?" she whispered.

Letitia stood up, glanced at both of them, then slid open the door to the balcony and stepped out. What a turn of events, she thought. She had so meticulously searched and planned the abduction of the woman who had stolen the painting, only to now discover that the deeds were not there.

What happened? Where were they?

A stiff breeze blew across the valley floor and ruffled her hair as she stood leaning on the railing of the balcony.

T H E   P A S T ;

Period 13

The year 1998–Near Silver City, New Mexico

Felicity Smith stood with her arms folded and ignored the wind that was plucking at her long blonde hair. She looked at the names carved into the handle of the sculpture.

The sun was high overhead, but the many clouds that drifted along the sky regularly brought shade and a reprieve from the heat.

There was no one around.

Other than the wind, there was no sound. At least for quite some time after she had arrived by car, parked a little way from the site, and had walked along the fence to where the noticeboard and sculpture were placed. But her ears picked up a new sound. A motorbike. It sounded like a big engine. Frowning a little she thought it must be either a Harley or an Indian.

She turned as the rider appeared and stopped next to her car.

An Indian.

The engine was cut and the silence returned.

She watched the rider, a man, a tall man, take of his helmet, revealing brown wavy hair that touched his shoulders. He swung from the bike in a fluid movement, left the helmet on the seat, then unzipped his leather jacket and walked over towards her. Keeping her arms folded, she watched him attentively as he came closer. He was taking his gloves off and looked directly at her.

She was wondering who he was, but thought that he had a kind face and his green eyes set in a tanned clean-shaven face, were friendly and warm.

Felicity shivered ever so slightly and briefly.

"Hi," he said, his voice sounding as warm as his eyes looked.

"Hi," she replied, not sure how to proceed with the conversation.

He stopped close to her and looked at the sculptured spade.

Neither said anything for a moment, then he turned towards her.

"Josie was my girlfriend," he said.

Felicity looked at the spade, then turned to him, "Kathryn was my sister."

He in turn looked at the engraved names, then again turned to her, "Simon, Simon Lightfoot," offering his hand.

She took it, looked into his green eyes and said, "Felicity Smith, but please, call me Fliss."

He smiled and nodded, released his hand from hers and sighed as he looked again at the names on the handle of the spade.

"Ten years ago now. Must have been true love," she said, watching him and thinking how crazy it was that she should have feelings for a guy she had only just met.

He turned to look at her, said nothing for a moment, then, "It was, but, there is more to it, to this whole, event, if you will, the tornado, the deaths, the injuries, the mystery."

"Mystery?" she queried, looking at him.

Simon turned to again look at the noticeboard and the spade, and looked around the surroundings, the enclosed ground within the confines of the white fence. It had been ten years since the tornado struck. It had been nine years since he had stood here. He took a deep breath, then turned to look at the woman. He had already noticed her lovely blue eyes, her long blonde hair and that she was not wearing either a wedding or engagement ring. She was pretty.

He smiled at her, she was quite a bit shorter, petite, probably no more than five two in bare feet. But he felt, something.

"A mystery," he replied, then continued, "a mystery that, well, ruined a couple of relationships. I can't let go, especially after what

I found out two years ago. I thought I'd come here on the tenth anniversary, though, not sure why. Anyway, a mystery."

She looked at him, intrigued, wanting to know more.

She watched his face, and waited for him to explain.

"Buried treasure," Simon said, then took an envelope from his jacket pocket.

Deciding he liked her, had a feeling about her, he handed the envelope over. "Read this, and it will help to explain."

Simon walked over to the gates, studied the ground and could see no obvious disturbance. Turning, he watched as the young woman read the letter. She folded the letter, placed it back in the envelope and handed it back.

"Her folks didn't like you," she said as he took the letter.

"Hair, bike, high school dropout," he answered, smiling. "No, they did not like me."

"And this, gold? underneath the mosaic tiles, sounds intriguing. You think it's still there?"

"I don't know. At the time, when I first received the letter, I came here, for the first anniversary. Wanted to see for myself. Wanted to see who might turn up. Did some research before I came, got a list of all those students who were here. According to Josie, only the professor, herself and a guy named Conrad knew of this find. They were the ones to cover it up as you read.

"The tornado struck that very same day. The prof and Josie were killed. That left this Conrad, but, who knows, the professor might have made some calls, probably had notes on the find. I decided to wait and see what might happen. So far there had been no mention of this find. I checked to see if any mention of the discovery was ever published. As it happens, the university did publish an article on the dig, including a tribute to the professor. There were some sketches and some photos of the find, but there was no mention at all of the mosaic tiles and the gold coins. The area, as you see, was quite quickly fenced off and designated a memorial ground. So, my assumption is that they indeed did this in all good faith as a memorial and knew nothing about the find or…"

"Or?" she pressed him as he had stopped talking and was gazing into the distance. Simon, heard her question, turned to look at her and said, "Or, they are covering it up."

After a few moments of silence, the wind picking up strength, Simon again turned to look at the blonde woman next to him, seeing her long hair blowing in all directions and noticing that she just let it.

"This whole thing" he said, and she turned to look up at him, "I can't seem to let it go. Not so much about Josie. Yes, I did care. I did love her, but this mystery, it's like an itch, I keep scratching it, wanting to know more."

Then after a pause, Simon went on, "As I said, it ruined a couple of relationships, my attention being elsewhere. I was finally concentrating more on my work, my business, but a couple of years ago, I picked up a newspaper headline, 'Local family's son killed in Rome, Italy'."

"It drew my attention and upon reading the article, found out it was the Shelton family, a wealthy family in Albuquerque. It had been Conrad who had been shot and killed, in daylight, in the centre of the city…"

Taking this in, Felicity asked, "Do you think there is a connection?"

"Maybe, but there is something else. The day after the tornado, one of the other students disappeared. I had the list of all those who were here. I did some sleuthing. Found out he had gone missing. His name was Eddie Philpot. To date, as far as I know, he has not been found, so, an unsolved mystery there. Was he connected to Conrad, I don't know?"

"I might have an answer," Felicity said. "My sister's diary. We received her belongings, several days after the tornado. Mum and Dad left it all packed. She was my older sister. I saw her diary, took it out of the box, kept it, but I never read it. Just wanted it, to, well remember, you know. Anyway, just as your … Josie, wrote to you, she may have written something in her diary. Now that I think about it, I'm sure she and Josie were friends."

Both were silent for some time, each with their own thoughts.

It was Simon who broke the silence,

"I came here today, for a final time, in order to move on with my life. However, meeting you… well, maybe there is more information to be found. I do believe that someone out there knows about the tiles and the gold"

Two days later in Albuquerque

Felicity walked into the bike showroom and repair shop, noticing an array of great motorcycles outside the showroom window, and spotted Simon, the owner, who in turn saw her and smiled.

"You need to hear what my sister wrote," she said, smiling at him and acknowledging that he definitely caused a sense of attraction within her.

Simon smiled at her, thinking that she was sure a pretty bundle of a girl and said for her to follow him.

"Right," she said, sitting herself down onto a comfy couch in what she assumed was his office. He sat in the chair beside his desk, which she noted was quite tidy and organised.

"You mentioned a Conrad Shelton," she began, "that he was one of only three who were present when the mosaic tiles and the gold were discovered, this according to what Josie had written and that he was shot and killed in Rome a couple of years ago…"

"Indeed," Simon answered.

"You also mentioned a guy named Eddie, who disappeared."

"Indeed, again" he replied.

"Well, having read through my sister's diary, written at the time of the dig, I found out something interesting. First of all, this Conrad guy was a bit of a charmer, but, a bit sleazy and slimy, according to my sister."

"But, get this," she continued, "the company that was hired to transport equipment and so on, to and from the site, was called Shelton Transport.

"Daddy's firm, and, by all accounts, as you mentioned, a quite wealthy family.

"Now, this Conrad was on the dig, not because of his academical prowess, but because daddy insisted to get him to actually do some studying. There are a few notes about him in her dairy, and, get this, this was written the day before the tornado, also the day that, by my calculations, the mosaics and gold were discovered. He, Conrad, was seen to be chatting animatedly to another student, Eddie, who my sister describes as a bit of a sleaze-ball."

"Well now" Simon said, going to the coffee machine, and asking her if she wanted a drink, to which he received an affirmative reply, "Now there's a connection for sure, a charmer and a sleaze-ball."

Handing a drink to the petite blonde to whom, he acknowledged, he was attracted, he asked, "And, did you find out if your sister and Josie were friends?"

Taking the drink from him, looking up at the man she had only met a couple of days ago, she felt herself blush a little and was in no doubt that she was attracted to him.

"Her name is mentioned along with others, they were friends, but not close friends."

Simon sat down and both of them were silent for a few moments. He thought back to when he first saw her, only two days ago, and how there seemed to be a bond already. The silence between them was comfortable.

Simon reached for a biscuit from the packet on his desk, offered one to Fliss, who declined, and bit into it.

Having giving up smoking only a few weeks ago, he had created a new habit.

Biscuits.

THE PRESENT;

London

Friday 31st May

Desmond Peter Janssen was a man of habits. He rose every morning at seven, had the same routine, same cereal for breakfast, same time for a morning cup of coffee and the same time for lunch, which he enjoyed every day, including Sunday, at the same cafe.

Eighteen years.

Eighteen years ago, he had been late. Eighteen years ago he had missed a call. He had been in the pub, had talked himself into another pint.

He had arrived back at his work, back at his desk to see a message, a note.

When he had called the number, when he had rushed away, when he had arrived on the scene, he had been too late. Detective inspector Janssen's life changed that day. He went through a divorce, and watched his wife take their children, three of them, away to go and live in Wales.

Desmond had been an angry man. At the time, he blamed everyone but himself. He had become irritable, impatient and difficult to get along with.

That day, afterwards, he sat at his desk, and it was as if he was struck by lightning.

He sat frozen, stunned, and then a lot of thoughts began to run chaotically through his brain. He became dizzy, disorientated, then, as suddenly as this strange feeling had appeared. Clarity.

He realised he had been the one at fault. He realised he had been the one that caused the marriage breakdown. He had been the one that had pushed others, including his own family, away.

He also realised that had he been at his desk, had he but answered the phone, he would have arrived on time. Would have been able to prevent what happened.

Though no blame was put upon him, he knew, he was sure, if he had been on time, the child would not have been killed.

He had been unaware that Robert Pentegrass had died.

Their paths had crossed some eleven years ago, when he had received a detailed e-mail from this Robert, saying he worked with the Portland police specifically in the tracing of missing people. Robert then proceeded to list some detailed information, names and addresses and the possible whereabouts of three young women, from a small town just outside Portland, who had gone missing during their vacation in Europe fifteen months ago.

Desmond had not hesitated. He'd immediately followed up on the information given. The subsequent raid was hugely successful. A band of human traffickers were arrested, in total seven girls were located and returned to their families, including the three from Oregon.

Since then, Desmond had on occasion sent Robert a greeting and informed him that he would be happy to be of help anytime if he could.

Through a communication with the, at the time, Captain of the Portland Police department, he had found out a little more about Robert and also his condition of Asperger's.

Desmond retired from the police force three years ago. Had no further contact with Robert since then, but then, quite by chance, had witnessed what he felt sure, was an abduction.

Sipping his regular ten o'clock coffee, Desmond read again the brief e-mail.

'Abductee rescued, need transport back to UK, help, TK'

He was relieved she was safe. He was impressed that she had been rescued so quickly. He had been sad to hear of Robert's passing and he wondered who this TK might be. He hadn't replied earlier to the e-mail for the fact that life, as it so often can, threw him a curveball.

The very moment he had realised something was amiss; the moment he realised that the woman was being abducted, was being forcibly coerced; the woman he had seen a few times in the cafe where he had lunch every day.

Though she was always alone and showed no signs of being engaged or married, he had not plucked up the courage to speak with her, though she had caught his eye once and had smiled.

The very moment that he knew that he needed to act, to do something, his phone rang. The call was from the police force in Cardiff, Wales. There had been an accident.

Listening to a female officer from Cardiff, seeing the woman being escorted from the cafe, Desmond suddenly thought of Robert.

Over the years, since he first had that information from Robert, he had learned more about him and knew the best way to communicate with him was to be brief, even cryptic. Desmond had figured that this must be the way his mind worked due to his condition. This was an answer.

The call ended and he cursed the world for such bad timing.

What to do? He had been in the vicinity, and though retired, his policeman's brain had picked up and stored some of the information that he had overheard.

It had all taken but moments. There was no way he could get word to his old police force, to any of his former colleagues. The only option, was to send of a quick e-mail to Robert.

All the while still digesting what the Welsh police had told him.

His ex-wife had been in a car accident and was in hospital in Cardiff.

Desmond closed his eyes for a moment, concentrated on what he had heard and seen, then sent the following to Robert;

'Robert, probable abduction, female, depart Plymouth Mon noon, arrival Bilbao Tue 1.30, company J. Inverno, send help, DP'

Then, concerned about the situation with his ex-wife, Desmond set off home to pack and travel to Wales.

That had been on Sunday. He had just returned, his routine totally out of the window.

But, he felt good about himself. His ex-wife was in a stable condition, had spoken to him, had thanked him for coming, had hugged him and had gently kissed him on the cheek.

Desmond read through the communications again, very happy that the woman was safe, but what could he do to help with transport? He would have to investigate. Time first though, to send an e-mail.

Myrtle Creek

Once again a 'ding' on her phone aroused Claire from her sleep.

She stirred, picked up her phone, noticed it had just gone 6 am, then was suddenly more alert as she saw it was an e-mail from DP. She had transferred the contact address from Robert's computer to her phone in order to monitor any incoming messages.

She sat bolt upright in bed and opened the e-mail.

'Sorry to hear about Robert, sorry for delay, emergency elsewhere, excellent news about woman, well done, will work on transport but need details, from where? And names?
Await your reply,
DP'

Claire flung the duvet aside and headed for the shower.

Fifteen minutes later she was dressed and eating a bowl of cereal whilst on the main computer in Robert's study sending a message to Thomas.

THE PAST;

Period 14–Part 1

The year 2002–Chicago–two weeks before Christmas

Felicity came out of the Rosemont train station on the Blue Line, felt the cold wind as she walked along the road heading to her apartment and looked up at a passing plane, which had just departed from O'Hare, wondering where it might be headed.

Twelve minutes later she entered the lobby, rode the elevator to the fourth floor and reached her apartment.

Taking off her winter coat, she noticed the clock on the wall in the hallway, quickly checked herself in the mirror, then headed for her kitchen. She would make herself a cup of tea, and have a quick bite to eat before leaving to start an evening shift in a restaurant at a nearby Hilton Hotel.

Felicity, though she preferred to be called Fliss, stripped, showered and changed for her evening waitressing job, drinking her tea and consuming a small portion of beef carbonnade before once again donning her winter coat and setting out.

Three evening shifts a week, plus her job in the city as a clerk in an insurance company kept her in the apartment with ease, and she could even afford to put a little aside each week. Braving the cold wind once more, she walked as the hotel was less than a mile away.

She smiled to herself. She wanted to be happy, to be fine, to be self-sufficient. Not to be home, not to be in a relationship, but to be free and happily single.

She thought back to two and half years ago.

Deciding to use her holiday to visit the site where her older sister had died had been a good decision.

Her parents had been, and had visited the site on the first anniversary. She had not gone with them, much to their disapproval, but that was nothing new. She could do nothing right according to them.

Whatever she had done with her life had not been supported by her parents.

Why can't you be more like your sister was? She was academic, bright, confident, with a goal. They even organised a date for her once, with a young man from a well-to-do family, a man with prospects.

One date, even only halfway through the date, she had known.

He was handsome, sure. He was well dressed, sure. He was smart, sure.

But he was not for her. He was self-absorbed, self-assured and seemingly took for granted that she was a lucky girl to be with him.

She took a week's leave from the two jobs she held, one in the Albuquerque Council offices as a processing clerk, the other as a waitress in a hotel restaurant.

It was time to go and visit the site, the place where her sister had been killed.

To make peace, to bring closure. She had directed all her anger at her these past years.

Booking into a motel in Silver City gave her a break away from her parents.

Meeting Simon was good too. He was nice, he was caring, he was kind.

She had delayed going to the site until the very last day. In fact as she was on her way back home.

Discovering that Simon worked and lived in the same city, she got his address and promised to drop in to see him soon, and that she would read her sister's diary.

He had smiled and had said he was looking forward to seeing her again as she got into her rental car that day.

As she was walking to work, Felicity smiled at that memory, but then thought back to the day she came to his work, his business, the day she shared what was written in her sister's diary.

He took her to dinner that evening, then dropped her off at her parents' place later.

He had taken hold of her face, ever so tenderly, had looked into her eyes, had kissed her briefly on the lips, but had then said, he wasn't ready. He wanted to keep searching for the truth. He wanted to assure her that though he liked her very much, he wouldn't be committed to a relationship until he had finished his quest to find the truth.

Was it all about finding the gold, she had asked.

No, it wasn't. It was about finding out what really happened, the truth.

What had been Conrad Shelton's part in it? Why had he been killed in Rome?

Was it all connected? He just needed to know.

Her parents, who had been none too happy to see her with a shaggy motorcycle rider, said he would not be welcome in the house.

Fine, she had said. And two weeks later had left home, headed for Chicago and had not spoken to or contacted them since.

She crossed the road, entered the staff door, took a deep breath and got ready to happily serve the waiting diners.

Meanwhile

More than 1300 miles to the south west in Albuquerque.

The winter evening was considerably warmer than in Chicago, and as Felicity was serving her first table of the evening, Simon had stopped his Indian motorcycle, had taken his helmet off and was walking up the path leading to the house where, two and a half years ago, he had softly kissed her and had left.

He had only just stepped on to the porch when the door opened.

First a man, then a woman, presumably Felicity's parents Simon thought, appeared.

"Where is she?" the man demanded.

Taken aback, Simon looked from one to the other, noting their angry and yet concerned look, then replied, "I take it then that Felicity is not home?"

"Isn't she with you?" the woman asked, showing more concern now, and less anger.

"I left her here, what, two and half years ago. There was something I needed to do. I haven't seen her or spoken to her since… You don't know where she is?"

"She left, couple of weeks after you…"the man said.

"We thought she was with you, she…was angry," the woman said.

Simon figured out what had happened. Though he had only known her briefly, he had an idea of how things were at home.

Looking at them both, he shook his head, then said to them, "You lost one daughter, through an act of God, you've lost another, because you…through an act of pride!" then turned and headed down the path.

"I will find her," he said, straddling his motorbike, then putting his helmet on, he fired the Indian up and rode away, not once looking back at them.

Riding through the city towards his house, Simon made a promise to himself. He'd messed up several relationships because of his determination to find out what had really happened the day the tornado struck. No more!

He had travelled to Rome to discover the circumstances surrounding the death of Conrad Shelton, as he'd been certain that the incident would be related. When he'd spoken to the police there, however, he discovered that it was the misplaced bravado of this young American, who, having lost heavily in some poker game held in a private club, had tried to flee the scene.

He'd confronted a man who had a small gun. The ensuing brief battle had resulted in the man being shot.

Mr Shelton had then fled the scene pursued by two men, who having caught up with him, had shot him down.

A vendetta. No connection to the events surrounding the dig in New Mexico.

On his flight home he was angry with himself. Angry he had let this stupid quest get the better of him. More than anything, he was angry at letting Felicity go. She had been lovely, bubbly, pretty and he missed her.

Simon focused on his business, worked long hours, and the days, weeks and months, passed.

Now, nearly two and half years later, he arrived back home. Not only angry with himself once again, but also with Felicity's parents.

Where had she gone?

He had a new quest, a new aim. Stalling his bike in the garage, he entered the house and grabbed a can of lager from the fridge. He was determined to find Felicity, but how? Where to start?

Later that evening, sitting on the couch with the television on eating a slice of pizza, Simon suddenly got up. He switched off the television, which he hadn't really been watching anyway, shoved the last piece of pizza in his mouth, then got ready to go out again.

Fifteen minutes later, deciding to use his pickup truck this time, he drove out of the driveway, made sure he had the letter and headed away. It didn't take him long to reach the address. Would they still be living there, he wondered.

He rang the bell and a man answered.

"Hello Mr Morton."

The man looked at Simon for several moments, then stood aside, "Please, come in."

"Thank you," Simon answered, then Mrs Morton appeared, and he gave her a nod.

"Please, let me take your coat," she said.

Simon took off his coat, handed it to her, then followed Mr Morton into the large open plan kitchen.

He had taken the letter from his coat pocket. This he handed to Mrs Morton as she entered the kitchen. "You gave this to me, a long time ago," Simon said. "You never opened it, you didn't destroy it, thank you for that, it has taken me on quite a journey, but I realised, well, you might like to read it."

Josie's mother, her eyes welling up, took the envelope, took out the letter, then sat down on the breakfast bar stool and began to read.

Her husband stood beside her and said nothing.

It wasn't long before tears rolled down her cheeks. She then handed the letter to her husband, got off the stool and approached Simon, taking both his hands she looked up at him.

"I am so sorry," she said.

Simon nodded, then released his hands from hers and moved forwards to give her a hug.

"Goodness," she said after a moment, "where are my manners? Coffee?"

"Please," Simon answered, holding out his hand as Mr Morton handed him the letter back.

"Not our finest hour," he said, his voice deep and Simon could hear the emotion.

Simon nodded his thanks for the coffee, declined any sugar or milk then looking at the both in turn, he spoke.

"Being a parent sure has its challenges. What to do for the best for your children? I have a similar problem at the moment, but first, about that letter…"

"Let's go through to the lounge," Mrs Morton suggested.

Simon followed her, taking his coffee mug and sat himself on the seat indicated by her.

"About the letter," Simon commenced again.

He then spoke about the contents, the part about the mosaic tiles and the gold, the visits to the site in New Mexico, the subsequent discovery of the missing young man Eddie and the young lad Conrad Shelton, who had been killed in Rome.

"That's quite a story," Mr Morton said, "and no mention anywhere, about this gold? This Eddie guy and Conrad, you say, was killed?"

"Eddie went missing. Never been found. I feel for sure he was involved somehow. Conrad was also involved, but, he was killed in Rome and that incident was totally unrelated," Simon answered, taking a sip of coffee. "I have found no evidence that the discovery made by Professor Emily Parker and your daughter Josie and this Conrad, was ever rediscovered. The tornado caused quite some damage. I believe it's still hidden there, which is good and well. I do believe though that there must have been some notes on the find, some information that the professor must have recorded, but it has been stolen, destroyed by the tornado, or, just kept secret. Anyway, I am finally at a point where I want to lay this to rest; move on with my life. I have spent far too much time on this crazy notion, not about finding the gold, but to find the truth surrounding the whole event. This is why I came to you, not just to show you the letter, which I should have done long ago, but I met someone last time I was at the tornado site. This was on the tenth anniversary.

Josie's friend, Kathryn, who also died that day, well, her younger sister, Felicity, was there. We talked and she had information that helped me in my, my quest. Subsequently, because of my, stupid determination, I said goodbye to her."

Simon paused, took another sip of his drink and gazed into space for a moment. He then looked at them in turn, and said, "I lost her. I called around to her family's house earlier today. She left home leaving no trace, and making no contact with her parents. Two and half years ago now. So, Mr Morton, I believe you are a big cheese in the tax department?"

Mr Morton smiled at the description, then said "You want my help to find her?"

"I should never have left, she was, the 'lesser' sister, from what she told me, always being compared to her sister who had been so, academic, so very much…well, anyway, you get the gist. Anyway, I have feelings for her, though I only spent a little time with her. She's no doubt got a boyfriend, maybe even married by now, but I need to find her, at least to apologise…"

Simon again paused for a moment, finishing his coffee, then said, "So, I wonder. Everyone should be paying taxes. She surely must be. Can you help me?"

Mr Morton nodded, "My help you shall have."

Simon nodded, put down his coffee cup and thought back, to the moment he, so stupidly, had left her.

THE PRESENT;

The Hacienda–Northern Spain

Friday 31st May

"We should go back," Cynthia said, her voice barely above a whisper. She was standing by the railing on the balcony. The sky was blue with an occasional white cloud here and there. It was warm in the afternoon sun. Frowning a little, she took in the view before her, saw the plane, the hangar, and her rental car, now parked directly below. She turned around.

"We need to go back" she said, her voice louder now.

Thomas, sitting in a cane chair on the long balcony sipping a beer was about to say something, but she turned to Letitia who stood, arms folded, in the doorway to the lounge.

"You said you discovered, in your father's office that the deeds were put on the back of the painting, which was then sent to the museum as a loan. A good idea, I guess. A safe place."

"However," Tia said, stepping towards the Spanish woman who was trying to comprehend, but was unable to say anything before Tia continued, "However, we have now discovered, from the horse's mouth, from the woman who stole the painting from the museum, who carefully took the frame off that, the deeds were not attached in any way or form."

"Si, yes," Letitia said.

"So, we need to go back, back in time. Back to when your father made the arrangements. You see," Tia said, stopping right in front of Letitia, "I was wondering. You weren't here, right? So, there was your brother, but, who else? When it came to these legal papers, who else was here that might have influenced your father to do this, and … There's something else, how did the man who asked Victoria to steal the painting, how did he know that it was in the museum? Something isn't right. Something else was happening.

"So we need to trace back, find out more about the circumstances in which your father agreed to send the painting to the museum," Thomas said, having got up from the chair, he was walking up to stand next to Cynthia, catching her drift and what she was thinking. He concluded, "Tia is right, we need to look into that."

Letitia looked at Cynthia, then at Thomas, then back to Cynthia.

"I understand, but I…why you want to help?"

Tia stepped up to Letitia, took hold of both her shoulders and looking directly at her, said, "Your intentions are, understandable, yes. They were perhaps wrong, but, we like a mystery, don't we Thomas?"

"Absolutely. Also, you have cleared our names with the police. So, where do we start Tia?"

She released her hold on Letitia, looked at Thomas, said, "You, get on your laptop. Victoria and this French woman, Sophie, are looking for the painting. See if you can't find a trail to where it was, and how it came to be here, with the Teremos family. Letitia and I are going to search her father's study, is that okay?" this to the Spanish woman, who nodded and turned to lead the way.

Thomas was about to enter the lounge from the balcony, the two women already halfway through the lounge heading for the door when his phone rang.

"It's Claire," Thomas said. "Hi Claire…"

Tia had stopped, both women waiting as Thomas listened, then said, "Okay, thanks Claire. Let us think this through and then I'll get back to you." Looking at the two women, Thomas said, "Finally a message from DP. Says he'll need names and retrieval destination in order to arrange transport. If it's okay, I'll think it through, then run it by you."

Tia nodded, then gesturing for Letitia to lead the way again, left the lounge.

She followed the Spanish woman and was pleased at how her and Thomas had bonded and how they were very much a team.

Having for so many years now, always been the one in charge, the one who made the decisions, the one who had control, she was pleased that Thomas, although taking charge in certain situations, was very much showing that he appreciated and trusted her leadership.

A little while later, both women searching through drawers and bookcases, it was Letitia who spoke, "You and Thomas?"

Cynthia turned around, "Me and Thomas?" she asked, knowing full well what Letitia meant.

She looked at the Spanish woman who sat behind the desk rifling through a drawer. She had noticed her looking at Thomas, noticed also that she was an attractive woman, and, judging by all her gym equipment, Tia could see she was very fit. Was the question loaded? Was she genuinely asking? Did she see something, was she interested in him?

Letitia looked up, smiled, "I think he likes you, very much. When I first see you, I think you were a couple. Put you together in guest room, this was…alright?"

still smiling but with a cheeky grin on her face, strangely feeling quite relaxed with her new guests.

"We've only just met. Well, not exactly. We knew each other at school, though not very well, and that was a long time ago. He's…very nice …" noticing the grin, "yes, the guest room is just fine."

Cynthia turned around again, feeling herself blush a little, and carried on looking through the various books on the shelf.

Not much later two things happened in quick succession. First Letitia called out something in Spanish and produced a folder which she placed on the desk behind which she was sitting and opened it.

Cynthia looked, then noticed the picture on the wall.

As Letitia was thumbing through the various sheets of paper she had found, Tia asked, "Are these your grandparents?" She was looking at the framed photograph of an elderly couple standing in the orchard.

It was a black and white shot, and Tia estimated it would have been taken somewhere in the thirties.

Letitia quickly looked across to where Cynthia was standing beside the bookcase admiring the photo.

"Yes, Abuelo Gregor, grandfather, he started the orchard, with grandmother, Consuela…"

"I wonder," Tia said. Reaching up she unhooked the picture, looked at the back and then shook it. She then turned and placed it on the desk, "There is something in there. I can feel it move…"

Letitia took hold of the picture, like Tia, she shook it, then quickly placed it face down on the desktop, and using a pair of scissor that were tucked in the pencil box, began to lever the tabs upwards.

They were both looking intently as Letitia lifted the cardboard backing away.

The deeds.

Letitia was overawed for a moment, then got up from behind the desk, came around to Cynthia, and hugged her.

Cynthia who was nearly lifted from the floor, gasped at the strength of the hug as Letitia kissed her cheek and said thank you several times.

The Spanish woman then took hold of the few sheets of paper and began to look at them closely.

"I'll go and tell Thomas" Tia said and left the study.

Whilst in Paris

"Caprice Jeanne Castagnet was the woman who sold the painting through the Franck Huysen & Son auction house in Boston, in 1895," Sophie said.

She was in her office, sat behind her desk and computer, speaking to Victoria who sat on the two-seater couch sipping a glass of wine.

"My friend Sam, who is looking into the Castagnet family history for one case, has come upon the information that relates to our case, or should I say your case."

"So, we need to find out how that painting, sold in Boston in 1895, unfortunately to an anonymous buyer, but, apparently someone from Paris, ends up with the Teremos family in Spain, and how Johannes

Acker knew about it and, moreover, how he knew that the painting had been loaned out to the museum," Victoria said.

"Exactly," Sophie replied, also taking a sip of her wine.

It was the middle of the afternoon, her work, as the manager of the Paris Fine Arts Auction House, was under control and the few little jobs she had on her agenda, she had delegated, so now, together with Victoria, they could focus on tracing the painting.

"The name you gave me, Johannes Acker, was a great help, though we have now discovered that he died in a boating accident in Switzerland. This was in 1990. He had worked with the French authorities in the locating and returning of art stolen by the Nazi's in the Second World War., I believe there is more to find, because I have discovered a name."

Seeing Victoria sit up and look at her quizzically, Sophie explained, "I was up late last night, and did a little digging, but wanted to get my work done today before totally focusing on this. The name I found, in connection with Johannes Acker, is Roberto Solari."

THE PAST;

Period 14–Part 2

The year 2002–Chicago–one week before Christmas

The snow was falling lightly as she left the station. Another day in the city, another day at her desk. Earlier she had lost herself as she looked out the window overlooking the lake. Her work was up to date. She shared an office with four others, but she had the desk by the window.

She had drifted off in yet another daydream. The snow falling was picturesque. She watched the people below, dressed up warm, either walking or cycling. It was getting ever closer to Christmas ever so fast.

She briefly thought about her mum and dad, but shook the thought away.

In the company she worked for there were two men who had on several occasions tried to come on to her, inviting her to a party here or a party there, catch a show, perhaps dinner. But she had declined them every time.

There was a man she saw regularly who worked in the same building. He too had plucked up the courage to ask her out, and though out of all of them, he was, to her, the nicest. She had not been persuaded.

Now, walking away from the Rosemont station heading to her apartment, she began to think that maybe she should give it a go. Give love a chance, what could be the worst to happen, she wondered.

Then, nearing her apartment, she looked ahead, saw a familiar vehicle, and as she drew closer, the drivers doors opened, and a man stepped out.

All thoughts of any others, vanished.

He was here. He was in Chicago. He had found her.

She quickened her pace. He walked around the back of the vehicle, stepped on to the pavement, and was smiling broadly.

She smiled back and rushed into his arms which enfolded her in a tight and warming embrace.

As the snow fell, they hugged for several moments, neither saying a word, until he said, "I am so sorry Fliss, I should never had left"

"It's okay. It's okay," she managed to say, trying hard to keep the tears at bay. "You had to go. How did you find me? I'm so glad you did. I should have contacted you, but," Felicity said, pulling slightly away from him to look up and into his eyes, "I was angry, then … well," she said, then once more, unable to speak, she placed her head tight against his chest, felt his chin resting on the top of her head and his strong arms around her.

She felt good, she felt safe and she sobbed softly.

Simon was overjoyed. She had rushed up to him. She had embraced him and as he had looked into those lovely blue eyes, he knew.

She didn't belong to anyone else.

He felt her sob, felt her body tremble ever so lightly, and he held her, promising to himself he would never let her go. He kissed the top of her head and held her until she stopped trembling.

"What does a guy have to do," Simon said, "to get a coffee around here."

She pulled away from him, looked up, smiled through her tears, then answered,

"Come on, let's get inside."

"Okay, may I grab my gear? May I stay?" he asked, releasing his hold on her, realising again how much he cared for her.

"Get your stuff," she said, smiling and planting a kiss on his cheek.

As they were riding the elevator up, she said, "So sorry, but I have a shift tonight, at the Hilton, just down the road. Need to get ready for that."

"No problem. I'll drive you there, pick you up later?" Simon said, his heart beating quite rapidly in his chest.

"It's just down the road. I'll walk there, but, yes, if you can pick me up around quarter past ten?"

"Absolutely."

Half an hour later it was Simon who was looking out the window at the falling snow, trying to see past his reflection in the glass.

He felt relieved and thankful. She had greeted him warmly, she wasn't married, didn't have a boyfriend, and he could see she was very glad to see him.

This will be a great Christmas, he thought, turning away from the window as he felt the need to eat something.

Felicity arrived at her work, ready to serve the customers and thinking she had not felt this happy in quite some time.

This was going to be a great Christmas, she thought, giving the chef a broad smile as she entered the kitchen.

10:25 pm that evening

"You flew to Rome?" Felicity asked, as she unlocked the door to her apartment. Simon had been waiting to pick her up, gave her a kiss on the cheek and opened the car door for her.

The snow had stopped falling, the drive home was short with little traffic around. Just as they had entered the building, he said that he had had travelled to Rome.

"I did. I felt I had to. I still couldn't let go of the, well mystery, if you like. I know, in hindsight, I should not have just left…"

She took her coat off, looked up at him as he took his off and gave him a smile, "It's okay, really. So, what did you find?"

They entered the lounge. "I wasn't there long actually. Went straight to the police station, explained my connection and what could they tell me…"

"Coffee?" Felicity asked, interrupting as she headed into the small kitchen.

"Yes, please, black, no sugar."

"Sure, sorry, carry on…"

"Well, unfortunately, not much to tell. It took the police nearly three days to find out who it was that had been shot. A subsequent investigation managed to trace Conrad's movements and it was found that he was into gambling, had boldly walked into a cafe he should never have ventured into, got into a card game he should never have got into and lost a ton of money.

"Then apparently, and, according to the coroner he had been taking drugs, he decided to do a runner, was stopped by this guy who had a gun, they struggled and the guy was shot, Conrad fled, but they soon tracked him down, chased him, and when he was cornered, the police told me that they just simply shot him, took whatever he had on him to make it look like a robbery and left him.

"After some investigation they tracked which hotel he was staying at, this too they discovered had been stripped of personal belongings, as they obviously took his room key-card. Anyway, they did discover who he was and his mother came to Rome to identify the body and arranged to have it flown back to the States."

"So, unrelated to the events at the dig?" Felicity asked, bringing in the mugs of coffee.

"Unrelated, yes, so though it didn't solve anything for me, I knew, flying back that I had to now just let it go, but, I wanted to try one more thing. I went to the Shelton family home, thinking that perhaps chatting with his mother or father, might throw some light on the events surrounding the tornado strike, but, well, I chickened out really. It was a large estate, gated property and all, so that was that. Went back to work, thinking of you."

"How did you find me?" she asked, sitting next to him on the couch and looking into his eyes, realising, surely confirmed by the butterflies in her stomach that she'd missed him and had stronger feelings that she'd allowed herself to accept.

"It took a while," Simon answered, looking at her. "I just couldn't bring myself to go to your house. I felt, well that I had blown it anyway, any chance of a relationship with you. Another mistake, another opportunity lost so. So I buried myself in my work. I had only just purchased the business when you came to my office that day, there was a lot to do to make it run better and make it a profitable business.

"I also felt, you being so pretty and all, I was afraid to find out that you'd moved on. That would have been… well, anyway, I worked and worked, then, the other day, I was just walking from the shop to my house. It was cold and getting dark, snow was falling a little and I realised that you were still on my mind, almost every day…"

Simon paused to take a sip of his coffee.

"Almost every day?" Felicity said, smiling broadly sensing his feeling for her.

Simon smiled back, "So," he said, ignoring her teasing question, "I had an idea. I went over to Josie's folks, Mr Morton is chief director of an income tax branch. I thought he would have access to information I needed to find out where you were. I asked him and he was happy to help."

"And you drove all the way here. That's quite a journey."

Simon had taken hold of her hand with his free hand and was looking at her, feeling thankful that she hadn't married, nor was she involved with anyone. Feeling thankful that he had a chance to be with her and feeling thankful that, as she looked at him, he could sense and feel that she liked him.

"You like it here? In Chicago? This is a nice apartment. What is it you do in the city?"

"I do like it here, yes. The apartment is nice. I work for an insurance company, then three nights a week as a waitress, I…I like you being here…"

They moved towards each other. Simon, without looking, managed to place the mug on the table, then, keeping his eyes locked onto hers he moved closer. The kiss was inevitable, it was natural, and Simon and Felicity were for long moments unaware of anything around them, drifting into a space and time where there wasn't anything, or anybody, just the two of them.

Felicity felt that she was floating, drifting, and could feel and sense her heart thumping away.

Simon felt positively upbeat. He was in the company of someone who had captured his heart, and captured it fully.

Outside the snow again began to fall softly upon the city of Chicago.

"So," Felicity asked, eventually pulling away from him, once more looking into his eyes, "who's looking after your store, and those fabulous bikes?"

"I took on a store manager, a chap I knew from my schooldays. He's fine," Simon answered, remembering his coffee which, upon taking a sip, he realised was only just warm, "As for the bikes, you like bikes?"

"I do. I recognised your Indian when you arrived at the site that day. You still have it?"

"Oh absolutely, fancy a ride in the spring?"

"Right now, I fancy you," Felicity answered, grinning, then flung herself back into his embrace.

For Simon, as once more they kissed, Albuquerque was a million miles away.

THE PRESENT;

Albuquerque

Friday 31ˢᵗ May

Millie Parker had parked the rental car opposite the gates that led to a large mansion style house.

The very gates that Simon Lightfoot had stood at, over seventeen years ago.

Sat beside her was Alison Hudson…

Upon returning to her own home later that Wednesday evening, after saying a huge thank you to Alison, and after they both hugged, each reflecting on their own memories, Millie had made up her mind as to what needed to be done.

The following day she caught an early flight back to Albuquerque, and armed with the all the information she had from her research at the university and with the very important, blood stained folder that Alison had retrieved from Portland, the one that Eddie had posted all those years ago, she went to the central police station.

Millie had subsequently been taken to a senior detective in a secure office where the two of them then had gone through all the information that she and Alison had gathered, and through all the police reports that had been made at the time.

Having done so, he then asked if it would be possible for her friend Alison to fly over from San Francisco, and for both of them to return later that afternoon or early evening?

He also stated that he might be able to reimburse her for any costs incurred.

Millie said not to concern himself with the latter and that she would call her friend straight away. Leaving him with her number, she left and called Alison.

Millie received a call just after 4.30 pm just as Alison's plane was landing.

"Good timing detective," she said in answer when he asked if she could possibly come in at 6.00 pm and if had it been possible for her friend to come over.

"My friend has just arrived. We will see you at six."

A clock on the wall in the reception area of the police station said it was 5.54 pm when Millie and Alison arrived.

They were escorted to a large room.

"Ah, good," the detective said, moving forwards and extending his hand. "Miss Parker, good to see you again, thank you, and this must be Miss Hudson." Shaking hands with both women, he said to Alison, "Roger Mantell, thank you for flying over."

The detective inspector gestured for them to be seated, then introduced them to another person in the room, "This is Michelle."

Then, both women having sat down, he again spoke, "So, good. Yes, well, again, thank you so much for uncovering the information that you have. Also, I didn't mention this earlier today, Miss Parker, but we have come across the name Robert Pentegrass before. Sorry to hear about his passing also. Please thank his assistant, Claire, when you speak with her next."

Both Alison and Millie nodded in the affirmative.

"Good, yes. Well, with all the information to hand," he continued, "we returned to the events of that day, the day the tornado struck. Michelle here," he said, indicating the woman sat behind her laptop, "will talk you through what she has found."

The woman, whom both Alison and Millie felt could only just have left high school, began to report…

They all focused on a large screen television screen …

Back in the car, where Millie and Alison sat quietly waiting, a phone rang.

"They are here," Millie whispered, reading the text on the screen.

Alison saw them.

Their instructions were to wait for their signal. She too thought back to yesterday, to the report Michelle had given them…

"With the information you have given," the young lady behind the laptop said, "We have dug into the archives. We have found meteorological records and satellite images of the tornado that struck near Silver City, back in 1988."

They all watched the big screen as, in the first sequence, they saw the swirls of the large tornado.

"As you will see, the tornado was more or less following a direct path, then, right about here…There, you see, it just veered at almost ninety degrees. That's when it quickly reached the dig site. It happened so quickly there was virtually no time to react or find safe shelter…"

Michelle stopped at this point, and knowing the circumstances, looked at Millie, "Sorry for your loss." Then she clicked some more with the mouse, and another image appeared. "So, here we now have satellite footage, unfortunately, not from that day and time. This was shot as the satellite passed over that area the following day. I've enhanced the picture and focused on the actual site."

All eyes were on the screen once more.

The screen showed the devastation, the upturned caravan, the debris from the tents, the litter from everywhere else that the whirlwind had collected and deposited.

The light was fading and, going by the time displayed on the screen, it was early evening.

Then Michelle spoke again and the screen shot froze.

"There, just on the very top right of the screen, see a vehicle, a Land Rover. See a light shining on the ground, a spotlight of sorts, and there are three people, just vague figures really, and as I slowly play it forwards, watch…"

"Okay, we can go," Millie said, starting her car and following two other cars into the driveway, through the gates towards the big house.

At a signal they stopped and stayed in the car, turning the engine off.

Several men and women had bolted up the steps to the front door, another group had left the second vehicle and were heading around to the back of the house.

Millie and Alison looked at each other, then sat and waited.

Millie gripping onto the steering wheel, tried to make sense of her emotions…

On the screen back at the police station, they had watched footage, not a lot, but enough to see what had been going on as the satellite passed high overhead.

Then there had been the final sequence of footage. "Here is another satellite video, this one was from only a month ago," Michelle said. "It was the most recent I could find which covered the property. I hoped it would give us answers. We got lucky, but we knew that we had found it, thanks to the sketch you mother had made…"

The front door opened. A woman stood there and one of the policemen was talking to her and showing her a search warrant.

Even from their car, both Alison and Millie could see the woman pale significantly as she took hold of the notice and was moved aside as the team entered the house.

Three minutes later a policeman appeared from around the side of the mansion and beckoned them to come.

They quickly got out of the car, then followed him around the side of the large house to the back, walked along a path that led up to a sizeable back porch, then, he showed them.

They looked over the railing that ran along the porch, leaving a wide gap where a set of four steps led down to the garden, and saw it too.

Surrounded by a low hedge was a tiled area, about a metre square, in mosaic tiles depicting the picture of a swallow.

Meanwhile, across the Atlantic

As Millie and Alison were looking at the mosaic-tiled square in the rear garden of the Shelton residence, it was the middle of the evening in Paris.

Earlier Victoria had spoken at length with Cynthia in Spain, was told of the new message from the mysterious DP and the offer to get her back to the UK. However, it was suggested that she remained in Paris a little longer, first, in order to help Sophie track down the painting by Titian, and second, to give them, meaning Cynthia and Thomas, time to think through the situation.

Victoria was furthermore informed that the deeds had been found, but it was still important to find whatever information they could on the painting.

Victoria related the conversation to Sophie and asked if it was all right for her to stay there. Sophie answered with an emphatic yes, so they set to work together, searching for the painting of King Charles standing by a horse.

The manager of a renowned fine arts auction house working alongside a one-time art thief.

Some 980 kilometres to the south

Cynthia was searching for Letitia.

Thomas had spoken to Claire, had composed a response to DP, and she had spoken with Victoria. Letitia had disappeared some time ago, so she went in search of her. She heard the sounds coming from the gym. The door was slightly open and she walked in. There she was, the slim Spanish woman, pummelling the large leather bag that hung from the ceiling.

She could see the strength of this woman, a power she had felt when they had hugged earlier, and seeing Letitia now, Cynthia was glad she wasn't a foe.

Though several inches shorter and lighter, Cynthia felt sure that Letitia was more powerful. The Spanish woman suddenly realised she was not alone.

"Oh, hello," she said, her breathing heavy.

"Sorry to intrude. I noticed earlier, you seemed, a little withdrawn,…"

"You and Thomas, good people. I am sorry for, well, and to kidnap this woman, to string her up, in here. It was, not very nice, for that too I am sorry."

Cynthia could see the genuine concern and regret in Letitia's face,

"Your home, your livelihood, it was in danger. You, needed to do what you thought best," she said.

"I guess, but, what now? I have the documents, I, read them, but, I think…"

"If you can have those documents translated, I may be able to help," Tia suggested, walking up to where a towel was draped over one of the exercise bicycles.

"You think…how?" Letitia asked, catching the towel which Cynthia threw at her.

"I have a degree in law."

T H E   P A S T ;

Period 15

The year 2015 – Brisbane, Australia

Stay ahead of the law.

Victoria waited in the first class lounge. Her flight was less than an hour away. She was going home, back to the United Kingdom, back to London, her home town. It felt like she was going home, even though she had been in Australia now for a little over twenty five years.

She had been careless, she had been to carefree and had let herself be swept away.

Swept away by a younger man, a handsome man. He was a 'hunk'. She was sure now that he had targeted her.

Three days ago she had been in the casino, a place she frequented from time to time. It had been going well. She was well up in earnings.

He had bumped into her, lightly. He had been apologetic. He had smiled, offered her a drink and the connection was made.

He had been charming, had with interest allowed her to speak, and had been interested in her life, her journey.

Later, the following morning, she was sure he had spiked her drink.

He was nowhere to be seen. She awoke alone in the five star hotel attached to the casino. She was angry with herself. What a fool she had been.

It wasn't that he also stole her money, several thousand in Australian dollars, but, she recalled the many things she had told him, recalled her detailed and self-praising accounts of her cat burgling days.

Sitting up in bed that morning, she recalled everything in detail.

He hadn't taken anything else, just the cash, and her dignity, she mused, but he knew who she was, knew what she had done in the past, and had targeted her for the money of that he was sure. But now, now he knew so much more. Knew things about her that could prove costly. What a fool she had been.

She needed to stay ahead of the law.

Deciding immediately to uproot, she gathered her belongings, placed a few things in storage and made the travel arrangements. She had more than sufficient funds, in fact, not only did she have close to half a million in the bank in Brisbane, but she also had an offshore account holding at least as much again.

She had been careless. Now she had to move, move away, move out.

There was no way she was even risking a chance of him blackmailing her.

After some thought, and after arranging flights and money transfers, she began to feel a lot better. She felt that the time was right to move back.

Though she had loved the Australian climate, the lifestyle, all through these years, there had been something missing, something more permanent in her life.

She had over the two and half decades had several relationships, but none for very long. She had acquired a dog at some point. This had been good for her, a companionship that lasted just over twelve years before her beloved Rascal had died.

That had been a couple of years ago now, and whilst the companionship had been good, she had not considered getting another pet.

Now, she'd sorted out termination of her house rental, gathered many of her belongings and taken them to a charity shop, and then she had packed.

Sitting in the airport lounge, awaiting her flight, she felt comfortable, relaxed and rather excited to be heading back to London.

Lesson learned, she told herself and smiled. No more hunky men!

But it wasn't being tempted by him that would prove costly, it was her careless talk as she sat with him in the lounge bar at the casino that evening, for sitting directly behind them, a woman was listening. She was intrigued. She too had noticed the young man. She too had thought him attractive and handsome.

But she had seen him charm the older lady and knew then he was only after getting something from her.

Listening to the conversation they had, she was glad she hadn't even tried to make eye contact with him. He was, there was no doubt, a con man, and, as she listened to the woman talk, she was fairly sure that he had drugged her, for her chatty conversation, was tinged with a slight slur, as if she had been drinking too much.

She thought about doing something, but what could she do. Thinking this through she realised the conversation had stopped, and taking a quick peek over the high-backed settee, she saw they were gone.

She decided that she ought at least to find out the woman's name, though still not sure what she could do with that information. She saw them. They were checking into the hotel which was part of the casino complex.

Making her way there quickly, she overheard the woman's name. Victoria Lange.

Making a note, using a hotel pen, she then left the casino, and headed for her own hotel. Her thoughts turned to herself, to her own weaknesses and vulnerability, and how it could have easily been her. She had been so lavish in spending her father's money, she had been so irresponsible, so very selfish.

The overheard conversation resonated with her, and changed her.

The following day she left where she had been staying, booked a flight and was going home.

She flew to Singapore and from there to Madrid. Then she took a national flight to Bilbao where her father, very pleased, picked her up.

Juliette Inverno was pleased to be home.

THE PRESENT;

Teremos Hacienda

Saturday 1ˢᵗ June

Thomas was reminiscing as he walked through the orchard. It was early in the morning, the sun, though having merely risen, was already pouring out the warmth of springtime.

So much had happened, in such a short time: Robert dying, inheriting a house, meeting Claire, discovering what Robert had been involved in these past decades, the urgent call for help from London, the quick departure and flying to Spain, being driven off the road, being attacked, being rescued by the lovely Cynthia. Then the daring rescue–how his heart had pounded, how exciting it had been–the return flight, the open conversation with Letitia; the reason she had for having planned the kidnapping of Victoria.

Thomas jumped over the low fence as he had done not long ago, but then he'd been carrying an unconscious Victoria.

He was retracing the route, heading for the forested area, heading for where Tia had parked the car that evening. It was there, where in the confusion she had left the handbag. Would it still be there, Thomas wondered, continuing his reminiscence.

That time they had returned. That time when they had been invited in as guests. That time when the housekeeper, Maria, had prepared the guest room. The assumption by Letitia that they were a couple. She had left them in the lounge to finish the coffee that had been prepared.

Cynthia had looked at him, smiled and said, "Who will have the bed?"

Thomas reached the road, and crossed it. There was no traffic about at all. Then he walked to where the car had been parked and lo and behold, there it was, the handbag.

On his return to the hacienda, Thomas thought about that first night, when they had entered the guest room. The bed was at least a king size, the room had an en suite, a large wardrobe, a dresser and dressing table, a couple of side tables with lamps and an easy chair.

As he drew nearer the house, Thomas smiled at the thought of that night: the moment they looked at each other. He had said nothing, though did look at the chair and how comfortable that might be.

Then she had smiled and said to him, "It's a big bed. Stay on your side, won't you."

His pleasant thoughts of their first night together, were interrupted as he heard a car coming up the drive.

Thomas entered the house, and went straight up the stairs into the lounge where he saw Cynthia on the three-seater, with a pile of papers on her lap.

"Got it," he said, smiling and holding up the bag.

"So that's where you were," Tia said, smiling, putting the paperwork aside and accepting the bag he handed her. She opened it.

"Usual stuff, credit cards, keys, perfume, manicure set, brush, handkerchief, …"

Then looking up at Thomas, "You look slightly flushed, did you run?"

"Err, no, I was just thinking back to that first night here" he said, looking into her eyes and once more feeling his heart thumping in his chest.

He leaned closer to her, she lifted her head towards him, each holding the other's gaze.

The kiss should have been inevitable, however, as their lips almost touched …

"This is Juliette," Letitia said, entering the lounge.

They pulled back from each other. Thomas straightened up, turned and looked. Then both nodding a greeting to the newcomer.

Letitia spoke, "You may have wondered how it was I managed to find Victoria. Well, it was because of Juliette."

Cynthia gathered the papers, again placing them on her lap making room for Thomas to sit down next to her.

She briefly glanced over to Thomas next to her, her heart still pounding as she had anticipated the kiss that almost was.

He was looking at the newcomer.

Cynthia also sized up the new woman in the room. She was slightly taller than Letitia, but shorter than herself, she was slim, had long red hair and blue eyes behind fashionable glasses.

She smiled hello in return, let her eyes settle on Thomas for a lingering moment, then turned to Letitia, who took up the conversation again, "It was not long after I had found out about my father's notes on the deeds that he had, supposedly, placed on the back of the painting which he had loaned out to the museum. I was in town, with Juliette. We were just walking by the museum, so, I mentioned what I had found, told her about the painting, and that it had been stolen. She stopped in the street because she had just then remembered something…" She looked now at Juliette to continue the story.

Letitia sat down, her friend sat beside her and looked at Thomas and Cynthia in turn as she spoke, "I was in Australia, in Brisbane on the Gold Coast. I was, as Letitia had been, a bit of a wild child. I was in this casino, I was tired, felt a little lost and generally felt sorry for myself. Anyway, there was this guy, really hot, really handsome, but he made a beeline really for this, older woman. I could see so clearly that he was seducing her, charming her, then … later, I was sitting in a sort of bar and lounge area, slumped a little on a comfy couch, almost lying down. Had kicked off my shoes, then this guy and this older woman, sat themselves on the couch behind me. I'm pretty sure they hadn't seen me. Didn't think anyone was in close proximity, and I listened.

It was the woman who spoke the most. The guy was just, well, listening to her, paying attention, being really interested.

I later found out that she had been rather successful on the roulette wheel, picked up around $4000. Anyway, it was what she was saying that was interesting; what she had done, in the past. She told this guy that at one point, she had been a great cat burglar."

Juliette turned to Letitia, then faced Thomas and Tia again, "I don't know if the guy was really listening, or whether he thought she was just telling stories. I knew that he was after her money. Just knew that he was a con artist. Anyway, when they left, they headed for the adjacent hotel reception. I followed. Somehow, I wanted to warn her, tell her to, well, wake up and smell the coffee, but I had a feeling that first of all that wouldn't work. She was hooked, and secondly, I think she might well have been drugged. Her drink spiked or something, so I listened as she booked a room, a small suite as it happens. She was obviously well off. I got her name, even used a reception pen and wrote it down on a slip of paper, then went back to where I was staying. The whole event, had stirred in me, well, something. I booked a flight back home and left Australia two days later."

"Are you saying…" Thomas asked, having listened intently.

It was Letitia who answered, "Juliette told me the story that day that her name was Victoria, Victoria Lange."

"Wow, but, she was in London," Thomas said.

"Letitia and I searched together," Juliette said, again taking up the conversation," we looked up articles of art thefts in Europe all around that time, the late eighties and early nineties, found a couple that mentioned the likelihood of this thief being a woman.

"We also discovered, when trying to locate her whereabouts in Australia that she left, in fact the day after I had left to come back home."

"She went back to London," Letitia said. Then seeing from their expressions that they were probably wondering how she might have found this out, Letitia looked at her friend.

"I have a cousin in Brisbane. It was with him I was staying whilst over there, and he has a friend in the airline industry," Juliette said, smiling a them both.

"Also," Letitia said, "having the name, I did some searching and found out that a Miss Victoria Long had arrived in Bilbao, from

London, way back in 1989, four weeks before the painting was stolen. It didn't take much to figure out that this was the same woman. It had to be."

"After stealing the painting, she must have gone to Australia, then changed her name slightly," Juliette added.

"That all makes perfect sense," Cynthia said, "based on what we now know about Victoria. Still, London is a big place, how…"

"How did we find her?" Letitia interrupted, smiling and then again turned to Juliette.

"My cousin, in Australia, he was the one who had discovered she had gone back to England. Keeping in mind this was well over five years ago now. But, as well as finding that she had flown back the day after I had left Brisbane, he also found out that she had used an international removal company to ship her stuff over to London." Juliette pausing briefly as she looked across at Letitia, then over to Thomas and Cynthia who were listening intently. "As you know now, my father started a transport business. I run it now, but cousin Enrico has a courier service business in Brisbane. Must run in the family, and through some contacts he found out the address to which Victoria's goods were shipped."

"From then on," Letitia spoke, again taking over the conversation, "I personally searched her out, stayed a week in London, saw her, watched her and looked for any regular routine. Then, again working with Juliette here, we formed a plan."

"Which all went well until we discovered you on our trail," Juliette said, looking across at Thomas and Cynthia.

"But, just as well," Letitia said. "Without your help we not only wouldn't have got anywhere, but would have had a kidnapped woman on our hands and, well, we hadn't really planned any further …"

Silence fell in the room for a moment or two. "Oh my goodness," Cynthia suddenly said. She had glanced down at the papers on her lap, papers that had been in a box file in Letitia's father's study. Something had caught her eye.

There was further silence in the room, but now all eyes were fixed on Cynthia.

Trying hard to read what exactly it said in Spanish, she looked up, stood up and walked across to Letitia, "Look here. I think it says that the painting by Titian, Charles V, standing by a black horse, was purchased from a Johannes Acker in 1947! It was the name Johannes that stood out for me, is that right?"

Thomas, Juliette and Cynthia watched as Letitia read from the sheet of paper.

Looking up at Tia, then at the others, spoke, "Cynthia is right. The painting was purchased in 1947. My father bought it, from Johannes Acker."

"Then," Thomas said, thinking it through, "Then, surely, the Johannes Acker that asked Victoria to steal the painting, over forty years later, can't have been the same guy?"

"A son perhaps?" Juliette suggested.

"Or just a con," Cynthia said, "using a name that was known to be working with the authorities in returning stolen Nazi loot. We should ask Victoria what he looked like and how old he was."

"Give her a call," Thomas suggested.

"Good idea. I have the number belonging to this Sophie woman. I'll ring her now"

Cynthia reached for her phone and punched in the numbers.

Standing up she moved to the balcony doors, then turned to see Juliette leaning forwards and striking up a conversation with Thomas as she waited for her call to be answered.

Not one Spanish woman, but two to contend with, she thought, then a woman's voice answered.

Cynthia turned to face the window, "Hi, Sophie? This is Cynthia…"

The conversation lasted for some time, then Cynthia ended the call, turned and headed back to the three-seater where she sat down next to Thomas. Looking at the two women across from her she began to talk, also taking hold of Thomas's hand whilst she did so. An action that didn't go unnoticed.

"Well, they say timing is everything. It sure is, because just as I was speaking to Sophie, she and Victoria discovered something. More on that in a moment. I spoke first with Victoria, asked her for a description of the Johannes Acker that blackmailed her into stealing the painting. Turns out it might well have been the same man. She says he was in his mid-sixties, had thin greying hair and wore glasses, so it is possible that it was Johannes who sold the Titian to your father. However," Cynthia continued, briefly glancing across at Thomas whose hand she was still holding, then back at the two Spanish women, "Sophie, who works at this auction house in Paris, discovered a ledger that mentions the painting by Titian, Charles V in red tunic, standing by black horse, so, we know it was sold in Boston in 1947, to an anonymous buyer from Paris, but, it was sold later that same year in Paris, to a Sebastiaan Haan." Cynthia let all that register for a moment.

Then she continued, feeling Thomas's gaze upon her and his hand holding hers quite firmly, "With this information, Sophie rechecked something she had discovered earlier, a connection between Johannes Acker and a Roberto Solari, who was a renowned forger. Looking at the timeline, she now concludes that it could be that this Sebastiaan Haan and this Johannes Acker knew each other.

"The upshot is, they have a name and Sophie is going to involve a friend of hers and see if they can find the whereabouts of this Sebastiaan Haan.

"Finally," Cynthia went on, "something else to consider. If this guy Johannes sold the painting to your father and had a connection to a known forger..."

"Our painting could be a fake," Letitia finished.

"Still, 1947," Thomas said, not only liking it that Tia had grabbed his hand, but making sure to hold it firmly, "that's some time ago. Is this guy still going to be alive? Sebastiaan Haan, sounds Dutch or German."

T H E   P A S T ;

Period 16

The year 2017–Dusseldorf, Germany

Ninety-four-year-old Sebastiaan Haan had died, though his real name was Hess, and he was distantly related to Rudolph.

He died in a secure rest home attached to the prison. He died a lonely man.

Three days later, Lotte Gruthart received a package.

She was the only one who had sought him out and visited him, and this had been nearly three years ago. A one-time visit.

There had been very little in the way of any sort of conversation. She had found him to be a bitter and angry man, though she felt that perhaps his outward reflections were put on to hide an inner shame.

She was a relation. Her grandmother was his sister.

He had been a high-ranking Nazi in the war, had managed to reinvent himself from Hess to Haan, but had to eventually flee to Brazil.

That had been in 1948.

Eighteen years later however, he was captured when he had taken a holiday and had flown to Caracas. Later that year, in 1966, he was tried in the court in the Hague for war crimes and sentenced to life.

Lotte opened the package and began to read the letter that was on the top of a pile of handwritten papers. Later that evening she discovered that these were his memoirs. At first she was hesitant to even read the handwritten notes, knowing his crimes, and knowing what he had done and had been sentenced for.

To her relief his action during war time were only brief notations, a very short summary.

It was obvious to Lotte that he hadn't wanted to dwell on this part of his life.

She came to a part in his ramblings where he had arrived in Paris …

April, 1947

I took a liking to this painting…Lotte read and was soon absorbed into the narrative. Her imagination took her along with the words, took her to Paris, to an auction house…

Sebastiaan waited a while, listened and watched as the price rose, then, when he sensed a hesitance, he raised his paddle.

He was well pleased with himself. The war was behind him, he had managed to integrate into the French lifestyle, had made some useful connections and had not only secured himself financially but with the skills he had developed during war time, had reinvented himself, false papers and documents, and so had gone from a German Nazi to a Dutch industrialist with connections to the underground freedom movements.

He was pleased with himself, for having read the provenance of the painting he had purchased and having some knowledge of art, he knew the price had been good and he would easily resell it at quite a profit.

He was in the process of heading for the sales office when a man, of a similar age to him, suddenly stood in his path.

"Sorry. Couldn't get here sooner. The painting you have purchased, it's stolen Nazi loot and I have instructions to return it to its rightful owners"

The young man's voice had been firm, assertive and full of confidence.

But Sebastiaan, pausing only momentarily, was not to be denied. He was also assertive and confident, and looking this newcomer straight in the eye said, "Sorry, you have the wrong painting. This work by Titian has been in the Americas since the mid-1860s, so can't possibly have been Nazi loot."

"So," Sebastiaan continued "who are you exactly and what's your game." He did not once lose eye contact with the man before him.

"Johannes, Johannes Acker," the man replied. "I work with the French authorities. I have this painting on a list of stolen art. Are you sure about the provenance?" Though he had been more than a little stunned at the response, he felt he had recovered well and quickly, while maintaining eye contact with the man.

"I'm sure. Check with the auction house. It was sold only a month ago, in Boston. You need to amend your records. Good day to you," Sebastiaan said, and moved past Johannes to head to the sales desk.

Thrown off stride for a moment, not expecting a response as assertive as that, Johannes had to regroup and rethink.

Fifteen minutes later, as Sebastiaan stepped from the auction house, Johannes once more approached, "How about we make a deal," he said. "How about we make a copy?"

Sebastiaan stopped and once more sized up the young man before him. Then he replied, "You work with the authorities, at least, so you say, yet, you suggest making a forgery?"

"I work with the authorities, yes. It gains me access to places, but I have my own agenda, as I believe you have too."

Then, seeing he had this man attention, he went on, "You know this painting's provenance, but you don't look like a collector of art, more like, someone who knows how to make a deal," Johannes said, hoping he had read the man before him correctly.

"Meet me in Cafe Orleans in Montmartre; one hour," Sebastiaan said then, hailing a taxi, left Johannes Acker standing on the kerb.

"Paintings, forgeries? What were these two up to?" Lotte said to herself, putting down the memoirs to prepare her dinner.

THE PRESENT;

Cannes

Sunday afternoon 2nd June

Roberto Solari sat in the warm sun in a comfy chair on the balcony and was smiling as he looked out over the glossy Mediterranean sea.

He was in the company of two women, and the now ninety year-old was fondly reminiscing.

Sophie had easily tracked him down where he lived in the apartment that had belonged to his sister who had passed away three years earlier.

She had introduced herself, had asked if he spoke English in order to relate to the woman she had brought with her, Victoria Lange.

She had added that Victoria was a renowned cat burglar from the mid-eighties and he had only been too pleased to talk to them both, saying his English was adequate.

Not long after their arrival Victoria told him his command of the English language was more than adequate and both women helped him prepare some drinks to take to the balcony, noticing his right arm was constantly shaking from Parkinson's.

Settling down on the balcony in the sun, Sophie explained the reason for their visit.

"I know," Sophie began, having taken a sip of the cool wine, "that you knew a Jan Smettens, copied a Gauguin for him. I was involved in locating both the original and the copy, thanks to a friend of mine. Now, I want to know if you also knew a guy called Johannes Acker."

The old man looked at Sophie, then at the other woman in his presence, Victoria, then looked out to sea and began talking.

"The Gauguin. I remember it well, because it was the first copy I made. Jan Smettens, yes, I recall him too, from what I heard and read, the painting, the original, was used to smuggle diamonds."

"And yes," Roberto said, glancing at the French woman, "I read also about you ma'amoiselle. As for you," this directing at Victoria, "I heard about a woman cat burglar, mid to late eighties, yes, never caught…"

Neither Sophie nor Victoria spoke. They glanced at each other then waited for the forger to continue.

"But, this other man, Acker," Roberto said, shaking his head. He looked at the women in turn, saw they were attentive, and knew by now that they weren't here to arrest him, so again looking out to sea, he went on, "came to me. Heard about me. Never introduced himself. He was young, only a little older than me I think. He was arrogant, but I was interested when he asked if I wanted to make a copy. I had a studio apartment in Monaco, at the time.

"But, this place, originally it was mine. Many years later I gave it to my sister. When she passed a few years ago I took the opportunity to come here to live as the sun is warmer, better for me. Anyway, this Acker guy," Roberto continued, shifting slightly in his chair, his bad arm not shaking quite as much as earlier, "he had a nice painting. I know my art and artists. This one was a Titian, the subject was Emperor Charles V, standing by a big black horse. When I first saw it, I thought maybe it was the son, King Phillip, but the face was Charles, so, I made a copy."

Roberto fell silent for a moment. Sophie asked, "So, if he didn't introduce himself, how…"

The old man turned and smiled at Sophie, then answered, "I do research on artists. Of course, I love painting, love to learn techniques, learn new pigments, how to mix how to blend how to make, when to first sketch then paint, or just straight into paint.

I study books, and for this one, had to study horse. Never done a horse before, always people–portraits.

"I also research this young man. I find out he had partner, Sebastiaan Haan. I remember the name. He was a forger, documents, passports and so on. He was to make copies of sales record, provenance for painting.

"I went to this cafe every day for my lunch, my wine, my coffee. Owner became a friend over the years. He told me, saw the two men together."

Again Roberto drifted off into silence, taking a sip of his wine and staring out to sea.

Sophie noted the expression on his face had changed. The smile had gone. "Roberto?" she prompted.

After another moment or two, he turned to look at Sophie and Victoria, looking from one to the other, his eyes settling on Sophie, then said, "Acker, not a nice young man, but Haan, he was not a nice man either."

"My friend at the cafe," the old man went on, "he had been in Paris during the war. He recognised this Haan man. He was not a Dutch industrialist, as he claimed, but he was a Nazi, he told me. Then he told me of the time that he had an opportunity to speak with Acker, but as they were talking, this Haan chap saw them talking, most likely saw the concern of on their faces."

Another brief pause, "The police were informed, but, before they could get to him, he was gone. Never heard from again … my friend says that Acker knew."

"That sounds about right," Sophie said. "Johannes Acker used this knowledge, just as he used knowledge he had on you Victoria, to steal that painting. By the way Roberto, we are talking about the same painting by Titian here."

"Bilbao," Roberto said, interrupting Sophie, looking at Victoria, "you took it from the museum in Bilbao!"

"I did, yes," Victoria answered. "As Sophie said, this Johannes Acker had information on me, blackmailed me into stealing it. Now that I know this other story, I am so glad I decided to move away straight away. He was no doubt going to have me arrested anyway, what a b … I'm glad he's dead."

"Yes," Roberto said, "boating accident in Switzerland."

"Is there anything you don't know?" Sophie asked, surprised.

Roberto had his smile back, "Oh, many things, but this I knew. He was, not a nice man, but I am a forger of paintings, and you are a thief, or were a thief," he said, smiling at Victoria.

Victoria smiled back, taking a liking to this old man. Despite his illness he still had a twinkle in his eyes, and, according to what Sophie had told her on the train journey down from Paris, he had been an accomplished artist.

Taking a sip of the cool wine, and enjoying the warm sun as she sat on the balcony, she reflected on these past days. In fact, only a week had passed since she was drugged and kidnapped from London.

A week!

It seemed like so much longer. A ferry journey she didn't remember at all.

Then waking to find herself tied up in the back of a van, with just one light on the ceiling to prevent total blackness.

The time those doors opened and she had been bundled into the house, having been blindfolded first.

Then, as the cloth came away, her hands were tied together and two young men, one with a ladder, attached the rope to a rafter. A woman was standing before her, one hand grasping her hair at the back of her head, the other hand clasping her upper arm.

She was still dizzy from whatever drug they had given her. She recalls the strength of the young woman, her arm in a vice like grip, the hold on her hair preventing her from struggling as the two men tied the rope.

They then left. Her hair and arm were released.

So much had happened, in such a short time.

Knowing why she had been taken and brought to Spain, she felt a little confidence growing. They needed information, She would give this Teremos woman something.

To gain time, to think things through. Then, again she passed out. Perhaps the drug was still having some effect on her. Perhaps hanging there sapped whatever energy she might have still had.

Then she woke up in a hotel room, and realised she had been rescued, but who were her rescuers, and how had they found her.

The escape by plane. The drive through a dark French countryside.

Victoria glanced over to Sophie, who was chatting to Roberto, recalling when she had stepped out before her as Victoria was about to enter the British Embassy.

So much had occurred, in so little time. And now, a week on her new friends and rescuers, had couriered her house keys to a man in London who would go to her house and fetch her passport.

This man, apparently the one who had suspected and warned of her abduction, would then travel across to Paris so that she would have documents to get back to England with.

It was arranged that he would be there on Tuesday.

She was looking forwards to meeting him and thanking him for his part.

But first, she was on this trip to Cannes to speak with a known art forger in order to hopefully track down a painting belonging to the woman who had organised her abduction.

Crazy, she thought to herself, you couldn't make it up.

Taking another sip of white wine, she tuned into the conversation Sophie was having. Realising that they were now conversing in French, she picked up something about being on the Mediterranean coast and tuned out again to take in the view.

Then after some moments of silence, each quite relaxed in the warm sunshine watching the many boats that were on the water, it was Sophie who broke the silence, "So, you definitely made a copy of the Titian, you say in 1946, for this Johannes Acker who you believe was working with a Sebastiaan Haan. What we can't figure out is why this Johannes should ask, or I should say, persuade Victoria to steal it from the museum in Bilbao in 1989, and, how, if the painting was originally bought by the Teremos family in 1946, probably not long after you finished the copy, did Johannes know it was now in the museum. And, was this the original or the copy, and where is the other one?"

"Ah, good questions. Well, talking with you today, it has given me a chance to think things through. As you know, I like to do my research. I know that this Haan man, was indeed a Nazi. I also believe that Johannes knew this, but he needed Haan's help with forged papers. I also think that Haan would have been suspicious of Johannes Acker.

"So, maybe he double-crossed him. Maybe Acker wanted to sell the copy to the Teremos family, and somehow get his hands on the original that, according to your findings, Miss Sophie, was purchased by Haan." After pausing briefly, Roberto continued his reasoning, "Then, somehow, Haan switched them, but having being identified as a Nazi, he had to escape quickly, probably leaving the painting behind, figuring that it had been Acker who betrayed him. But, the original was now safely with the Teremos family.

"Somehow though, Acker found out many years later that he had been duped by Haan that he had the forgery, so, sought out the whereabouts of the original Titian and found a way to have it stolen, by you, Victoria, as it turns out.

"But that is my thinking, it may not be right."

"It does make sense. It could well be as you just imagine, but, it still does not get us closer to where the original or copy of the Titian is now," Sophie said.

"And we know that Johannes Acker died." Victoria added.

"I think you should look into that accident. Find out where in Switzerland he was; who he was with. The answer may lie there" Roberto said.

Meanwhile, over 900 kilometres due west

"I think we should go to Switzerland. The answer may be there," Cynthia said.

Thomas was finishing packing his suitcase.

Cynthia was already packed and ready to go.

The previous day Thomas had formulated an e-mail to DP in London, heard back almost immediately, and Juliette offered to post the keys to the address given using a courier that would guarantee delivery the following day.

DP had responded again and informed them that he himself would deliver the passport to Victoria in Paris on Tuesday.

Thomas had been thinking through all the various aspects of their adventure, but heard her voice and registered what she had said.

"Switzerland?" he queried, lifting the suitcase from the bed to the floor and looking at her.

Her light green eyes were studying him. He studied her: her brunette hair, her tall figure. She was smiling at him.

They had shared this guest bedroom since they arrived in the early hours of Thursday.

Thomas recalled that time, when she had asked the question, "but who is going to have the bed?"

He smiled back, but then asked again, "Switzerland?"

Cynthia looked at the man before her. The man she had, when he was a boy and she a girl, been unkind to, badly so, even having him beaten up.

The man who had without hesitation set out to follow up on trying to rescue an unknown woman. A man who had daringly flown the plane out of here and even more daringly had flown back.

A man who looked for the best in a person. A man who forgave her. A man who, this last night here in the hacienda, had made love to her, so gentle, so sweet, so unselfish and with such caring and love.

Cynthia took a deep breath, then said, "Yes, it's where this Johannes Acker died in a boating accident back in 1990. Now this was less than a year after he asked, or really forced, Victoria to steal the painting. I feel this needs to be, let's say, investigated more deeply. Why was he there? Did he live there? Did he have a house there? More importantly, who was he with? Hopefully it will help us to find out why, the man who was involved with a forger in 1947, persuaded Victoria to steal that very same painting, in 1989, over forty years later."

"With Sophie and Victoria seeing this forger in Cannes, and with the tornado case all wrapped up back home, thanks in the main to Claire, this is really the only avenue left to investigate. I see what you mean," Thomas concluded.

"Will you sort out flights to get us to Lucerne. I'll find us a hotel."

EPILOGUE

Wednesday 5ᵗʰ June 2019

The powerful jet engines droned on relentlessly in the night sky over the north Atlantic. Far below lay the vast area of Greenland.

Thomas was awake. Beside him Cynthia was asleep in the comfortable business class seat. He smiled and looked at her fondly for a moment.

Less than three weeks ago, he had been asked the question, "who are you?" as he had walked up the path towards the house. A house he had been bequeathed.

A good question he thought, reflecting on these past weeks. He certainly felt he was a different person now. So much had happened in such a short time.

Like a small rock rolling down a snow covered hill, gathering speed and gathering snow. Growing bigger and bigger, until it reached the bottom.

He felt a little bit like that.

The momentum had gone, the action had stopped.

Thomas closed his laptop, looked across at the sleeping woman beside him, then recapped in his mind all that Claire had written.

All about case file 1988. Robert's letter to him, giving him the house, had asked him to investigate case file 1988. It's where it had begun.

He recalls the moment he first stepped into that room, the room with the keypad lock. The room with the shelves and shelves of books and folders.

Then he'd discovered the file, right there on the main desk, in front of the computer that Robert had named. 'Search Engine'.

A file he had opened, had started to read, then the e-mail that had pinged through. The e-mail that had started that rock rolling down the hill.

The cryptic message; the call for help.

Thomas sighed, carefully leaned across Cynthia and brushed a few strands of brunette hair from her lovely face, then sat back again and thought back.

How to put things in order in his mind. His school friend Robert had sure set him a task, but what an adventure.

It was night time and the cabin lights had been turned off. Most people seemed to be asleep, here and there Thomas noticed a reading light as the British Airways jet flew to its destination, Vancouver.

Lucerne had not been necessary. Just as he was about to search for flights, and Tia was scrolling on her laptop to find a hotel, a call came through to her from Victoria.

Early on in the conversation, she held her hand up in a stop motion, he ceased looking for flights and waited.

When she had finally finished with the call she explained all.

Victoria and Sophie had travelled to Cannes, to visit an old man by the name of Roberto Solari. He had been a forger of paintings, apparently quite a good one. He was able to relate the story of how he came to copy the Titian, told of his knowledge of Johannes Acker, as well as a chap named Sebastiaan Haan, who was really a Nazi by the name of Hess.

With this information Sophie had contacted her Dutch policeman friend. He, already on the trail of the Titian, was ahead of them. Together with the German police, and with the help of information they had received two years earlier from a relation of Sebastiaan Hess about his with Johannes Acker and the location of a house in Lucerne where many paintings were found, including both the original and copy of the Titian.

Letitia would now, thanks to proof that Sophie and her could supply, get the painting back. The copy was destroyed.

They took all that in and related it all to a very joyful Letitia. As they had already packed, they had driven to Bilbao where Cynthia returned her rental and Thomas had to fill in numerous forms with regard to the rental he had crashed.

They then flew to Paris.

The image of a little rock rolling down the hill gathering snow and speed again came to his mind as the plane flew through the night.

Cynthia had picked a hotel in central Paris for three nights.

Though Thomas wanted to reflect on those nights, memorable and wonderful nights, he focused on retaining some order of his thoughts, to get the whole story sorted out in his mind.

On the Monday they had met up with Victoria and been introduced to Sophie, who wanted to know the full story in detail as she told of her connection to the whole case. In fact, of course, Thomas reasoned in his mind, the central connection in all of it, was Robert.

It had been Robert's tireless efforts that had brought about the rescue of over thirty missing and taken people, men and women, and children as well.

It had been his delving, figuring out and pursuing that had saved Claire.

Claire who had asked him that question, "who are you?"

Claire, who, when Thomas spoke to her at length on the Sunday evening, had related all that had happened on her end.

He had thanked her profusely and asked her to write it down so he could digest it all. This she had done, and this he had read on the plane, as Tia slept.

In the overall picture, Thomas thought, it had been Claire's work on case file 1988 that had brought about the connection to Sophie that had brought about the conclusion, and found the Titian.

It had been Claire's work that had connected with Millie and subsequently led along a trail that solved the case of her mother's death and the location of the gold coins that had been stolen.

Another little rock that had gathered speed, Thomas was thinking.

But now, now the rock had stopped. The momentum no longer required, the adrenalin subsided.

No wonder Cynthia was fast asleep, but he wouldn't be able to sleep himself until he had the whole story sorted in his mind.

He thought back to Tuesday, when they had met DP. Desmond Peter Janssen, the man who had started that little particular rock rolling.

His meeting with Victoria resulted in blushes from both and they flew back to London together later that day.

Victoria hugging them and crying a lot.

He and Tia had stayed one more night. Again he wanted to linger on thoughts of that, but again he pushed those memories away, for now.

They said goodbye to Sophie and flew to London where they boarded a flight to Vancouver. From there they would return home to Myrtle Creek, via Portland.

This adventure had come to an end, but Thomas thought about the many files in Robert's room.

Who am I Claire? He thought, almost aloud it seemed. I am a different person, as are you, as is Cynthia, as are many others, all because of you Robert, my friend. The searcher.

May you rest in peace.

Thomas closed his eyes, now he allowed himself to think of those nights…smiling he fell asleep almost immediately.

BOOK 2

The Ornate Box

PROLOGUE

Leiden

The year 1744

The sound of the horses hooves echoed around the buildings in the Pieterskerk area of the city on a rainy and slightly misty afternoon as the day grew to a close.

A group of children were playing with a wooden hoop and didn't let the rain stop their fun.

The wagon driver shouted a command and the horses stopped.

Christoffer Rosenborg stepped from the covered buggy and looked up at the facade of the house.

His residence for the next three years.

A man came from the house, approached, bowed a greeting and gestured for the new arrival to enter the house. In the doorway a woman was waiting.

Seventeen-year-old Christoffer nodded and smiled at the man who then saw to the driver and the luggage and made his way up the path towards the waiting woman.

Born in Copenhagen into a wealthy family, Christoffer, the youngest, had an urge for adventure. He'd realised early on that, as the youngest, he would be the least likely to take over the family estate and business.

His two brothers were several years older than him, and with his father mostly away and his mother involved in a variety of organisations and clubs, Christoffer would regularly be found by the docks.

He watched the ships come and go, made notations, and would find out where they had come from and were going to.

He was a regular at the shipping offices and, as he was known to be from an influential family, he had the run of the place and was welcomed and given whatever information he was asking for. And so, by the time he was sixteen, he knew what he wanted to do. Sail the seas of the world.

Armed with letters of introduction, other correspondence had already been sent ahead, with his parents' backing, financially secure, he boarded a Dutch merchant vessel two days after his seventeenth birthday.

This particular ship he had already seen and boarded for a look around as it regularly plied between Amsterdam and the Danish city. He had befriended several of the crew and knew the captain. Christoffer was now enrolled in the University of Leiden, an institution that had been founded back in 1575 by William I of Orange. He would study shipping and trade for the next three years.

He nodded and said "Hello" to the woman who showed him to his rooms, three in total, occupying the whole of the second floor.

Over the next few days he familiarised himself with the surrounding area and the route to the university and it was on a Sunday afternoon, the day before he was due to begin lessons at the university that he spotted her.

She was sitting reading on the steps of what he presumed was her house in the Kloksteeg, a narrow lane opposite the big church, a block away from where he resided.

She had long dark hair, more unusual as a vast amount of the folks here were blonde. She wore a printed cotton dress, and white socks in black shoes. Christoffer figured it was her Sunday outfit, probably as she had been to church in the morning.

She looked up at him as he approached, and he was attracted to her pretty face. Her eyes were somewhere between dark green and brown and she gave him a smile.

The reaction made his heart flutter. It seemed, momentarily not too sure what to say. He stopped and after a moment, began, with the little Dutch that he knew, to start a conversation.

She smiled some more, then gestured for him to sit next to her on the stone steps.

Nearby a group of younger children were playing marbles. A young couple, obviously courting, walked by and a clock chimed the hour twice whilst he was with her.

She was curious and interested in his story, as he was in hers.

Later, as it was beginning to get darker and a little cooler, he got up, nodded a thank you, said he hoped to see her again, and walked back to his accommodation.

He figured her to be about the same age as him. He'd learned from her about her ancestors, known as the Pilgrims, who had escaped from England, settled here, had purchased land, and had lived in this area for about twelve years before around half of them decided to move away to travel across the sea once more and head for North America.

The girl, whose forefathers stayed, loved to read history. Her name was Tineke and she told Christoffer how her ancestors, the ones that decided to leave, had sailed on a ship called the Mayflower, back in 1620, over a hundred of them, then another group left the following year on a ship called the Fortune.

Further ships sailed in the year 1623, and the second Mayflower journey left in 1629.

Tineke enjoyed relating all that she had learned to this young man whom she not only found handsome, but who was such an interested listener.

Christoffer found this history fascinating and was in awe of the pioneering spirit of these Pilgrims. As he walked up the path to his dwelling, he smiled to himself. Whilst what she had told him was interesting indeed, it was her smile, her face and her eyes that were far more captivating.

He was also thankful that his little knowledge of the Dutch language had been helpful, and he recalled the time when the captain of a ship that regularly docked in Copenhagen, had spent time with him.

He had, over time, befriended some of the crew, and had once before set foot aboard the schooner, the very same that would take him to Amsterdam three years later. The captain had spent well over an hour with him walking around his ship and explaining the way it worked, the various tasks necessary to sail, the equipment used, and he had shown the boy, only fourteen at the time, the many decks, cabins and cargo spaces.

It had been that day, when walking home that Christoffer had decided that he wanted to be part of that, to experience sailing the seas, to visit foreign lands.

He wanted adventure.

The first part of that adventure had begun. He had left home and was about to start studying at the university. He would make sure he focused on learning, though as he entered his rooms that Sunday afternoon, his thoughts were on the young girl he had just met.

On 3 October of his first year there, when the city was celebrating the end of the siege in 1574 which had ended Spanish rule, he came upon a store.

One of several book stores as the city was known for its printing works.

He had been drawn to what he saw displayed in the small window of the store:

a book about the various trade routes in the far east.

Explaining to his group of friends that he would catch up with them soon, he stepped inside the store.

Whilst the shopkeeper prepared to take the book he had asked for from the window display, Christoffer looked around and saw an interesting map.

Among his new friends, including Tineke who he had been seeing regularly but was unwell that day, there were several others who were also descendants of the Pilgrims that had come over from England.

The map he had found, a pencil drawing in fact, was of the city, dated 1627 and Christoffer noted a faint scribble of a signature, Mercator.

The name rang a bell. Then his eye was drawn to a wooden box.

Picking this up, he studied it for some time. The box was the size of a large book, around thirty centimetres in length, eighteen centimetres in width and about eight centimetres in depth.

The lid was hand painted and carved with a few scrolls either side of, what in the Dutch language was known as a 'Tafareel' a scene, in this case a landscape which looked to be a faraway land. In this landscape there was a horse and wagon, and a man standing by the wagon, speaking, it looked like, to the occupant.

Christoffer admired the details and the colours, and noticed the matching scroll and carvings along the sides of the box.

The lid did not have a clasp or lock, but fitted snugly and was hinged all along the back.

He opened the box, saw it was lined in a soft red coloured felt cloth, looked at it for some time. As the storekeeper had by now come over to him with the asked for book in his hands, Christoffer was told that the box was about eighty or ninety years old as it dated from around the middle of the last century. It was possibly used as a Bible box.

He purchased the book, the map and the box.

Two years later, in the year 1747, Christoffer, now aged twenty, and standing just over six foot tall, completed his studies and was taken on by the VOC, better known as the 'Dutch East India Company'.

He had knowledge of trading and bartering, knew about cargo and weight distribution, and had learned about trade routes, map reading and navigation. He now spoke several languages, for along with his native Danish, he was fluent in Dutch and could converse in Spanish, French and English.

He was taken on as a negotiator with the added role of managing the loading, unloading and weight distribution of cargo: a senior officer on board at just the age of twenty, quite a feat for the young man.

He knew he would have to work hard and show his mettle to gain the respect from the crew.

Additionally, he would document procedures, contacts, goods sold and received and journal the travels.

A correspondent for the company.

Just before Christmas, on a cold but snow-free day, he left the house near Pieterskerk, thanked and said goodbye to the people who had looked after him, and boarded the very same buggy that had brought him there.

Tineke, the only girl he counted among his groups of friends, was there to say goodbye. The hug was tight and long, then she pulled away, briefly planted a kiss on his lips and stood back.

Christoffer coloured a little, smiled back, then got into the buggy.

Three days later he settled himself in his roomy cabin on board a three-masted ship of the Dutch East India Company, and placed the ornate wooden box in the top drawer of a chest of drawers, inside which he had placed the old map he had purchased, along with some other bits and bobs.

When he put the box away, he thought back to the day he had purchased it, a day which he recalled he also spent with his new friends, several of whom were descendants of the original Pilgrims who had stayed behind as other had left to travel across the Atlantic.

Looking out of his porthole as night was falling he smiled and began to think.

His first journey was going to the east, to be to Java, and he was excited about the prospect. They were due to set sail the following day, but he wondered, where would his travels take him, and would he one day too sail to the west and visit the Americas.

One thing Christoffer did not know, or could not foresee, was that he would never return to his home town, or see his family again.

As he closed his eyes for his first night on board, his thoughts went to the lovely Tineke.

⤷

T H E   P R E S E N T;

Boston

Friday 27th March 2020

The city was in lockdown.

Christina Small sat on the leather sofa in the front room of her brownstone house that had been in her family for generations. Her laptop was open in front of her on the low coffee table and she had several sheets of paper, an old diary and two larger journals spread out around her, some on the table, others on the sofa beside her.

With her reading glasses perched on her forehead, she was looking at the screen.

Upstairs, having taken himself to the guest room, her fiancé, Sam, was asleep.

He had contracted the Covid virus, had a slight fever, a cough and a light headache. He wasn't unwell enough to warrant hospitalisation, and assured her he would be well soon and just needed sleep.

The pandemic virus had travelled the world. Already in some countries there had been outbreaks which struck the elderly and those with underlying health problems the hardest. The death tolls was rising. Thousand were being admitted to hospitals in Italy, in France, in the United Kingdom, in Canada and in the States.

Sam didn't smoke, and was normally very healthy. Christina, known to her friends as Chrissie, had not been infected, and though obviously concerned for the man she was in love with, felt that he would be fine.

They had planned to marry, but this had been put on hold for now.

Her good friend Tammy, who lived in New York, and was the chef and owner of a restaurant, had had to temporarily close her business as the city was also in lockdown. They had chatted on a video call for nearly an hour earlier.

Chrissie turned her focus away from the screen, slid her glasses down and picked up one of the journals that had recently arrived.

Sam and Chrissie had been in a strong and steady relationship since last June, so shortly after the new year Sam had asked their friend Sophie from Paris, and his policeman friend Martijn from Amersfoort, to oversee the packing company as they cleared his apartment in Rotterdam.

Sam had himself driven all the way to Moncton in New Brunswick to pick up his possessions from there as well.

The shipment from the Netherlands had arrived ten days ago.

Now, in lockdown, and limited to going out for essentials or exercise only, Chrissie had taken the opportunity to locate and begin reading the journals that had been written by Sam's great-grandfather, who had been a British ambassador.

Samuel Price, who Sam had been named after, had served as an ambassador in Copenhagen, Cape Town, Paris, The Hague and Vancouver, and was an avid art collector.

The journals were not only his life stories telling of his work in these cities and countries, but also a record of paintings he had bought and sold over the years.

Two of these painting had proved instrumental in catching a thief, discovering a forgery, and finding a cache of diamonds that had been stolen over a hundred years ago.

Chrissie turned the pages and read the life story of a man who's great-grandson was going to be her husband.

She was just about to go upstairs and check on Sam, when she was drawn to a painting, the photo of a painting in the journal.

She read the description and details. The ambassador had purchased it at an auction in The Hague in 1912. The painting, measuring 34"x39" was called 'The Lovesick Maiden' and painted by Jan Steen.

There was something in the painting that had triggered a memory, but, what was it?

Taking her reading glasses off and placing them on the table, she got up, leaving the journal open on the page, took a last look at the photograph then left to go upstairs and check on Sam.

Opening the guest room door slowly and quietly, she noticed he was sat up in bed, laptop open.

"Hey', you're supposed to be resting" she said, smiling at him and speaking only just above a whisper.

Sam smiled.

"I can't go out and visit clients at present," he answered, his voice still sounding a little rough, "but with the help of technology, I can provisionally view the items they have to sell, and do at least some provenance checks. I can then confirm everything when I can see the items, and, of course, once we can have auctions again. My feeling, though, is that we could still hold some sales, but do them online only. Anyway, I am feeling a little better and doing something is better than doing nothing."

"Okay then. Can I get you anything?" Chrissie asked, staying by the door as they had agreed no physical contact until he was better.

Sam looked over at the side table, noticed he still had plenty of water, looked back at Chrissie, "No, I'm good thanks. How is Tammy? You said you were going to video call her?"

"Yes, we had a good chat, her restaurant is closed for a while, so, like me, she too is going to do some research into the past. She wants to see what more she can find out about her great-grandfather, Percivald Quinton."

"That will be interesting. Hope she can find out more about when he came to Boston to purchase those two seascapes, and how Beatrice Parker fits in."

"Yes, she said the same. I still find it uncanny that he was at the very same auction as my grandfather that day way back when," Chrissie said. "I'm looking through your great-grandfather's journals, and something caught my eye in one of the paintings he purchased. It's another Jan Steen. We know about the 'Feast of St Nicholas', well, this one is called 'The Lovesick Maiden'. I know how she feels," Chrissie said, smiling.

"He bought it in The Hague, in 1912, before he went back to London, and then on to Vancouver, but I don't know what is was that drew my attention. Going to a have another look at it, Sure you're okay?"

"I'm fine," he said, then blew her a kiss and smiled.

She smiled back and left the room.

Bounding down the stairs, she first went into the kitchen, to get a fresh coffee as she had let the previous one get cold.

Preparing a fresh pot, she thought about Ally. She was once very much in love with Sam and a rival for his affection, but was now a close friend. She had, in this very kitchen, relinquished her chance with Sam, as she had seen how much Sam meant to Chrissie, and had also said she thought it was likely, very likely that Sam would choose Chrissie. It would be a decision Sam might have difficulty in making, and so Ally had left.

Chrissie smiled. Ally was such a lovely person. She'd gone through a lot and was left for dead at one point, and probably would have been, had it not been for Sam. Chrissie decided to give her a call.

Coffee made, she took a mug through to the lounge and picked up her phone, looking again at the photo of the painting in the journal.

Whilst the phone was ringing, Chrissie noticed the packing box Sam's books and journals had come in, noticed the label on the side, the destination and where it had come from: Rotterdam.

THE PAST;

Period 1

The year 1668–Rotterdam

Bibiana flicked back her long dark brown hair, opened the top drawer of the chest of drawers that was secured to the cabin wall, took out the ornate wooden box, closed the drawer with her elbow and sat herself down on the bench like seat that was placed at the end of the bed and opened the lid of the box.

She was already used to the movement of the ship as it plied through the waters of the Atlantic Ocean.

Taking some papers out, also several items of jewellery, she then came upon the black leather pouch.

Bibiana thought back…

Five days ago. It had been such a foggy day, with the sun barely penetrating through the mist making it hard to tell what time of the day it was.

She smiled as she recalled the eerily feeling of her surroundings as she headed for her grandfather and grandmother's cottage in the Haringvliet district of the city.

She had come to say goodbye.

Her grandmother had been quite ill and had not been able to attend her wedding in Middelburg two weeks earlier. Her grandfather, Karel, had stayed with her…

Bibiana took hold of the leather pouch and held it tightly, knowing what was inside. She sighed, looked out of the porthole and let a tear roll down her cheek.

Had she done the right thing, she wondered.

She had been attracted to him, having been invited to a dance at a country estate in the province of Zeeland.

He had talked with her, danced with her, had been charming, and he sure was a handsome man.

Johan De Reder, a wealthy landowner, almost forty years of age to her twenty three.

They were on their way to South America.

Together with a group of business men, Johan had financed a fleet of ships to set out and conquer Paramaribo in Surinam. This had been successful. Subsequently, a fort had been established to protect their conquest and the lucrative trade that could be set up, in particular sugar, a highly desirable commodity.

They'd taken over several plantations, and one of these was now to be her home.

Bibiana put the pouch back, put her jewellery and papers on the top of it, closed the box lid and stood up.

She was tall and slim, had olive skin and green eyes. She was well-educated, spoke four languages fluently and had good knowledge of the shipping industry, trade, cargo handling and finances. Both her father, who died when she was a little girl, and her grandfather, were mariners.

She opened the drawer in the chest, and put the ornate wooden box back.

She looked at the painted scene on the lid and thought about who had given her this present at their wedding. It had been her mother-in-law, who said she had it specially made for her, and that it had been painted by someone named Jan van Goyen, which meant nothing to Bibiana, but she thanked her moth-er-in-law for it as, despite having only met her once before, she liked her husband's mother.

The relationship with her husband however, was soon to deteriorate.

The year 1671

All had been well at first. The journey to Paramaribo, and her first time at sea, was smooth. The arrival at her plantation house, all good. She had staff and servants who were attentive and welcoming. Again, all good, then, got pregnant. Still all well and good.

But, when the time came for the baby to be born, it wasn't good any more. The birth was difficult, there were complications, the baby, a boy, died almost instantly and Bibiana was quite sick for some time.

Her husband did not respond at all in the way she hoped, or thought would be natural.

He was angry. With her. Blamed her for losing the baby.

Suddenly she saw a different side to him.

No longer the charming man she met and had fallen in love with. No longer the handsome gentleman she had danced with and gone to parties with.

He became bitter.

Then, one afternoon, a few weeks later the doctor had told her she would not be able to have any children. Upon her telling him, he flew into a rage, blamed her again, then struck her and left the room.

She was shocked, but became resolute. She had a fighting spirit. She moved into a different bedchamber, concentrated on getting better and healthier, and after an evening when he had been drinking and had once more slapped her across her face, she made up her mind. Time to plan, time to scheme and plot. Time to find a way to leave.

Fortunately he sailed back to the home country a few days later. Excellent.

She had built up a rapport with the staff and servants and they with her for she treated them with fondness and consideration.

As she often went to the docks to check out what had come into the trading post, she had also built relations with the workers there, as well as with many of the visiting ships and their masters and crew.

Her plan began to formulate.

She became fitter and fitter and was feeling more and more confident, both in herself and in her plan which was coming together.

He arrived back after seven months away, with a young blonde girl in tow. He made a point of doting on her, and even moved her into his bedchamber. This was all fine with Bibiana. He would leave her alone.

She would receive secret messages from time to time, with regard to ships due and their destination, and one such message was the one she had expected, and was waiting for. Perfect timing.

Her husband had thrown a party.

There was plenty of drinking and eating and merry making. She had, at one point, sneaked a look at the various people who had come. She noticed her husband's new blonde girl prancing about in an expensive dress and shook her head.

Poor girl, she thought, then got ready to put her plan, finally, into action.

The following morning, very early, she left her room. Her luggage was already in place and a wagon came around to one of the side doors of the plantation house on the opposite side to where her husband and his mistress lay sleeping.

The staff was tearful and helpful, and helped her load the wagon. Two young men drove her to the docks.

Here too, she had help. Folks assisted her on board a ship that had docked the previous afternoon. She was given a large cabin and when the sun had just made an appearance, the ship slipped its moorings and sailed away.

By the time her husband woke, a little before noon, he did not noticed anything out of the ordinary until late that afternoon, by which time the ship carrying Bibiana was nearly a hundred nautical miles away.

She had done it. She had escaped.

As the sun went down, Bibiana took out the ornate wooden box, the gift from her mother-in-law, who would definitely not be proud of her son.

The box was a memory of her, not of her husband. Opening the lid, she smiled as she took out a small satchel containing several gold coins. These Bibiana had found whilst searching throughout the house when her husband was away and she looking for anything of value she would take with her.

Placing some papers and jewellery out of the way onto the bunk upon which she sat, she fished out the leather pouch, the very precious gift her grandfather had given her. In the time she had been away, he had written to say that her grandmother had passed away. She wrote that she was well and missed him.

In the light of the lantern she sat very still, holding the pouch and letting tears run down her face, thanking her grandfather for all the stories and all the advice he had given her. She would most likely never see him again.

After a while, she took a deep breath, and realising that soon she would be joining the master for dinner, she put everything back into the box. After another look at the carved box with the beautifully painted scene on the lid, she got up from the bunk and placed the box carefully into a large trunk.

She was all right now. She had escaped. It was the year 1671 and she was on her way to Essequibo, a port in Guyana.

She wondered what might lie ahead as she took the small lantern and left her cabin to join the master and his officers for dinner.

THE PRESENT;

New York

still Friday 27th March

Tamara Wilson, known to her friends as Tammy, looked out of her panoramic window of her 28th floor of her apartment overlooking Central Park.

It was the middle of the afternoon. She can't ever remember the city being so quiet.

Locked down. Only go out for essentials or for exercise. Wear a face mask or covering. Wash your hands often and drink fluids.

Her restaurant, where she had once worked as a waitress, but which she had, after receiving the inheritance from her grandmother, purchased, was closed due to the coronavirus lockdown.

She had worked hard, had studied for three years to be a chef and to learn about hospitality management, had then revamped the restaurant, changed the décor to Parisian art deco, had developed a new menu and had changed the name to 'La Petit Tresor' the 'Small Treasure'.

And what a treasure it was, winning awards and a loyal clientele.

With time on her hands, and having spoken to her friend Chrissie earlier in the day, it seemed they both had the same idea, look into the past.

Tammy knew a lot about her grandmother, Rosemary Quinton, but hardly anything at all about her great-grandfather. Percivald Quinton. How did he acquire his wealth? What did he do? Why was it that he had gone to Boston and why had he purchased the two seascapes, which, along with a third, were hanging in the long hallway, and who was Beatrice Parker.

This, she hoped to discover.

She turned away from the window and crossed from the large living room into the separate dining room where she had placed an assortment of papers onto the table.

There were also a collection of photos, some letters and an old diary.

"Get these in order and establish some sort of timeline," she said to herself.

After about twenty minutes, she decided on a starting point.

"Got to start somewhere," then reached over and grabbed a scarf. Her grandmother's scarf.

In one pile of papers she had placed everything she had that was related to her grandmother, Rosemary Quinton.

Holding the scarf in her hand, Tammy flicked through the pile and pulled out the birth certificate.

Date of birth, 1922. She was born in New York. Fathers name, Percivald Quinton. His occupation was listed as architect.

She had not spotted that before. Architect.

Reading on it stated he was also born in New York, in the year 1898.

Mother's name was Catherine. Mother's maiden name–Winter, place of birth–Chichester, England, date of birth–1901.

"Well, well, England," she said aloud, and wondered where exactly Chichester was.

Still holding the scarf in her hand, she placed it close to her nose and sniffed it, thinking back to the amazing and yet troubled journey this scarf had with its owner, her grandmother Rosemary.

Tammy knew so much about Rosemary, and knew the detail of the adventure she had undertaken, all through the letters and the commission Tammy had been given.

Still, it would have been great to have known her grandmother in person.

With the scarf draped around her neck, Tammy went to the kitchen, poured herself a glass of wine and returned to the dining room. She thought back to the time she herself had flown over to Europe. This was in response to a quest she had been sent on, eventually leading to Antwerp, in Belgium, where she had met Samantha, a friend of Sam.

There she had visited the house where her grandmother had once stayed for a brief time, and where she had met and fallen in love with Bastiaan Bouten.

Together they had then sailed to New York, but, it had been her great-grandfather who had intervened, had made the young Belgian return to his homeland and had written his daughter, a very brief note, simply stating that this Bastiaan was a bounder and already married.

Tammy was sure, though that Bastiaan was her mother's biological father.

When she'd visited the house, she'd met up with a likeable young man called Adriaan, and discovered that it had not been true.

Bastiaan was not married at the time. So why had Percivald said he was?

Taking a sip of wine and placing the scarf on the table, she opened her laptop, sat down and with paper and pen to hand began to search for more information on Percivald Quinton, starting with his birth date in 1898.

Three hours later she had an admiration for the genealogists who trawled through old, mostly illegible, documents, and who would follow up with searching old newspaper articles and reading complicated wills, day after day.

Three hours and she was dizzy with concentration and had developed a slight headache.

A second glass of wine was required as she took herself to the lounge, noticed it was getting dark outside, switched on the lights and sat herself down in a leather two-seater.

Tammy placed the glass on the small table beside her and looked at the sheets of paper she had written up.

❧❧❧

THE PAST;

Period 2

The year 1674

Bibiana stood on the wooden jetty and watched the Dutch vessel disappear into the distance. The sun stood high in the blue sky and the heat was oppressive, but she was good with that.

Her olive skin shone in the sunlight, her green eyes sparkled and she was half smiling as she was in deep thought. Three years ago.

Three years ago she had arrived here. Three years ago she had noticed the young man, with his ruffled hair and crumpled clothes. He had later that day called upon her to introduce himself, had tried to speak to her in broken Dutch, and had been awkward in his explanation that he was the doctor. She could speak four languages, spoke to him in his native English and reassured him that should she need a doctor, she would know where to come.

It hadn't taken her long to find out all about him. Robert Ward.

In next few days after her arrival, she spotted him twice and briefly spoke to him once. She had quickly observed that he was smitten with her.

She liked him, but wasn't ready, not yet.

Standing in the hot sun on the jetty, she thought back to the journey that had brought her here.

On the second day she had written two letters, the first, to her grandfather, explaining her situation, what had occurred and thanking him for his guidance and council. She also gave him the address of the trading post to where he could send a letter.

The second letter was to Catherijn De Reder, her mother-inlaw, whom she had found a likeable person and who had given her that lovely wooden box.

It was a long letter, detailing everything that had occurred. Her baby boy who had died, the subsequent change in Johan, the anger and the beating he gave her. Everything.

Two days ago, when a Dutch three-master had sailed into port, there had been letters for her.

One from her grandfather, which she was overjoyed to receive. The second was a bulky envelope containing a letter and documents, was from Catherijn.

It was quite a read. She had sat down in a corner of the Trading Post where a few tables and chairs had been set up creating an eatery for the staff and visiting mariners.

In the letter, Catherijn had apologised profusely. She told Bibiana she had confronted her son when an opportunity arose, had heard the truth and had immediately declared she would disown him.

Furthermore the envelope contained papers absolving her of her marriage to Johan and on top of that, there was a letter that stated, upon the death of Catherijn De Reder, the house in Leiden would come to her.

There was a reason she liked the woman, she thought at the time.

Bibiana had written back, with gratitude, love and thankfulness a letter that was now sailing in the vessel which was now just a speck on the horizon.

That afternoon, having digested the lovely letter from her grandfather who was fit and well, and all that the bulky envelope from Catherijn had contained, she had stepped into town and gone to a large building, which was partly the hospital and partly Robert's quarters.

She had found him talking to a few patients. A nurse, one he had trained, was also present.

"Can your nurse take over for a while? I need to speak with you," she had said, trying to keep the excitement from her voice.

He had nodded and she took hold of his hand, practically dragged him to an office where all the medical records and medicine was kept, closed the door and said, "Robert, I am now a free woman, do you want to take me as your wife?"

Bibiana turned and walked back down the jetty, smiling at the memory. That was two days ago. They would be married the day after tomorrow.

Five years later

Robert Ward said a tearful goodbye. Fourteen years he had been the town's doctor. Fourteen years. Where had those years gone?

He couldn't believe all the folk that had come out to say thank you and goodbye. The villagers, the elders, the people at the trading post, the Dutch mariners and the operators of the harbour and trading post.

He had healed many and had delivered many babies.

Bibiana stood a few paces away. So proud of the man, now her husband, who was such a caring and gentle man, so loving and so kind. She knew he loved her very much. She loved him, more than she could ever say. He was so different from the man she had married before. The master of the ship had already ordered their luggage to be taken on board. A cabin had been made ready for them.

The Dutch three-master, 'De Barendrecht' had called into the port twice before. It was due to sail for Amsterdam.

They would travel via Cadiz in southern Spain as there was a peace treaty now in place between the Dutch and Spanish, and the bulk of the ship's cargo would fetch a good price there.

Free passage, the first officer's cabin, and the best service they could get was theirs for two reasons.

Firstly, Karel Maas had died. Bibiana's grandfather was well-known in shipping circles as he had run the Dutch trading port in Java for over thirty years.

Secondly, Doctor Robert Ward, Englishman, but he was an honorary Dutchman, for he had taken care of the well-being of all who had visited, lived in or worked in the port at Essequibo.

The letter telling Bibiana her grandfather had died had arrived three weeks ago. Robert had insisted they go back to her homeland; it was time for a change.

The ship sailed just around mid-afternoon and Robert stood on the aft deck until he could no longer see land.

"You are so kind to agree to go back to Holland," Bibiana said, brushing her long hair. The lantern was lit in their cabin and they had just returned from dinner.

The sea swell was gentle. Robert had been concerned about becoming seasick as he hadn't been at sea for many years, but felt good.

He stood by the porthole, looking into the darkness, or trying to. In the reflection of the glass he could see her.

He was a lucky guy. She was just so beautiful. They had been seeing each for some time, since not long after her arrival when she had told him, one sunny afternoon, all that had happened to her. About her cruel husband, about losing the baby, about not being able to have any more children.

He was in emotional turmoil that day. Anger at the man who had treated her badly. Empathy for her for the loss of a baby. He was determined to ensure that he himself, would always treat her well, if she would one day have him as her husband.

He turned from the porthole, and was about to speak when she spoke again, "But what about you. I know you told me you had written home several times, but you never received any letters back? Don't you want to see them?"

"Maybe. As I have said before, never got on good with my father. Perhaps he died? Perhaps that's why I haven't heard anything. My mother could neither read nor write you see," he explained.

"Well," Bibiana replied, putting her brush away and knowing that she had to lead the way, to guide him, to push him even, "Once we are settled, we'll make a trip."

"Very well. Sounds good," he answered.

"Good, then. Blow out the light and come and keep me warm," she said, smiling at him.

Two days out and an afternoon when the seas were very calm with hardly a breath of wind, the first officer, Albert van Rijn, knocked on the door to what really was, his quarters.

He knew that the Englishman, the doctor, was helping the ship's doctor at that time and, not having a grasp of the English language, wanted to speak to the lady in Dutch. She opened the door.

He was slightly red in the face, and, almost stammering, when he asked if he could speak with her, about her former husband, about Jan De Reder.

Bibiana invited him in. She guessed he was in his late twenties. He was gangly and tall. She figured he was not a ladies man and sensed he was rather uncomfortable.

"Please, go on"

"I met him, once. Not a very nice man, but what I think you don't know, is that he is dead."

"Really? No I had not heard, when?"

"Only a few days before we set sail to Guyana. I also know that he was, in trouble, he could not go back to Holland, he would be arrested."

"Arrested? Why?" Bibiana wanted to know, indeed very curious about this turn of events.

"He shot one of the servants, in the plantation, in Paramaribo. It's also where he died. He was attacked in the night and killed."

Bibiana took all this in, walked over to the porthole and watched the calm seas for a moment, then turned back to the officer, "do you know which servant he shot?"

"No ma'am. I do know that his mother, I mean De Reder's mother, told the authorities about his behaviour to you and to others. A woman had written a letter to Mrs De Reder that's all I know, sorry to tell you this."

"Thank you very much. No need to be sorry, not for him anyway, but if you can find out who it was he shot?"

"I will try," Albert said. Then as he was about to turn and leave the cabin, he spotted the ornate wooden box on the top of a chest of drawers.

"That is so beautiful," and with a confidence he had not shown until that point, he boldly said, "May I look?"

Bibiana nodded.

The young officer walked over, looked at the sides, at the top, studied the painting, then turned and asked, "This is very fine workmanship, do you know anything about the painting?"

"The lady you mentioned, Catherijn, Jan's mother, gave it to me. She did mention who painted it, but I can't recall. It is very nice. You seem to know about it?"

"Not about the box, ma'am, but I do recognise the scene of the painting. It is from the Bible. It is about the apostle Philip, speaking to a traveller. I'm sure that is what the scene is."

Bibiana stood next to the officer and looked at it.

"Thank you," she said.

When he had left, she picked up the box, studied the lovely carving and took in the scene that was so beautifully painted. The strange landscape, the horse and wagon, the man standing by the coach seemingly speaking to the occupant. The small pond of water in the foreground.

"Very interesting," she whispered.

❦

T H E   P R E S E N T ;

Boston

still Friday 27th March

Chrissie turned the television off. More deaths, more people in hospital. Everywhere.

A little earlier she had made some soup and toast which she had taken to Sam. He sat up and enjoyed it, saying he was feeling quite a lot better.

He was asleep again now. She was thankful he was on the mend.

Making something for herself, she then decided to take another look at the painting in the journal that had triggered her curiosity.

Why had it done that? What was it that had drawn her attention.

'The Lovesick Maiden' was the title of the work by Jan Steen, was it that?

She looked again, going from left to right, from top to bottom.

Then she saw something, and wondered if it was that which had drawn her attention.

Putting the journal back on the table, she got up and went into the kitchen, rummaged around for a bit, then gave up. She then went upstairs, to one of the guest rooms which she used as a hobby and craft room as well as a bit of a dumping ground for some unwanted ceramics and glassware.

She found what she was looking for, bounded back down the stairs, sat on the floor by the low coffee table, and taking her reading glasses off, looked at the photo of the painting with the magnifying glass.

Her phone rang.

"Tammy?"

"Chrissie, hi, can you talk right now, or, actually, rather listen?"

"You've found something? About Percivald?" Chrissie asked, knowing Tammy was going to research her great-grandfather.

"Yes, yes, but, more than that…"Tammy began and Chrissie could hear the excitement in her voice.

Though Tammy was eleven years younger than her, they had so quickly become very good friends. They had bonded over the fate of her own grandfather and Tammy's grandmother, and it had been an instant liking for each other. Chrissie was smiling as she got up from the floor and sat herself on the couch, picturing her excited friend.

"I began with birth certificates. Had Grandma's, so, this led me on and on and so, believe it or not, I found out the name of my seven times grandfather! He was William Quinton, and he was born in 1738!"

"Wow," Chrissie interjected.

"Indeed, but now it gets really interesting. I noticed that on the certificate I found, so hard to read some of these you know, practically done my head in. Anyway, first of all, he was born in Plymouth, England, so that was cool, but, I noticed, his mother's name was Virginia Powell. That was her maiden name. Well, the name rang a bell with me…do you remember, you told me the story of how you and Sam were hunting for this miniature, the one that Grandma… well you know, Now, didn't you tell me about a journalist, from the New York Gazette. He was from England, he was a Powell, a Thomas Powell, right?"

Chrissie was about to agree, but Tammy had continued to speak.

"So, what I did was, I looked up this Virginia Powell, found her records and guess what?"

Again, before Chrissie even begin to formulate and answer, Tammy had continued to speak.

"She, this Virginia, Thomas's sister!"

Sensing that her friend was taking a breath, Chrissie said, "Goodness that's some sleuthing girl, very interesting indeed."

"But that's not all," Tammy continued, still sounding very excited. "By chance, I found a newspaper article. In fact I found several. The upshot is this. Now, let me get this straight in my head."

"Okay, ready for this?" Tammy asked, but didn't wait for a reply, "Thomas, brother of Virginia, was the journalist that went to New York, working for the Gazette. This we know. Then, he met, fell in love with, and married an English girl he met whilst reporting on a play. This we know. I recall the story you told me. Then he took his wife, and by then their son, back to England. Now, we come to the part, which you didn't know. Sadly, and I practically cried when I was reading this, his wife died shortly after reaching England, reaching Plymouth. So, what happened then was that Thomas left his son with his sister who offered to raise the child. Thomas went back, I believe to the north, a place called Shrewsbury.

"So, Chrissie, my seven times grandfather, William, grew up with Thomas's son, whose name was John Robert…"

"That is so amazing, wow, you have done a lot of research today!" Chrissie said, impressed with the findings and managing to get a word in…

"Aah, but that's still not all. There is more, much more… that's why I wanted to call you, so exciting; so sad too. Tell you why," Tammy said. "I remember also, when you told the story of what you and Sam had found out, actually, I believe it was Samantha and Sam that found all this out from what I recall?"

"Yes, this was early on in the search for the miniature. Yes, you're right, and by the way, what a great memory you have!"

"Thanks, comes with remembering people's orders in the restaurant I reckon. So, anyway, yes, they found out that a John Robert Powell, obviously having kept his father's name, sailed for Philadelphia in the year 1763, then they lost the trail.

Well, I have something to add to this. Something rather sad. I discovered that a body was found some six months after John Robert had supposedly sailed away out of Plymouth. The body was that of John Robert."

"Whaaat?" Chrissie exclaimed, "Really… so who…"

"Who indeed? The young man had been battered and robbed and thrown in the river just outside of the town, so the police figured that whoever had done this, had also taken his travel documents and had sailed in his place. Now, get this, my seven times grandfather, at the age of twenty five, decided to sail to Philadelphia and search for the killer of his cousin. Though, having grown up together no doubt he was more like an older brother as there was a four year age difference, and that must be, how the Quintons came to the States, because I know that all the other ancestors after him, were born in New York!"

"That's amazing Tammy. I will tell Sam all about it. Great work, but what now? Will you continue to see what, if anything, this William found out?"

"Absolutely! Not only that, but how it was he stayed in America. He might even be the one who started building up the wealth that eventually came to Percivald and to my grandmother."

"Take a break first. I suggest," Chrissie said, "you get some rest from reading all that stuff. Well done you, though. I hope I can be as successful in my research."

In New York Tammy replied, "I hear you" then, suddenly feeling rather exhausted. Saying her goodbye to Chrissie, she flopped down on the leather two-seater, but she didn't stay seated for long and after a few moments, went back to her laptop, looked at the various sheets she had printed out and made a decision.

"Let me see" she said to herself, "if I can find out more about William's father, Rene Quinton."

After a while of searching she came across the name and discovered something quite surprising.

It was a ship's manifest and passenger list. It listed Rene Quinton, arriving in Plymouth aged sixteen, and listed a woman, Evonie Dupois Quinton, age thirty three.

No doubt, his mother, but no other Quinton's arrived from Le Havre, France.

"France! Wow, what is the story there?" Tammy said aloud.

Her nine times great grandmother was French!

But what happened for her to leave her homeland and come to England.

Landing in Plymouth in the year 1729.

T H E   P A S T ;

Period 3

The year 1729

Doctor Robert Ward waved goodbye one final time, then turned and walked back up the path. He could hear the sound of the sea behind him. His cottage in Plymouth was only some two hundred yards away.

His visitor had been a young man, Thomas Powell, a relative, the grandson of his sister.

Robert stepped inside, closed the door behind him and sat himself in his favourite chair by the fireplace in the lounge.

Thomas was a journalist, with a nose for a good story and the gift of investigation.

Three years earlier he had travelled to New York where he had been taken on by the New York Gazette.

Thomas had come back across the Atlantic to see him especially as Thomas's mother had suggested that her uncle could relate a story to him that his New York readers would find interesting to hear.

Robert closed his eyes. Thomas had been a great listener and he had felt good telling the story, but it had taken it out of him. He was tired, and missing his wife, Bibiana.

Thomas, carrying an ornate wooden box under his arm, walked back into the centre of town. He was glad he had come.

When he had received a letter from his mother to suggest talking with uncle Robert, he at first thought it a ploy to get him home so she could see him, which, he had to admit was nice anyway, but then he had travelled down to Plymouth, visited his sister where he could stay a couple of days and had gone to see uncle Robert.

His mother had been right. His readers in New York would like the story. Seeing the time on the church clock, Thomas was surprised how much time had gone.

Nearly three hours!

Once back at his sister's place he would rewrite the many notes he made. He was due to sail back to New York in two days' time.

His journey to his sister's house took him past the docks where a schooner was unloading it's cargo.

Thomas noted a few passengers coming ashore: a woman, shortish dark hair, who certainly, from a distance, looked to be rather attractive, a lad, already taller than the woman, was right behind her, carrying two cases. No doubt a son, Thomas surmised, then a building blocked his view as he continued walking to where his sister, eight years his junior, now lived with an aunt on his father's side.

Standing on firm ground, Evonie Dupois took a deep breath. She was glad she had arrived safely, unlike her husband who had not been able to avoid being arrested and imprisoned, for being a protestant.

Religious warfare was rife in pockets around the European continent.

It was beyond her understanding.

A man approached them. "Mrs Dupois Quinton?" he asked. He'd taken his hat off and smiled at her, then gave the tall lad a nod.

Meanwhile Thomas walked on towards his aunt's house, running through all the things that doctor Robert had told him.

Once indoors, he made himself a fresh pot of tea, then sat at the dining room table, placing the ornate box on the cotton tablecloth and taking out his notebook.

It wasn't long before he was once again, totally absorbed in the story, not even noticing that his sister had arrived home from work, She saw the freshly made tea in the kitchen, poured him a cup and brought it through, placing it on the table.

She noticed the ornate wooden box and wondered what that was all about, smiling as her brother wasn't even aware that she was there.

Thomas was reading and writing, getting to the part where the doctor and his wife Bibiana left Essequibo, where they sailed, via Cadiz, to Amsterdam, arriving there in the late summer of 1679, fifty years ago…

Bibiana opened the gate, then froze for a moment, recalling the time she had left through this very gate, the time she had said goodbye to her grandmother Salee and to her grandfather Karel.

Eleven years ago.

So much had happened in that time.

She had travelled to Rotterdam by herself. They had acquired lodgings in Leiden and her husband Robert had already found work in the hospital as they were very short-staffed.

She assured him she would be fine as she set off to sort out the affairs with regard to the cottage which had been left her.

A neighbour had met her, had given her keys, had spoken warmly of her grandparents, and had given her details of where they were buried and the address of the notary who was dealing with the property and finances.

She closed the gate behind her and walked up the path, feeling tearful.

Doctor Robert Ward was thankful when his wife returned safely after four days and for several years they lived an existence far removed from the hot sunshine that they had been used to.

But Bibiana eventually made a decision. She knew she would have to be the one to do so. He was so kind and caring, but would always make sure her happiness came first. It was again time for a change.

She organised it all, and it was shortly before she had arranged all these things that her former mother-in-law, Catherijn De Reder, died.

As promised, the house and property was bequeathed to Bibiana.

A substantial house, and funds. Very timely.

Three weeks later, having herself informed the hospital, where he had fitted in so well and was, not surprisingly, well-liked that he would be leaving. They set out for Plymouth, England…

… Thomas drank some of his tea, not even aware that it had been his sister who had placed it there, noted down the year they had come to Plymouth. 1686.

Forty-three years ago.

He took hold of the box, opened it and took out the black leather pouch, then sliding its contents into his hand showed it to his sister who had just come back into the dining room.

"This is the heart of my story," he said to her.

"It's beautiful," she answered, "so is this box."

THE PRESENT;

Boston

Friday evening 27th March

"It's the box!" Chrissie exclaimed, sitting upright in bed.

She switched on the bedside lamp. Twenty minutes to midnight.

She had only just switched the light off and closed her eyes when the thought struck her.

Sam was still sleeping in the other room, his health improving slowly.

Knowing what it now was that had drawn her to that particular painting, she slipped out of the bed, threw a dressing gown on and barefooted headed downstairs.

Moments later she grabbed the journal, opened it up to the page, found the painting and placed the journal on the table. Then, again using the magnifying glass, she focused on a dressing table in the scene of 'The Lovesick Maiden'.

There it was. The box. It was closed, but she could see the ornate scrolls were the same; she was sure of it, and though barely visible, she noted that there was a painted scene on the lid.

Getting up from the floor where she had kneeled, she headed for a tall bookcase. At the bottom there were two doors. She opened the left-hand side and there it was.

Retrieving it, she stood up and was utterly amazed.

It was identical. She was sure of it.

Placing it on the table, beside the journal, then sitting on the floor once more, she looked from the box in the painting, to the box on the table. In her mind there was no doubt, it was the same.

Sam entered the lounge.

"Hey, heard you were up," he said, his voice still a little hoarse. "Everything all right?"

Chrissie turned and looked up at him. His colour was back to normal, his eyes seemed clear, and it was good to see him on his feet again.

Chrissie stood up and walked up to him.

Time for isolation and separation was over. She practically flung herself at him and he embraced her.

Then, releasing herself from him, she said, "It's the box. You remember the box, the one I found under the stairs which had belonged to my grandfather, to Eddie? Well, I'm sure it's the same as the one in that painting, the one in the ambassador's collection.

The question is, how did that box, painted by Jan Steen in sixteen hundred and something, come to be here, come to be in the possession of Eddie, here in Boston? I mean, like well over two hundred years later?"

Sam reached down, picked up the journal, studied the page, looked at the box on the table and then looking at Chrissie, said, "Could be a copy of course, a replica, but it sure does look the same."

Placing the journal back, he said, "I know a guy who can check it out, date the box, but we need to also find out exactly how your grandfather came into possession of it."

"Absolutely, this is intriguing. I love it."

"All good and well my wife-to-be, but it's past midnight, I'm feeling tired again, so how about we go to bed?"

"Together?" Chrissie asked.

"According to what I read, the transmission period for this virus is by now well over. I'm safe to sleep with." Sam answered, smiling.

"Mmm," Chrissie said. "I'm not sure that I am though!"

Then taking his hand she led him out of the room, switching off the lights and heading up the stairs.

THE PAST;

Period 4

The year 1744

The shopkeeper took the book from the window display as the young man was browsing around in the store. He watched as the well-dressed man picked up a map, studied it for a bit, kept hold of it and walked over to where a wooden box was sat upon a shelf.

Stepping over to the counter, he told the young man about this box, how it had only recently come in, how it must be quite old already, more than eighty years and that the 'Tafareel' was hand painted by a local artist.

Christoffer purchased the book, the map and the box and left to rejoin his friends celebrating the independence day feasts.

Later that evening, when Christoffer went to visit Tineke, who had been feeling unwell and was unable to join the festivities, he showed her his purchases. She was particularly taken by the lovely wooden box and wondered about the scene on the lid, about who might have painted it, who might have carved it and made the box and, as Christoffer had told her it was over eighty years old, she wondered who it might have belonged to and why would anyone sell such a lovely item.

The ornate box was about to go on another journey, having already travelled to South America, Spain, England and North America before finding its way back to the very city in which it had been crafted and painted.

Fifteen years earlier, in the port of Plymouth, England, doctor Robert Ward was tired. It had been wonderful to relate his story to the young Thomas, to once again reflect on the life he had led, in particular all those years with the most beautiful woman he had ever seen.

Sitting back in the chair by the fire he knew he had done the right thing, to give Thomas not only the pouch with the miniature, but the box too. It was time for them to be looked after by someone else.

Three days after Thomas had sailed back to New York, Robert passed away peacefully in his sleep.

Thomas heard this news and was saddened as Robert would never get to read his article.

Whilst the article, all about the painted miniature ivory, now in his possession, was very popular and had attracted many new readers for the paper, even talk of a special journalist prize, something else happened that overshadowed all of that.

He fell in love.

Covering an event in a local theatre, a play, the first of its kind, he was drawn to one of the actresses.

After a short courtship, they married in New York.

All was well for some time, a baby boy was born to them. But then his wife became ill. They needed to get back to England and Thomas, not having quite enough funds, sold the ornate box to the captain as part payment for the voyage and, in the year 1737, sailed back to England.

The captain gave the box to a lady friend, who, after several months and after the relationship had petered out, sold the box in a market in Amsterdam.

Several years later it was sold again, this time to a man from Leiden who, less than a week later, sold it to Christoffer in the year 1744.

He had wanted to give the box to Tineke a few years later as he was about to set sail in his new role with the VOC, but she insisted he keep it to put the letters she would write into it.

And so the ornate box, in the year 1747, travelled to Java.

Saturday very early 28th March

Eddie Philpot was about to die.

He knew he was about to die, he must be, he thought. His life was flashing before him, images, pictures, scenes. Surely this meant he was dying?

He felt shivery, his body ached, his head hurt.

The scene that kept repeating in his mind was when he hit her.

He hadn't meant to kill her, but he did.

All because he had been in debt; all because he had gambled and lost; all because he had fallen in with the wrong crowd.

They had wanted the papers. They had wanted the information she had with regards to what she had found out: the discovery.

All documents had to be retrieved.

Eddie sat in a dark corner of the metal boxcar, only a sliver of light entered through a slit in the sliding door. It was the only one, or rather the first one, he had found to open when he tried the handle.

Though if push came to shove, he had the ability to pick a number of locks.

Huddled, his arms folded, he tried to remain as still as possible, but he was cold yet sweat was on his brow. He could feel it. He couldn't rest, couldn't sleep. He was absolutely sure he had caught the virus. His breathing was laboured, his head throbbing.

The scene came around again, where he had tried to take a folder from the woman. A folder she was clutching to her chest…

She was bleeding from a cut on her head. In the violence of the tornado, she had struck her head on something. She was a little dazed, but he recalled her eyes as he approached her–shock, dismay, then anger and determination–she wasn't going to let go of the folder.

He struck her, with what he couldn't remember, but in the same spot where she was bleeding. She went limp.

He took the folder and ran out of the trailer. In the chaos of all that was going on around him, he slipped away.

He hadn't realised that he had killed her until he heard it on the news the following day...

The wheels of the train clickety clacked onwards. The sound did have a soothing effect, but the pain, though having retreated slightly from the forefront, was still there.

He was dying and knew it, but that was not important. What was more important was to pass the information he had found, on to the right person. The only person. For along with the sheets of information he had with him, inside a worn satchel, was also a letter. A letter he had written many, many years ago.

Over thirty years ago, the year was 1988...

When the realisation struck, Eddie had to think quickly. He had the information they had asked for, but now everything had changed, he had killed the professor, Emily Parker.

His regret was enormous, she was a nice lady.

The previous day, having taken the folder the professor was clutching, he shoved it under his sweater and left the trailer. Amidst the confusion of ambulances approaching, two police cars arriving, students crying, walking about or sitting on the ground, the shredded tents and plastic chairs everywhere, along with loads of paper and clothing, he had walked, head down, towards the parking lot.

He noticed, and was thankful that the twister had, in the main left most of the parked cars and vans, virtually untouched, save from the dust blown about.

He needed to get away. He needed to think. He had felt awful striking the woman.

He got into his old battered Ford, sighed with relief when the engine kicked into life and drove towards Silver City.

He booked into a motel for the night, and woke up to hear the news and the fact that the professor had died. He was sick with worry.

He had killed her.

Quickly grabbing his gear, he drove away, this time, heading for Albuquerque. A plan began to formulate. He had the folder; they wanted that, but he had killed for it, he needed to get away, far away, away from this scene, away from Conrad and his friends.

Upon reaching the city, he first headed for a post office. Here he placed the folder into a parcel bag, quickly scribbled a note and sent it to his younger sister.

He then used a public telephone, spoke to her, breaking down in tears, sobbing and telling her what he had done. He asked her to hide the parcel, and not tell anyone.

After he had done that, he took a deep breath, pulled himself together and left the phone box.

Time to run. Time to hide.

He first drove his car to a parking lot near the train station, made sure he took out all that he needed, then left it, throwing the keys in a nearby flower garden.

He took a bus back into the city centre, walked to the bus station where he bought a ticket for Phoenix, going via Flagstaff.

Two hours later the Greyhound bus pulled away…

Eddie realised the train had stopped, he had, at last and to his relief, fallen into a slumber of sorts.

With great difficulty he got up, carefully slid the door a little further open and in the dimness of the morning he saw that he was back in Phoenix.

It had been from here that he left by freight train, back in 1988, more than thirty years ago. It was to here he now had returned, by the same way.

What goes around comes around, he thought to himself, suddenly feeling a little stronger, a little clearer in his mind.

He thought back to all those years ago, when he felt he had cleverly hidden his tracks. He'd arrived in Phoenix in the early evening, and set about to find out about the freight train movements. A little before midnight he had successfully entered a boxcar on a train that would be leaving within the hour, heading for Tucson.

He still sensed that death must be close, but he had to get the information to the woman, to Millie Parker, the daughter of the woman he had killed.

Eddie slipped from the wagon, surveyed his surroundings, and saw where he needed to go to get out of the large goods yard then set off.

From here he would again take the bus, and head for Albuquerque. There he would give himself up to the police with all the information he had.

Why hadn't he been braver when Conrad had grabbed him by the collar amidst the roar of the tornado, he thought, as he reached the perimeter fence.

THE PAST;

Period 5

The year 1762 – Boston, Massachusetts

Late afternoon, with the sun well on its way down giving the skyline of Boston an almost silhouette like appearance, Christoffer stood on deck, a fresh breeze on his face as the French galleon slowly sailed closer to the entrance of the port.

He had given over thirteen years of service to the VOC, in the main plying the seas from Amsterdam to Persia, Indonesia, Java and the Philippines. It was time for something different.

He smiled as he recalled the thoughts he had when he was with Tineke in Leiden, and remembered the stories she told of her ancestors, stories she told of the Pilgrims sailing to North America, and how he wondered if one day, he might cross the Atlantic too.

Taking in the fresh air, seeing the city in front of him, and seeing the coast of the North American continent, made him feel good.

He had decided to leave in order to pursue what he discovered was his real passion. To visit other lands, to visit other cultures, especially war-torn countries to report, journal and investigate.

Christoffer had learned of skirmishes between the French and English in Canada, particularly in the region of Nova Scotia, with added trouble from local tensions thrown in.

This would be interesting. It would make good story, which would be of interest, especially to the French.

He had made contact with a Parisian newspaper, and outlined a proposal. He would send weekly updates in return for a passage to Boston, and for someone there to sort out initial accommodation upon his arrival.

This had been fully accepted. If he could find his own way to the port of Rouen, he would then be able to board a vessel bound for Boston. He was also informed of a local contact that would see him through customs upon arrival.

Christoffer had smiled when he received this communication. He knew about the contact in Boston, he was an astute man, a learned man able to speak several languages.

After years of bartering and dealing, he had come to know people who could prove helpful, even in places he had never been to.

He had another motive for entering North America without too much fuss.

Lucrative sales.

Over the past five years he had been planning for this next phase of his life and had purchased an array of goods. Furs and silk, copper pans and tea, various items of jewellery in silver and gold, and, just a week prior to leaving Rotterdam, he had purchased three paintings in an auction.

He knew he would sell all these items well, and thus needed someone with some knowledge to help him through customs.

Hence the smile on his face when he had read the reply back from the Parisian newspaper.

The three-masted galleon slowly entered the harbour area.

He watched as the vessel docked, and had he looked at a nearby mansion house on the waterfront at the right moment, he would have spotted a large man briefly standing by the window. A man he would be seeing in only a couple of days.

Christoffer was met by a thin man in his late fifties, whose name was Patrick. The very man whose name he had heard before.

Patrick wore baggy trousers, and a thick cotton shirt, cream in colour, over which he had a green tweed waistcoat.

His feet were in some sort of moccasin shoes and he smiled a lot and talked even more, quite rapidly, which caused a little difficulty for Christoffer, but he smiled back, nodded often and followed the man.

Going through customs was a breeze. Christoffer's papers were stamped and he was on his way through. Less than an hour later all his belonging were loaded upon a cart, and he was sitting next to Patrick on the horse-drawn wagon, and they rode away from the harbour.

His lodgings were fine. A whole house to himself, where he could stay as long as needed.

Christoffer thanked the man and gave him two gold coins from his collection, for which Patrick was enormously grateful and repeatedly said so.

Eight days later, Christoffer would be on his way north into Canada and towards Halifax.

In just those few days he sold much of his merchandise.

The furs and silks were sold through a local market, and being good at sourcing contacts and with the help of a very willing Patrick, he found a buyer for the copper and some of the jewellery.

On the afternoon of his third day in the city, a man called on him.

A jovial man. A very large man. An influential man.

Charlie Parker.

Christoffer greeted him warmly, and invited him into the lounge where a crate stood in the middle of the room.

With a flourish Christoffer pulled the side of the crate away.

Into view came a large painting. A seascape, beautifully painted.

Charlie Parker was mesmerised. He loved it, walked up closer to it and studied it.

Christoffer then moved up to the crate and took the painting out to reveal another behind it.

Charlie Parker looked at the painting, looked at the man, back at the painting.

Then another move was made, the second painting was moved out of the crate to reveal a third.

Charlie Parker was impressed.

Three days ago he had celebrated the birth of his first child, a son.

The two men bartered for some time as both were experts in negotiations.

A deal was made, and Charlie bought all three, and Christoffer promised to deliver the paintings the following day.

It was when Charlie Parker was leaving the lounge that he noticed an ornate wooden box on the mantelpiece and stopped to take a closer look.

Christoffer didn't hesitate. He saw the man liked the box, went up to it, opened it, took out the contents and then said, "For you, a gift."

Charlie Parker smiled, thanked Christoffer and said, "For the little lady." The two men shook hands, said their goodbyes, then Charlie, carrying the box, left the house.

Afterwards, having carefully repacked the large oil painting back into the crate, Christoffer briefly thought about the box he had given away.

Several letters from Tineke had found a home there for some time, but over time, he had written less, then not at all. Though unsure as to why, he put the thought of her aside.

That ship has sailed, he said to himself.

THE PRESENT;

Boston

Saturday morning 28th March

Chrissie stirred, lifted her head up from his chest, then snuggled down again. She was warm and content. Closing her eyes, she thought back to the day he had knocked on her door.

Her mind conjured up a myriad of memories since that day, but suddenly a thought struck her. Lifting her head up again, she said, her voice soft, "Sam?"

"Aha," came the reply as he encircled his arms around her, and thinking how good it felt to have her lying on his chest.

"You know how Tammy is trying to put together her family tree, and also how it was that her great-grandfather, Percivald, came to be in Boston where he purchased the two seascapes, and how he and Beatrice, we think, knew each other?"

"Aha," he replied, now running his fingers through her hair and looking into her eyes.

"Well, I just thought about this. You said that this Beatrice was in the Parker family tree, and that it was her son, Joshua, only a child at the time, who would later inherit the mining company, and that it was him who eventually sold the business to that Rozzini chap, right?"

"Aha" Sam replied, his free hand caressing her back.

"Well, you told me about all those photographs, in the boardroom, all taken throughout the mine's history. You said there were many and you took pictures…"

Sam drew himself towards her, and muted her conversation by placing his lips upon hers.

It was some time later, with Sam now lying on top of Chrissie and smiling at her, when he said, "Yes, I took pictures of the walls.

There were, from memory, around forty-eight photos. I separated them out into individual shots, and took them along to show Joe. He was the old guy at the railway goods yard I met when I arrived in Moncton. We spent some time looking through them. It was the same day that I took Ally to Halifax airport I recall. What is it you hope to find?"

She smiled back at him, quickly raised her head, kissed him briefly, then answered, "If they are a history of the mine, then there could be a picture of Beatrice, or her son Joshua, maybe, because I think you said each picture had a description?"

Sam thought for a moment, then rolled off and in a fluid movement got out of the bed, heading for the en suite shower, he turned his head and said, "I would have thought of that, but you distracted me."

"I…" Chrissie began, then grabbed a pillow and threw it at him, but he had slipped through the door and she missed.

Laying back down, she grinned.

San Francisco–Saturday 28th March

Ally Hudson was tossing up whether or not to get a dog, or whether or not to move.

She was alone in her apartment on the north side of the city.

She felt a little lost. She realised, she didn't have many friends, not really, what you might consider good friends. Acquaintances, sure, a few work colleagues, yes, but not really close friends.

She thought back to when Chrissie had called her yesterday, from Boston.

She was a friend.

There was of course Millie, and the search for her mother's killer that she had been involved with, already some nine months ago now.

A mystery unravelled that had also brought her back in touch with a two girls she knew at high school, which had also brought back bad memories.

Barbara Philpot, whom she had gone to confront, whose brother Eddie, whom Barbara had never heard from again, had fled the scene of the tornado strike.

It had been him who had caused the death of Millie's mother, Professor Emily Parker.

And then there had been Cynthia Barnes, who, together with someone else from her high schooldays, a guy named Thomas Klaassen, had been following a mystery trail of their own.

They had spoken on the phone, Cynthia having initiated the call, a brief chat, both perhaps remembering the bad old days and not wishing to go back there.

Puffing out her cheeks, Ally went to the kitchen to prepare some lunch. Her daughter, Theresa, Terri to her friends, had finished her schooling at the girls' boarding school, where Millie had been one of her teachers, the place she had been taken to when she had been kidnapped from her mother at the age of seven.

Ally had spent over ten years trying to find her daughter, trying to figure out where the father of her child, along with his wife, had taken her.

Ten years!

During that time she had not been able to make friends, not been able to settle into any place, not been able to be relaxed, not even remotely considered a romantic relationship.

But her persistence had paid off, though she nearly paid for it with her life.

A puppy? Or move?

Terri had been successful in obtaining a role in the city's art museum, in administration initially, cataloguing and research, with the aim to one day be a curator.

With funds, mainly from a substantial court payout, she had moved into her own apartment near the centre, close to the museum.

Though Ally had, thankfully, bonded well with a daughter she had not seen for over ten years and who had been told that her biological mother had died, she also realised that she had to let her lead her life the way she had thought fit. And more importantly, to let her go in the direction she had for years in school been working towards.

Ally made herself a coffee, prepared a sandwich and a salad and thought about her situation.

With this worldwide virus gripping every continent, it was all rather a worry.

Wear a mask, wash your hands, only go out for exercise, or essential shopping.

Laboratories around the world were working towards vaccines.

A puppy would mean she would need to go out, force her to exercise, force her to get that fresh air.

But with Terri now so involved in her new work, she felt alone.

Chrissie was her, really only, friend.

Eating her sandwich, she smiled, recollecting when she had first met Chrissie.

It had been after a call from Detective Sergeant Karen Saunders from the Royal Canadian Mounted Police, who informed her that Sam was missing.

Sam.

The man who had saved her life. The man who had been so instrumental in finding her daughter. The man she had totally fallen in love with.

She had been let into Sam's apartment in Moncton, by Chrissie, who had been the one to raise the alarm that Sam had gone missing.

They had met, as rivals, yet with a common interest, finding Sam Price.

They had bonded, had worked together, had become friends.

A puppy or a move? Ally wondered, tucking into her salad.

Her phone buzzed, she answered it.

"Hello?"

THE PAST;

Period 6

The year 1763-Philadelphia

Young William Quinton, armed with a sketch, entered the large trading store at the dockside.

First of all, he looked around in awe at all the goods on display, then, struck by the hive of activity as he slowly walked about taking it all in, William eventually spotted a man who seemed to be in charge.

Approaching the silver haired man he asked if he was.

"Zecheriah Strauss, at your service young man. Just of the ship from Plymouth?"

"Yes sir, I wonder…"William began, then showed the man the sketch he had in his hand. A sketch that had been provided by the constabulary in Plymouth, who after a bit of investigation, had come up with the likely suspect in the murder of John Robert Powell. They had identified a stocky man, known to the police as the Oxman. They described him as a nasty piece of work.

"Do you recall a man who looked like this coming here, earlier this year?

Zecheriah studied the sketch, then handing it back said, "Sure do. He was here. Strange fellow, sold a miniature painting to me. Painted on ivory. Nice piece, sold it on the very same day. He didn't look the smartest tool in the box, if you know what I mean, but I had no reason to be suspicious of him. What's the story?"

William tucked the sketch away, "A bad man, killed my brother, well, cousin really, but more a brother, any idea where he went?"

Zecheriah thought for a moment then said, "I recall some folk heading down to Louisiana around that time. Might be he went along."

"Thank you so much. At least you've confirmed that he came here on John's ticket and with his possessions."

Then, William once more facing the proprietor of the trading post, asked, "I don't suppose you could tell me who purchased the miniature, could you?"

Zecheriah thought for a moment, then nodded and headed for the counter.

Fifteen minutes later, carrying two large holdalls, William stepped from the trading post and walked into the city, wondering what adventure might be in store for him.

He thought about his cousin, John Robert, his uncle's son, who had been a journalist for the New York Gazette, but who had, sadly, been killed in Yemen when covering the war there.

That had been in 1752. Even though he was only fourteen, he recalled when aunty Evangeline had come down to Plymouth to inform John Robert that his father had been killed.

Perhaps this had been something he had in mind to do, to find out about his father's life in New York, where he had met and married his mother.

With tears in his eyes William thought back to how excited John Robert had been to have purchased the passage, yet, because of some useless thug, he never even left.

William stopped briefly to check his bearings, then composed himself and took a quick look at the map that would take him to his lodgings.

He promised himself as he walked up the steps to the large house that he would find out what happened to the thug known as the Oxman.

William never would fulfil that promise.

Three days later he fell in love.

THE PRESENT;

New York

Saturday evening 28th March

Darkness had fallen. Another day indoors. Fortunately her apartment was large. She could move about. Sipping another glass of wine, she looked out over Central Park, trying hard to see through her reflection in the window.

Tammy had stopped her research for a while, for fear of worsening a headache she had developed from all that scrolling and reading.

She had, however, found another link in her quest to trace her ancestors.

William, who had sailed to Philadelphia, had married there. She had come across his marriage certificate.

The year was 1764, about a year after his arrival in the city, and the lucky girl was a Dorothy Baker. He was twenty six, she twenty one.

Tammy left her research there, trying to imagine the young couple, the young Englishman and, presumably, an American girl. Young love.

Tammy tore herself away from the window. Glass in hand she strode through the hallway and stopped briefly to look at each of the three seascapes that adorned the wall.

Two of them her great-grandfather had purchased in Boston, the third had been given to her by Sam. It had been part of an assessment he had done, one that involved the rescue of a woman she had heard of, but not yet met, Alison Hudson.

She had been told the story her by her friend Chrissie, whom had she also met through Sam's research. The pictures were beautiful seascapes, all by the same artist.

It had been a woman called Beatrice Parker who had sold them, back in 1938, at the very same auction where Chrissie's grandfather had purchased the painted ivory which had been at the very heart of an investigation that had brought them all together.

Sam, in his research, had discovered that Beatrice Parker was once married to a Nathaniel, who had left her, leaving her with a small child, Joshua, but how her great-grandfather Percivald was connected, wasn't known.

Why was he in Boston at that time? What made him buy the seascapes?

More detecting to do with regards to her ancestors.

William and Dorothy married in 1764, so, what happened next?

Tammy pulled herself away from the paintings in the passage way and headed for the kitchen.

Time to prepare some dinner for herself, then she would telephone each of her staff members, feeling it was important to keep in touch and show loyalty and determination in view of the lockdown circumstances.

Then, she would again have a crack at delving into the past.

A little later, coming from the kitchen and heading back through the passageway towards the lounge, she again glanced at the three seascapes and thought about what Sam had discovered, recalling the time when he had been here, and had taken the backs of the painting off to discover that all three had been purchased, in Rotterdam by a man named Christoffer Rosenborg. If she remembered correctly that had been in the year 1762.

T H E P A S T ;

Period 7

The year 1803–Caracas, Venezuela

Christoffer Rosenborg walked slowly with the aid of a stick.

He was at the port.

He was often at the port, he would come and sit and watch the vessels coming in, going out.

He would think of his daughter, Sofia. It was well over a year ago now that she and he husband Rene and their little boy, his grandson, had sailed from here.

He had received no news from them as yet.

He knew he would not see them again, would not see his grandson, who they had named Christoffer Junior, grow up.

But he was resigned to that fact.

He himself had left home to go travelling when he was just seventeen. He had, in all these years of journeying, never returned home, and never saw his parents again.

As he sat, the sun shining upon him, the reflection of the sunlight on the water creating an almost magical scene, he watched as a Spanish galleon entered the harbour.

He thought about the many lands he had visited, the many people he had met, the occasional confrontation with pirates, and the numerous and varied trade deals he had been part of.

Why, he wondered, had he never ventured back home?

He knew nothing of the lives of his two brothers and a sister.

Had they married? Did he have a score of nieces and nephews he knew nothing about?

He was dying.

He knew he was dying.

Each day it got a little harder.

It was perhaps why, in these recent days, he had all these questions popping up in his mind.

He smiled as he thought about the day he had arrived in Leiden, ready to study at the university, and the day he met the young girl, Tineke.

Sitting with her on the steps.

The memory took him to another place and another time, to an auction room in Rotterdam some eighteen years later.

He had successfully just purchased three paintings, three seascapes, very likely by the Rotterdam artist called Jan Porcellis. Along with silks and furs and an array of other goods, he was aiming to sell these when he travelled to Boston a few days later. It was when he was just leaving the building that he saw her.

It was unmistakeably her, it was Tineke.

After departing Leiden to begin his career with the VOC, he had kept up a communication with her for nearly three years. He wondered briefly if it had been him or her who had stopped writing.

Christoffer was about to approach her when a man arrived alongside her.

He could see, by the familiar way they were with each other that they were a couple.

Sitting on the wall overlooking the harbour in Caracas, watching the Spanish galleon tie up to the dock, he recalled the pang of pain he felt in his heart, and remembered how he had quickly departed feeling quite a loss.

What could have been; what, perhaps, should have been.

Christoffer stood up, got his frail body to move and headed towards the trading post where he often would wander to and look around. He noticed a couple of large schooners anchored as well as an English galleon that had also recently docked.

As he was about the enter, when a man, quite seriously sunburned, came out, noticed him and held the door open for him.

Christoffer nodded his thanks. It never occurred to him that in this man's possession was the very same item he himself had purchased in Philadelphia, forty years ago.

Around twenty minutes or so later, beginning to feel tired again, Christoffer left the trading post and headed home.

He thought of his daughter, Sofia Camille, thought back to how wonderfully proud he had felt walking her down the aisle, only a couple of years ago, and, for some reason wondered where the three paintings he had purchased and sold would be now.

Perhaps it was because it was the event in his life, when seeing Tineke that day, he realised he wanted to have companionship, love, children, a woman to come home to.

Christoffer smiled as he slowly walked home. It had been only a month after purchasing the item at the Philadelphia trading post that he had sailed to Venezuela, had met, had fallen in love and had married.

The rest, Christoffer thought, smiling to himself again, is history.

THE PRESENT;

Albuquerque

Sunday 29th March

Simon Lightfoot stood by the large window of the lounge in his house on Loretta Drive, overlooking the Rio Grande.

His Harley Davidson Dealership and motorcycle repair shop was closed. Though unlike other places, the city was not in total lockdown, he had four members of staff who were ill with the virus. One of which was in hospital and in a bad way.

Despite Saturday being the busiest day of the week for him, Simon had closed the store. It was now early Sunday morning.

He stood and watched the water of the river flow past for some time. To his left he noticed that traffic on the Alameda Bridge was sparse.

His staff member, the senior mechanic he had known now for over thirty years and whom he had made a manager of his establishment several years ago was in poor condition, on a ventilator. No visitors allowed.

Fifty-year-old Simon, turned away from the window, sat on his favourite leather chair and looked at the various sheets of papers, several books and reports, a number of photos and an array of pens and pencils that lay strewn across the large coffee table.

He had trouble letting go of the past.

Long, long ago, when he was nineteen, he had a girlfriend. Josie Morton.

She was a student at the university and deeply interested in archaeology. She had been on a dig just to the east of Silver City, when a tornado had ripped through the site. She, along with three others, had died.

He wouldn't have thought any more about it, other than that it had been an act of God, a force of nature, had it not been for a letter.

A letter that had been among her possessions, but had initially been returned to her family, who, at the time, had no time for him.

A long-haired high school dropout who rode a motorcycle. Moreover, he was a white guy, and she was black.

But through circumstances, the letter had come to him. It had not been opened.

It was this letter that then took him on a quest. A quest that for several years he had not been able to let go of. A quest that through more circumstances, he had returned to.

In the letter, apart from the many lines revealing her love for him, and her anger at her parents for not liking him, there was also something else. Something she had been asked not to talk about. But she had written it down in the letter, thinking it would, by the time he read it, no longer be a secret.

It was about a find. About a discovery unlike what might be expected in the dig for ruins of Mayan settlements, for it was an area of around a square metre of Roman mosaic tiles.

Which wasn't unusual in itself, however, what the professor had discovered hidden underneath these tiles was even more astounding.

Gold coins, and many of them, it seemed at first glance.

There had also been a thin leather pouch containing a letter written in Spanish.

It was this fact that made him suspicious, because there had been no mention of this find at all.

Simon sorted out the memories in his mind, recapping thirty years in just moments.

He had received the letter from Josie's mother, only two weeks before the first anniversary of the tornado strike. He had then visited the site on the first anniversary. There had been a memorial service held at the time as well and by then he had investigated a little and had obtained a list of names, all who were connected with the dig in that site near Silver City.

But a great investigator he was not.

Time passed. He was busy establishing his motorcycle repair and dealer store and when ten years had passed, all he had was that a guy named Eddie Philpot had gone missing on the day of the tornado strike and had not been heard from again.

He knew of the three people who had known about the mosaics and the gold.

These were the professor herself, his then girlfriend, Josie, and a guy named Conrad Shelton, who was the only one left alive. He had also found out that the wealthy Shelton family were in charge of all the transport and vehicles hired by the Albuquerque university for this dig.

Then, in 1998, visiting the site on the tenth year anniversary, he met Felicity Smith, the younger sister of Kathryn Smith. Kathryn, Josie, the second in charge, Donald Alfredo, and the professor were the four people killed that day.

Simon got up from the chair and once more stood himself by the window, watching the flowing river. He briefly thought again about his friend in hospital, then his thoughts returned to the past.

Felicity. The bubbly blonde, just five foot two, with long blonde hair and very blue eyes. How stupid he was. After only one date with her, knew he was smitten, yet, he had not let go of trying to get to the truth of what happened at the dig.

He had found out that Conrad Shelton had been shot and killed in Rome.

He told Felicity that he needed to follow up on this.

What a fool he had been.

The incident in Rome was unrelated. A dead end. He even had intended to visit the Shelton residence, but got as far as the big gates to the mansion and no further.

Just as well he was a good mechanic, just as well his business was doing well, for he surely wouldn't cut it as a detective.

Several years went by.

Then, in December of 2002, with the help of Josie's father, he was able to locate Felicity, who had left home in anger and was now working and living in Chicago.

It was such a relief that she was happy to see him.

Refocusing on the present, Simon stepped away from the window, went over to the table and picked up a sheet of paper.

The name at the very top was that of the Professor's daughter. Millie Parker.

He needed to speak with her.

Meanwhile

The importance of wanting to get the information he had, and the letter he had written, to Millie Parker, drove Eddie on.

Wearing a face mask, he had been shivering slightly as he stood in a short queue waiting to purchase his bus ticket to Flagstaff, wanting to travel a stage at a time.

Once there he would see how he could get to Albuquerque. Knowing that there was a large truck stop there, he would see if he could hitch a ride.

Taking in a deep breath and making sure his voice was as confident as it could be, he bought the ticket.

Then, a little later, sighing with relief, he again began to shiver.

Hang in there! He told himself.

Clutching his satchel, he boarded the greyhound bus twenty minutes later.

The burger, the coffee and a bar of chocolate had given him some much needed energy as he watched the landscape roll by.

He thought back; back to the time he had fled…

To the time he had successfully reached Phoenix, to the night journey on the freight train that took him to Tucson.

Here he kept a low profile, called himself by a new name and slowly, ever so slowly, built a new life for himself. Then, recently, he had found some interesting information. He came across a diary. An old diary, written over two hundred years ago.◻

T H E   P A S T;

Period 8

The year 1816–South of Acapulco

Eleven-year-old Angelina promised she would be careful and left the house. She strode quickly across the yard towards the large barn, and a little later walked her horse out, leading the horse by the reins, with no saddle. She liked to ride bareback even though recently she had fallen and knocked herself unconscious. The kind stranger had picked her up and taken her home.

She led the horse to a wagon which she climbed onto, and then onto her horse, a beautiful animal. It had been her horse that had found the stranger and brought him back to where she had fallen.

She rode away from the farmhouse and towards the coast.

Her father, her uncle and aunt, and the strangers, though by now they were much a part of the family, had left early on this beautiful day. Angelina knew where they were headed, had heard stories, was inquisitive, and really needed to see what they were going to do.

The stranger's name was Philippe. He had been washed ashore after his ship had been battered in a violent storm that had cost the lives of all of his men. He alone had somehow survived.

He had later travelled to Acapulco and collected a woman who was to be his wife. Her name was Caprice, and Angelina thought she was not only pretty but very nice.

Angelina rode her horse steadily, making sure she would reach the coastline a little away from where her father was heading.

The dark grey horse strode easily up the hill and reached the top.

The sea lay before them.

The young girl stopped her horse and looked over to her left.

There, on the sandy beach, was her aunt, Chantale, standing beside a pile of equipment.

Then she saw the little boat returning from a rocky outcrop some fifty metres from the shore.

She had noticed as the group had left the house that between them they were carrying a small boat and quite a lot of other stuff, like ropes and things.

She also knew, by overheard conversations, that they were going to try and recover some treasure form the sunken ship. She heard of gold coins.

Angelina rode her horse a little bit back from the top of the dune, then slipped off and sat down, watching, making sure she wasn't spotted.

Uncle Marcos helped Chantale onto the narrow boat, a very lightweight craft made of straw, and then paddled back towards the rocky outcrop.

The ship had been blown onto those rocks and had broken up and disappeared below the waves.

Angelina had heard Philippe speaking of the event and how somehow, he had been thrown clear, pushed through the various rocks and had then been washed ashore.

Angelina saw the little boat reach a large area of rocks and then vanished from view. It was obvious that she would not be able to see what was going on from the dune. Like her aunt who had taught her, she knew how to swim.

The bay was usually a very quiet and sedate spot to swim and escape from the summer sun. There were several outcrops of rock that also sheltered the bay a little. Angelina told her horse to just stay there, patted the nose of her beloved animal, kissed it, then strode determinedly towards the sea.

She was more than curious. She wanted to know.

She swam towards a group of rocks that lay slightly to the right of where the others had landed, reached it in no time, carefully climbed around the rock almost to the top, then got on to her belly and slid the rest of the way and suddenly had the view she had hoped for.

In the little boat, she saw her aunt and the other woman, Caprice, had both taken off their clothing and were just in their underclothes. Both had already been in the water, for she could see their bodies glistening in the sunshine.

Then Caprice rolled over the side of the boat and into the water, diving below the surface.

She seemed to be under for such a long time Angelina was thinking. How she wanted to be able to swim like that some day.

In the little boat Chantale kept watch.

Caprice resurfaced and Chantale helped her back into the little boat. It would be her turn again next, but the smile on the other woman's face told it all. Caprice hugged the other woman and then waved frantically to the shore.

Lying on her belly, ignoring the hardness of the rock, a mere sixty metres away, Angelina watched it all. She saw the blonde woman wave, watched as the group on the rocks all looked to be very excited.

For another forty minutes, Angelina watched as both Chantale and Caprice in turn dove beneath the surface, this time with rope, which they had in the boat with them, until they had secured what it was they had been searching for.

Then her aunt paddled back to the group whilst Caprice made sure she held fast to the rope.

Angelina watched until the three men on the rock had pulled and tugged and strained to finally pull a chest out of the water.

The little girl smiled. A treasure chest, a real treasure chest.

She slithered back down the rock upon which she had lain for quite some time, then went back into the water and swam confidently back to shore.

She was hungry after all that exertion. She ran up the beach, up on the dune and called her horse who came at once.

She greeted him, then put her arms around his neck and with a movement she had done before climbed upon his back and steered for home.

That evening Angelina carefully wrote everything down that she had seen and heard that day. It took her almost two hours.

THE PRESENT;

Albuquerque

Sunday 29th March

Detective Sergeant Jose Rodrigues looked at the notes he had just written down.

Then, logging into his computer screen, he clicked and scrolled and found what he was looking for.

Reading it through carefully, he picked up the phone, dialled reception and spoke to the operator.

Just under forty minutes later, Detective Inspector Roger Mantell walked into the office.

"Hey, what's up Jose?"

Just as his colleague was about to speak, his own phone buzzed.

"Hello?"

"Miss Hudson, yes, I remember you…okay, yes, go ahead, I'm writing it down…"

Roger listened and, having taken a pen from his jacket pocket, he began to scribble on a pad that was on the desk.

Four minutes later, he thanked the caller, promised he would be in touch soon and finished the call.

Jose gave him an enquiring look, then said, "Miss Hudson?"

"Yes, why?"

"It's what I wanted to speak to you about. I just had some information with regard to a Mrs Constance Shelton. Just read the case. This is uncanny."

"What about Mrs Shelton?" Roger wanted to know.

"Gone missing from the Camino Nuevo correctional centre, early this morning."

"Miss Hudson had a call yesterday, from a Barbara Philpot, she's the sister of a Mr Eddie Philpot, missing presumed dead, over thirty years ago. He's wanted for murder. Well, it seems he is alive, though apparently not well. He's on his way here, with new information."

Roger pondered for a moment, then said, "Will you look into the breakout?"

To which Jose nodded affirmatively.

"I'm going to delve into the old case. Something there I found a while back, which might be of use now, but before that, there is a bus I need to meet."

In San Francisco

Alison puffed out her cheeks. She had already spoken to Millie before contacting the detective.

Barbara had called yesterday, tearfully, having received a distressed call from her brother, and she had related all of that conversation. She had not been able to get hold of Millie until earlier this morning, had not slept terribly well, and though Millie couldn't get away just now, Alison promised her she would fly down to Albuquerque and keep her informed on the proceedings.

THE PAST;

Period 9

The year 1866–Harris, New Brunswick

Henry's sculpture stood in a far corner on the back porch of the big house. He had finished it many years ago, had chiselled a square plinth for it out of hard white stone, and had secured the sculpture on to it.

The two foot high piece of rock had a mainly light grey sheen to it, but here and there quartz showed through in colours ranging from a translucent orange, through to shades of yellow and even a light green streak could be seen.

Henry had polished it, smoothed the edges and had roughly carved the title of this work on one side of the plinth, which was about three foot square and six inches deep.

The title had come about, after his wife, who, at the beginning of his work on the piece, had asked, "Henry, what's the point?"

After some thought he had smiled at her and had said, "Hopkins Point", and so it was and so it had been carved into the base.

Under Sara's supervision, four men lifted the piece and placed it on a hand cart. Together the group walked over to the main building where Sara had chosen a spot, on the paved square by the entrance, for it to be placed securely.

"Well Henry," she whispered to herself, when all was in place and she stood alone, "here it is and here it stands"

It was a strange sort of oblong shape, and about two thirds of the way up and no more than two inches from the left-hand side, Henry had drilled a small hole into which he had inserted an emerald.

Sara noticed early on that often the rays of the sun would catch that pale green precious stone and it would sparkle and gleam.

What it was meant to represent, she did not know. Perhaps only Henry knew. Maybe he had written about it in one of his journals.

Journals that he had already passed on to her several months back, perhaps having an inkling that his health was ailing.

She hadn't, as yet, started to read them, but promised herself to begin to do so soon.

Almost every day when she came to work, before entering the building, she would put her hand out and touch the sculpture.

Good morning Henry, she would often say in her mind.

Two weeks had passed since his death and since the death of Rebekah, his wife and her grandmother.

Sara had arrived with a photographer in tow. The first photograph she wanted taken was of her standing by Henry's sculpture.

Not much later she entered the big office. Her office now. It had been her father's, Charlie Parker the third, and as she walked over to the large desk she took in the beautiful seascape that hung on the wall behind it.

It had been a gift to her father, by his grandfather, also named Charlie, who, she knew, had purchased it way back in 1762.

Then it had been Henry's office when her father and mother returned to Boston to take on the company business there, leaving the mine to Henry and Rebekah.

Now it was hers.

Sara sat herself in the comfortable leather chair and thought just briefly about the change of circumstances. She still grieved over the loss of Henry in particular, who had spent so much time with her and had so thoroughly taught her all she needed to know to run the business.

In the top left-hand drawer were the journals that he had written, and once again she inwardly promised herself to read them soon.

On top of the desk were only a few items: a large ledger, a smaller ledger which was used for the day-to-day running, a wooden set containing two inkwells and an array of pens.

There was also an ink blotter and a wooden stamp, and a box, a lovely ornate carved box with a painted scene on the lid.

It had once belonged to her great-grandmother, but had been passed down the line and was now hers.

It contained two things, both bequeathed to her by Henry: his Bible and his beautiful watch and chain that he wore every day.

Whilst still grieving over her loss, Sara was also inwardly excited for it was not long now, before she was going to be married, to Carl.

Later that same day there was a knock on the door.

The photographer.

⚜

THE PRESENT;

Boston

Sunday 29th March

Eddie Philpot was en route on a bus going from Flagstaff to the Albuquerque bus terminal.

Alison Hudson was on a flight from San Francisco heading for the same city and same bus terminal.

Constance Shelton, having escaped, was determined to get to that bus terminal, and Detective Inspector Mantell was also making his way there.

Another person who would also end up going there, would be Simon Lightfoot.

Unaware of all of this, Chrissie was sifting through the photographs that Sam had spread out on the kitchen table.

"Hey look" Sam said, holding a photo up for Chrissie to see, "I stood by the very same sculpture"

"Who's the woman?"

Sam turned the print over and read what it said. "Sara Parker."

"Oh my goodness," Chrissie exclaimed. "Here it is!" then holding what she had found up for Sam to see.

"It's that same woman, Sara, in this office, but look, there, on that wonderful desk, see?"

"The box!" he said, "and there, on the wall, the seascape, the very one I went to assess."

"Now hanging on the wall in Tammy's apartment," Chrissie added.

After another closer look at the old photograph, she said, "So, this Sara Parker, had the box, in…1866…"

"Wait a minute!" Sam interrupted. "I know, from my research that it was a Charlie Parker, who, in 1762, bought the seascapes from Christoffer Rosenborg. Remember, his name was on the back of the paintings? Now, this same guy could have had the box as well, and perhaps also sold that to Charlie. It makes sense as it is still in the same family, so that's very likely how it came across the Atlantic."

"Yes, I remember. You're right, it does make sense," Chrissie agreed, thinking back to the time when Sam took the back off the two seascapes in Tammy's apartment.

"Now we need to look into how it came into your grandfather's possession. When did he acquire it?"

"I don't know," Chrissie answered. "I found it under the stairs. I had never seen it before. It's unlikely that my dad, or mum bought it, so it must have been granddad. I went to see the housekeeper about it. Unfortunately, she could not recall the item."

Chrissie noticed her husband-to-be was totally engrossed in the selection of old prints.

"Interesting record of the mines history?" she asked.

"Very. Looking at the range, and at the dates and descriptions, I think it must have been this very same Sara who initiated this whole record. Here she is again. Look, this is dated 1889 and titled 'Steam comes to Harris'."

Chrissie took the picture. It was the same woman, nearly twenty years later, but still looking very attractive, stunning even, Chrissie thought, alongside a tall and handsome blond man, and a younger man, with a smile on his face.

She turned it over to read the details.

"Henry Charles Parker, with mother Sara, father Carl and sisters, Rebekah and Charlotte." Below that was written 1889 and 'Steam comes to Harris.'

"Sam, can you show me that family tree that you drew up. The Parker dynasty?"

Sam looked up, smiled and said, "Sure, I'll fire up my laptop. In the meantime, could you rustle up some coffee?"

THE PAST;

Period 10

The year 1924–New York

Nathaniel Parker was feeling a range of emotions. He was angry, that was for sure. Angry at himself. He was also a little afraid; afraid of why he had come to New York, why he had found this office building, and why he had approached the receptionist who was looking at him expectantly as he strode across the marble tiled lobby.

On top of that he was feeling guilty and a little nauseous.

He managed a smile as he spoke to the lady behind the imposing reception desk, was told him to go straight up, indicating the elevators, to the eight floor.

Here another smartly dressed woman was awaiting him and escorted him to an office.

Percivald Quinton stood up from behind his walnut desk and came around to greet Nathaniel. Offering his hand, which was shaken, Percivald got straight down to business.

"All laid out for you here, Nathaniel," he said, indicating the various documents on the desk. "Just need your signature, and all will be well."

Less than twenty minutes later Nathaniel was on his way to the railway station heading back to Boston.

He reflected on the past, instilled in himself a new aim, a new attitude and promised himself, to get over this hurdle and carry on.

Seventy percent!

Seventy percent of all the profits his business in Boston was going to make, would now go to Percivald Quinton. All because of the turn of a card.

All because he had gambled, and lost. In the casino in Monte Carlo.

At one point all had been going so well, then it had all fallen to pieces. The turn of a card and he had lost, lost everything.

But Percivald Quinton had been there, had suddenly appeared at his shoulder and had whispered a deal.

Seventy percent!

Time passed.

Eight years later, when his wife Beatrice gave birth to a baby boy they named Joshua, Nathaniel could not face it any more.

He had worked hard, had even grown the business, but he began to realise more and more that the better the company did, the more Percivald would put in his pocket. Nathaniel had never told his wife that he had gambled the company away, never told her many things. No more.

Nathaniel left one morning and never returned; was never heard from again.

He left a heartbroken woman holding the baby.

Four years later, in the year 1938, Percivald sold the Boston business, making sure that Beatrice was financially secure.

It was at an auction, where some of the assets of the big house were sold, where he purchased the two seascapes.

It was at that auction where Beatrice received funds from the sale of those paintings, along with the proceeds of much furniture sold as well as some smaller items.

Included in these items was the ornate box.

It was also at this same auction on that day that Zeta Bell sold the miniature which ended up being purchased by Chrissie's grandfather Eddie.

Furthermore, it had been a few days earlier when Zeta took the miniature in for placing in the sale that she came across three smooth black covered journals, written by Henry Hopkins, which in later years she posted to her father Carlos in San Francisco.

The same journals that years later would be thoroughly read and enjoyed by Emily Parker.

Finally it was at that auction where Chrissie's grandfather, having already purchased the miniature ivory, also took a fancy to the ornate box, stuck his hand up and ended up winning the bid.

Percivald, satisfied that Beatrice Parker now had sufficient funds to live on and knowing she, with her son, were going to travel to the town of Harris to reside there, left the auction room, left Boston, and returned to New York.

THE PRESENT;

New York

Sunday 29th March

"Yes, yes, yes, who's a clever girl then!" Tammy said, to herself. She got up from the dining table, which was totally covered with a huge array of sheets of paper, folders and notepads, not to mention two empty glasses with a residue of wine, two cups and saucers, showing a residue of coffee, and a selection of pens and pencils.

A small mantelpiece clock that showed the time to be a little after eleven.

Picking up her phone, she pressed a couple of buttons and placing the phone down on the table, the speaker on, she began to tidy up the numerous sheets of paper and documents.

"Tammy?" answered a female voice.

"Hi Chrissie, how are you, and how is Sam doing? Is he getting better?"

In Boston Chrissie smiled at the thought of being with Sam the previous night and answered, "Oh yes, much better thank you. You sound, a little excited. Don't tell me you've found out some more page turning information?"

"Why yes Chrissie, dear, so pin back your ears, and listen," Tammy replied, smiling and happy to be able to share what she had discovered.

"I know the connection between Percivald and Beatrice Parker!" she commenced. Then, again she began to rattle out her story without seemingly taking a breath.

"So, it turns out that my great-grandfather inherited an already lucrative business in New York, in the form of a couple of factories that manufactured flour and syrup, and a large bakery that made cookies.

"Then, I found out that he owned, or at least had bought out, a large shipping and retail business in Boston, one that was started by a Charlie Parker way back in the mid-1700s." Not giving Chrissie an opportunity to speak, Tammy continued,

"Now, I found this out, mainly by working backwards. You see, I found that he sold this business, in 1938, and according to the ledgers, there was a part owner, none other than Beatrice Parker. Actually, after some deeper digging, the company had belonged to a Nathaniel Parker, but he had gone AWOL. Gone; disappeared one day, so his wife, Beatrice, then ended up owning it, or at least thirty percent of it from what I can make out. I'm not an accountant.

"So," Tammy went on, Chrissie, smiling at the tone of her excited friend and the rapid discourse, "there was an auction, selling goods from the family home, including the seascapes. Now, here's the thing though, Percivald seemingly already owned most of this stuff, but he purchased the paintings.

"And with a substantial offer, from what I can see, anyway. I think it was to raise some more funds for this Beatrice, whose husband, Nathaniel had left them, and she had a baby, although by then a four-year-old. His name was Joshua, and, if my memory serves me well, and I listened properly to that husband-tobe of yours, it was this Joshua who eventually sold the mine in Harris to that Rozzini guy."

It seemed Tammy had run out of breath, for there was a longer pause, one Chrissie used to jump in, "Goodness Tammy. Have you even slept at all? Yes, you're right, about the Joshua connection..."

Tammy must have taken a breath because she once again began. "Right, yes, thought so. Well, anyway, it turns out that Percivald, with the funds of the sale of this business in Boston, bought the apartment, this apartment, my apartment. It also helped me in further connecting my family tree, though I still have to connect young William, who came over from Plymouth, to the ownership of these manufacturing plants and bakery..."

It was Chrissie who interrupted and asked, "Did you say the goods from the family home, as in the Parker family home in Boston, were sold at auction? The very same auction my grandfather attended?"

"Yes, why?"

"I don't suppose you would have any idea as to what these goods might be, would you?"

"Hang on," Tammy replied, beginning to sort through the papers on the table.

"Yes, here we are. Furniture and stuff, why?

"Is there by chance the mention of a box, a wooden box, an ornate box, anything like that?" Chrissie asked, feeling rather excited about the possibility of it being there and helping her with her own riddle.

Tammy glanced down the list on the document she held in her hand, "Yes, yes, here it says wooden ornamental box, with scrolled decoration on all sides and a painted scene on the lid…"

"That's it! Yes, oh well done Tammy, you're a star!"

"I know that, but why…"

That box that very box, without doubt, is what my grandfather bought that same day. I have it here. It's right in front of me…

THE PAST;

Period 11

The year 1988–Near Silver City

All of a sudden Conrad was right in front of him.

There was noise, there was chaos. People crying.

Conrad had grabbed the passing Eddie by the collar and was shouting as the wind roared.

"Go, get it now. An opportunity like this does not happen often, so go! Get those papers."

"Okay okay, but you're bleeding."

"Just a small cut," Conrad answered, wiping the blood away from just above his left eye with his hand, "Now go!"

Eddie made his way through the carnage, ignoring the moans and cries, ignoring the students who were seemingly wandering around aimlessly.

He got to the Professor's trailer just in time to see one of the students come out, the Mexican girl, Nueva, he believed her name to be …

Already some distance away he saw the dust and swirl of the tornado. He opened the door of the trailer, noticed the second trailer, that of the professor's assistant, on its side and leaning against the professor's trailer. Then he stepped inside.

Sirens were heading their way.

A girl, bruised and bleeding from a cut on her arm, walked up to Conrad.

"Your little friend, Josie," she said, her breathing laboured, "the one with the biker boyfriend" she added, then, with a half-smile, "taken care of."

"Good, mingle and help now. I can see ambulances coming. I'll come back, maybe tonight, probably tomorrow night. I'll let you know."

He then nodded at her, pleased with himself. He ought to perhaps check on Eddie.

But he saw an opportunity, as the girl turned around, and grabbed a steel pole that lay right beside him.

Eddie was perspiring. Sure it was the middle of the day, it was hot, but it was more than that.

He was afraid.

In his desperation to get the folder, discovering the professor, barely conscious, holding it firmly clasped to her chest, was the first stumbling block. She just wouldn't let go. Her eyes looked up at him, and registered confusion and anger.

He hit her.

Coming out of the trailer, having quickly stuffed the folder under his sweater, he looked around and felt that no one had seen him. It was time to leave, to leave the scene.

His heart was thumping. Sure, he had the folder. He had what he had been asked to get; made to get, really; demanded, because of his weakness, because of his debt, his gambling debt.

Conrad Shelton. Rich boy, nasty.

He formed a plan in his mind, a plan, to level the field.

The police were arriving, ambulances, two of them, appeared on the scene.

He needed to get away, to get away from Conrad to start with, to further formulate a plan. Get away from this chaotic scene.

He walked through the carnage, the blown around tents, the books, the plastic tables, the chairs. He walked through a trail of destruction left by the tornado.

Looking up, he saw the violent twister far in the distance, though it had by now severely diminished in size.

He passed several students, in shock, suffering cuts and bruises.

Paramedics walked around quickly, sizing up how badly people were wounded.

Several cars and vans were parked in a field adjacent to the dig site. Amazingly as the twister had cut a path through the landscape, the parking area was virtually untouched.

Eddie saw, to his relief, that his battered old car was in one piece.

Conrad, on his way to the trailer to make sure that Eddie had the folder that he knew existed, saw him coming out of the trailer, but Conrad was suddenly stopped.

A paramedic was right in front of him.

"You're bleeding sir" the man said, taking hold of Conrad by both shoulders and looking directly at him, "Let me check this out."

Conrad had no time, "Please, I'm good. See to others. Some serious injuries, over there," he pointed to where he had come from.

The paramedic had a quick look into the young man's eyes, then nodded and said, "Okay," and headed in the suggested direction.

Conrad thanked him, then made his way to the trailer, seeing no sign of Eddie.

A short time later, he once more headed for the chaotic scene where once had stood the main tent, the hub of their site.

Fellow students crying, in shock. He had been so focused on using the opportunity, he had not even considered the devastating effect of what had occurred.

He looked on where a paramedic was hunched over a body. It was Kathryn Smith.

There was another lifeless body. Already having been examined and with a blanket covering her.

This was Josie Morton.

Her wounds seemed only superficial. An autopsy later would conclude that she had been hit in her stomach by flying debris, which had rendered her unconscious. Her body seemed to have gone into shock and she had simply stopped breathing.

A news van arrived, photographers descended.

"Tornado kills 4, 17 wounded", would be the headlines the following day.

It was also on the small television in his motel room.

Eddie listened and watched in horror.

What had he done!

He had driven away from the carnage. He hadn't been stopped. He had reached Silver City, booked himself into a motel and had, eventually, fallen asleep.

He had wanted to play it cool, make a deal with Conrad for the information that he now had.

But all that changed when he heard the news.

He had killed the professor.

Gathering his stuff, he left and drove to Albuquerque, all the while trying to think clearly and come up with a plan. By the time he got there, he had made a decision.

He left his car in a large parking garage in the city, went to the post office and bought a parcel bag and stuffed the folder inside. He addressed it and then made a call. To his younger sister in Portland.

No other option; he had to run.

THE PRESENT;

Albuquerque

Sunday 29th March

Constance felt she had no other option.

She had received a message the previous afternoon. A message she hadn't conceived possible.

Eddie Philpot was alive.

Not only that, he was on his way to give himself up; to reveal all.

According to the message source, this Eddie was coming with new information.

All overheard as a phone call was made, an emotional phone call, all overheard by a former inmate, someone who knew Constance Shelton.

Information that was surely worth something.

He was going to be on the bus from Flagstaff that would arrive around lunchtime.

She had no option.

She needed to get to him first.

What other information did he have? Where had he been for all these years?

She had calmly and quietly slipped away from the Correctional Centre in Industrial Avenue in the very early hours of the morning.

It hadn't been difficult. She had made friends inside; friends with connections; friends with pull and know how.

She was a wealthy woman, they knew this. They counted on this. Their friendship was based on this.

She wouldn't be missed for several hours.

All she had to do was to get to that bus. Apparently he was quite unwell. It would be easy.

Until then, she just had to lie low.

Meanwhile

Eddie, clutching the satchel, was dozing in a seat near the back of the Greyhound bus. Though still unwell, he no longer felt that he was dying.

Speaking to his sister had helped. It had been a relief to hear her voice. It had been a relief to talk.

Not much longer now, then he could tell all, bring closure, and accept whatever lay ahead.

The weather was fine as the bus drove smoothly along the highway.

He thought how providential it had been to have come across a diary, written by a young girl so long ago, back in the early 1800s that had, in combination with what he knew about the discovery at the Shelton residence, given him the information he now had.

Back in Albuquerque

Simon Lightfoot had perused the various documents once more, then gathered them up and placed them in a leather case.

The documents contained the findings that had turned his world upside down, again.

He was still getting his head around what Raphael had found out all those years ago, when the young man had come to see him one day.⊠

T H E   P A S T ;

Period 12

The year 2002–University of Albuquerque

Raphael Morton was stunned. He paused for a moment, then set about to re-examine the tests he had performed, for a third time. Checking and triple checking.

But every time, he came to the same conclusion. It had to be the answer.

The only answer.

He had been there for three days. Time out from his training, time out before being deployed to Afghanistan in the next few weeks, before Christmas.

He had asked to come to the laboratory and to use their facilities as, he explained, wanted to learn more about the forensic side as his aim was eventually to be a medical examiner.

Currently he was a corpsman in the marines, already close to completing his studies as a doctor.

He had a few contacts at the university which gave him the opportunity to use the laboratory. The real reason was different.

As a boy, especially a black boy, he had often been picked on, not just for the colour of his skin, but because he was small of stature.

It had been one day, coming home from school via a route he didn't normally take that he was being targeted by a trio of teenage troublemakers.

Raphael was eleven at the time.

It had been outside the motorcycle repair shop where Simon worked.

Simon who had been his sister's boyfriend. Simon who was cool. He had a bike; he had long hair; he smoked.

He was cool in Raphael's eyes.

Simon had come out that day, and had walked over and confronted the trio, who, at first were hurling insults at him, but Simon merely looked at them. They backed off and retreated.

Simon had looked at him. He had looked up at Simon who had simply nodded and had gone back inside the workshop. He had not uttered a word.

He had told his mother when he came home. The only reason he wanted to, despite the fact that he had not come home the direct route and could be in trouble, was to let her know that Simon was a good guy, knowing they had disliked him and him seeing Josie.

It had been only recently that, upon coming home for a few days from his military training, his mother had told him that Simon had been to visit.

She showed him the letter that his sister had written.

It fired his imagination and so he had come up with plan to examine all the evidence that had been recovered and recorded from the tornado strike.

With this to hand, he set about to work.

He took samples, tested and digested all the information he could get his hands on.

The police reports, witness reports, medical reports.

He completed his findings, then rechecked them.

He was sure he had found some anomalies.

But what to do next?

Raphael was deployed less than a week later, to Afghanistan, where he served for three years.

The year 2005

Raphael was employed by a medical clinic as a qualified doctor, in Yonkers, New York. Though he often thought about his findings, he had told no one, until the day he left home in Albuquerque to settle into his new apartment close to the clinic where he was to work. On that day, he drove over the motorcycle showroom and repair shop, now owned by Simon.

He was there and Raphael shared his findings, feeling that, perhaps if anyone should know, Simon should as he had all along wanted to uncover the truth of what really happened that day, though what he was about to share, would certainly shock him.

After a week in his new place, and having settled very well into his new role, he noticed the law firm that was almost across the road from where he worked.

He made an appointment. He needed some legal advice.

Just as he was entering, a young lady was coming out. He noticed her. She was pretty, petite and blonde, and though she was in deep thought, when he held the door open for her to exit, she looked at him and smiled.

He entered, then, after introducing himself to the receptionist who had asked him to wait, he watched the young lady cross the street.

She had on a brightly coloured top tucked into faded blue jeans, the denim jacket she wore was too long in the sleeve, apparently fashionable, she had a green coloured handbag, was holding a smart looking leather case and got into a battered Volkswagen beetle.

"Mr Morton?" the receptionist said, standing up, "Mr Stratford will see you now. If you will follow me?"

Raphael tore his eyes away from the pretty blonde and turned around.

T H E P R E S E N T ;

Albuquerque

Sunday 29th

Simon picked up the photograph that was on display on the low cabinet. A picture of himself with Felicity. She was smiling, her blue eyes bright, her long blonde hair a wild mess.

So pretty, he thought, then put the photo back.

"It has to be done. It just has to come out, Fliss," he whispered.

Then he donned his leather jacket and left his house. He placed the folder into one of the saddlebags.

With a heavy heart he straddled his Indian motorcycle, brought it to life and headed into town.

"She's heading for the bus terminal. She wants to meet with Eddie," Detective Sergeant Jose Rodrigues said, almost breathless, as he entered the office and spoke to Detective Inspector Roger Mantell. "She had information about a call yesterday."

"Mmm, now what could Eddie know that might be a threat to our Constance," Roger said looking at his watch. "Let's go. The bus is due in twenty minutes. Get a patrol car to go out and meet the bus, without making it obvious. Make sure no gets on or off before we get there." "On it," Jose answered and picked up a phone.

Alison Hudson left her overnight bag in a locker at the airport.

If she ended up staying the night, she could easily retrieve it.

She joined the queue for a cab.

Poor Barbara, she thought. She had had such a difficult upbringing, had to hold on to a secret when her brother had called, over thirty years ago, and had to hide the parcel he sent.

Then she had received that call, just two days ago, from him, from a brother she had thought long-gone and dead.

Alison got into the cab and gave the driver instructions.

Simon arrived at the police station. According to the newspaper articles he had kept about the gold coins and the subsequent arrest of Mrs Constance Shelton, the leading detective was a man called Roger Mantell.

It was him he was hoping to see.

A car drove away as Simon, and the cab with Alison, arrived.

She paid the driver got out, noticed who was in the car that was driving away and spoke to the motorbike man, thinking he was part of the police force.

"Was that Roger Mantell just driving away?" she asked walking up to him.

Simon looked at the woman, then at the vanishing car, then back at the woman. "Was it? He is the man I came to see…"

"You're not the police?" Alison interrupted.

"No…"

"I need to get to the bus terminal, do you know where that is?" Alison said.

"Sure, but…"

"Look, take me there, okay. You want to see Roger, well that's where he is going…"

"Really, but…"

"No time to explain… go, go" she pushed the man towards his bike.

Simon could see the determination in her eyes, heard the urgency in her voice, "Jump on, and hold on!"

In the unmarked police vehicle, Roger received a call from a colleague that the bus was under surveillance and ahead of schedule, due to arrive within the next five minutes.

Roger spoke to Jose, who was driving, "Have you got men on the ground by the terminal? Bus coming any minute."

"We're there. Keeping an eye, but staying back," he answered, closing in on the bus terminal.

Alison held on tight as the man easily manoeuvred his big bike through traffic, taking several sharp turns, speeding along quieter side streets and they reached the terminal at the same time as the detectives.

"There he is," Alison shouted above the roar of the Indian's motor.

Simon drove deftly, and very capable of handling the bike he had owned for several years now, caught up and stopped right by the car as Detective Inspector Roger Mantell got out.

"Roger!" Alison shouted, leaping from the motorcycle and walking towards him.

"Miss Hudson? Right, glad you're here. Mrs Shelton is here, somewhere. The bus is due any minute. You know what she looks like, be careful!"

Turning around, Alison approached the motorcycle man, "Okay, you, come with me. There's a woman here, somewhere. Could be armed. Need to find her, so stay close, okay."

Simon, quite impressed with this tall blonde with the clear blue eyes, said nothing but followed her as she headed for the terminal building.

He glanced at the man he knew now must be Detective Inspector Mantell, who seemed pre-occupied, then made sure he kept close to the woman, who apparently was a Miss Hudson. What intrigued him most though, as he followed her through the crowd, was that a Mrs Shelton was mentioned.

He knew who that was, so what was happening here? A bus due any minute, who, was on it?

The bus from Flagstaff pulled in. A police car pulled in behind.

Alison looked among the crowd, then spotted her, and without hesitation made her way towards her.

Passengers began to step from the bus and the driver had pushed a button to open up the side panel to the luggage compartment.

Alison worked her way through the crowd. It was quite busy, she thought, despite the restrictions, despite the call to only go out for essentials, and, even though the recommendation was to wear a mask, hardly anyone did.

She realised that she was not either, but she had an excuse. She was on a mission!

Then she spotted Mrs Shelton in a dark rain jacket, jeans, baseball cap. She had only caught a glimpse of her, from a distance, but knew it to be her.

She reached her.

Several people had by now stepped from the bus and some were retrieving their bags.

"Hello Mrs Shelton," Alison said, now right behind the woman who was intently watching the disembarking passengers.

The woman in front turned quickly, paled and started to withdraw her right hand from the pocket of her jacket.

But just as she did, a hand suddenly appeared and grabbed her wrist. In her hand was a makeshift knife.

Simon's grip was secure and tight. She dropped the weapon, tried to break free, but two policemen who had been alerted and also spotted Mrs Shelton, arrived.

"We've got this sir," they said in unison, to the man who had grabbed the woman's wrists in such a timely manner.

Simon nodded, released the arm and looked at Miss Hudson.

"Are you okay there, Miss Hudson?"

"Yes, thank you. I was prepared for her to do something, but she was very quick. Phew, I'm glad that's over."

Then, taking in the tall man before her, said, "And call me Ally."

Meanwhile Roger Mantell entered the bus as no more passengers were emerging.

Walking carefully, advising the driver now to get out, he walked towards the rear of the bus.

There, near the back, a man sat, slumped, clutching a satchel.

Roger sighed, and leaned forward to check for any signs of life.

Then, carefully taking the satchel, he made a call.

⌘

EPILOGUE

Police station–Albuquerque

Sunday 29th March 2020

The Covid Pandemic was rife around the world. Vaccines were being worked on and tested frantically, but it would be more than eight months before they were ready to be used…

Thousands of people were in hospital; flights were being cancelled; cruises were put on hold.

Travel restrictions were beginning to be put in place. There were more lockdowns, more guidelines, more restrictions. Everywhere.

They were together in the big air conditioned boardroom. The very same where Alison and Millie had been when Detective Inspector Mantell, with the aid of Michelle, had explained all their findings, with regard to the tornado path and subsequent theft.

That had been nine months ago.

Present this time, were Detective Inspector Roger Mantell, Detective Sergeant Jose Rodrigues, Alison Hudson and Simon Lightfoot.

Then there was a young lad, who was just introduced as David, who was in charge of the recording equipment as well as making notes.

It was almost four pm.

"Well," Roger, the last one to enter the room, said looking at Alison and Simon who sat together. He glanced at his colleague Jose, then gave a nod to the young lad.

He had in his hand two large folders. These he placed on the table, then sat down next to Jose and opposite Alison and Simon.

"Mr Lightfoot," he began, "thank you for coming forwards with the information you had. I'll get to all of that in a moment.

In fact, I'll let you explain it, but first, sadly, Mr Eddie Philpot is dead. He succumbed to this dreaded virus." Then looking directly at Alison, "Miss Hudson, I wonder, could you inform his sister? Seeing as you…well, would you?"

"Yes of course. I spoke with her earlier, so she knows I'm here I told her I would speak to her when I knew something. I knew he had died, but felt I needed to wait for your approval to tell her."

"Thank you, again. You have been most helpful in all of this." Then, looking at both her and Simon, he said, "He did have important information with him, and we also found a letter he had written and a diary, a sort of journal written, quite some time ago by a young girl, probably only about eleven or twelve. It was written around 1816 to 1818."

He paused and again looked across at Alison and Simon. "How Mr Philpot acquired it, perhaps we'll never know. We do know that for the past thirty plus years, he had been living just outside Tucson.

Roger picked up the weathered item. "It seems that he figured out from information in this journal, this diary, and from information in the papers about the arrest of Mrs Shelton, and the gold coins and the mosaic tiles found in her back yard, that we didn't find everything.

"According to the girl's notes, written in here–by the way, we know her name was Angelina–there had been 720 gold coins. Now this girl says she had received a letter. It had been written by a lady called Lena Castagnet." The detective paused briefly, before continuing, "It was written in Silver City. Now this letter is in Spanish, as is the diary. Eddie, obviously had a knowledge of the language as he translated it. We have that in his written notes." The detective placed the diary down on the table and picked up the very notes he was referring to, then, after taking a quick sip of his glass of water, he continued. "The letter tells that this Lena and her husband buried the gold coins as the weight of having the Spanish coins was too much pressure. They had all they needed and to have nothing left to strive for was not for them. They wrote that they had buried the all that they had retrieved from the sea, which is another story. The upshot is 720 gold coins were buried, with the mosaic tiles depicting that swallow, covering them. This was then further covered by soil back in the year 1862."

Roger took another sip of water, looked at both Alison and Simon and then went on to further explain.

"When we uncovered the stashed gold coins in Mrs Shelton's backyard, there were only 400. That leave 320 still unaccounted for.

"This was the information Eddie wanted to bring to us, and he also wanted to confess to his part in the sad affair. In the letter he wrote, addressed to Millie, she is the daughter of professor Emily Parker," Roger explaining the connection to Simon. Then looking at Alison, "Again, I wonder Miss Hudson,…"

"Of course, I will get that letter to Millie," she answered, anticipating the question.

"Thank you,…in it, he expresses his enormous regret and apologises."

Roger paused for a moment, took another sip of water, then giving both Alison and Simon a quick look, he continued, "Sadly Mr Philpot died, for although, yes, he did take the folder from the professor, and yes, he did hit her, while he thought that it had been him that had killed her, this, in fact, was not true."

The detective let that sink in for a moment, before explaining, "I later discovered an anomaly. Sad to say that in the chaos of it all, there had not been due diligence in fully establishing the cause of death of Emily Parker, of her assistant Mr Donald Alfredo, and of course the two students, Kathryn Smith and Josie Morton."

The detective specifically looked at and gave a nod to Simon, before saying, "After Conrad was shot and killed in Rome, I took a look at all the evidence and information gathered myself. I had a feeling that I should, anyway. I found a blood spot, found it belonged to Conrad. His prints were on file as he had a juvenile record which had been sealed. Anyway, from what I can reconstruct, Eddie went into the trailer, hit the professor, took the folder and left, but Conrad, no doubt wanting to check up on Eddie, entered the trailer afterwards, and it was he, I'm sure, who killed the professor. I'm sure she had been alive when Eddie left."

He again let that sink in for a moment.

"The reason I feel confident now that this is the case, is due to other facts that have since come to life. Again, I must thank you Miss Hudson, and of course Miss Parker, for all the information you found and brought to us, which, led to the arrest of Mrs Shelton. However, Mr Lightfoot's finding, well, they puts a whole new light on the matter. I think at this point Mr Lightfoot, perhaps you can explain."

Simon looked across to his left at Alison, a woman he had only met earlier in the day, who had so commandingly got him to transport her to the bus terminal. A woman who was a rather attractive, tall blonde, he had also noticed, and who was now looking at him with those lovely eyes. He was momentarily distracted.

He then looked across at the two detectives and began to tell his story.

"Okay, well, I had best begin at the beginning," he said, "especially for you Miss Hudson," turning to look at her again, and giving her a quick smile. "To put you in the picture, Josie Morton, one of the students killed that day when the tornado struck, was my girlfriend.

"She was also one of three people who initially knew about the gold. You see, it wasn't until some time later that I received a letter from Josie's family, a letter that Josie had written to me.

"It had not been opened and, well anyway, I didn't get it until quite some time later. In it, she tells of a discovery that the professor, her and this guy Conrad, made, the mosaic tiles covering the gold coins. Anyway, she was told at the time not to tell anyone, but she wrote the letter figuring that by the time I got it, the discovery would be public knowledge."

Simon paused, this time himself taking a sip of water. "So, of course, when I read it, as I said, quite some time later, there had been no mention at all about the gold. I decided to investigate, to discover the truth of what happened."

Again he paused, then, taking a breath. "Unlike you, Miss Hudson, I'm not such a good investigator. Also, I should have, at the time, perhaps, shown the letter to the police. Anyway, I decided to do some sleuthing myself. I felt it had to be this Conrad guy who might know more."

"According to Josie's letter, he was one of the three who originally found the gold, also now, he was the only one that was still alive.

"My research had also discovered that there was a student who had gone missing. This was of course this Eddie. Anyway, I assumed that the gold was still there. The area had been quickly fenced off and made into a memorial. Was that perhaps because whatever notes had been made were lost in the destruction of the tornado and nobody knew about it, or was it to cover this information up, for whatever reason? But if so, what about this Conrad guy, because he knew…"

Simon took a sip of water, looked again to his left at Alison, who was hanging on to his every word and then said, "I was stumped really. Didn't do any more about it, then one day, I found out that Conrad had been shot in Rome. Thinking it might be connected, I resumed my investigation. I flew over to Italy, but found the shooting wasn't related. I even thought the Shelton family was involved and was going to visit that big house, but only stood at the gates and, well, already I had spent too much time on this. Several relationships suffered, so I never went in."

"Then, I met this girl. It was on the tenth anniversary of Josie's death. I went to the site, met Felicity Smith, younger sister of Kathryn who was also killed that day. Anyway, eventually this led to a relationship, this was in 2002."

"Then," Simon paused for a moment, "one day when I was at my business, I run a motorcycle showroom and workshop here, a young man came in, his name was Raphael Morton. He is the younger brother of Josie, and he felt I ought to know some information that he had found out, though, he didn't know what to do with it, as the persons who were all involved were all dead.

"He really felt that it would be best to let sleeping dogs lie, he said to me, but as I was Josie's boyfriend, and, as he, as a young boy, thought I was cool… his words by the way," Simon elaborated, looking at Alison, "anyway, he is a doctor now, studying to be a medical examiner. In view of the letter that Josie wrote to me, which his mother showed to him later after I had returned it to the family, he wanted to do some forensics. He got the material and evidence together at a lab in the university here, then set to work. What he found really upset and stunned him."

Simon took a break, realising that everyone was listening very closely.

"The upshot is, to quote Raphael, 'the only person to die directly from the force of the tornado is the assistant of the project, Mr Donald Alfredo, when the trailer he was in was lifted and tossed against the trailer of professor.'"

"The professor, Emily Parker, as we know, and I believe you are correct inspector, died at the hands of Conrad. Now here's the kicker, according to Raphael. Josie Morton, was killed by Kathryn Smith."

Simon paused briefly, staring at the table, then quickly glanced around the room as he let that information sink in.

"This is what he believes," he continued breaking the hush that had descended in the room, "Kathryn was Conrad's sidekick. Though she pretended to not like him, they were in fact, a couple. Conrad, I believe, had obviously told her about the gold, and told her also of a plan to have that gold for themselves.

"Perhaps he left it at that, Raphael was only deducing here. But when the tornado hit, Kathryn saw her chance. Josie had been wounded, hit in the stomach by flying debris. Raphael believes that Kathryn pounced upon her. She was, apparently a junior wrestling champion, often using a body scissor and choke hold to win a match, according to research he had done on her. Such a hold usually resulting in the opponent being tapped out."

"Kathryn wore a cashmere pullover. She was the only person who wore anything cashmere that day. Raphael found traces of cashmere in Josie's lungs. He believes Kathryn put a choke hold on Josie, and, wounded as she was, Josie didn't have the strength to fight back." Simon again paused to let that sink in, whilst he tried not to think of how his girlfriend must have briefly suffered, all because she knew about the gold.

"And," he continued, after drinking several sips of water, "that's not all, for we know that Kathryn too died. Raphael believes that it was Conrad who killed her. She was struck with a steel pipe that the tornado had plucked up from somewhere in its destructive path. The reason he feels sure that this is what happened is the fingerprints he found on the steel pipe. They were Conrad's." Simon finished.

"He must also have told his mother about the gold coins, probably not about the killings, because later that same evening, he, with the help of his mother and a third person that we have not located yet, took the mosaic tiles and the gold coins," Roger said, taking up the conversation.

"Wow," Alison managed to say, sitting back in her chair and digesting all that new information. "So, you didn't come forwards with this?" she asked, again breaking the silence in the room. Then seeing the concern on his face, added, "I'm sorry, I just…"

"No that's okay, and, you're right. I should have. Perhaps Raphael should have, but as he said, all concerned are dead, could it be helpful in any way, or would it just be more harmful? He thought about Kathryn's parents. Did they really need to know this, and his own parents, he knew how he himself felt about it all.

"And, well, he was right in a way, because, as I was in a relationship with Kathryn's sister, and I felt I needed to tell her at least, the truth and all… she told me to go. Couldn't possibly continue a relationship with me, knowing that her sister had killed my girlfriend…"

"Oh Simon, I am sorry. I shouldn't have…"

"It's okay, really. It was a difficult decision, but well, in the end, it was only a few days ago that I felt that the truth must be told, must come out…"

Then, looking directly at Alison, said, "You are right, I really should have come forwards with this…" then, his voice only a little above a whisper, Simon said,

"My good friend and the manager of my business, was in hospital, because of this virus thing. Sadly, I just learned, only an hour ago, that he passed…"

The room fell silent again for a while.

Alison reached out her hand, gently squeezed his shoulder, then looking across the table, asked, "What does Mrs Shelton have to say for herself?"

"She's not saying anything, but her sentence will be extended, by quite a bit. We'll find the rest of the gold, or whatever might be left of it," Detective Sergeant Rodrigues replied, speaking for the first time.

Meanwhile–in Boston

The ornate box was now on proud display in Chrissie's lounge in one of her glass-fronted cabinets, alongside the collection of Japanese netsukes that her grandfather had collected.

Chrissie was pleased that she had now traced the journey that the box had made once it had been purchased by Charlie Parker in 1762.

She was still wondering how she could find out who made the box in the first place, and who had painted that lovely scene on the lid.

Furthermore, how was it that the artist Jan Steen had included it in his painting of 'The Lovesick Maiden'. and where would this painting, once owned by Sam's great-grandfather, the ambassador, be now.

Sam was sat in an armchair by the front window, the very chair he had sat in the first time she had met him when he had arrived at this house on the trail of the miniature. He was now reading the Bible passage that the scene on the lid of the box depicted.

Meanwhile in New York

Tammy sat curled up on the sofa.

Whilst she as yet had not connected all of her family tree, she was very pleased to have discovered how her great-grandfather Percivald was connected to Beatrice Parker, and how the sale of the business in Boston had paid for the purchase of this, now her, apartment right here in New York, right by Central Park.

She had also uncovered the fact that their financial well-to-do was due to the manufacturing plants of flour and syrup, and the factory that produced thousands and thousands of cookies.

She had yet to figure out how all of that had started, but was pleased with what she had found out.

She still would like to find out more about the woman, her so many times great-grandmother, who had fled from France to England, and to find out the fate of her husband who had been imprisoned.

Sipping some more white wine, she looked out through the vast panoramic window and sighed. As everything was going to be in a lockdown for a while, she would have time to do some more delving into the past.

The sky was getting darker and she thought about what to make for dinner.

Across to the West Coast and in a small town called Myrtle Creek

Claire had received a telephone call from Millie Parker. The conversation had taken some time as Millie explained all that had happened. She told Claire about the missing lad, Eddie, who had, at the behest of his mother, been the starting point in Robert's research, which had led to the initial discovery of the fate of the professor and the importance of the missing folder.

She had thanked Claire for her work on the case.

Thomas had, upon his return spent some more time in what was once Robert's work room, his 'search engine', and had found several folders, several 'cases' which as yet had not been resolved.

Cynthia, who had moved to a house not far away when first working with Robert, was all for continuing his work. Thomas was very happy to have her as a sidekick, though perhaps, he thought, maybe he was her sidekick?

In Albuquerque

After the meeting Ally found a quiet spot in the police station, and spoke at length with Barbara. She promised to call and see her some time as she told the story of how Eddie had discovered information helpful in the case and how, according to the inspector, it had not been Eddie who killed the professor, though sadly, her brother passed away not knowing that.

Finally

Alison Hudson had flown back home. On the flight she had been amused at how she had behaved when she had taken control of the situation and ordered Simon about.

He had taken her to the airport, on his trusty Indian motorcycle.

They had embraced, and he kissed her on the cheek.

But the look in their eyes surely suggested, 'to be continued'.

THE END

THE AUTHOR

Hendrik Hoitinga was born Leeuwarden in Friesland, the Netherlands, and emigrated to New Zealand at 10. After travelling extensively during his teens and twenties, he married his wife in Auckland, before relocating to the UK. They have two children. Hendrik worked in retail for 26 years. He and his wife were then commissioned and ordained as officers of the Salvation Army in 1995. They have since served in England, Belgium, Wales and Scotland. Hendrik has been able to focus on his writing since he retired in 2017. Now a grandfather, living in Wick in Scotland, he still loves travelling, music from the sixties and seventies and he collects Dutch comic books.

Hendrik Hoitinga
The Item

"The Item" is the story of a missing work of art. The story jumps from past to present, bringing to life the lives of those linked to the item, as Sam Price examines its provenance, solving linked crimes, and looking for new love.

www.ingramcontent.com/pod-product-compliance
Lightning Source LLC
Chambersburg PA
CBHW021019310726
48969CB00006B/1459